THE FALLEN FRUIT

A NOVEL

—

SHAWNTELLE
MADISON

THE

FALLEN

FRUIT

AMISTAD

An Imprint of HarperCollins*Publishers*

THE FALLEN FRUIT. Copyright © 2024 by Shawntelle Madison. All rights reserved. Printed in the United States of America. No part of this book may be used or reproduced in any manner whatsoever without written permission except in the case of brief quotations embodied in critical articles and reviews. For information, address HarperCollins Publishers, 195 Broadway, New York, NY 10007.

HarperCollins books may be purchased for educational, business, or sales promotional use. For information, please email the Special Markets Department at SPsales@harpercollins.com.

FIRST EDITION

Designed by Yvonne Chan
Illustrations © Chanthima Saenubon/stock.adobe.com

Library of Congress Cataloging-in-Publication Data has been applied for.

ISBN 978-0-06-329059-4

24 25 26 27 28 LBC 5 4 3 2 1

This book would've never existed without the inspiration from the late Walter "Toby" Madison Jr. Thank you, Uncle Toby, for introducing me to my family's rich history. I can only hope someday to match your passion to discover our ancestors' untold stories.

THE BRIDGE FAMILY

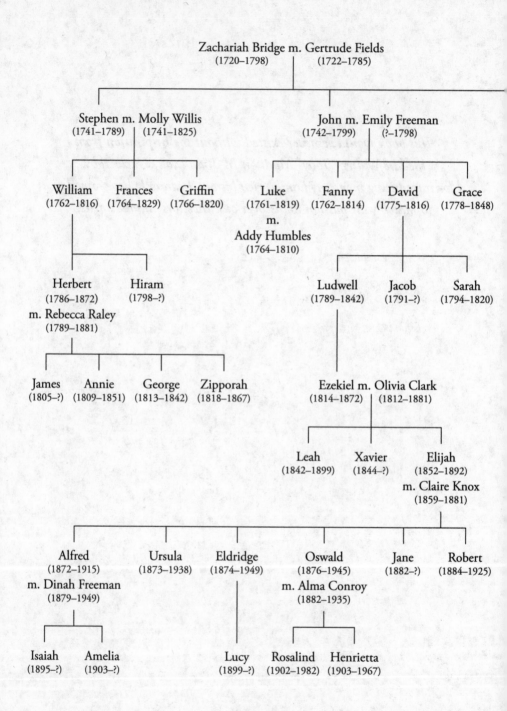

Zachariah Bridge m. Gertrude Fields
(1720–1798) (1722–1785)

Stephen m. Molly Willis
(1741–1789) (1741–1825)

John m. Emily Freeman
(1742–1799) (?–1798)

William (1762–1816)
Frances (1764–1829)
Griffin (1766–1820)

Luke (1761–1819)
m.
Addy Humbles
(1764–1810)

Fanny (1762–1814)
David (1775–1816)
Grace (1778–1848)

Herbert (1786–1872)
m. Rebecca Raley
(1789–1881)

Hiram (1798–?)

Ludwell (1789–1842)
Jacob (1791–?)
Sarah (1794–1820)

James (1805–?)
Annie (1809–1851)
George (1813–1842)
Zipporah (1818–1867)

Ezekiel m. Olivia Clark
(1814–1872) (1812–1881)

Leah (1842–1899)
Xavier (1844–?)
Elijah (1852–1892)
m. Claire Knox
(1859–1881)

Alfred (1872–1915)
m. Dinah Freeman
(1879–1949)

Ursula (1873–1938)
Eldridge (1874–1949)
Oswald (1876–1945)
m. Alma Conroy
(1882–1935)

Jane (1882–?)
Robert (1884–1925)

Isaiah (1895–?)
Amelia (1903–?)

Lucy (1899–?)
Rosalind (1902–1982)
Henrietta (1903–1967)

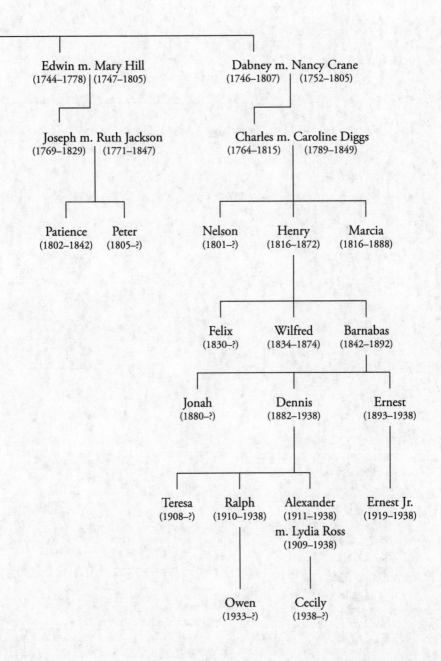

Edwin m. Mary Hill
(1744–1778) | (1747–1805)

Dabney m. Nancy Crane
(1746–1807) | (1752–1805)

Joseph m. Ruth Jackson
(1769–1829) | (1771–1847)

Charles m. Caroline Diggs
(1764–1815) | (1789–1849)

Patience
(1802–1842)

Peter
(1805–?)

Nelson
(1801–?)

Henry
(1816–1872)

Marcia
(1816–1888)

Felix
(1830–?)

Wilfred
(1834–1874)

Barnabas
(1842–1892)

Jonah
(1880–?)

Dennis
(1882–1938)

Ernest
(1893–1938)

Teresa
(1908–?)

Ralph
(1910–1938)

Alexander
(1911–1938)
m. Lydia Ross
(1909–1938)

Ernest Jr.
(1919–1938)

Owen
(1933–?)

Cecily
(1938–?)

PART ONE
AMELIA

Cecily Bridge-Davis

MAY 1964

My family tree has poisoned roots. Secrets from generations ago sank far into the earth where truth and lies tangled in a polluted snarl. Over time, those deep roots—the ones that couldn't stay buried forever—writhed to the surface like new saplings and contaminated the earth around them.

I discovered one of those saplings when my aunt Hilda—who'd raised me like a daughter right outside Charlottesville—died. Her will stated I had an inheritance: sixty-five acres of Bridge family land. Since I hadn't heard a word from my father or his kin, I didn't know what I'd find. With my luck, the apple trees would be termite infested and any haphazard shacks would be unfit for human occupancy.

I should've sold the place, sight unseen, but the hunger to learn more about my father's side of the family propelled me from the home I'd made for myself in Nashville to return to the Virginia woods. Five miles north of downtown Charlottesville, a heavy downpour left me lost in the countryside. I had no choice but to stop my car on a rutted dirt road and approach an old bungalow where an elderly Black woman sat in a rocking chair on the porch. The moment I showed up, her middle-aged son emerged with a stiff nod.

"Stay away from that godforsaken place," the woman said, waving away a mosquito from her cloud of white hair. "You'll find nothing but trouble. A long time ago, one of them Bridges killed a bunch of people before he kidnapped an innocent child."

"Are they still around here?" I asked.

"Who knows," the woman replied. "They come and go."

"Those Bridges kept to themselves," the man said. "Sell that land and wash your hands of it. That's what I'd do."

My granddaddy told me I never knew when to back down from a challenge.

"I still need to see it," I said. "Please tell me the way."

Reluctantly, they gave me directions. From years of teaching history to college students, I knew too well how folks always wanted to share these sorts of tall tales. Vendettas among the countryfolk passed from one generation to another, sowing animosity over amity between neighbors. But all stories and legends had their roots in the truth.

After leaving the bungalow and taking two wrong turns, I finally came upon a hidden opening to my right. Back when I was small, my grandfather sometimes stopped here on our way to church. I would sit in the idling car, playing with the hem of my Sunday dress, until he came back. Grandpa never went farther than the entrance itself. Neither did I, until the day I steered my car down the winding path, which ended at a house next to overgrown apple trees. Wildflowers and tall grass filled the pasture while a stubborn oak stump jutted out in the middle. Rotted fence posts leaned away from the single-story house, perhaps to escape from the clinging neglect. Decades ago, this long-forgotten place had been someone's home, their sanctuary from summer's heat and winter's bitter chill. Now only daddy longlegs, mice, and cobwebs lived here.

After shutting off the car, I hurried through the rain and side-

4

stepped the missing floorboards on the porch. I pushed open the door with ease, at once slipping into the past. I pulled the collar of my blouse over my nose to dampen the odors of mildew and musk of wild animals and left the door open to bring in some fresh air. It was a damn shame no one had thought to take care of this place.

Carefully, I walked through the empty living room with only the storm's pitter-patter and my breath to keep me company. From the living room, I made my way to the summer kitchen, then the two bedrooms off a narrow hallway. Broken-down and dusty furniture filled both rooms. I sighed, imagining the scrubbing and hauling someone would have to do. I was better off tearing down the whole house. There was nothing for me here. Anything that might've been interesting or useful had long rotted away, and I resigned myself to return to my car when a glint from something on a shelf across the living room drew my eye.

I had to at least take a peek. Tucked away on the ledge, I discovered a cerulean tin box. With trembling hands and a hope that this would be my reward for coming all this way, I picked up the tin and wiped away the dirt and grease on the lid to reveal the bouquet hidden beneath. My pulse thrummed as I unhooked the rusty latch, loosening the lid's stiff hinge to lift the top, and revealed a spool crafted from maple and a Bible carefully protected by the lambskin wrapped around it. Turning the spool between my fingers, I could tell it was old—very old. I exchanged it for the Bible. The pages were yellowed and nearly transparent in their thinness, but the tin had preserved the Bible from worse decay. The flyleaf held a wealth of information—someone had consigned the names and birth dates of every Bridge born on this farm, beginning in the late 1760s and ending in the 1920s. A set of initials denoted the first family scribe as "R. B."

"Who's that? Hmm." I stroked the handwritten letters.

I had a lot to look through, but I could do it at another time. As I began to close the Bible, I spotted two pieces of paper. One was tucked securely between the Bible's pages, but the other fluttered to the floor, and on it, someone had drawn a map of the property. There were X's marked here and there. Were those more houses? Though I'd planned to book a motel room to rest, the marks on the map implied more Bridge secrets. Would any of them tell me more about my father? I had to know.

Using the cabin as a starting point, I searched the pasture adjacent to the family's orchard and followed the map until I came to an aged elm. Circling the tree, I compared it to the map. This was the X-marked spot closest to the house, but why? I ran my hand down the trunk in search of an answer, then I noticed the cavity hollowed in the base. I dropped to my knees to clear the dead leaves and brush until my fingers grazed something within that I desperately tugged free: an old mail carrier's tote from the Civil War. Time had stiffened and cleaved deep creases into the leather while the elements had tarnished the brass hardware. With a brush of my hand across the grungy front flap, I traced the stitched words: UNITED STATES. Below that was a name: WILFRED BRIDGE.

This man had been my relative. Many years ago, he'd slung this bag over his shoulder and trudged from town to town to deliver news of births, marriages, and losses. I caressed the leather bag and shivered as our hands connected through time.

Inside the tote, someone—perhaps Wilfred—had left the necessities for survival: a flint-and-steel kit, a compass, hole-filled mittens, a folded knife, and the crumbled remnants of old hardtack. When I reached the bottom, my hands scraped against a sheepskin pocket. The soft material still held its shape, having uncannily protected the faded piece of paper within. The paper held words penned with a shaky hand.

"Bridge Family Rules," the first line read.

The next line added, "Never interfere with past events."

I scanned faster.

More rules followed. And none of them made sense. Not a single Bridge family member had spoken to me since my birth, and yet this single piece of paper resembled an urgent warning from generations past.

But what did these rules mean? Why had this bag been hidden and marked on a map? Who was meant to find it?

A tendril of the Bridge family tree wrapped around me and tugged, and I eagerly followed it down to the rotted roots.

―――――――

The next morning arrived and decisions needed to be made. I would have to put the farm up for sale, but I couldn't resist learning more about my daddy. If I could find one thing about him before I returned home, just *one* thing, this whole trip would be worth it.

Within a couple of weeks, I should have an ad posted in *The Daily Progress* and an offer in hand. Sounded easy, if you asked me. But first things first, like Aunt Hilda used to say, I'd have to put in the work to part the grass to find the weeds hidden underneath.

The Carver Inn on Preston Avenue proved the best place for my new home away from home. I imagined most travelers would forgo the hotel because of the overgrown shrubbery and chipped white paint. Time had not been kind to the Carver, even though the receptionist boasted of lodgers as renowned as Duke Ellington and Louis Armstrong. Either way, I'd slept in less appealing accommodations during the bus station protests in '61. The Freedom Riders had blazed a trail across the South, and my husband and I had joined them after we heard about the horrific attacks against the civil rights activists at the bus station in Rock Hill, South Carolina. Back then I'd rested on couches or slept on stiff-backed seats. A rundown hotel with a lumpy bed and four walls suited me just fine.

Not even a day into settling in, I called my husband to reveal plans had changed.

"How long you gonna be gone?" Winston asked. The sounds of my family's early morning routine seeped through the crackly phone line.

"Shouldn't take longer than a week or two," I replied. *Or four*, I couldn't resist thinking.

I pressed my hand over my other ear to hear my eldest child, six-year-old Jason, complaining about how his younger brother had yanked a button off his shirt. Winston always got them up on time—me, not so much.

"Lloyd . . ." he warned.

A mumbled "Sorry" from the four-year-old filtered through. Most likely after he got a deathly glare from his daddy. Winston Davis didn't play games in the morning.

"Go apologize to your brother." My husband switched gears with ease. "You don't talk about the Bridges much, Ceci, but I know you've always wanted answers."

"And I'll get them *today*." I blew out a short breath. "I'm heading to the library later."

The call ended with I-love-yous and a brief chat with my boys before Winston gave me one last warning not to let my search get me too far into my head. I had a family in the past, sure, but I needed to remember my family in the present too. Still, it wouldn't hurt to try to find out something. Maybe I'd learn that my daddy's orchard had been a profitable business before the farm's fall to ruin. Perhaps there'd be a photo or two in *The Daily Progress* from my father's youth in the 1920s. The possibilities pushed me out of my room and down the steps. I hurried through the parlor, grinning far too widely as I passed the boarders reading papers and eating breakfast. One gentleman glanced up with disapproval, only to quickly return to his meal. Smiling never hurt anyone, I say.

The rain had retreated, but a fog clung to the city streets, leaving low visibility. The drive down to McIntire Library didn't take long—I had walked these streets for years as a child and knew the way. With each turn, my excitement grew, until that elderly woman from yesterday came to mind.

A long time ago, one of them Bridges killed a bunch of people before he kidnapped an innocent child.

Those murders could've happened before my father had lived there. Maybe they weren't even true. Didn't people spread other folks' private business all the time? For all I knew, that old lady and her son in that shack probably couldn't stand the Bridges.

Yet my rational thoughts didn't stop the peculiar tingle along the back of my neck. The sensation traveled to my stomach and formed knots. My grip on the steering wheel tightened until I passed the white-columned brick building deeper into downtown. I kept going until I pulled up in front of the Albemarle County office building.

I sat in the car for ten minutes until I gave up and went inside. Tomorrow was another day. Another opportunity. I'd walk right into *The Daily Progress* and the library to handle business, but for now, I clutched the family Bible to my chest. I had names to research. The Bridge family had a story to tell.

Winston's parting words this morning followed me inside. "Be careful what you hunt in the dark," he'd said. "You might not like what's waiting."

CHAPTER 1

Amelia Bridge
FEBRUARY 1919

Wintertime in central Virginia tricked the senses—especially along the low-lying Southwest Mountains. On bleak days, the gusts wrestled the powdery snow from the evergreens and blinded foolhardy travelers. At the highest point on nearby Wolfpit Mountain, one could see for miles unless a blizzard gripped the countryside. It was in these whiteouts that the line between reality and purgatory blurred. Those lost to the haze wandered, seeking out familiar landmarks but finding none.

During such a time, Amelia Bridge's kin rarely traversed the one hundred acres of the Bridge family farm, or "Free State," as the locals called it. She feared for any souls who meandered through places like these. They'd find a desolate landscape with a cutting wind that bit bare flesh.

Millie and her older brother, Isaiah, always waited until the late February snow melted before they bundled up, drew their packs over their shoulders, and ventured out of their home. At the ages of sixteen and twenty-three, the pair had more than daily chores to do.

They were never alone. Isaiah's foxhound, a one-eared dog who rarely barked, accompanied them. Felix trotted close to his master and alerted them to any danger.

The mud-speckled path from their cabin weaved through the pasture to the Bridge family orchard. At this time of year, the pippin apple trees had shed their green coats and now their naked limbs extended to heaven. Millie marveled at them—every one of these trees bore branches grafted from the original saplings her ancestors had planted over one hundred fifty years before. Over a century of land ownership was a rarity for Negro families in the area. Before the American Revolution, her free forefathers had settled here and created a community, a haven for other free colored folks.

But such a wondrous place held dangers too. The apple trees' spindly branches were a reminder that something once alive and vibrant appeared dead—just like the deceased colored man Millie and Isaiah came upon not long after leaving the orchard. The poor man was curled up on his side under a cluster of evergreens. His skin was mottled, and frost added bulk to his six-foot frame. The cut of the man's dark-green coat was unfamiliar, as well as its shiny, smooth-to-the-touch material. She sighed. He wore nothing more than a coat, paper-thin trousers, and footwear better suited to the city than the countryside. This wasn't unusual for those who succumbed to the family curse.

Felix sniffed around the evergreens and avoided the body. Her brother's dog had a keen nose for hunting, but today perhaps the animal detected the otherness of the man they'd discovered. The dog never liked to help them search for fallen Bridges.

"I was hoping we wouldn't find anyone again," she said as her brother stooped to examine the man.

"You say the same thing every year." Her brother fished through the man's pockets for identification. Millie preferred not to bury and pray over a stranger—especially if they were kin.

Usually they didn't find anything, but this time Isaiah discovered a folded piece of paper hidden in a coat pocket. His thick brows drew together as he read. "These are his freedom papers. Says his name is Crawford Bridge—or that's the name he'd planned to go by."

"At least he remembered to carry them." Every Bridge child was advised to carry fabricated documents stating they were freemen. Falling into the past—the Bridge family curse—held too many perils, including the possibility of enslavement.

Isaiah retrieved a tarp from his pack. The soil was still frozen around this time of the year, so the Bridges did what they could. With reverence, they extended the tarp over the snow. Once they were done, Millie stood over Crawford, pondering how such a fate could snatch away dreams. The man appeared to be between twenty and thirty years old. Had Crawford left behind a wife and child? Perhaps he owned a cabin on this land—far off in the future. His fields would remain fallow, never to be tended again. His cattle would go hungry. The travelers weren't the only ones affected by time travel.

Nearly one hundred forty years had passed since the first Bridge, a man named Luke, slipped back in time, and questions still tainted the air as to how the family had been so cursed in the first place.

"You ever wonder what would've happened if the first Bridge had fallen into the wintertime?" she asked.

Isaiah's gaze flicked from Crawford's body to the unforgiving land. "For all we know, Luke might've."

"He must've been terrified." She shivered and wished it were merely the cold. "Back then, Luke could've been standing not far from here. Maybe he was eating his dinner or walking to Ivy Creek. Maybe he was talking to his mama. Then he was gone—whisked away twenty-two years to the past. It's hard to believe he managed to survive and get home in one piece."

Every Bridge child knew of Luke's journey. He served as a lesson. Not to frighten them but to prepare them. Millie often thought of Luke's circumstances, but even more so, she couldn't help but feel for his siblings. His mother, Emily, too. How much pain had the woman endured after she lost her child?

The pain felt all too real as Millie thought of her brother. As the children of a Bridge man, only one of them would fall through time. The other would be spared the same fate.

"It's always hard to be the first of anything." Her brother picked up the man and placed him on the tarp. Then they draped the thick fabric over Crawford, covering the man from his ashen face to his stiff legs. After that, they searched for stones to protect his body from predators. He would be buried once the ground softened. The whole task ended in minutes—far too short a time. She glanced up to see her brother bleary-eyed and leaning hard on his walking stick.

"Why don't you return home?" she asked.

Isaiah shook his head, wheezing. He turned his back on her as if that would make her forget all the times he'd collapsed while running. Or every time he'd clutched his chest when his heart stuttered.

"Your stubbornness isn't bravery," she said gruffly.

"And treating me like a child won't get the job done, Millie."

She considered returning home, but Isaiah walked away. Felix obediently followed. Her older brother had always been stoic when she faltered, pragmatic when she was idealistic. She'd tried to sleep in this morning, but Isaiah would have none of that, stomping through the house, banging pans loud enough to wake their ancestors from six feet underground.

His heart was weak, but he had a bear's courage. Even when it came to the war in Europe two years ago, Isaiah answered the call without fear. He was twenty-one when the first registration opened that June. He wanted to go overseas, but the military deemed him unfit for service and sent him back to the farm.

She wished he could've left—seen the world and what it might offer.

Her brother shifted to accommodate his large pack. Though it was cumbersome, he never dared go out unprepared. Millie didn't carry hers as often, much to her brother's disapproval, but she always had her freedom papers.

Millie approached him to adjust his backpack's straps. "It's too heavy, ain't it?"

He grimaced. "I'm fine."

She reached for a strap, finding it difficult since Isaiah towered over her. He was birch-tree tall like Pa, while she was short like Ma. "Why can't you take it off and rest?"

He shrugged. "Because I don't want to."

"Why are you so stubborn? You're going to hurt yourself." She'd given this lecture before, and he always took it. But this time he strode away. "It ain't natural to live this way—all bent out of shape over a moment that might never come."

"No, it ain't," he bit back, "but it's all I got."

"Isaiah, I'm sorry. Look, I don't want to see you like this. You should be happy."

"I told myself no regrets. Ain't no way Ma or you are gonna make me believe otherwise." His deep-brown cheeks reddened with his rising frustration. "Until I fall, I'm half a man."

"I don't understand."

"Either you or I will end up in the past—which means, right now we are dead folks walking. Half of us are in the present while the other half have already left. We just don't know who it's gonna be or when."

She shook her head. "But we're *here*. The past has already happened, and we're living *now*—"

"Don't matter." His lips lifted into a half smile. He accepted things too easily. "Anyone we love should be with someone else."

She snorted. "And while she's with someone else, you can live like a hermit in a cabin, wasting away."

"You're the hermit." His smile deepened. "Especially when Sam comes around."

She stifled a retort. Her brother's best friend, Samuel Ross, had taken a liking to her. Based on how often he'd asked if she planned to attend the dance in town tonight, he hadn't given up.

As much as she wanted a beau, she didn't want to deal with the aftermath. One minute a boy would come courting, and in the next, she'd be married and stuck at home with babes circling her skirt. Now wasn't the time.

"And I'm not wasting away," he added, staring at her like he could steal her apprehension and keep it for himself. "I'm preparing and providing for my family."

He turned his back on her and walked away with his dog. Far too often she saw his retreating back. She feared he'd disappear without saying goodbye.

———

Hours later, the doors opened to the dance hall, but Millie never arrived on time. All the boys sauntered in as they pleased while the girls waited outside well before the dance began. Last year was the first time Isaiah had dragged her to the Negro dance hall in town. She'd been the new girl at the time, fresh-faced in one of her mother's dresses. She spent the entire time gawking at the gleaming oak floors and sweet-talking band members. After hiding away from the Spanish flu, folks couldn't wait to slow dance with one another. But once or twice around the dance floor with boys who wouldn't keep their hands above her waist had left a bitter taste in her mouth. About as bad as the foul odors from the boys' mouths after their moonshine drinking and cheap-cigarette smoking.

So she took her time and waltzed in an hour late. Might as well make an entrance.

The crowd outside the doors had thinned, and she strode through the entryway into the thrum of a pulsing drumbeat and a trumpet's trill. She hadn't worn one of her mama's dresses this time but an almost-new hand-me-down from her well-to-do cousins up in DC. Eyes from all across the room swept over the sage-green and lace affair. The gown had a cinched waist with chiffon flowers and sheer scalloped sleeves with beaded trim. Anyone would say the dress bordered on perfection. Even her hair had been brushed and pulled up into becoming coils. But as she walked over to the nearest wall, she decided to leave after she listened to a song or two.

This was all a fantasy, and she soaked it in—the couples strutting and swinging to the music; the girls laughing and chatting at the small tables. Life continued here in Charlottesville while she waited for the inevitable back at the farm.

Before the next song—a slower number—began, her brother made his entrance with a fresh cigarette between his lips and Samuel at his side.

Millie spotted Eloise, at the other end of the room, glancing in Isaiah's direction. The girl had turned seventeen not too long ago, and the glow from her dimpled cheeks and her soft laugh had drawn many an admirer. Isaiah had shown up in the only suit he owned, a frayed dark-brown garment with an old gray tie and too-long trousers, but Eloise's gaze sipped at him with anticipation.

Sam, on the other hand, limped in grinning in his linen pin-striped suit. A wound from the war had slowed him down, but he flashed his toothy grin while Isaiah glowered.

Millie abandoned the wall to go to her brother. Might as well tease him a little before she left.

"Hey, Millie," Sam called out to her. "You gonna dance with me tonight?"

"Maybe," she said.

"You always say maybe." Sam turned to Isaiah. "Is she trying to let me off nicely?"

"All women are letting you off nicely." Isaiah tugged his friend to follow him. "I say you need to find Gladys."

Sam shuddered with a mischievous smile. "Oh no. Not tonight, my friend. That woman is as scary as they come. Maybe even scarier than them Germans."

Isaiah laughed. Seeing her brother smiling, and without his pack, set Millie at ease. She returned to the wall and pressed her sweaty back against the cool surface. Whether the liquor or the company he kept lent to his happiness, that didn't matter. They needed nights like this one to taste the world outside their prison.

Two songs came and went. While Millie stood at her spot, she tried to keep her left knee from shaking, her fingers from flexing. Her chest tightened, then relaxed. She fumbled with her purse instead of glancing at the doorway. Couples formed. New relationships bloomed. While Eloise tried to coax her brother into conversation, Sam joined Millie at the wall.

"Looking beautiful tonight, Millie."

"Thanks."

Over the years, Sam had grown taller, his shoulders broadening, and he'd splashed an enticingly spicy aftershave across his dark-skinned cheeks, but she could still see the filthy boy who'd followed her brother around and teased her.

"Care for a dance?" he drawled. "I won't take no for an answer this time."

She held in a laugh. "Guess you'll have to hear no again."

"Why not? Didn't you come here to have fun?"

Good question. "I don't know."

They stood beside each other for some time as the party continued. Gladys hovered nearby with a near-empty cup of lemonade in her hand, almost within earshot.

"You should go to her." Amelia bumped her shoulder against Sam's side. "She's probably still thirsty."

Sam snorted. "She's still thirsty for something."

"Be a gentleman and refill her cup at least."

Sam's shoulders slumped as he abandoned the wall for the refreshment table.

Not long after Sam's attempt, another gentleman, a light-skinned fellow, asked her to join him, but she declined and made her way to the door. The fantasy had to end sooner or later. There would be no happily ever after.

CHAPTER 2

Amelia Bridge

FEBRUARY 1920

illie startled awake with sweat drenching her back and
her hands clenched in fists. Again, she'd dreamt of that
dead man from a year ago. Crawford Bridge. She closed
her eyes and grimaced from the sunlight flooding through the single window above her head. Behind closed eyelids, she returned
to stumbling onto Crawford curled up beneath those trees—the
dead man's frozen eyes wide, and his lips parted in the middle of a
scream. The dream was too fresh, too vivid. Turning onto her side,
she faced her brother's bed across the room. As expected, his bed
was empty. Long before the sun rose, Isaiah's usual routine was to
prepare breakfast. Based on the buttery smells wafting under the
door, he'd cooked hotcakes and fried eggs again. Her favorite. Even
their ma, who rarely left her room, gobbled up his eggs. He was
likely lumbering around that kitchen with his survival pack on his
back. He even slept with it slung over his shoulder.

Millie swung her socked feet off the bed and twisted to stretch her weary muscles. Her own pack lay within arm's reach. Today, she wanted to be free of it.

A dull thud from outside the closed door tugged her out of bed. She caught the sounds of Felix's muffled whimper as she crossed the room in two steps. Beyond the bedroom lay the summer kitchen—or what could be called a kitchen for a cabin as small as theirs. She listened. Something scraped along the wood floors. Was Isaiah struggling to stay standing? She reached for the doorknob, then froze. Through the door, she heard a faint wheeze, her brother fighting for each breath. He'd taxed himself again. She murmured a prayer for their hearts to beat in time, for his heart to match the strength of hers. But she knew the human body didn't work that way.

"He needs heart medication," the county doctor had told them. "And I'm not talking about herbal tinctures like foxglove leaves or nightshade berries. What he needs is expensive manufactured medicine."

She pressed her forehead against the door's cool wood and counted each breath her brother took. One, two, then three. He kept moving. Someday he wouldn't.

An ache formed behind her eyes, a familiar sign of stress. She had to get the hell out of here, perhaps find a job in town or Richmond, but she wouldn't find much. Most factories wouldn't hire Negroes—whites got the best positions first. Over the last couple of years, many parishioners at their church left to seek work, never to return. Now and then she'd heard rumors they'd resettled up north in New York or Massachusetts. Some even relocated to the Midwest. Millie didn't want to go that far away. Plenty of well-to-do ladies in Charlottesville would hire an educated colored girl like her as their housegirl. Whether she fell through time in town, instead of at the farm, didn't matter. Hadn't her brother said they were half in this world and half in the next? All this standing still and waiting got them nowhere. A couple months of double shifts scrubbing floors and tutoring children could earn her enough money to pay for Isaiah's pills. And if he fell—no, he *wouldn't* fall through time. God wouldn't be so cruel as to thrust him back to a past where nothing could save his heart. She would be the one to go.

Eventually, her brother shuffled back to the stove. By the time she got dressed, she'd made her decision. Come Monday, she'd head down to Charlottesville to find work.

————

When the sky finally cleared and the wavering brush quieted, Millie and Isaiah patrolled the farm again. Just like last year and the year before that.

Each spring, she held on to the hope they'd encounter someone alive and well. That the provisions her family left for time travelers would be discovered and save a life. During her more pleasant dreams, the ones from which she woke feeling refreshed, Millie and her brother would turn a corner and see smoke rising. There'd be a campsite right over a hill. The sun would be shining without a single cloud overhead. The smiling face of their kin would feed her soul, and all the wrongs and sorrows in the world would disappear for a moment.

How she wished their efforts weren't for nothing.

The unsettling feeling pressed on her shoulders, circling like the chilled air seeping through her coat.

They passed a copse of evergreens, and she couldn't help but stare at the spot where they'd buried Crawford once the soil yielded to a shovel. The man had died no more than one hundred yards from a satchel with life-sustaining tools.

This time they didn't find any bodies, so they set about another task: replenishing the survival packs the family stowed away inside wooden boxes. After restocking three packs, they returned to the spot where they'd found Crawford. With a knife, she nicked his name into the evergreen trunk—so she could pay her respects— but a part of her wished she could send a message to the future: *Don't rest here. This marks your end.*

"He'd almost made it," she remarked.

"A year ago, we couldn't have seen our hands in front of our faces. He was doomed," Isaiah replied somberly. "What's done is done."

She expected her brother to say more, but they continued in silence to the next container, a weathered maple one. Millie lifted the cover and withdrew a twenty-year-old doctor's bag. Carefully, she surveyed the contents. The velvet-lined interior had held up well. If Crawford had stumbled upon this, he would've discovered flint, dry kindling, and beef jerky. A fire would've warmed his face and the food would've nourished his belly, but all these things meant nothing if their kin never found the packs. She replenished the supplies—at first cramming them inside, before her heart settled. Then she nestled them in with care. The final touch, a folded piece of paper, contained a reminder of the Bridge Family Rules:

Never interfere with past events.
Always carry your freedom papers.
Search for the survival packs in the orchard.
Do not speak to strangers unless absolutely necessary.

Over a century had passed since Luke, and then many others, had disappeared. Back in the 1830s, the Bridges established the rules and devised the packs to protect those who'd fallen. For those who had time traveled earlier, they wouldn't have found any of these things—only an unfamiliar landscape filled with confused ancestors. She shuddered to think of their fate, and that it could be hers too.

"You done yet?" Isaiah touched her shoulder.

She gave a nod and tapped the top of the box for luck. If God heard her prayers, and half the time she suspected He didn't, He'd see fit to send her instead of her brother. Maybe she'd return to this very box in 1901.

Isaiah gave her a lopsided smile and drew her back to the present. "You'd put a winter coat into that thing if you could."

She chuffed. "I would if we built bigger boxes."

"Too much work." He chuckled. "You reckon Uncle Oswald will return to Free State this summer?" He removed his hat and rubbed his bushy hair. She'd chased after him with scissors, but he disappeared every Sunday morning before church.

"Hope so," she said. "Feels like he's getting too busy to see the likes of us."

"Plenty busy, Millie. Now that he knows he's not gonna fall, he should move on."

She nodded. Her uncle hadn't forgotten about them, but she'd still felt trapped as she watched him leave. Many Bridges tried to forget about the family curse and settle elsewhere, but they'd learned the hard way. Grandpa Elijah loved to tell Millie the story of the Bridges who'd fled the farm to head west. Back in 1842, they'd escaped through the mountains into Kentucky, crossed the plains in Illinois to reach the Missouri River. Once there, they built a house, along with a new orchard of apple and peach trees. In the beginning, they'd always carried packs on their backs like Millie and her brother, but over time, they grew complacent. They left their packs at home. But they could never deceive time. And when the tides of the past plucked away one of their children, that poor child fell through time to the prairies of Missouri, a wilderness they still knew little about. In all their wisdom, they could never predict how the landscape would change. When the land would flood. When the forests would burn from a lightning strike. Or how some rivers had bridges built across them in the future but none in the past. Death awaited the foolhardy—if they fell in the wrong place.

Millie never forgot the stories or the rules. But even as she stayed on the farm, resigned to her fate, she found bright moments, especially every summer when Uncle Oswald paid a visit from Washington, DC. He brought gifts, including shoes and clothes for the other kids living in the houses scattered across Bridge land. While the smaller children wanted toys, Millie received books, paper, and pencils. She hungered to learn more, maybe even attend college if she ever saved up enough money. Perhaps that was also why she had made the decision to leave and find work.

The thought of money elicited a sigh. There'd never be enough.

"You're always sighing like Ma." Her brother stooped to stroke Felix's side.

"I'm sighing 'cause you're a pest."

"Liar." He flashed a smile again.

She couldn't help but grin in return. Her brother's easygoing nature made it hard to stay angry with him.

"C'mon, let's get out of this cold." She pulled his arm to get him moving. "I need to get a lot done if I plan to be in town come Monday."

He stopped, and she couldn't pull him any farther. "What are you talking about, Millie?"

Damn her mouth again. She'd planned to sneak away. After taking in the swaying barn door near her uncle's house, she sucked in a breath and admitted to Isaiah that she planned to earn money.

"No." He spoke before she'd finished her last syllable. "You ain't going."

She cocked her head, then shook it. Was her brother in any position to tell her what to do? Wasn't he the same man who went out traipsing in the middle of the night to see girls? With a shake of her head, she tried to walk away. Her brother shifted to stand in her path.

"When the time is right," he said, "you'll go."

"Let's go home," she murmured. "Don't say another word."

"I'm praying I'll be the one to go so you can move on with your life." He'd said that casually, but underneath every word, she knew he was serious.

"Oh no!" She'd had enough and advanced on him. "I told you to stop saying that."

"I can say what I goddamn want."

Millie opened her mouth to chastise him for taking the Lord's name in vain, but she stood her ground instead and glared at him. This fight had been festering between them for years. Only one child born from each Bridge man would fall. If Isaiah fell, she'd be safe.

"You can't tell me I'm not the one." His tall form blocked the sun, and she could see every pockmark from when he'd had chicken pox. "I can see it. Feel it. I never told you I had a dream about you a year ago. You were sitting in a nice house."

"Don't do this to me—"

"You were smiling and happy 'cause you got accepted into one of them nice Negro colleges—"

She plowed into him, briefly forgetting how fragile he could be, but her brother didn't budge. They'd both had dreams, but none of hers included him leaving.

"You don't get to do *that* to me." She reached for him again, but instead of colliding with him, she collapsed to the ground, her knees throbbing from the impact as her hands sank into the damp dirt.

Felix sniffed in frenzied circles and searched the ground around her feet before throwing back his head in a pained howl. The dog sprinted off into the woods, but he'd never find his master.

"Isaiah . . ."

Millie's voice quivered. Her brother had fallen. By God, right in front of her, he had fallen in time. He'd gotten what he'd always wanted: a hero's victory. There'd be no formal goodbyes or regrets to carry into the next world. That burden was hers now.

CHAPTER 3

Amelia Bridge
MAY 1920

From March to May, the mornings became a time of stillness in Millie's house. Her kin dropped by now and then, but she rarely noticed them. Instead, she took the time to stoop in the doorway to the bedroom she'd shared with her brother, hoping the ghost of his presence would brush against her shoulder. May had brought warmer weather, so she waited patiently for a wandering spirit's chill to pass through her.

Isaiah's dog refused to step into the house, preferring to watch for his master from the porch. It was just Millie and her mother, and Ma had surrendered to loss long ago. Years of losing kin had chipped away at the woman until there was nothing left. Most of the time, she kept to her room.

Now Millie wandered through the house, her footfalls heavy and her hands never ceasing in their labors to seemingly entice her brother to return home. She'd washed his bedding, scrubbed the muddy prints he'd left near the front door, and sorted his collection of rocks and metalworking tools. With painstaking care, she arranged his mallet and tweezers. Over the years, he'd scoured the mountains with Sam and pocketed shiny, crystal-like goethite and white chunks of limestone.

"Don't know why Sam loves the shiny ones," her brother had said. "He told me he's looking for a diamond for a pretty lady, and I reckon there's nothing wrong with searching."

The rocks were tiny, insignificant things, but that was all she had left of her brother.

Among his metalworking tools, she brushed her fingertips against the rough surface of forceps and the needles for stitches. She'd never touched them, feeling unworthy.

"Can't practice what you learned in those medical books without the right tools," he'd said offhand.

Isaiah had dreams far more vivid than hers—almost as if he could glimpse beyond the horizon to conjure a brighter future for his sister. Yes, she wanted to become a physician. Yes, she yearned to leave the farm someday. But not like this. Not without her brother.

So she waited.

It was as if she expected him to appear at the front door—just like the old stories about Luke Bridge's journey home. Perhaps Isaiah had gone back in time only a year or two, and soon enough he'd waltz into the house hungry and weary from his wanderings. But the door never opened with his arrival, and the only sounds in the house were the wind winding down the chimney, the persistent bubbling of the kettle on the stove, and, underneath those sounds, the tiny voice that whispered he wouldn't come back. That she wouldn't have a chance to ask him where he went.

Millie poured herself a cup of hot water for chamomile tea and abandoned the kitchen to sink onto the bed across from his. They'd always shared this room, but her brother had left few traces of himself in here. She'd swallowed the empty space with books and a chest of clothes. Isaiah had always been the less sentimental one, having no need to cling to trivial belongings. She thought him stronger for that. After all, he carried his world on his back.

For many hours, she sat there, until her tea cooled and visitors appeared. Aunt Betty slipped into the house. Her mother's sister said nothing while she added coal to the empty stove, washed the dishes, and warmed porridge to ease their hungry bellies. After Betty left, more Bridge women arrived. A parade of saintly women fed the neglected chickens, collected the eggs, and swept the dusty porch. Most of Millie's family moved silently through the rooms, but her birdlike aunt Ursula burst into the bedroom, smelling of lavender and the cornbread muffins she left at the house every morning.

"Time to get on up now," the woman said in her no-nonsense, high-pitched voice, "or you'll be mourning for the rest of your life like your mama."

Millie gave her a spiteful stare, but Ursula ignored it.

"Your cousin Lucy fell two years ago today, God protect her soul," her aunt said. "Before that, my great-uncle and then my uncle and sister. On and on. The Bridges endure, and you must do the same, child."

Millie didn't want to endure. She only wanted to exist in a numb place where she herself could fall away, drifting from the world and time, but her aunt wouldn't allow for self-pity. Every morning, Ursula arrived and forced Millie to wash her face, change her clothes. Attempts to also rouse Ma only resulted in cursing and the familiar murmurs of a lost mind.

"I told you to leave me alone," Ma would spit from her filthy bed. "I was up too late searching for your uncle Bertie."

During the day, Ma slept, while at night, she escaped the house to search for a man who'd flitted in and out of their lives. Unlike Pa, who'd worked at chopping down timber from what few trees remained in the northern woods, his brother Bert had lived here for a while, then wandered from state to state. He'd come home once in a while but then leave again. From what Millie had heard, her uncle had seen—and lain with—loose women from here to California. That man probably had left one of his unsuspecting offspring unaware of their horrific fate.

Now that Isaiah was gone, after her pa had died years ago and Ma hid away in her room, Millie had only herself for company—which made visits from her aunt less bearable. If she had her way, she'd surrender and live in the past like Ma.

In late May, Ursula said brightly, "I can't have you looking this way when your uncle comes."

"Uncle Oswald's on his way?" Millie hadn't expected him to return, and yet he did from time to time. After Aunt Jane had fallen, Millie's aunts and uncles had moved on with their lives.

"His letter said he'll be here by Monday." The woman winked. "I'm sure he'd like to see you, if you want."

Millie smiled, and this time it wasn't forced.

"I'd like that very much," she whispered.

———

Uncle Oswald arrived before the summer heat. Millie waited on the bottom porch step. The moment her uncle's head popped up on the horizon, she sat up and smoothed her checkered skirt's fabric.

"Amelia" was all he said.

She shifted to get out of the way. Her uncle strode up the steps and eased onto a worn chair. He pulled off his black hat and rested it on the rocking chair's armrest. An early morning train ride had added wrinkles to his tailored day suit, but Millie couldn't find a single hole or scuff on his shoes. He even used a fancy handkerchief to wipe the sweat off his brow.

"Mornin'." She'd tried to add strength to her voice, but to her ears she'd sounded frail. "Want me to go get Aunt Ursula? She's inside."

"No need. I'm not here for her."

"You need some rest then?"

He leaned forward. "I came for you because of your brother."

"Why?"

"You remember that summer when your mama twisted her ankle?"

"Yes, sir."

"You were about eight years old. All of us were sitting on this porch." Her uncle pulled a cigarette from the inner pocket of his suit. Before he lit the smoke, he stared at the glen beyond the house. "Your mama was in this seat." He tapped the one next to his. "And your brother was where you are right now."

"Where did I sit?" Nobody had wanted to bake in the stuffy house.

"You were right in front of me, listening to me go on and on about Howard."

She smiled. "I remember that day. You made that place sound like another world."

"It is in a way." He retrieved a match and lit the cigarette. "You were grinning and laughing, and your eyes lit up."

"I've always wanted to go."

"We saw that. Ever since you were twelve or so, your brother started sending me a letter every season. He told me how you were doing, what you needed. I'd expected the boy to come up to DC after his schooling." Sweat had formed under his chin, so he wiped himself again. "Course things didn't work out that way."

Millie picked at her memories, searching for a time when Isaiah might've dropped a letter in the post or hid away in a corner to write, but she couldn't think of any.

Her uncle continued. "He told me, if his letters ever stopped coming, he'd fallen and I should take you to the capital."

Millie swallowed past a lump in her throat. God help her, Isaiah had kept that secret all these years. The wind shifted, sending the trail of cigarette smoke her way. She blinked and waited for the world to shift back on its axis.

"And the last letter said you'd passed your . . . Amelia, are you listening?" her uncle asked.

At the sound of her name, she turned to him. "Yes, sir."

His lips twisted with disapproval. "Get in the house and fetch your belongings. We got a noon train to catch."

He hadn't asked if she wanted to go or if now was a good time. Questions rested on her closed lips. Did he expect her to abandon her home that easily? What would happen to Ma? What about the farm? She took in her uncle, expecting him to say more, but he leaned back in the rocking chair and set the seat in motion.

She sat there for a moment. Shouldn't he try to convince her to go? Why convince someone to do something when they already know the answer?

She scrambled to her feet, then she slowed down to walk inside.

Millie found Aunt Ursula in her room. The woman had already taken out Ma's suitcase and stacked Millie's clothes on her bed. Her aunt expected her to go too.

Ursula handed Millie one of the few housedresses she had. "Go put that one in."

The woman eyed a plaid dress with a frayed hem and loose stitches. She set it off to the side.

"How long have you known about Isaiah's letters?"

"For a while now. He'd give me the letters and I'd mail them. In each one, he wrote about how much you'd grown and how much you loved Ozzie's gifts."

Millie reached over and touched her brother's things. Tomorrow morning, she'd wake up somewhere else. She might never see them again.

Aunt Ursula drew one of the dresses—a faded blue garment Ma had worn—up in the air.

Ursula sighed. "Dinah was absolutely beautiful in this. Mmm-hmmm. Your daddy couldn't take his eyes off her when she wore it."

The brief light in Ursula's eyes raised Millie's spirits. She loved to hear that Pa had once been so in love with Ma. She'd never seen that.

"This is a rag, Millie girl." Her aunt tossed the dress onto the bed. "You're going to the city, and you should be at your best."

Millie's gaze swept over what she considered her best: four housedresses, two petticoats, a faded chemise and camisole, a single corset with worn straps, and two pairs of stockings. She'd inherited a lot more than many of her kin, who'd had only a threadbare housedress or two to their name.

"There's something else you should take with you," Ursula said softly. From the kitchen cupboard, on the very top shelf, she retrieved a cerulean tin box. Ma kept valuables inside. A bit of dust covered the embossed bouquet on the top, but the metal glinted after Ursula wiped off the lid. From inside, she retrieved a single antique pearl hair comb.

"But that's Ma's." Millie had never touched such a precious thing.

"Dinah got this as a wedding gift from Granny Claire. And now it's yours." Her aunt ran her fingers along the small shiny pearls ad-hered to the comb.

"What should I do with it?"

Ursula's thin lips pursed together, revealing the sharp lines of her face. "Wear it?"

"But—"

"You're going to Washington." She pushed Millie to hide it in the suitcase. "Your mama never wore it. A shame, I say. She was always scared she'd lose it or somebody'd steal it."

Millie took the gift and folded it in a handkerchief. Then she tucked it into the suitcase. It amazed her how quickly she'd packed her life away. How little she owned.

With a sigh, Aunt Ursula patted her shoulder. "C'mon now. If you keep standing there, you might grow roots, girl."

When she thought about it, perhaps she should sprout roots and stay. Who'd take care of Ma? What about the many tasks around the cabin? "Maybe I shouldn't go. What about my mother?"

Ursula placed the suitcase in her hands. "I'll take care of her. She'll be fine. Young folks like you should move on." She added, "Don't let anyone or anything keep you from enjoying what life has to offer."

———

By midday that Tuesday morning, Millie and her uncle boarded a train in Charlottesville for Washington. It was a whirlwind of goodbyes, and as she perched on the train seat next to Uncle, she didn't feel nervous until the train pulled away from the station. She'd waited for this moment for a long time—this all didn't feel real. That perhaps her brother hadn't left and given her such a beau-tiful gift. Would she wake up tomorrow back at home?

The four-hour train ride from Charlottesville to Fredericksburg and then finally Washington was shorter than she'd expected. This was her first train ride, and she couldn't help but watch through the window as the scenery passed and listen to the conversations bubbling up around her.

A different world existed outside the long country roads and fields she'd seen. While the Blue Ridge Mountains rose to the west, their train weaved through towns no bigger than a speck, but they had names like Gordonsville and Lorton. The passengers who boarded and disembarked didn't openly stare like she did. They had far more interesting lives.

Conversations in the colored section bounded up and down the aisles. Much of the chatter related to the upcoming election. Whether they supported Cox or Harding, they all wanted change. Especially those who hated the nation's current leader. Two Negro men discussed Woodrow Wilson's failure as president.

"If that man had his way, we'd be in chains again," one gentleman said. "Last I heard, he's still segregating the capital."

"My uncle lost his job at the post office," the other said. "All them so-called promises of fairness during the election in 1912 was nothing but fruit rotting in the sun."

"Politicians will say anything to get the Negro vote."

On the far side of the carriage, an old biddy and her grown granddaughter spread their family's business.

"When I get off this train, your daddy's gonna get it," the older woman hissed.

In a quieter voice, her granddaughter replied, "Granny . . ."

"That dirty fool has been sleeping with your cousin under our very noses." She made loud smacking noises. "Our neighbor told me he noticed Henry coming and going while everyone was at work. Bentley heard both of their voices coming out of the bedroom window. Lord knows my son ain't a Christian man no more—now he's a filthy philander."

Millie stole a glance at her uncle, but he kept his eyes on his book. Perhaps he'd heard it all. Dirty gossip hung from every clothesline on the farm, so she wasn't one to judge.

At least she would've kept private Bridge business to herself.

To take up the time, Millie considered pulling Oswald into a conversation, but he crossed his legs and closed his eyes. His dark skin appeared dry and wrinkles lined his brow so she let him sleep. The last time she'd seen Uncle, he'd looked like Pa, or at least a younger version of him, without the creases alcohol had cleaved into his face. Perhaps if her father hadn't taken up liquor, he would've worn a tailored suit and expensive shoes like Uncle.

Uncle Oswald slept until they reached Union Station. The conductor's call startled him awake—and brought Millie's apprehension back. Now her new life would truly begin. Without a word, Uncle got off the train and she followed. Commuters spilled around them. She couldn't help but stare down the long, covered train concourse.

Colored men, women, and children wearing fine clothes or the simplest garments strode away from them while three women waited. The woman at the end had to be Aunt Alma. She had a stern expression, about as stiff as the pleated wool poplin dress she wore. The two younger women beside her, who appeared to be around Millie's age, took after their light-skinned mother. They brightened at the sight of Uncle. Those had to be her cousins.

"So this is Alfred and Dinah's girl?" Aunt Alma's gaze jumped from Millie's worn shoes up to her faded gingham housedress. Her aunt's stony assessment came to a stop at her waist, where two black buttons were missing.

Uncle gestured to the women. "Amelia, this is your aunt Alma and your cousins Henrietta and Rosalind. Girls, greet her."

Unlike their mother, Henrietta and Rosalind smiled. Henrietta appeared statuesque, with wide eyes, narrow hips, and long arms. Her shorter older sister, Rosalind, was stockier, her hips fuller.

Like their mother, they were dressed in fashionable dresses with ribbons and shiny buttons. Extravagant wide-brimmed hats adorned their heads. Millie touched her straw hat, hoping her braided hair hadn't escaped the flat bun Aunt Ursula had made.

"Where are her things?" Aunt Alma asked, her voice wispy. "Mr. Parks is waiting to collect them."

"This is all I have." Millie slipped her scuffed suitcase behind her back.

"She doesn't have any trunks, Alma." Uncle began to walk away. "Let's go."

Millie had always assumed Uncle Ozzie was a man of means, but she had no idea how much money he had until they reached the family car, a Model T. The jalopy her brother had used to drive back and forth to town never shined like this one. She gawked until Mr. Parks, who now held her suitcase, opened the passenger door. Uncle got into the front seat while the others got into the rear. Millie scooted onto the back seat last, and her aunt sniffed with displeasure.

"Smells like the farm arrived with you, *my dear*." Barbs covered her endearment.

"Don't listen to Mother," Henrietta whispered to Millie. "She's trying to work her way into the Lenox Social Club, but at the rate she's going, she'll never make it."

Uncle Ozzie didn't live outside the city but near a busy street. Every house and building had electricity.

Henrietta must've seen Millie's widened eyes, for she said, "This is U Street. Isn't it amazing? Rosalind said the main drag in Harlem is better, but nothing compares to home."

She was grateful for the seat at the end—she had the best vantage point to take in the other vehicles and carriages honking and avoiding the pedestrians lining the streets. They drove past a hot sandwich vendor on the sidewalk and a truck selling tamales. The wonderful scents wafted through the car. They passed a YWCA, two banks, and even a hotel. A sign displaying the afternoon viewing times for a local theater's showing of a Charlie Chaplin movie stood tall beside an advertisement for The Stocking Store. From one end to the other of the wide boulevard lined with shade trees, Millie saw mainly Negroes, many of them finely dressed. She breathed in the city and sighed. This colored neighborhood felt like a town tucked away in a vast metropolis.

Millie and her brother had always wanted to visit the capital.

Thank you, Isaiah, she thought.

They left the bustle and turned eventually onto a quieter street called Willard. Elegant yet narrow three-story houses were lined up on both sides of the street. Even though the homes were uniform, they had charm, with iron fences and ornate doorways. The car pulled up next to a beautiful light-green house. Mr. Parks opened the door and Millie peered at the many windows until Henrietta touched her shoulder.

"C'mon!" she said.

Millie got out of the car, and Henrietta clutched her hand to pull her up the steps to the small porch. Aunt Alma and Rosalind followed as they entered a parlor. Right beside the door, a set of steps led up to the next floor, while the rest of the first floor lay ahead. Every surface in the parlor gleamed.

"Etta, see that she changes into more suitable attire before dinner," her aunt said stiffly before the older woman marched up the steps. "Rosie, fetch the maid to bring me some tea."

Millie never got a chance to say another word to her uncle either. He disappeared down the hall off the parlor.

It was Henrietta who tugged Millie again to climb the stairs to the second floor. "You'll be sharing the room with me," she said. "Are you seventeen, like Father said?"

They reached the landing and headed to the second door.

"Yes," she murmured. "I turned seventeen back in January."

It was the last birthday she'd celebrate with Isaiah.

After Henrietta opened the door, Millie slipped into a room she wouldn't even have known to dream of. Henrietta had two beds covered with pink-and-yellow paisley bedspreads. Matching curtains adorned the single window, which brought in late spring light. Between the beds stood a single chest of drawers, a desk, and a wooden chair with a padded seat.

"You can have the bed closest to the window," Etta said. "I emptied the two bottom drawers in the dresser." Her cousin explained where to find the bathroom and such, but Millie missed much of it as she collapsed on her bed. She leaned up to search every corner of the room, but she couldn't uncover a single sign of an emergency suitcase, pack, or bag.

She'd just arrived, and the topic of the family curse had yet to come up. The one thing she'd learned from her elders was that every Bridge man bore someone who'd fall. Did that mean her uncle's family already had lost a younger or older sibling? Or even worse, were they oblivious?

"Was the trip rough? How early did you have to be at the train station?" Henrietta asked, pulling Millie into the present. Millie had also missed Rosalind's entrance into the room.

"Not early," Millie replied. "I get up before dawn on most days."

"I'm sure you would," Rosalind quipped. "Have to milk the cow and all."

Millie leaned toward Henrietta. "Do you have a brother or sister who has fallen already?"

Etta stole a glance at her sister. Rosalind hurried to the door and closed it.

"We don't talk about that," Etta whispered.

"Why?" Millie asked. "What happens if—"

"Mother said it doesn't matter *anymore*," Rosie said firmly, her brows drawn together. "And I say it's backcountry foolishness. Mother doesn't want to hear it and neither do I."

Henrietta reached out and patted Millie's hand. "Rest easy. I *promise* that everything's fine."

Fear pulsed through Amelia. Did their mother truly believe the curse wasn't real? Had her uncle failed to convince her?

Etta gave her a forced smile. "If you're my age, then that means you just finished high school, right? Rosie couldn't pass Howard University's entrance exams last year so she's trying to take them again in September."

With that remark, Etta's older sister glared at her.

Etta grinned at Rosie. "Father told us you came here to take the exams and attend Howard to become a physician?"

Millie's breath faltered. Not only did she have a willfully ignorant aunt, she had another problem. She'd assumed she'd attend college someday, but she'd thought she would have more time. Maybe she would find a job, work in a factory for a year or two. But was she even ready for the rigors of college? Other than studying the books Uncle Oswald had sent, she'd completed only two years of high school.

Rosie must've caught Millie's apprehension, for she said, "You've been studying all this time, haven't you?"

"Of course." Her smile faltered and Rosalind caught it.

"I'm sure you'll do well." Rosie folded her arms. "A smart girl like you won't need to find a job." She shrugged. "And if all else fails, you can work with Clara as one of our housemaids."

The bite in her cousin's tone nipped at Millie, but she simply forced herself to smile and get up to unpack her bag. She presented her back to them. It was better that way. Telling Rosie what she truly thought—that the girl should mind her viper's tongue—would get her into trouble.

Mother, did you hear what our dear cousin said to me? Rosie would probably say over their supper. *She's a heathen, I tell you.*

Millie stuffed her dresses into the drawers to still her trembling hands. She kept working. Her uncle had brought her here for a reason.

From the corner of her eye, she caught Rosie waltzing out of the room. Millie expected her to take her backhanded comments with her.

CHAPTER 4

Amelia Bridge

JUNE 1920

A re you certain you want to walk, Miss Amelia?" Clara asked Millie that morning. "Didn't you walk last week?"

"It's absolutely beautiful outside," Millie replied. "The fresh air will do me some good."

The others had departed for the day, leaving only Millie and her uncle at the dining room table. Clara whisked away the dishes before Millie could offer a hand. While her uncle continued to read the latest news from *The Washington Bee* and drank from his never-empty cup of coffee, Millie got ready to leave.

"Young ladies shouldn't be out in that heat." The woman—who appeared to be no older than Millie herself—put her hands on her ample hips and looked Millie up and down as if Millie would come back five shades darker.

Ever since Millie had arrived, Aunt Alma had droned on and on about parasols and how Millie would never find a nice light-skinned gentleman if she kept gallivanting on her little trips down the street.

"Amelia doesn't have to walk." Her uncle took a ghost's sip from his cup. "She can go with me."

Millie edged closer to the door off the dining room. The spears of summer sunlight beaming through the parlor's bay window beckoned for her to explore.

Before she could throw a gleeful goodbye over her shoulder, Uncle Oswald abandoned his newspaper and headed out of the house. She hurried after him.

"Miss Amelia, you forgot your parasol." The sharp-eyed maid put the light-pink umbrella in Millie's hands before she could reach the door. "Have a pleasant walk, Miss."

Once outside, Millie spotted Mr. Parks scurrying out of the car to open the back door.

"Is Miss Amelia joining you at the clinic already, Dr. Bridge?" the driver asked.

"Not today," her uncle replied. "My niece wants to go to the park."

Mr. Parks's head tilted to the side in amusement.

They settled inside. After Mr. Parks started the car, her uncle asked, "Will you be carrying on with all this wandering once your schooling begins?"

"You think I'm wandering?" she replied.

"Feels like you're searching for something."

"I guess I'm a bit restless."

"You're searching for the middle ground, but you'll never find it. Mark my words, the life you had at the farm is no more."

The car cruised down U Street until the tiny park appeared. She waited for Uncle Oswald to say more, but he didn't fuss like Aunt Alma. He had even fewer words after she got out of the car.

"Stay out of trouble" was all he said.

"Yes, sir." The car pulled away, and her quiet march into the park began. She passed a gentleman in a threadbare suit. She gave him a nod but got none in return. Not everyone brushed her off, but the city added grit to most folks' eyes. In many ways, the capital was like the Virginia countryside, full of sinister and kind creatures, but she missed the sounds of home. Every morning Millie woke before dawn and waited to hear the rooster's call. She waited to feel the darkness pull her back into slumber, but she lay there and couldn't sleep. In this land of perpetual light and little starlight, she longed to lose herself on the farm with the familiarity of her pack on her back. If she closed her eyes, she could still hear Isaiah trudging around the cabin, preparing breakfast before they did their chores. The muscles in her hands recalled the weight of the milk bucket, her back the pressure from the worn sack. But most of all, she heard Isaiah's voice rise like a choir, singing of the things she needed to remember the most during their morning walks through the orchard.

"What can you eat here?" Isaiah had always asked her.

Millie had searched the forest floor, past the fungal dead man's fingers, over the poisonous crawling berries to the oyster mushrooms. The pearl-white mushrooms spread out like umbrellas protecting the lichens from the rain.

"Those," she'd said, pointing to the oyster mushrooms. "And those too," she'd added once she spied the wavy tops and golden-brown stalks of chanterelles hiding among the ferns.

Her brother had towered over her and drawn the branches away so she could pass under them. "Which plants are better for stomachaches, garlic or mint?"

"Both," she'd said proudly.

Millie missed those days. Here in the city, the patches of greenery were smaller. She only had to turn her head slightly to glimpse concrete and stone. Gone were the plentiful cottontails. Gone were the bears. Edible plants were here, but she found fewer of them. In many places, she uncovered green-speckled poisonous mushrooms and deadly fruit on the spiny stalks of horse nettle plants.

Millie was as far from home as she was from her brother.

Before Millie could take her college entrance examinations, or even have her expensive tuition paid, Aunt Alma had an ultimatum.

"You'll learn proper etiquette, dear. I won't have you sully the Bridge name among my friends," she said crisply.

As Henrietta had mentioned upon Millie's arrival, Aunt Alma wanted to get into the Lenox Social Club, an elite gathering of the upper-class Negro women in the capital. To ensure Millie fit her standards, Auntie had hired an etiquette tutor from New York. That stern mulatto tutor drilled lessons so deeply into Millie's head, she couldn't sit still without hearing a particular instruction. "Keep your chin up," she often heard. Or the lovely order for her to: "Cross your legs at the ankle."

The rules bit at Millie worse than early summer mosquitos.

"Mimic your aunt," the tutor had instructed. "When you court a fine gentleman someday, you'll thank the heavens for her connections."

She found it laughable how Aunt Alma could give advice to anyone. The woman cared more about what others thought of her than her less fortunate peers did.

Especially when it came to Millie's attire.

On an early summer afternoon Aunt Alma had ushered them out of the house for shopping.

They strolled down U Street, having just departed from Ware's Department Store. Pedestrians hurried around the four of them, including a keen-looking gentleman in a double-breasted gray suit. Rosie's head tilted with interest, but she kept in time with her slow-going mother. After three hours of shopping and fittings, Millie was in no hurry either. So she lazily strolled beside Etta behind a chatty Rosie and her aunt.

"Granddaddy Foster worked himself to death as a laborer in Boston," Etta said to Millie.

"Your granddaddy sounds like mine. Most of my kin only know the farm. Some folks left for the city but"—Millie gestured toward the flashy businesses lining the boulevard—"none of them lived like this."

"I suspect Mother cared more about the company she kept after she married Father and moved here," Etta said. "Over the years, she's lost herself in making sure Rosie and I go to the right schools. That we vacation in New York or Martha's Vineyard. That we join the right social circles so we can meet the right people."

Even with her rural upbringing, deep down Millie understood that there was an "us" and a "them." Especially among the colored folks. Ma hadn't needed to mention the invisible line in church separating parishioners in polished shoes from those who walked in barefoot.

What she didn't understand was why some Negroes needed to separate themselves. Whether they had fair or dark skin, curly or straight hair, folks still needed to breathe, and in the end, they died too. Just like everyone else.

"Aunt Alma ain't—isn't lost," Millie said, quickly correcting herself. "She knows exactly what she wants to do: keep up appearances through spending money."

Etta flashed a smile. "Shopping wasn't that bad. Didn't you have fun? You'll need those clothes for school."

"I have clothes."

Etta gave a half shrug. "You'll see. When you go to college and associate with those people, you'll understand why you must look different."

As Auntie had told her repeatedly over the last three hours, she didn't have the proper attire suitable for an "educated" young woman. Last she'd heard, folks learned just fine without fur-lined coats, velvet cloche hats, and leather lace boots.

"I'm here to go to college," she said. "That's all."

Aunt Alma must've heard her. She replied, far too loudly, "Agreed. Good girls do not associate with the riffraff that comes out at night."

"Goodness forbid she associate with that element," Rosie added.

"Yes, ma'am," Millie murmured.

"Rosie's been down to Murray Palace Casino many a time," Etta whispered with a conspiratorial smile. "She sneaks out of the house after Clara goes to sleep."

Millie hid her grin and kept pace with Etta to hurry around a man campaigning for Harding. The gentleman belted out promises for a return to normalcy—which she welcomed after the war and the flu pandemic. Around them, U Street writhed with activity, its occupants carrying more than parcels and purses. They carried burdens. Whether she lived in the woods or the city—one thing was certain: everyone kept secrets.

CHAPTER 5

Amelia Bridge

AUGUST 1920

As temperatures rose, Aunt Alma shaped and molded Millie into "one of Dr. Oswald Bridge's girls." During those summer months, her cousins frolicked and socialized without a care—it was as if the family curse never existed to them. Millie hated to admit it, but she felt the same way. As August swept in, the birch tree forests and Virginia mountains began to feel more distant.

Much to her surprise, Aunt Alma finally gave Millie permission to join her cousins for a movie. The young women ran off to U Street again, eager for an afternoon of laughter. While *Shoulder Arms*, starring Charlie Chaplin, played on the big screen, she grinned like a fool. She'd never seen a movie before, and she almost pinched herself in delight. Nothing compared to the fine leather seats and the theater's gleaming overhead lights. The audience devoured every quirky mannerism Chaplin threw at them. A couple to her left burst into laughter. Four men shouted protests when the actor bumbled down the wrong hallway.

She carried the laughter and joy with her right up to the entrance examinations in September. And she not only passed but also excelled, receiving a far more favorable score than dear Cousin Rosie. After the young women learned the results a couple of days later, Rosie stood in the kitchen and complained to Aunt Alma. She didn't bother to lower her voice either. Millie heard every syllable from the parlor, where she sat with Etta.

"She told us she only had two years of high school," Rosie said. "Makes no sense."

Her aunt harrumphed. "You can't take the backwoods out of girls like her. She probably cheated off Etta."

Millie swallowed a laugh, but Henrietta couldn't resist snickering. Why bother cheating when Millie knew the answers? And Etta hadn't scored as highly as she did either—Millie had worked hard to reach this point. Over those five years her brother had written to him, Uncle Ozzie had sent her book after book. During the long winters when Ma, Isaiah, and Millie were stuck indoors, she'd learned geography, Greek history, and biology.

She wasn't lucky, and she most certainly wasn't a backwoods fool. She simply had put in the work.

After they'd passed their exams, the young women only had to wait a few days for autumn quarter to begin. On the morning of move-in day, Millie could think of nothing else but starting her studies in biology. After she obtained her degree, she planned to attend medical school. All those dreams began with her uncle. She never forgot that fateful summer when she was eight and Uncle Oswald had spoken of his time at Howard University. Day after day he'd trudged from his dormitory at Clark Hall to the Medical Building. And now it was *her* time. Nothing would get in her way—unless she faltered on her own.

While everyone ate breakfast, Uncle Oswald said, "Focus on

your studies, and after you've adjusted to your first quarter, you can join me at the clinic."

"But I'm not a doctor . . . yet," she said to him.

"Don't need to be a doctor to fetch supplies or do secretarial work," he replied stiffly. "Will be good for you to listen and learn."

She bowed her head and departed the house with lighter shoulders and joy in her step. None of the girls spoke while Mr. Parks drove them to campus, but soon enough they reached Miner Hall. A throng of chattering ladies surrounded them, for Rosie and Etta had many friends here. Millie faced the imposing brick building, with its columns and three stories, and marched up the steps. The girls' dorm should've filled her with fear for all the long hours of studying to come, but she was ready for anything. There would be difficult days, but today no one could take her exuberance away.

CHAPTER 6

Amelia Bridge

JANUARY 1921

Winter swept in not long after the autumn quarter had ended. Millie had gotten high marks for her labors. Everything was as it should be until she stepped into Professor Patricia Mayberry's classroom the next quarter.

Henrietta had taken Professor Mayberry's Medieval European History course the previous quarter and she had warned Millie to stay away. "She's the strictest teacher I've ever seen."

Millie had tried to help her cousin study, and she quickly discerned Henrietta couldn't remember dates if her life depended on it. So her poor cousin had fumbled through the verbal exams and barely passed. Millie, on the other hand, eagerly registered for the course. Mayberry's teaching style didn't frighten her. She *wanted* to learn from someone who required memorization and the strictest standards. Even though she was safe from falling through time, she'd learned that knowledge of the past was of the utmost importance.

It was a dreary, snowy day in January when she stepped into Main Hall. The previous quarter, the four-story building, perched on the summit of a hill, had intimidated her—for it represented years of exams and lectures. But now she marched inside with the rest of the students, her mind open and ready to focus on her studies.

Warm air from the building's steam furnaces fogged up the glasses of one of her classmates as he hurried into Mayberry's classroom to secure a front-row seat. She followed the less eager students and settled into one of the middle rows.

Millie wasn't *that* eager to be a target for the teacher's attention.

The woman in question scribbled classroom rules on the chalkboard. Her crisp handwriting was punctuated with each scratch and tap. From behind, Patricia Mayberry could've been any colored woman on campus. Her silk blouse, with the feminine lace border along the collar, softened the stiffness of her back. In contrast, the professor's muted gray skirt reflected the bleakness of the expression she presented when she turned around.

"Good morning," she said.

"Good morning," the class repeated.

"Welcome to—" Mayberry's words were interrupted when a student hurried into the room with murmured apologies.

"Your name?" the professor asked, her voice devoid of emotion.

The student froze. He turned around and sucked in a breath. "Harold Sims, ma'am. I had to—"

"Your excuses are irrelevant." Mayberry pointed to the rules she'd written on the first of two chalkboards. The first rule: ALL TARDIES WILL COST HALF A POINT. "Life as a student happens, but unlike you, I'm expected to do my job to earn a wage. Your tuition and your place in this school are sacred. Remember that next time."

He removed his bowler hat and inclined his head. "Yes, Professor."

"Be seated." Mayberry paced the front of the room while she pressed on. "Mark and remember my rules. A laborer late for work will lose his job, but all you'll lose is half a point."

Millie had already written down the rules, noted the readings for the week, and tucked a bookmark in at the first page in the textbook. At least she got something accomplished.

For the rest of the hour, not a single student sneezed or made a peep unless the teacher asked a question. Millie glanced around and noticed, like in her other courses, that only four other women sat in class. She recognized two of them as fellow freshmen.

After a lecture on the barbarian invasions during the late first century, Professor Mayberry concluded the class. "I expect you to read the first two chapters in the Hargreaves book. Your homework is simple." Her gaze swept over the classroom. "This is a medieval history course, but I want you to consider the past and the present. Do you believe history repeats itself? We will have a debate during the next lecture, and I expect everyone to participate."

When Mayberry said "everyone," she looked right at Millie, then she dismissed them. Millie hurried out, the weight of the woman's stern eyes following her.

Class met twice per week, so she had only forty-eight hours to answer the question. It seemed simple: Did history repeat itself?

And yet from what she'd experienced, a simple answer didn't suffice. Giving examples from the many failed Russian invasions came to mind, but she couldn't help but consider the deeper meaning behind the question.

Wednesday morning snuck up on Millie, and she didn't have any answers other than the ones she'd scribbled last night. This morning not a single person walked in late.

As on Monday, Professor Mayberry got right to the business at hand. "We will begin with our discussion on your homework topic."

A few of Millie's classmates sat up straighter, some adjusted papers full of notes. The woman beside her had three pages of arguments and rebuttals.

Her paper had five measly sentences.

"Let us begin our discussion with a practical example. If any of you have read George Santayana's *The Life of Reason*, you will have read the line, 'Those who cannot remember the past are condemned to repeat it.' Consider the fall of the Roman Empire, as well as the demise of Han dynasty China. Each of these civilizations had a corrupt government, social unrest, and invasions from other countries. Yet they were thousands of miles apart, with differing philosophies. Why did this occur? Why couldn't any of them have learned from the past and changed the outcome?"

Three hands shot up. Millie's wasn't one of them.

"Man is inherently flawed," one man said, eager to make his point. "Power corrupts, and with that corruption, we make the same decisions we believe will benefit humankind, but these decisions only benefit ourselves."

Professor Mayberry ignored the other two hands and pointed at Millie. "What do you think, Miss Bridge?"

All heads turned to her. *Damn*. She should've raised her hand like the others. Millie touched the papers on her desk, but the answer she had in mind didn't come out. "We're supposed to learn from the past, so we don't repeat our mistakes, but what if every option will result in the same outcome?"

The professor approached her desk, weaving around the others. "True, but 'in the midst of chaos, there is always an opportunity.'"

"Sun Tzu," Millie dared to whisper.

"Correct," Professor Mayberry said, her gaze flicking to Millie's notes—or what few notes she had. With a nervous smile, Millie clasped her hands together and rested them on top.

The woman pressed on. "One of the greatest tacticians of all time also said, 'There are not more than five musical notes, yet the combinations of these five give rise to more melodies than can ever be heard.' Think about it." She tapped Millie's desk twice. "The Romans or the Han didn't have to make the tried-and-true choices. Nothing is inevitable."

"Nothing is inevitable," a classmate murmured.

Millie begged to differ, but she listened while the professor continued.

"One alternate decision," she said, "at the right moment, can change everything. Consider the late 300s Visigoth invasion you read about in chapter one. If their leader, Alaric the First, hadn't sacked Rome in 410 AD, would Rome still have fallen?"

The discussion progressed over the material they'd studied. A few of Millie's classmates eagerly jumped into the conversation, but she held back, her thoughts swimming with ideas she'd often thought about back at the farm: Who'd cursed the Bridges? How had all this madness started?

By the time the class ended, she had her book and notes stowed away. She rushed out of the room with more questions than answers.

CHAPTER 7

Amelia Bridge

NOVEMBER 1924

F ive years came and went. Sixteen short seasons full of sunshine, rain, and snow. Millie completed her biology degree and began her first year in medical school. Much to Aunt Alma's disdain, she didn't bring home a swanky suitor from a fine family.

Etta had far bigger ambitions. In the time it had taken them to finish their undergraduate studies, she'd waltzed into Uncle's house on the arm of the heir to one of the richest colored manufacturers in town. Rosie had less luck, but she still secured a position as a secretary to one of the few Negro-owned law firms in the city.

Millie returned home during Thanksgiving recess to a silent house.

Clara greeted her at the door with a stiff nod. The girl fetched the bag the driver had left nearby. "Welcome home, Miss Bridge."

"It's wonderful to see you again. Are you excited about the upcoming holidays?"

"Of course, Miss."

Millie smiled, but there was nothing exciting about the holidays in this house. This place rarely stirred or twitched, which was nothing new. Over the years, she'd never heard their radio playing music. Occasionally, the electronic tinny sound in the form of a news broadcast had come from Uncle's study. He seemingly lived at his practice while her aunt spent evenings at charity functions. He and Aunt Alma had separate bedrooms, ate at opposite ends of the dinner table, and never laughed or kissed. They were two ships that rarely shared the same port.

But today they were in the same room.

A heated conversation bounded down the hall and crashed through the parlor. Millie stood wide-eyed in the foyer. Clara beat a hasty retreat up the stairs with the bag. Usually, Millie didn't eavesdrop, but when Uncle Ozzie growled out the word "dalliances," the bitterness in the air drew her closer.

"This circus show between us tires me," Uncle said, his voice smeared with drink. "I refuse to be seen with a two-faced adulterer."

Alma's sigh floated through the closed door and slipped down the hall. "I was weak back then."

"You were more than weak." A chair groaned as someone, likely her uncle, got up. "You were willing to lie with another man to get what you wanted."

"I wanted what you didn't care for: an heir." Footsteps approached the door. Millie stumbled back, but Alma must've crossed the room. "Thanks to me, our daughters are respected. Our friends speak highly of your practice."

"Those are not *my* children—"

The older woman harrumphed before she spoke again. "I did what you asked. I *never* had a son by you—to appease your far-fetched curse, the supposed legacy of all you foolish Bridge men.

But make no mistake, husband, those girls are yours. They have your name and you will respect me in public and not destroy what we have built."

Millie retreated until her back hit the far wall. A painting jostled, but she reached out and steadied it.

Dear God in heaven, she thought. No wonder her cousins didn't live in fear. They weren't Bridges after all. She stumbled up the stairs.

Relief should've followed her, but as the fall quarter progressed, new feelings settled in. Doubt. Fear. For now every time she met her cousins, she knew why she never saw features similar to Oswald's.

Just like Millie's features didn't resemble her father's.

Millie took after her mother more than her father, Alfred. Ma had always been short, unlike Bridge women, who were usually taller with square shoulders. Wherever she went, she was the shorter one, the petite woman with feet too small for grown women's shoes.

"I never seen someone so tiny until I saw your ma," Pa always used to say. Millie could still imagine her mother cooking in the kitchen when she was a child, but she never considered how she didn't have Pa's wry smile or his wide nose.

Alfred had raised her and instilled in her a drive to work hard. That inner strength had carried her through her studies. The stubbornness he'd passed on flared once in a while. Like this morning, when Millie left the house to trudge to the corner market. Clara could've done the errand, but Millie's feet worked just as well. Five years ago, she could step out of the cabin to fetch what she needed nearby. The snow would crunch under her boots as she hurried to the chicken coop. Her path to fetch eggs was different now. Sludgy snow covered the roads, leaving vehicles trapped against snowdrifts. She darted around them, sure-footed in her boots, coat, and overalls. Farther down the street, men attempted to dig out a Model T from its wintry grave.

From Willard Street, she made her way northward to U Street. Even during the holidays, pedestrians huddled together to head to work or hurry home. Powdery snow partially covered signs and advertisements, but the flashing lights from the Murray Palace Casino still shone. The door to a restaurant opened as she walked by. Millie lingered, letting the rich smells of fried eggs and grits pull her away from her distracted thoughts. Before the door closed, the lively horns and piano from Bessie Smith's "The St. Louis Blues" filtered out. That woman's rich voice, singing about an unfaithful man, lulled her as she reached the busy intersection of U Street and Florida Avenue. Millie could still hear and feel the weight of loss. She'd never been to St. Louis, but she had her own blues. It was too easy for her mind to wander. Perhaps that was why she took a misstep on the curb and fell forward. She reached out to catch herself, but jagged glass in the road sliced through her glove and cut her hand. The blood pooled in the snow, and she stared at it—just like Bessie kept singing in her head about hating to see the evening sun go down.

Back when she was seven, she'd glimpsed another pool of blood, but it'd been Ma's, not hers. Millie and her brother had never liked their lonely Sunday dinners after church. Before Pa started drinking, their mother used to wake up before the sunrise to prepare the meal. By the time the family returned home from church, everything would be ready. All that ended when Pa picked bottles of booze over church. His absence was marked by the empty space in the pew between Isaiah and Ma.

Their family got constant reminders from their pastor. "We'll pray for him," Pastor Harris said at first. Then a month later they heard, "We sure do miss Brother Bridge."

Later, the deacons said they hoped he'd find the church again, but they knew where to find him. Most of the men Pa drank with were laborers who gathered near the old mill to smoke, listen to music, and drown themselves in moonshine. The foul-tasting fluid blurred Pa's mind and soured his temper.

It also changed how he looked. Alcohol drew wrinkles along his cheekbones and etched worm-like veins into his eyes. A foul stench followed him around. No employer wanted a man who arrived at work on time but couldn't think straight. Week after week, he grew angrier and more frustrated with his circumstances. And that was when he started to lash out. Sometimes when Millie and Isaiah were sound asleep, their parents would argue until Pa beat Ma. Isaiah stood up to their father first, and when he fell from Pa's blows, Millie tried to protect Ma. Night after night, Pa beat them too.

During those long summer nights, she waited for family to come take Pa away. For one of Ma's sisters to intervene and save them. But at the age of seven, she learned a hard lesson that what happens in a man's house often stays there.

After living for so long in a broken home full of arguments and bruises, Ma didn't care how much her words angered him. One July evening, right as the sun was setting, she perched on her chair on the porch, itching for a fight. Pa lounged on the other end.

Ma bit out, "Why you still here? I know you don't trust me, Al. You might as well get out."

"*I* should leave?" Pa asked, incredulous. "I'll drag you and those bastard kids of yours to sleep in the dirt before I let you stay on my daddy's land."

Ma slowly shook her head. "You own nothing here but the shirt on your back. Your brothers own everything!" She cackled, the sound bouncing off the nearby trees.

Pa growled, his face contorting until the monster pricking under his skin came to life. For the second time that day, he punched her until she couldn't talk back. Millie and her brother wrapped their arms around her, and like earlier, he hit them too. Once he exhausted himself, he left the house. The siblings were left holding on to Ma as her blood pooled on the porch floorboards.

After the beatings, Ma never cried. She only grew more distant. That night, with her lip busted open and her eyes swollen shut, she muttered words Millie had since cast aside. "That man will never be like Bertie," she'd whispered. "My husband is useless in my house, and in my bed too."

The words she said that night came to mind as Uncle Oswald stitched up Millie's arm in the kitchen. She'd never thought about why her father had said his kids didn't belong to him. Hadn't he been drunk at the time?

But now that she stared at the neat rows of stitches and thought about it, everything came together.

"We should go to a hospital, Millie," Uncle said with his glasses resting on his nose. "The laceration isn't deep, but there will be a pretty bad scar from your forearm down to your palm."

"We all have scars" was all she said. Uncle hadn't seen the ghastly mark on her shoulder and didn't know why the pinkie on her left hand didn't bend all the way. One more scar wouldn't matter beside the others Pa had given her.

Millie took in her uncle, the man with features so different from her cousins'. She considered how often Ma had rushed over to Uncle Bertie's house. Back then, her uncle'd had no wife or kids and fought Pa over the beatings. And now it was obvious why Millie shared Bertie's smile and his small hands, while Isaiah had Pa's height and wide nose. He was Alfred Bridge's boy, surely.

She sniffed and the weight of it all pressed against her chest until she struggled not to cry. If Bertie was her father, then like Isaiah, she was walking half in this world and half in the next.

CHAPTER 8

Amelia Bridge

DECEMBER 1924

Paranoia returned and smothered her like the winter storm raging outside. Safe inside the dormitory at Miner Hall, Millie should've rested before fall exams. And yet she'd startled awake with sweat drenching her back and a tremble to her fingers. Millie tried to turn over in bed, and the crinkle of the freedom papers tucked away in her pocket sounded like a rising alarm. She couldn't ignore the impending doom settling into her stomach. Didn't she have school to attend? Sprinkling doubts on her thoughts helped—there was no way to prove Bertie was her father.

One of her teachers often quoted Occam's razor: The simplest explanation is the most likely.

And yet she couldn't close her eyes without remembering the last time she'd seen Bertie. He'd sauntered up to the house with that lazy smile of his. She was twelve at the time. He'd leaned against the doorframe and asked a question he knew the answer to. "Your ma home?"

"She ain't home," Isaiah had said.

Bertie had smiled, winked at his nephew, then reached over to her and brushed his fingertips along her forehead. "Tell her I'll come back later. You take care now, sunshine."

Her heart tugged painfully at such a simple goodbye.

Millie forced herself out of bed and got dressed. Then she retrieved the satchel she'd stowed away under the bed to collect what she would need. She stole flint from Thirkield Science Hall. One of the groundskeepers outside Main Hall sold a pocketknife to her. Kindling scattered across the quad between the men's and women's dormitories filled her pockets regularly. And after each meal she tucked away pieces of bread and wrapped them in handkerchiefs. She felt foolish at first, but with her luck, she'd fall headfirst into an eighteenth-century swamp filled with mosquitos and hostile settlers. Not once had she studied a map or scoured the books in the library to learn DC-area history. She strode into battle without knowing the lay of the land.

As Christmas recess approached, Millie knew a decision had to be made, whether to leave or to stay and finish her degree. She could fall through time at any moment, but she could also move on with her life. Over the next few weeks, she ran through scenario after scenario, but her fear finally won after she finished her Histology final. She strode into Union Station and purchased a one-way train ticket to Charlottesville.

It was time to go home.

I'm so sorry, Isaiah, she thought.

If her brother were here, he'd tell her she hadn't wasted her time. She had an education, even though she hadn't obtained what she'd always wanted: a medical degree. She wouldn't take over her uncle's practice or settle down here and marry. Leaving the city also meant she'd return to the farm with no job prospects other than teaching children or working in one of the many businesses or farms around Charlottesville. Home was a prison in the guise of a sanctuary.

But Millie had also experienced what life had to offer. She'd seen the Washington Monument at dusk, eaten the finest French and Italian cuisine, and heard esteemed Howard University musicians play the most beautiful melodies in a concert hall. Once she'd even dared to sneak out of the house with Rosie. They'd sipped giggle water and enjoyed a night of dancing until Millie's feet hurt. Over the past couple of years, she'd experienced golden moments to last a lifetime.

During her first semester, Professor Mayberry had said a single decision could alter one's destiny, but Millie wouldn't have changed a thing. Everyone had to make choices.

She was determined to leave the capital with her head held high, but she knew regret would follow her.

———

With several feet of snow outside, Millie feared the train wouldn't depart tomorrow, but she still packed up her trunks. Just like last year, the house was decorated for the upcoming Christmas holiday with fresh evergreen wreaths, but no one gathered in the parlor to mark the occasion unless Aunt Alma invited friends over.

Piles of clothing and Millie's precious textbooks littered every nook and cranny of her room. While she arranged chemises and camisoles into a trunk compartment, she could practically hear Isaiah teasing her.

Are you gonna need all them clothes and books where you're going? he'd say. *You're too tiny of a thing to think you can hoist that over your shoulder and drag your belongings to the next world.*

No, she couldn't drag all her belongings back in time, or other people, but she could haul each bag, trunk, and box down to the farm. These books would benefit someone else, and the medical supplies from Uncle would come in handy for those in need.

A soft knock on the door interrupted her packing. Clara popped in with a smile. "Miss, you have a visitor."

"I wasn't expecting anyone," she said, putting down the dress she'd worn when she arrived in DC.

"It's a Mrs. Mayberry. She said you'd know her."

Millie's stomach dropped. Clara's face fell when she caught her expression. "Should I tell her you're not accepting guests?"

"No . . . I'll see her in the parlor." Millie smoothed down the wrinkles in her skirt. "Thank you."

"I'll prepare refreshments." Clara escaped out the door, leaving Millie wondering why her former professor would pay her a visit. After she'd taken the woman's class, she'd rarely seen her. Every so often, she'd spy her professor's retreating back on campus, but her teacher had never spoken to her.

Millie fussed over her disheveled appearance and hurried out of the room. To still her fast-beating heart, she took her time to descend the stairs. She found Professor Mayberry sitting on Aunt Alma's preferred seat in the corner, a divan covered in rich dark-brown leather. The woman crossed her legs and placed the teacup she held back on its saucer.

Several years had passed, but Millie could see the university professor still had the same stiff demeanor.

"Good morning, Professor Mayberry." Millie's words had faltered, but she got them out.

"It's wonderful to see you again, Miss Bridge," the woman replied.

Millie eased onto the chair opposite the divan. "The pleasure is all mine. I'm sorry you had to wait—"

"Well, you weren't expecting my visit, so that's fine." Mrs. Mayberry turned to gaze out the parlor window for a moment. "I thought we'd never have to have this conversation, but after I heard you'd withdrawn from school, I knew we'd have to meet."

Millie tried to read her face, but she couldn't discern what the woman hid behind her eyes.

For the first time, she caught her professor's slight smirk. "All these years I thought I'd crossed paths with the wrong woman . . ."

"The wrong woman?" Whatever was she talking about?

"You were sitting for your Embryology final, and I noticed the bandages on your hand. That's when I knew I'd found the woman I'd sought."

The hairs on the back of Millie's neck twitched. She edged off the seat, fearful. Had this woman lost her mind?

"I know what you're thinking, but let me finish." The woman's smile was gone and only an iron resolve remained. "I will make my point, and you can decide if we should talk further."

Millie eased back onto the seat, glanced at the clock on the mantel. "Ten minutes, but no more."

"I will be brief then, Miss Bridge, but I hope you'll listen since we're family, you and me."

Millie scoffed. *Should I get up now or after she tells me we have the same mother?* she thought.

She folded her arms. "How are we related?"

"I wasn't born with the name Patricia Mayberry. I acquired it over ten years ago . . . after I arrived in Virginia. I used to be Cecily Bridge."

Her emphasis on the word "arrived" made Millie's stomach

clench. She peered at the woman closer, searching for a face she might recognize.

Her professor continued. "It wasn't until I'd reached the age of twenty-six that I learned about our family's *circumstances*. Unlike you, I didn't know the rules or how to prepare myself. All of that had been taken away when my cousin . . ." She paused and blew out a deep breath.

Millie's hand rose, for they'd dived into dangerous territory. "Please stop. I shouldn't know about any of this," she said softly. If her professor was a Bridge, the woman had to know she was violating one of the most important family rules: Never interfere with past events.

Millie added, "You don't know what damage this could do."

"But I must. My granddaddy said something I'll never forget. 'Don't be afraid to find your truth, if few are doing so.'" Mrs. Mayberry's features softened briefly. "I've wanted to recite that to you for a long time now."

"He sounds like a wise man." Millie shifted, unable to find a comfortable position.

"He was indeed, and his words fit right now. We all have a choice to stand still and accept our circumstances as they are or enact change, dear *Emily Bridge*."

"Emily?" The woman had used the name of her distant ancestor, Luke Bridge's mother. She'd only heard that woman's name when family members recounted the Bridge legends. Over time, she knew the stories had changed, but the names had always remained the same.

"Yes, and I know without a doubt you are *the* Emily Bridge," Professor Mayberry said with conviction. "On February 5, 1771, Emily Bridge stood before the court in Albemarle County, Virginia, to request a new set of freedom papers. In that document, her description was given: five foot two inches tall, thirty-five years old, a Negro of a dark complexion with a scar from her forearm to the middle of her right hand and a mark on the nape of her neck."

"That can't be true," Amelia lied, knowing very well Mrs. Mayberry had described the scar on her arm and the birthmark on her neck.

The woman who called herself Cecily stared out the window again. Silence darkened the room until the clock on the mantel dinged nine times.

"You are Emily Bridge and I have proof that you will be the first in our family's long history of time travelers." She took a deep breath. "I know all this because not only am I one of your descendants, but also I've studied our history. The Bridges will continue to suffer and fall through time—unless you hear me out."

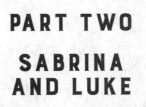

PART TWO

SABRINA
AND LUKE

Cecily Bridge-Davis

JUNE 1964

When you coming home, Ceci?" Winston's voice bled through the Fifth Street pay phone, along with other familiar sounds from back home in Nashville. Jason's and Lloyd's raucous laugher—they'd hung out at the pool all day—and the clinks and soft thuds from Winston's mother setting the table for dinner created a sweet symphony. The rich scents of her chicken potpie seemed to waft across hundreds of miles.

They were holding yet another dinner without me.

"Can you hear me?" he asked. "You've been gone for a month now. Something's wrong, isn't it?"

The smooth timbre of his voice drew me back into the conversation. Instead of the late afternoon traffic, I wished he were in front of me to assure me everything I'd learned about my family's history up to this point wasn't true. He'd wrap his firm arms around me, the smell of his Old Spice aftershave close and intimate as he whispered promises that everything I'd discovered couldn't be real.

Aren't you a woman of science? he'd once asked me.

Yes, I'd been that bright-eyed child who'd attended every science fair. That child who'd tried chess but ended up falling in love with history. And through archeology and research, history revealed truths about everyone and everything. Because of facts, history was immutable. I could trust history.

"Took some time to negotiate the sale, but I should be back soon," I lied through a hard swallow, before reminding him, "Can't stay forever since my leave of absence ends in September." I held the phone close to my mouth as if he'd hear me better as a crowd of college students passed by the booth, but what I said didn't matter.

I might not be in 1964 tomorrow. I could be decades in the past. Centuries. I'd scoured the family Bible, calculating the ages of those who'd fallen. Sixteen. Twenty-two. Twelve. None of the ages were over twenty-seven. At my current age of twenty-six, I had little time left. Every clock I passed ticked with a deafening roar.

Tell him the truth, echoed through my mind. *Tell him you might disappear and never return.*

But I didn't have the heart to—or rather, the evidence that he'd need to believe. Though I'd covered a lot of ground, figuratively and literally, I'd married a fellow academic with as much skepticism as I had. After researching the Bridge family's history, I'd pieced together the family curse and my place within it. I also had suspicions about Amelia Bridge, but I had no proof of her *true* identity—yet. This search had consumed me, and I wasn't ready to extinguish the flames.

"If there is something I need to know," he said carefully, "you should tell me before—"

"Everything's fine." I coughed to clear my tightening throat as I imagined myself kissing my babies' foreheads, smelling the scents of summer and the shea butter Mama Davis applied to their scalps.

He blew out an exasperated breath. "You've never been like this before."

"Like what?"

"You've always been reserved, but you've never kept secrets from me."

"There're a lot of memories here, and many of them aren't good. They're . . ." The truth bit the tip of my tongue.

"If you're hurting, then what can I do to help?"

"Nothing. Give me space." The churning in my stomach bubbled forth. "In all the years you've known me, have I *ever* given you a reason to believe I'm untrustworthy?"

"No."

"Then let me finish what I've started. Answers are coming. I promise."

The conversation ended with strained goodbyes and a set date to speak again at the end of the week. While I sagged against the booth's glass wall, I held on to hope that I had more time. No one else would do this critical work. I had to be the one to figure out why Luke Bridge's entry in the Bible stood out among the other finely penned words. Someone had scrawled his name with reverence, in large and sloping letters, as if he had been deliberately set apart from my other kin. He even had two distinct lines under the date he fell. His name held power and weight, and I needed to find out why.

CHAPTER 9

Sabrina Humbles

APRIL 1780

Grandma often said the land around the Bridge family farm had a kind of magic. Unsettled spirits lurked in the low-lying, early morning fog. Ominous forms, not man or beast, slipped between the pitch pine and pignut hickory trees' thick foliage, and an ever-present silence in the forest gathered in one's chest when one expected the morning birds to sing.

Less than a year ago, Grandpa had told Sabrina about a boy who'd vanished a couple of miles away from the nearby prisoner encampment. Even with all those British soldiers roaming about, it didn't surprise her how one person might disappear. There were far too many hiding places. To the east, living in the foothills of Wolfpit Mountain, an entire Negro family had abandoned their cabin. Uncle Stephen had said they got smart and fled before the slave catchers noticed they'd forged their freedom papers. When frost formed on the ground in the fall, Grandpa loved to frighten the children with the tale of a wandering man who never found his way home.

Ever since Bree and Addy were taken in by Grandma and Grandpa Bridge twelve years ago, Bree had heard all these stories and believed they were nothing more than tales to quiet the children before they slept. And yet she was still careful—one never knew what might be found around the corner.

The morning had crawled along, like it always did, with fetching water from the creek and far too many chores. At their ages, seventeen and sixteen, Bree and Addy couldn't dally, but they still idled here and there with their pails swinging. Dawn had yet to embrace the horizon, and dew dampened their boots. All around them crickets sang their final chorus.

Like always, Bree's little sister didn't say much. Even Addy's delicate footfalls murmured when hers shouted. The *swish-swish* from Addy's pail skimming the tall grass beside the footpath told Bree her sister followed two paces behind. Addy hummed a soft hymn while Bree searched for flecks of color in the grass. By the time they reached Ivy Creek, marigolds and daffodils would fill Bree's apron pocket. She could already imagine the sunshine bleeding into the wool she liked to use for embroidery. She also used these walks to commit the shapes of wildflowers to memory. Bree loved ruminating on the delicate, bell-shaped honeysuckle vines. Or how the meadow rue flower extended its purple petals to the heavens like Aunt Molly raising her hands in prayer.

Her fingers itched to complete a border of violets on the hem of a petticoat for Grandma Bridge. With a month until Addy's wedding, one would think she had plenty of time, but she had other garments to complete—Addy's wedding dress in particular.

The sky above the tall birch trees blushed orange and pink once they approached Ivy Creek's banks. The creek wound its way northeast to Rivanna River. On cooler spring days such as this one, they'd often find other Bridge women drawing water or scrubbing shifts and petticoats. Today, the sisters discovered a clean-shaven man, who brought a flush to Addy's light-brown cheeks and elicited a sigh from Bree.

Luke Bridge, the eldest son of Grandma Bridge's second offspring, lay sprawled on the creek bank, his breeches rolled up to his knees while his bare feet dangled in the water. His open shirt revealed defined muscles and smooth brown skin. The small smile on Addy's cherubic face widened at the sight of her betrothed's carefree grin and long limbs. Bree glanced elsewhere, but the beguiling curves of Luke's cheeks and his finely constructed nose were etched in her memory as vividly as the last dress she'd made. Maybe even more so.

"This is no place to bathe," Bree said curtly. "Cover yourself."

Luke fell into an easy smile, then he took his time to fasten the front ties.

Bree's heartbeat skittered. She searched for a distraction and found none. At the age of nineteen, that boy had a nonchalant nature that bothered her to no end.

"Oh, Bree." He sighed. "You could've gone farther downstream." His drawl didn't reflect annoyance but amusement.

"That water is not fit for pigs," she muttered while he stood. "Last time we brought a bucket home from that spot, Grandma made us get rid of it."

Luke gently took the bucket from Addy, then he tugged Bree's from her tight grip. He filled Addy's bucket to the brim and hers barely had a sip's worth.

Bree exhaled between clenched teeth. She had always been the subject of his pranks.

In a huff, she collected more water and returned to march up the riverbank before she could hear their conversation or Addy's giggle. The pair followed her uphill, and she walked ten paces ahead instead of their standard two.

Somehow their trio had withstood the test of time. Early on, they spent each springtime playing in the pastures or doing penance for Luke's troublemaking.

Another spring had arrived, but soon their trio would dwindle down to a pair. A familiar hollow feeling coursed through Bree. She quickened her steps, but Luke's wide strides caught up with her. His rough palm brushed against hers as he took her bucket.

Addy hurried to keep up with him and soon the pair walked ahead of Bree. The light from the rising sun briefly blinded her. She focused on the wet grass darkening the hem of Addy's blue petticoat instead of the gentle sway of her sister's hips whenever he was near. If she blinked often enough, she'd miss the complimentary sweep of his gaze as his betrothed approached him.

But the view never helped, so Bree shielded her eyes behind an invisible cloak. This cloak kept her smiling whenever she thought about Addy leaving home to go live with him. But most of all, it would shelter her heart at the thought of her friends leaving her behind.

"Did you sleep well, Addy?" Luke asked.

"Well enough. Last night Ben kept barking at the raccoons."

The two chatted about Grandpa's ornery cocker spaniel while their path uphill weaved through the glen surrounding the homes of the Bridge family sons. Their cabins were nestled on over two hundred acres of land. In the middle of this property lay the family orchard.

They meandered past Uncle Stephen's cabin and the pasture where his cows grazed. Beyond the enclosed field, they strolled into a grove of apple trees. The sun kissed the tops of the trees and the breeze tugged at the branches holding fragrant buds. Addy loved the sight every spring—Bree not so much. Not that she didn't appreciate them. These first trees had taken the Bridge family five years to cultivate. It still amazed her how these plants had once been saplings, but she'd seen trees grow from seeds and the buds blossom into apples many times. Bree wanted to see new things. And that meant she had to leave the safety of Bridge land for less muddied waters, but the wilderness and the few cities she'd seen were no safe place for a Negro woman. Monacan Indians still lived in villages to the northwest. To the south was Hawkins land—a white merchant family. Even farther into the woods and east was Shadwell, the Jefferson family's plantation with over fifty Negro slaves working the tobacco fields along the foothills of the Southwest Mountains. Here, they encountered few traders and travelers—most of them didn't want the Bridge family's hard cider—but the one or two they did see came with rumors about Shadwell, along with Monticello, the Jefferson family's newest plantation.

There were far fewer free Negro families in the outlying areas too. Bree could count the number of farms on one hand, but if they had etched a better living for themselves, why couldn't she? Maybe up north, past the plantations and slavery, other Negroes had ventured beyond the restrictions of their freedom papers. Perhaps there she could start a new life.

"Are you coming, Bree?" Luke glanced over his shoulder. The pair had left her behind while her mind had wandered.

Bree gave a short nod and followed them to the cabin. Grandma and Grandpa Bridge's home was the oldest one on the farm. The walls kept them warm in the winter but retained far too much heat during the summer. She trudged inside to find Grandma's and Grandpa's chairs empty. This early in the day, even elderly folk tended to the orchard. Once the snow melted and Grandpa's aches in his knees quieted from the cold, the couple spent more time with their other children: the pippin apple trees.

Immediately, she got to work outside on the day's wash, trying not to pay any mind to the hushed chatter behind her.

Didn't Luke and Addy also have chores?

Uncle John, Luke's father, had complained the other day how Luke needed to start new stacks of firewood now that the families had used up their winter supply. And Addy had piles of carded wool from the spring shearing to spin into woolen yarn.

Once Bree finished hanging up the clothes, she went inside to mend some of Grandpa's shirts. The stone fireplace held nothing more than dying embers, but spite seared Bree's face. Here they were, chatting about the weather, not caring if Addy got a tongue lashing when Grandma returned home.

After some time, she said, "Addy, we only have so much daylight before Grandma returns."

Now that got her sister moving. The memory of Grandma fussing until Bree had to make excuses for Addy added haste to her step. Ever since they were little, Addy had never been in a hurry. Bree barely remembered their lives before escaping a plantation in South Carolina, but she did recall the day their papa let go of her hand while on the outskirts of Richmond. Bree was five. She had held on to her sister as the girls wandered away from town, searching for him without screaming out his name.

"Always, always stay by me," Papa had said. "Don't speak to anyone. We'll get to New York soon."

But he'd released Bree's hand and disappeared into the trees. Just like those people Grandma warned them about.

It was Grandpa Bridge who'd found them starving out in the wilderness outside Charlottesville. He still marveled at how Bree had kept her sister alive for so long.

When they'd first arrived here, Addison clung to her older

sister's dirty petticoats and sucked her thumb. Even then, Bree didn't need to be told how to wash clothes or tend to babies. Whippings and other punishments had burned a work ethic into her bones. She always did what was needed.

And right now she needed silence.

Bree wiped sweat off the back of her neck. Held her breath and forced a smile.

Jealousy isn't becoming for a godly woman, Sabrina, she reminded herself.

"After we finish our chores, I can make progress on your wedding dress," she offered.

While Addy busied herself with gathering the cards of wool she'd need for spinning at her wheel in one corner of the cabin, Luke lingered in the doorway. He stuffed his hands in his work apron's pockets. The weight of his gaze touched Bree's back, but she ignored him and sewed faster to close a hole in the sleeve. Eventually, he'd speak.

Luke Bridge always had *something* to say.

"I'll return after supper," he finally said with Bree's back still turned.

He'd left many times. Why should she bother seeing him leave? Wasn't Addy his betrothed?

But Sabrina was unable to resist peeking over her shoulder. She managed to catch his retreating back as he ventured west to the orchard.

With Luke gone, Bree and her sister settled into a familiar rhythm. The *whoosh-whoosh* of Addy's spinning wheel filled the cabin, and Bree perched on a stool to examine her stitches.

By the time the sun was high in the sky, Bree had to bring

Grandpa his lunch. Often he refused a midday meal, but then his hands would shake, and he'd stare at the ground before he sat down.

When the eldest Bridge ate, her aunts and uncles worried less about him during the workday. And whenever she brought him food, the others often sat with him to keep him company. Most of the time, Luke would join too, but lately he'd been taking off to wander the woods.

Grandpa munched on rye bread covered in blackberry jam as Ben rested his head against his master's boot. Meanwhile Uncle Stephen regaled everyone with his never-ending war tales from four years ago. Stephen's wife, Molly, complained that her husband used the time as an excuse to work his mouth instead of his hands, but she smiled with each jest. She sat among the other women who lounged underneath the birch trees lining the orchard. Grandma rested while Molly's deft fingers braided strands of her hair, as long as a river.

"There were men as far as you could see," Stephen said with flair. "Up in New Jersey, there are just as many hills like you see around here. The new Continental Army recruits were taking in the scenery while men like Papa couldn't load their muskets."

That got a laugh from Grandpa. "At least my aim is better than yours."

"True. Back at Brandywine, I was shaking worse than Papa on a good day." Stephen tucked snuff from a tiny tin box under his lower lip.

"One would think Stephen's aim would've improved with people shooting at him." Aunt Emily, Uncle John's wife, laughed, and soon they all joined her. Bree took in each face, each of them familiar and comforting. Every Bridge elder was here. Chatting. Laughing. Bree stooped beside Grandpa and let everyone's mood lift hers. If she ever left, she'd miss these moments.

"You brag too much, Stephen," Aunt Molly said.

"The only one of us that fired faster was Edwin," Grandpa said softly. "He could do it with his eyes closed, I say."

At the mention of Edwin, silence fell. The smiling face of his wife, Mary, stiffened. After the men had returned home without her husband, she'd rarely talked about him.

Once the quiet grew too thick, John brought up something else. It was for the best—Bree couldn't go anywhere around here without seeing land Edwin had helped clear or fences he'd repaired. It was Edwin who had sheared the sheep every spring and tended to the fall-lambing ewes. Every single cabin was painted with memories of him, but God saw fit to take his life during the war.

After the family heard about the men's enlistment—a tale Bree had heard *many* a time—she took what remained of Grandpa's meal and returned home.

She gathered the eggs from the coop, and even managed to clear out the rotten vegetables from the root cellar, but no more than a minute into embroidering another flower along the hem of Addy's wedding dress, Bree spotted Luke.

This time, he came to her instead of Addy with a simple request.

"Can I borrow your neckerchief, Bree?" With sweat lining his brow, Luke stooped on one knee before her. Hints of his labors tending to the apple orchard trailed after him.

Behind her, Addy paused, her sister's spinning wheel quieting at the sound of his question.

Bree trained her eyes away from the intricate stitches of bluebells she was sewing to meet his dark-brown eyes. To him, it was just another day. Another workday during which he likely had misplaced his neckerchief and now wished to take hers.

Bree bit her lower lip and retrieved the dark-blue neckerchief from her apron pocket. The frayed edges tickled her neck when she wore it, but the linen fabric kept her skin covered and cool.

"I want it back," she whispered stiffly.

He gave her his lopsided smirk. The long, pale scar along his chin from a tree fall winked at her. Bree wanted to glance elsewhere. If she stared at Luke for too long, she'd see he didn't look at her the way he looked at Addy.

Luke opened his mouth to speak.

One moment the April midday sun bled around him, causing the burnt-orange light to spill to the cabin's dirt floor and cast his shadow toward her, and in her next sharp inhale, the full breadth of the sun's rays left her blinking.

"What did you say?" she asked.

No one answered.

Addy gasped.

He wasn't in the room.

"Luke, I tire of your tricks." Bree rose from her seat and marched out the cabin door with heat gathering in her stomach. That man played far too many children's games for someone who planned to wed soon.

Nothing suspicious stirred outside. No footsteps trailed away from the cabin in the dark soil. She expected to glimpse his retreating back heading to the orchard, but she fixed her gaze only upon swaying pine and elm trees beyond the clearing leading away from their home. Chirps from nearby yellow-rumped warblers amplified in the open space.

"Where did he go?" Addy's quiet voice didn't calm Bree's hitched breaths.

"I don't know."

They circled the cabin. Traces of sweat from Luke's labors were the only evidence he'd been here.

Bree called his name, even whistling three times, a signal from when they'd played together as children.

They waited for his reply, but none came.

"Had we imagined him?" Addy asked.

"No." Bree reached into her apron, finding only the flowers she'd gathered. "He asked for my neckerchief, and I gave it to him."

They explored beyond the enclosure to their garden to the small field where Grandma's sole cow roamed. From there they ventured away from the cabin, down the beaten path between the trees to the orchard.

Did they miss him leaving the house to return to work?

At first, they walked, their necks craning, their gazes searching behind every nook and cranny. But soon enough, Addy's step quickened, then Bree's.

"This cannot be real," Addy whispered. "Maybe we got sick for a spell. That's all."

Had the bright morning light played with their senses? Grandma Bridge had warned them about how the mountains tricked the foolish. Those who left the warmth of the cabin in the winter without proper clothing lost fingers and toes. The imprudent ones who hadn't stocked up on kindling or who'd let their fires die ended up dead.

This felt different.

Bree gripped her sister's shoulder. "You saw him. I did too."

That was their truth. They could lie to their minds but not to their hearts. As they drew closer to the orchard, they began to run.

A sour feeling quaked in Bree's stomach as if she'd eaten spoiled fruit. The familiar faces tending the trees were too short, their shoulders too narrow. The curious stares of her aunts and uncles hardened. Many of them paused their search for pests and mold among the branches and trunks.

"Girls, why are you running? Are you searching for someone?" Stephen asked.

John approached them first.

"Have you seen Luke?" Addy asked.

"Last time I saw him, he was going your way," he replied, and then he looked Addy over with a knowing grin. "Did he pay his intended a visit?"

Addy's gaze flicked to Bree.

Bree sighed. How much could she say without sounding daft?

John noted their hesitation. "The wedding's coming soon. It's fine if he goes courting to see his intended and gets lost on the way."

"Luke came by to see us—I mean Addy, but he . . ." The explanation died in Bree's mouth.

"What's the fuss about?" Aunt Emily's brow furrowed as she descended a ladder from a nearby tree. She was the smartest person Bree had ever met. Maybe Luke's mother could explain what they'd seen.

"He's gone," Addy blurted. "He came to the cabin, just like you said, then he asked for Bree's neckerchief. After she gave it to him, he disappeared."

John guffawed. "Ran away, did he? A little early for that."

Addy's face crumpled and her lower lip quivered. "Not like that. You know how smoke rises from a fire, then you can't see it anymore? Like that."

John laughed again, but it was Aunt Emily's flat expression that sent a chill along Bree's back.

"Did you hear any horses or voices outside the cabin?" She stepped forward, her dark-brown eyes intent and mouth firm.

"Nothing." A tear dropped down Addy's cheek.

The urge to cry made Bree blink, but she clenched her right fist until her nails dug into her palm. Based on the hard line of her aunt's mouth, she wondered if Em thought slave catchers had slipped onto the farm and taken Luke. The family hadn't had any visitors from the local Monacan Indians in over a year either. Once in a while, travelers or traders came through, but most white men avoided the Negroes.

Emily reached up and brushed the tear off Addy's cheek. "Calm yourself, girl." She turned to Bree. "I want to hear every detail from the moment he came to the cabin."

Bree recounted the tale, which didn't differ much from what Addy had said, but she added how she witnessed his arrival but not how he left. The path to the orchard from the elder Bridges' cabin could be seen from over one hundred paces away. Even if he'd slipped outside, they should've seen him.

Briefly, Emily stood there, and the lack of answers along with her unsettledness seeped a cold fear into Bree's body. Perhaps Bree and Addy were mistaken. The elders understood many things. Aunt Emily was one of the few elders who could read and write, and every baby born on this farm fell into her small hands. She had to know what happened.

But Emily merely swallowed deeply and pivoted to walk away from them.

"Where are you going, Em?" Uncle John called.

"To search for our son." Her voice was thin and sharp.

"You know the boy is always playing tricks on those girls."

Emily tapped her chest. "I have a feeling this isn't a trick."

Uncle John's jaw twitched. "Luke will do the rest of my work if he's hiding in the trees."

But Luke wasn't hiding in the forest. Or fishing off the Rivanna. On the farm's northern side, the older children working the gardens outside Uncle Stephen and Aunt Molly's cabin hadn't seen him either. To the south, in John and Emily's cabin, the place where Luke slept in the loft was empty. The men sped away on horseback with promises to return before sunset. The women ushered the children into Stephen's cabin to watch for danger.

As the day marched on, Bree waited for Luke to appear with apologies. He'd have that familiar smirk and vow to never play tricks on her again.

But instead of Luke returning, night arrived with a clammy silence, leaving Bree and Addy staring into the forest. They waited patiently for a fleck of his shirt's light color to emerge from the shadows, but the only stirring was a suffocating darkness and the promise of Grandma's legends bearing their dreaded fruit.

CHAPTER 10

Luke Bridge
1758

The sun casting a honeyed glow on Bree's light-brown cheeks was the last thing Luke saw before day became twilight. He clutched her neckerchief—still scented by the wildflowers she tucked away in her apron pocket. When he glanced above, the warmth from the sun had vanished. Dusk crept in, slinking over the forest all around him, the stars shimmering overhead and crickets chirping. No smoke from fires carried on the breeze. Grandpa and Grandma's cabin was gone. Bree and Addy were gone too.

And God have mercy, his feet up to his calves were in the ground.

Luke struggled, panic gnawing within his insides. He clawed away at the grass. Scooped away handful after handful of chilled dirt, debris, and slippery worms until he freed his feet. His boots were stuck in the ground. He stumbled out of them and scrambled backward.

Then he searched the horizon.

From the purple sky above to the damp ground at his feet, none of this could be real. Had the midday heat baked his head? Or even worse, had he died? But the dirt caked under his fingernails was real when he picked at it. He smelled it to be sure. A chill in the air swept across his forehead, a signal fall was approaching. If this was a dream, he wouldn't have to be afraid, but if it wasn't a dream, then where had everyone gone?

Luke glanced down. *Grab your boots, fool.*

The sky continued to darken, but he easily spotted familiar landmarks. He was in the clearing where Grandpa and Grandma's cabin stood. Or should stand. To his left should be gardens, the pasture, and, farther to the west, a path to the orchard.

Beyond the untilled field, there was nothing but rolling hills and forest.

"Addy? Sabrina?" Only the scatter of frightened birds replied with their squawks. No one answered when he yelled for Mama and Papa either.

Think, think.

After huddling with his back against a knotty birch tree, Luke lost more precious light, but his unraveled common sense weaved back together. *Safety first. Questions answered later.* Before he lost any further light, he had to check for any of the other cabins. He ran as hard as he could to the northwest, then the south. There was no sign of his aunts, uncles, or cousins. Within minutes, Luke knew he was alone.

No cleared land or cabins. No fences or pastures. No one from the Bridge family was nearby, which meant he had to find fire-starting supplies as quickly as possible.

He checked his work apron, stuffing his hands deep into his pockets to discover he had one chisel, a folded knife, and his rolled-up freedom papers. With no one around, Luke wasn't sure what good those papers would do.

"I don't care how much you hate holding them," Mama had barked. "Let some white man catch you without them, and we'll see how far he can carry you away."

Point made, Mama.

Next, he set about getting a fire going to get rid of mosquitos and keep larger predators like bears and wolves away. He shuffled about like a fool, gathering dry kindling, sunbaked grass, and bigger branches to keep the fire burning all night. Once he had prepared his pile, his legs ached. He gritted his teeth and whacked his knife against a stone until sparks grew into gentle flames.

By the time the shadows ran so deep he couldn't see twenty feet away, Luke had a good fire and plenty of pitch pines gathered for additional light.

Covered in ferns and brush, Luke couldn't sleep. No matter how hard he tried, the outside kept shifting. Writhing. What should've been home became a presence so foreign he couldn't find peace. His whole body shook. He sucked in one breath after another, trying to hold back the rising panic squeezing his stomach. When the tears came, he let them flow, but he refused to cry out. No one heard his whimpers.

The glen and the apple orchard used to be beacons. They were never-moving North Stars. Whether he traveled ten feet or ten miles, he had a home to return to at the end of the day—right now, there was nothing.

After spending a few days foraging for wapato and other tubers along the riverbank, and fishing with a makeshift pole, he gave in to his need for answers and ventured south to find Charlottesville.

It wasn't there.

What should've been a town with a smattering of trading posts was the outskirts of an Indian village. Grandpa had said the whites chased out the villagers twenty years ago. So why was Monasukapanough still here?

Monacan women and children flitted in and out of wooden huts, all the while speaking in a tongue he didn't recognize. Luke peered deeper into the village yet kept his distance; Pa had said only a fool traipsed into Monacan territory uninvited.

The enticing scents of a meal frying on flat stones floated from a communal cooking pit. Luke's empty stomach rumbled in response, and he took a step back.

He had come here to find answers. Nothing more.

Luke searched, noting the land itself was familiar. All he'd had to do was follow Ivy Creek southwest from the Rivanna River to get within sight of Charlottesville. And yet it wasn't here.

He watched the Monacans for a spell before realization tightened his chest. He hadn't died. A nearby woman and her young children laughed and carried on about their day while an elderly man sat quietly with a babe in his arms. These people were flesh and blood. And if this was Monasukapanough and his family farm was gone, then he'd fallen into a fate far worse than he'd expected.

———

Luke really should've listened when Grandpa and Grandma talked about where they'd lived before they'd settled on the farm. His grandparents had briefly worked on Nicholas Lewis's farm over twenty years ago. After saving their pounds, they'd bought a parcel of land from him, built their first cabin, and then planted the apple saplings they'd purchased.

Hunger and thirst finally drove him southward, away from the Monacan village. They had crops and such, but he kept his distance.

He wasn't as familiar with the land beyond the Southwest Mountains and stumbled about, numb.

"Stay close to home and you'll stay alive," Papa had always said. "The white man doesn't want you meddling in their affairs." Occasionally, the family had traveled southeast to Richmond to barter for goods, but they never ventured any farther. Papa and his uncles were always uneasy—they never knew if they'd cross paths with the whites or the Indians.

Luke kept himself going through purpose: food, water, and shelter. With the rise of the sun, he checked his snares and drank water from the nearest creeks. He often sat and listened for his family, expecting them to appear over the horizon, but no one came.

So he took one day at a time. Day by day. Week by week. There was nothing else he could do. This far out in the wilderness, he encountered fewer homesteads, fewer mountains and more flat land.

He began to mark the days by scoring a notch in a branch he used as a walking stick, the blade of his knife flicking away a sliver of bark each day until he peeled away more than two years' worth. Luke told himself all he had to do was bide his time. Keep his head down and find a farm needing a strong hand with carpentry skills. Sooner or later, the Bridges would return. He prayed that much.

What he'd found, after a long period of isolation, was that his thoughts circled, and his fondest memories came to mind. He lost himself in a reverie of the Humbles sisters. How he'd chosen Addy to marry, but he hadn't expected things to happen that way. To be truthful, Bree came to mind more than her younger sister, and he often wished he remembered how they'd first met. Back then, the sisters had arrived at their farm and were nothing more than curiosities to him and the other Bridge children.

That changed when Luke was fourteen. He'd fallen off a rickety elm tree, cutting his chin. Bree found him at the base of the tree, her eyes and lips widened. While Addy cried, Bree rapidly untied her dandelion-yellow neckerchief and pressed the cloth firmly against his face—that was his most vivid memory of Bree. The deep yellow darkened to burnt orange; the bleeding refused to cease.

"Bleeding like a stuck pig." Twelve-year-old Bree snatched Addy's hand and held her sister's palm there. "You stay here," she added to her sibling. "You better not follow me."

"But what if he's dying?" Addy whispered.

Bree sighed. Here he was, bleeding all over God's green Earth, and Bree had already lost her patience.

She ignored Addy's question and said to him, "Don't move. I'll go get your mama."

Not long after, his mother came running. The entire time they'd waited, Addy continued her crying until she was red-eyed, snot-nosed, and barely helping. Instead of her holding the cloth against his wound, he had to hold it himself.

He didn't recall the sting from Mama's stitches or her chastising about climbing too high, but Bree's face over his stood out. Summertime patches of freckles speckled the sharp angles of her light-brown cheeks while her mouth parted to reveal a playful gap in her top front teeth. A hint of a thick, dark braid peeked out from under her green head wrap.

A couple of weeks later, it was sharp-eyed Uncle Ed, the only Bridge man who could see well and read folks, like Mama could read her precious books, who told him the obvious: "When are you going to tell Bree you've taken a liking to her?"

He shrugged but couldn't hide the subtle twitch of a grin. "She's pleasant."

Uncle Edwin nodded. "Every Sunday, I see you staring at her when you think no one's watching."

After his uncle's revelation, Luke couldn't help but feel shy. Whenever the sisters invited him out into the woods, he declined. When they needed help, he feigned needing to do chores.

But that was the thing about longing—the feeling churned deep inside him, and no matter how he tried, eventually Mama approached him in private.

"You will marry Addy." She'd spoken the words as if they were an instruction, as matter-of-fact as the Bible.

"I don't want to marry her."

He stood there looking down on Mama, feeling shame for speaking instead of obeying. She'd always been there, protecting him through the days when Papa drank too much, and his siblings didn't mind their errands.

"You see what you want to see, Luke," she said, "but the women-folk talk. We know what's in her heart. Bree is special—"

"I know that."

"Out of all the children I've taught reading and writing, she's excelled. She's always telling me she wants to learn more than I can teach her."

He turned away from his mother, but her fisted words struck his back.

She added, "If you let her go, she could become an apprentice with a milliner. Or even a seamstress of means."

"You told me never to accept an apprenticeship. Why should *she* do such a thing?" He kept respect in his tone, even if resentment touched his senses.

"We all have to make sacrifices for the greater good. And if you marry her, she'll remain here."

"She'll remain here with me."

"Is that what's best for her or for you?"

Luke didn't answer her question, nor did he speak to Mama for several days. She allowed him to sit with his disappointment and anger. When his feelings quieted, he made the announcement to his parents that he intended to marry Addy. From that point on, he'd lived life with a central purpose: to cultivate and protect the Bridge land. His inheritance. His legacy.

Now his home didn't yet exist. But as he traveled from place to place, never staying anywhere for long, he grew complacent while he waited. Then three errors on his freedom papers ended his meandering.

He'd stuck to what he remembered as Buckingham County, away from the footpaths and roads, but a young white man, dressed in buckskin breeches and jacket, spied him from afar. The man wasn't much older than Luke and tracked him with ease. With a musket trained on his chest, the stranger led him to an expansive mill, where he was duly arrested by the local parish's churchwarden for trespassing.

"Probably a runaway slave," said the young man's father from a rocking chair on the farmhouse's large porch. As Luke was hauled away, the old man's wife stood in the doorway of their cabin, a look of distaste aimed in her husband's direction.

After Luke's arrest, he attempted to present his papers. That was his first mistake. For the past two years, he hadn't needed them. Either way, he should've stayed calm and kept his mouth closed.

"Always think before you speak," Mama had said. "A boy playing a child's game in a man's world will get him nothing but a bear's open mouth waiting to swallow him whole."

The tiny township's churchwarden peered at the slightly yellowed piece of paper. When his brow furrowed and his head tilted, a sick feeling circled Luke's gut.

"This says you appeared before the court in Albemarle County in *1771* to certify you were born free." He laughed. "Last I heard, it's 1760."

Luke's chin collapsed to his chest and his jaw clenched hard enough to hurt.

The churchwarden eyed the paper again. "I know every single alderman in that county since my kin comes from that land, and I've never heard of this gentleman."

Luke opened his mouth, then clamped it shut. *Think before you speak.*

"You must believe you're smart, forging these papers," the man added, "but you're a fool like the rest of them."

Luke refused to glance up.

"We'll hold you," the churchwarden said firmly, "until we've determined your rightful place."

By "rightful place," he meant Luke would go to the county auction block. His family had always warned the children to mind where they went. The elders had told them stories of those who'd disappeared from the fields. They'd vanished on the way to visit family only a mile away. Those folks rarely returned and haunted the family they'd left behind more than the ghosts or river monsters their parents tried to scare them with.

The churchwarden spoke further. With each word, Luke trembled and his empty stomach tightened. Two days later, when they paraded him about the buyers and presented his scar-free back and legs, he still did not speak.

Memories of Mama trailed after him like a vigilant specter. He recalled the day she'd stood before the alderman for permission to stay in Albemarle County. As a boy, he hadn't thought much of how they'd measured her up: "five foot two inches tall, thirty-five years old, a Negro of a dark complexion with a scar from her fore-arm to the middle of her right hand and a mark on the nape of her neck." They'd assessed her like cattle to identify her later.

Now he faced the same treatment before a sale.

He imagined Mama sealing her lips with a fingertip while the auctioneer asked Luke if he could read and write. She shook her head when the urge to struggle against his chains and bolt for the door hit him.

He might've been mistaken, but he swore she shed a tear when Mr. Pinkham purchased him.

Or maybe it was him.

———

For the next eight years, Luke worked as an enslaved carpenter at the Pinkham mill.

For a Quaker family, no less. Not that his owner feared God. He feared only death and an empty pocket. His wife, God bless her, reminded Luke of Grandpa. She would read her Bible, perched with a tree-straight spine on their porch's harshest of seats, or spend her mornings praying out loud for the end of man's greed and slavery, all within earshot of her husband sitting in the parlor.

The woman stood no taller than Luke's tiny mama, but her voice carried the weight of two men. The overseer wasn't allowed to beat the slaves. The slaves never missed a meal either—even if the farm animals ate better than they did.

Mrs. Pinkham, just like Grandpa Bridge, excelled at waiting too. Luke had seen his granddaddy, ready to take down a buck, holding a musket as steady as stone until the moment to fire.

And strike she did one late-summer morning. News arrived that Master Pinkham and his son wouldn't be returning from a trip to Richmond. Bandits had attacked their wagon and left them for dead. With no heirs to immediately take on the role of master, she briefly controlled every strand of grass, as well as the barn and stables Luke had helped rebuild.

Mr. Pinkham had a younger brother, a supposedly godly man living in Massachusetts, but in the time it took the heir to saunter his way on down here, she made changes. By midday, on the day she learned her husband had died, the ten slaves, including Luke, no longer worked without wages. A month later, when a stiff-looking Mr. Samuel Pinkham, dressed in fine breeches and smelling of a musky perfume, stepped onto the property, she'd already petitioned the governor for permission to draw up manumission papers to free every enslaved man, woman, and child. No indenture, limited instruction required, and no payment for freedom necessary. Over half of the newly freed men and women left before his arrival, but Luke waited.

Where else did he have to go?

Luke now had valid freedom papers and a new name: Noah Battles. During his eight years as a slave working at the mill, everyone had called him Luke. Since he had a good Christian name, his master had never changed it. The choice to answer to another was his decision. Why continue to answer to a name connected with another life? Every time he heard it, the reminder of what he'd lost added a stumble to his steps. Somehow he had to move on and begin again. Might as well start with his name.

Therefore, it was Noah who left the rolling hills of Buckingham County and snuck back north again to find another haven. He'd reached the age of twenty-eight, and he had coins in his pocket but nowhere to go as a free Negro to spend them. Luke sought out the familiar rise of nearby Wolfpit Mountain to see if his family happened to reside in their former home on Nicholas Lewis's property northwest of Charlottesville.

Traveling those old Monacan footpaths gave him a sense of ease he'd missed. Even if he might not be able to see Mama's face again, hope tugged him home. If he were lucky, he could partake of her meals and feel the comfort of his bed.

Soon enough, he arrived home. While taking the long way from the south to the north around the farmstead, he spied himself from afar, standing in the woods. At seven years old, the younger Luke was mostly arms and legs with a tiny head. Seeing himself chopping wood shoved Luke back until he fell against a nearby tree. His stomach lurched and his vision blurred.

How was he standing there—and yet he was also over here?

Was the boy alone?

No, four younger boys no older than twelve toiled on the other side of the tiny clearing. Luke recognized his cousins. Each of their names came to mind—adding sorrow to his backward steps.

This farm still wasn't his home.

For the next couple of days, Luke stumbled south again, then east, making his way to the Southwest Mountains. He needed to add distance between the place where he wanted to rest his head and the outside world. But neither place was a fit for him. Not long into his journey, he encountered a peculiar sight: two girls, one holding the hand of the other, making their way northeast.

At first, the leaves obscured their faces, but the closer they drew to him, the more he could make out familiar features. The older girl, whom he knew to have only just turned five, wore a dark-gray dress—a slave's garments—while the younger child trailed after in a light-gray one. Mud and filth from their journey clung to the tattered hems.

It was Bree and little Addy.

Luke's breath caught. How long had they been alone out here? Hadn't Grandpa found them around this time?

He glanced around, almost expecting the elder Bridge to make a grand appearance, but the woods around them were tranquil.

Bree's downward gaze darted like a butterfly, jumping from one flower to another as she parted the tall grass. When she found what she sought, she examined her find. Her dandelions wouldn't feed a scrawny fly, but she plucked away at the flowers, giving Addy the larger portion.

Luke touched his haversack. When had they last eaten properly? He had recently caught some squirrels; they'd appreciate the cooked meat, but what girl on her own would trust a stranger? He took a step forward. The branch under his foot snapped. Bree's keen eyes flicked in his direction. He dipped deeper into the cluster of ferns he hid behind.

"Come now," she whispered to her sister. Addy took her hand, and they ran back into the woods.

Bree was far too clever to speak to strangers, but Grandpa had a way about him. It was best for Luke to leave things be. Sooner or later, they'd find him.

But with every step he should've taken in the opposite direction, he kept his distance and followed them, until Addy complained about being tired. Instead of chastising the little girl, Bree grinned and settled her sister into her lap.

"Just rest," she said. "We need to find water before the sun goes down."

Luke sighed. The girls were too far east and too far up the mountains to find water.

He watched from afar, waiting until Addy dozed away. While

the girls stayed put, he foraged along the mountainside, mustering up more dandelions, chanterelles, and bunches of tender field chickweed. Now he had to devise a way for them to discover it.

Luke wrapped the plants and strips of cooked squirrel into one of his old red shirts. When the sisters roused and began their journey uphill, he ran ahead of them. Based on their current trajectory, the rough path close to Wolfpit Mountain's peak would divert them south. He darted along the safest path and found the perfect spot near a sturdy maple tree. Carefully, he used the arms of the shirt to fashion a hook. A couple of seconds later the prize hung from a low branch of a tree, ready to be plucked by hungry hands. He expected Bree to find what he'd left for them, but it was Addy who pointed.

"What's that?" She took a step forward, but Bree yanked Addy's dress and tugged her back.

"Probably belongs to someone," Bree replied.

"Who?"

Bree glanced around. "Hush now."

The sisters edged closer, constantly checking over their shoulders. When Bree could finally reach for the shirt, she pulled it off the branch, grabbed her sister's hand, and they escaped west.

For the next week, Luke left them tiny wapato tubers he dug up from the riverbanks. Peppergrass, morel mushrooms, and violet petals appeared before them like manna from heaven. And when necessary, he watched out for danger, detouring their path from traders or travelers such as himself.

Inch by inch, he led them north again toward Bridge land. They walked downhill from the mountains and west toward Ivy Creek. When Grandpa Bridge did stumble upon them, Luke told himself it was God's hand that guided them. Not him.

Once the Humbles girls were safely in Grandpa's care, he was alone again, an outsider haunting his homeland. As he returned to the mountains, he carried his joy in his pockets, but he remained restless. Day stretched out into the evening. The night surrendered to the dawn, and with the dim light and fog creeping over the hills, shadows closed in. Luke sat in silence until a shadow the size of a muskrat shifted to his left, escaping into the thickening fog. Knife in hand, he made his way to the spot it had escaped, but he found nothing. Only a breeze wrestling at the canopy branches.

Somehow he slept, only waking to tend to his fire and eat. He should've fled this place, but every morning he rested and let the low-lying clouds swallow him.

Wouldn't hurt to fall away for a bit.

Sometimes, back on the farm, he'd caught Mama staring off into the trees—never toward home or the orchards. Had she been expecting something, or had she been like he was now—cast adrift in thought with nothing to tether either of them to the present?

There had to be a way home eventually. Living alone like this left his thoughts unhinged. The right opportunity would come, but he wouldn't find it near the farmstead.

When the time was right, he'd return.

CHAPTER 11

Luke Bridge
1768

Time had frayed the edges of Bree's neckerchief, but Luke kept it tucked deep in his pocket as he journeyed northward. At night, he slept before a fire with no one to hear his thoughts or troubles. It was during the fire's crackle and the hushed murmur of the nighttime that he worked on a smooth piece of maple the length of his palm. A tree had discarded the wood long ago—why not see if he could give it new life? So he whittled away at it, crafting a thread spool for Bree as he passed through land he'd never seen before and heard names he didn't recognize. Maybe it was best he had a new name too. Luke Bridge remained at home in Virginia while Noah Battles was a hatchling. No matter how much he wanted to stay close to the nest, he had to face new challenges.

Far from the safety of the Bridge farm, Luke had much to fear, but he had valid freedom papers and he'd seen his kin. That had to be enough, and yet he still wondered how Bree fared in the future.

It felt like a lifetime had passed since their paths veered away from each other.

During the late spring of 1768, he roamed like a migrating flock of geese, escaping from Virginia to the British province of Maryland. He had no final destination, only an unyielding desire to discover a less restrictive home, but even Maryland was no haven. The rough paths through the forests bordered endless indigo and tobacco plantations. Hunched slaves, their skin glistening with sweat, filled the fields, and their overseers watched them. He drifted past many Negroes—every one of them enslaved, based on how they avoided his gaze—as they went on errands for their masters.

"Move on, boy," a Negro woman warned when he'd stared at men working in an indigo field too long. "You got no business here." The weight of her sharp gaze told him plain and clear: there'd be trouble for everyone if he poisoned the air with notions they could be free too.

More ominous signs—as dark as stormy seaside clouds in his new home of Boston—erupted around Luke. Hints of an uprising brewed between the Loyalists and the colonists, and protests continued into 1770. Few wanted to allow British soldiers to quarter in their homes, nor did they wish to pay the increased taxes. Whispers of freedom flitted from the elite down to a simple man like him. He knew what lay on the horizon. All he could do was wait for the rising tension to culminate in the formation of the Continental Congress. Not long after that, war erupted in Lexington. Thirty miles away still felt like thirty feet.

From there, the very event that led to his elders leaving the Bridge farm occurred: the Continental Army of 1776 was formed. When Luke heard rumors about the call to arms for Negro men, he'd already departed for Virginia. He'd had enough of the Loyalists' actions and wanted to fight for the republic. Many Negroes had also heard about the promise of freedom for those who served either the Continental Army or the Loyalists. The time had finally come for a reunion with his kin.

When Luke arrived at a recruitment camp back in Virginia on an early January day in 1777, a frigid breeze dusted fallen snow along the Amherst County road. He waited patiently in line— for God rained fortune on his head: the Bridge men waited in line ahead of him. Seeing his uncles from a distance lightened his step. All of them were free, and yet they still joined to help the colonists' cause. He ambled into the line behind them, keeping his distance.

Oh, to never be alone on God's Earth, he thought.

If Luke had any sense, he'd return to Boston for the next three years, but he wanted to be with his family again, so he had to enlist. His breath caught to see Uncle Edwin. The man was as portly as Luke remembered him with his patchy facial hair and kind eyes. Aunt Mary had regularly griped about how often her husband groomed what little hair he had. Right next to him stood Uncle Stephen, the man who told a tale with any opportunity. Stephen stared down the road before he spat a ribbon of tobacco to the side. In front of him stood the eldest Bridge, Grandpa Zachariah, who waited closest to the beginning of the line, bearing a grim expression.

Luke stared at them, marveling at their similar features, their high foreheads, the thick eyebrows and square shoulders.

Luke didn't expect to see his papa. His father would've been here if he hadn't broken his leg, and at the time, Mama had refused to let Luke enlist with them.

"He's not old enough," she'd snapped to the Bridge men when they gathered to make the final decision.

They'd tried to remind Mama of her place in men's affairs, but she'd refused to listen. "We're not lying about his age either," she'd added. "Those rich white men can fight over their precious land without him."

At the time, Luke had stood taller than anyone and hungered to show them he could hold his own.

What a fool he'd been back then.

After Luke completed his enlistment as a private in the 10th Regiment, he was grateful Mama hadn't budged in her decision. He remembered, at fifteen, stumbling about like a spotted fawn—he'd been nothing more than a wide-eyed teenager from a farm who'd never shot a man, only animals. With years of wisdom, along with knowing what he'd face, Luke would successfully complete what little training the army offered. There'd be many losses on the Continental Army's side, and if he had his way, his uncle would no longer be one of them. He was willing to embrace the monotony and welcomed the supplies he was issued.

Luke had already learned about rank and file during his time in Boston, as well as all the commands necessary to survive. Negroes and whites worked side by side to follow Captain Franklin's instruction during the musket and marching drills. In a company as large as the 10th, with nearly five hundred men, Luke should've blended in. He had a new name, and years of working for the Pinkhams had added scars and bulk to his frame, but that didn't prevent any accidents. Once, while he was relieved of guard duty, Uncle Edwin strode in with the other fellows. His uncle glanced at him and froze. Luke hadn't prepared himself for the moment—and he often had imagined a reunion between them.

"Is there a problem?" he asked, afraid to hear his uncle's answer.

"You look familiar." Edwin's head tilted a bit.

"I do?"

"Indeed you do . . . It's your face. I feel like I've seen you before." Edwin chuckled and shook his head. "The cold must've played with my head."

Luke gave a nod, and the tension in his shoulders eased. On the outside, he stood tall, but other words rose inside him.

During the day he learned basic drills with the Bridge men, while at night he listened to the tales he'd heard many times from Grandpa. How Grandpa had met Grandma up in Pennsylvania to the first bleak winter the couple had spent on the Bridge farm. These stories carried him through the weeks that turned into months. Based on what Luke recollected about Stephen's recounting of his journey to Philadelphia, the 10th Regiment would meet the redcoats in battle. With orders from Major General William Alexander, they were to help defend the city.

Once they reached Philadelphia in September, fear finally seeped in. Tales were one thing, but the reality of standing in the line of fire was another. It was that real feeling—sharp and breath stealing—that propelled him forward as their general ushered them into battle.

And what a sight it was. He'd never seen so many people at one time before. Back in the wilderness, he'd grown used to hearing only wildlife. Now he stood among thousands of men ready to fight for their liberty against England.

And he knew they'd fail.

With each battle, Luke held his breath, trailing after Edwin as if any harm to his uncle's body would surely have to go through his.

A month later in Germantown, not far from Philadelphia, they tried to hold their ground against the British troops' divided army, but they lost again. The army didn't make progress protecting Philadelphia either, but each time, Edwin survived. His uncle's boots barely had any soles, and the man's clothes wore thin, but the good Lord granted him breath. Poor Uncle Stephen had far less. Stephen walked barefoot at one point, but he didn't go without for long.

For once in a while they came across dead redcoats who no longer needed their boots or jackets. The Continental Army made quick use of the goods.

Months passed, and after their loss outside Philadelphia, his weary brothers-in-arms needed rest for the upcoming winter. They received those orders as a searing fall settled into a morose and wet December. The somber march from Philadelphia lasted eighteen miles. Once they reached Valley Forge, they found no tents or barracks. No sources of water either. They'd have to build everything.

As temperatures dropped, the soldiers built over two thousand huts. Ten men—whites and Negroes mixed together—huddled in each cabin. As far as Luke could see, men tried to keep warm—all the while avoiding the growing piles of shit and piss.

Thankfully, the weather was mild that winter, but the cold rain soaked through the soldiers' clothing and left them ornery and miserable. From one day to the next, Luke watched men slip away overnight. Some deserters were found and hanged, their bodies on display as a lesson to keep fighting for the republic, but the hammer had already struck the weak-minded. Any man could see it wouldn't be the winter's chill that killed them off but sickness. Crowded in circles to keep warm, men coughed and hacked until their bodies shook from fever. For the less fortunate, red rashes formed on their faces. They moaned and writhed from aches no comforts could abate.

By February, many more of Luke's fellow soldiers succumbed. Far more than he could count. A camp crawling with men, women, and children turned into a cesspool with wards for the sick and weary. Those left standing dug trenches to bury the bodies. The Bridge men didn't escape the sickness. First, Uncle Stephen disappeared into the hospital, then Luke fell sick with fever. For over a month, he lay on that god-awful bed, surrounded by coughing, shivering, and dying men. Their foul breaths and bodily waste tainted the air. Not far from his pallet, one boy begged to die, while on the bed next to his, an older Negro man was delirious, mumbling in a tongue he hadn't heard before.

Murky thoughts swam in and out of Luke's mind. He wondered if he was the only one on this cursed journey through time or if there were others like him—unfortunate souls tossed on the fire to see if they burned or escaped. He shifted, unable to find comfort, and waited for Mama to return to him again. Maybe if he died, she'd welcome him home, but the good Lord never sent him back to the future or to heaven.

Not long after he had gathered his wits, Uncle Edwin succumbed to the flu too. Luke could stand before the man and take a bullet for him or even tend to his wounds with haste, but a sickness such as this one, which brought down the largest man to the smallest, was far more formidable than any enemy.

Luke often ambled to the hospital quarters he'd left to raise Uncle's spirits. But with each visit, a dread settled into his weakened body. Ed's dark skin paled and his bright eyes dimmed far too fast. The smile Edwin gave any stranger faded with each passing day. The Bridges tried to make him eat, but he often refused his meals. Over time, Ed's cheeks, which had been full, became gaunt and his breathing labored and wetly rattled.

After every visit, a thought came to mind Luke couldn't shake: *Is this the end?* Or had Edwin's course through time been forever altered—due to Luke's actions—and now his uncle had to suffer? Such thoughts plagued him and followed him incessantly.

Papa had scolded him more than his siblings when he was younger, but much of what Papa had said made sense now. "After you destroy something, you can never build what you had before. You can only start back at the beginning."

On a brisk morning in February, Grandpa, Stephen, and Luke returned to the hospital to find an empty bed.

Just seeing that filthy pallet punched Luke harder than any man had ever struck him. Uncle Stephen broke down sobbing. His uncle's body had been hauled off after he'd stopped breathing. There'd be no farewells. No prayers for his uncle's safe journey. The bridge Luke had hoped to rebuild collapsed before his very eyes. Edwin had died, not from a redcoat's bullet but from disease. Had he kept his uncle safe from a fast death by a redcoat's lead only for him to suffer for weeks in sickness? Was that better? And, God help him, did that mean his uncle was always meant to die during the war?

The Bridge men lived in a camp of mourners. Nearly two thousand others died that winter, so the Bridges didn't grieve alone.

For many days, Luke felt he was carrying the entirety of his grief on his shoulders. He was lost in thought and unable to anchor himself to the present, just like he felt back in the mountains. Time passed, and he often tried to distract himself through menial tasks. Every day, he sorted his belongings—far less than what he'd started with. Other than his weapon, along with his bayonet, he carefully gathered his tin cup, bowl, spoon, cartridge box, canteen, and such back into his haversack. Nestled at the bottom was Bree's neckerchief and three thread spools he'd crafted over the years. With a movement as familiar as walking, Luke pressed the fabric to his face and pretended he could still smell the wildflowers. Wrapping lavender between the folds helped now and then, but he couldn't capture that first time he'd sat alone in the woods and felt like Bree was seated beside him.

He needed time to heal, and he wished he were with her instead of here.

By May, Luke had fully regained his strength, and the new drills added a sharpness to the men. They now marched in time, and with the army's new alliance with France, their spirits rose. But the Bridge men had a haunted look in their eyes, a detachment he often glimpsed when Edwin's name was mentioned.

Luke understood their pain now.

Not long into June 1778, the soldiers marched to New Jersey to meet the British in Monmouth. The day's heat seared the backs of their necks, but they marched behind Washington, rallied, and held the line.

The British retreated.

The minor victory and abandonment of the redcoat camp the next morning heightened their resolve. Luke thought he'd have all the time in the world with Grandpa and his uncles, but their time in Monmouth brought an end to their journey together. The army honorably discharged each of the Bridge men, but Luke was given orders to march to Augusta with the rest of the troops. The army would need him and many others for what was to come. Watching the Bridges leave him again was bittersweet. Almost as painful as learning Edwin had died. But knowing they'd make it home, back to the farm, gave him a bit of peace, as small as the feeling was.

After Luke departed to Georgia, one day blended into the next. He chiseled away at time like he did to form those maple spools for Bree.

In December 1779, he earned his discharge. Three long years had passed, and somewhere, hundreds of miles away, another Luke hunted for winter fowl. The other Luke was unaware that in a couple of months he'd take the first step on a great journey. This younger version of himself would become the person he was now.

For over four months, Luke traveled northward, weaving his way home with a haversack and Bree's neckerchief in hand. Somehow he arrived safely. Seeing the familiar glen unfold added a band around his chest. His steps quickened until he rapped his knuckles on the rough wood of the stump next to Uncle Stephen's cabin. He heard movement inside and slipped away to the woods. From there, he stuck to the outskirts, marveling at how twenty-two years had passed. And yet every smell and sight and even the memory of tasting Aunt Mary's bread with fresh honey from the late-summer harvest came to mind.

He skirted along the dense foliage, making his way toward the orchard. And it was there he found the Bridge family. Every mid-day they gathered around Grandpa. Uncle Stephen stood in the center, probably spreading more lies about his fighting prowess now that Luke knew the truth. Mama stared off to the west, her face ashen and withdrawn.

Bree spotted Luke first. He couldn't sneak up on a woman with an eye as sharp as her needles.

"Who's that?" He couldn't hear her but caught the movement of her lips just the same.

Luke glanced from face to face, not seeing his own this time. He'd made it, but for them, how many days had gone by since he fell through time?

No one greeted him. No outstretched arms or smiles. Grandma's face grew pale, and her head slowly shook. Did she recognize him?

"Can we help you, stranger?" Grandpa called out. Ben barked and circled before his master.

When Uncle Stephen spotted the haversack Luke set at his feet, he let out a loud guffaw. "It's Sharp-Eyed Noah!"

"Now, that's a sight," Grandpa added. "Never thought we'd see you again."

"Who's that?" Aunt Mary asked with a frown.

"He's one of the men we served with in the 10th." Stephen patted Luke's shoulder. "You're looking well."

Luke waited for his mama to see her son underneath all the changes he'd gone through over the past twenty-two years, but it was Sabrina, sweet steadfast Bree, who edged forward. She was limping. A scar he'd never seen before streaked down her freckled cheek.

Bitter ash bubbled in his stomach. When did *that* happen?

She peered at him, her gaze sweeping downward from his bearded face to his dirty leather breeches.

"Luke?" she whispered.

CHAPTER 12

Sabrina Humbles
APRIL 1780

The man in front of Bree stood at the right height. The top of her head met his broad shoulders. She'd always had to tilt her chin upward to meet Luke's eyes with a bold glare, but this time she could only bear to stare at the middle of his chest. There was an intensity to his demeanor she hadn't seen before, a lower baritone to his voice only time and experience could add. Her breath hitched, and the questions gathering in her lungs wouldn't course up her throat.

Why couldn't she speak?

Bree had prayed for his return. She'd hoped he would come home so she could let go of him for good, but this man looked as old as her uncles. White curls peppered the hair above his ears, and the beginnings of wrinkles gathered at the corners of his eyes. The smooth skin on his forearms was now scarred and rough with muscle.

Stephen spoke first. "That isn't Luke." His voice rose. "I *know* this man. We last saw him two years ago."

Emily took a step toward them, but John caught her wrist. They exchanged a brief glance as her features darkened and his softened.

Grandpa released a long sigh and tried to soothe his growling dark-brown spaniel. "Don't search for what isn't there, child."

Emily freed herself. "Heaven and hell, including my husband, cannot keep me from my boy." She marched up to the stranger and inched between Luke and Bree.

Without a word said, the man bent on one knee before her aunt. Emily grasped his chin and searched his face like Bree had, perhaps finding details everyone had missed.

"Luke . . ." Emily whispered. There was a tinge of sorrow in her voice.

"It's me, Mama," he said.

Then she smiled, pulling him into her arms. "Thank you, God," she cried. "My baby. My child."

Bree clutched her chest. Was it him?

"Now, Em, you're too close." John reached for her again, but venom pooled in the woman's eyes.

"Don't you dare touch him," Emily hissed.

"I don't know what kind of knavish trickery you're practicing, but an honorable man wouldn't come here saying he's someone he isn't." Stephen inched toward them.

More Bridge men made their move. John lunged forward, sneering as he snatched his wife's wrist. He yanked Emily back while Stephen withdrew his pocketknife.

The man they had called Noah froze. "Rest easy. I don't mean any harm."

"If you mean no harm," Grandpa said, his voice steady, "why would you come here bringing the devil's lies?"

Noah blew out a long breath that lifted his shoulders. "I've waited a long time to return home. Over the years, I considered what I'd say to explain everything, but the words never made sense."

"None of this makes any—" John snapped.

Grandpa's hand rose to silence his second son. He clutched Ben to keep him back.

Noah pressed on while he stood. "I am Luke Bridge but . . . How do I say this? You believe I disappeared not too long ago, but the truth is, I ended up twenty-two years in the past."

No one spoke a word, but from where Bree stood, her heart fell. This couldn't be Luke. Only a man deprived of reason would say such crazed things. John shook his head while Stephen clenched his knife. They waited within striking distance. Grandma trembled from where she sat next to Grandpa.

"I understand how I must sound right now." Noah's voice broke. "I was confused too. But I swear on Grandpa's Dutch Bible that I am Luke Bridge. All I ask is that you hear me out."

Stephen tugged at Bree's apron strings to draw her back. His message was clear.

"I don't want to hear a damn thing you have to say." John struggled to keep Emily away. "You did something to my son."

Bree swallowed deeply, catching the glint from Stephen's blade.

"Don't touch him!" Emily used her free hand to point at Stephen. "You'll have to fight me before you strike a blow."

"Already swayed by the devil?" John said to his wife.

Not far from them, Grandma whispered a prayer in her mother tongue. Low and menacing, the sounds stretched out and unfurled. She rarely spoke of her childhood in Africa, but she still knew the ways of her people, even after her former master had forbidden her to speak what her heart knew. Bree feared God, but she feared the gods Grandma worshipped just as much.

Protests rose around them with curses Bree dared not repeat.

Noah remained with his head lowered and back straight, his speech softened to soothe those around him.

"Steady now." Noah retrieved a switchblade, a pistol, and an ax from his person. Slowly, he lowered them each to the ground. "I don't mean any harm."

"You already harmed us, son," Grandpa said. "Thanks to you, my daughter cries on your behalf and my wife curses your name for bringing unclean spirits to our home. I do not trust you or your promises."

"Haven't you always told me 'And the truth shall set you free'?" Noah asked.

Stephen smirked. "It shall, but even the devil's demons know the Bible better than any man."

"That is also true," Noah said, "but I ask everyone to hear my truth, then decide whether I'm Luke and Noah Battles or a stranger. If I remember right, our family always talked through our problems."

John again tried to pull Emily away, but she refused, muttering words only her husband could hear.

The newcomer lowered his head. "We met as kin and we conversed as kin. Only the Luke you know would remember the time when a pine tree fell on our roof. It left a crack this wide." He opened his arms to show the span. "A couple years ago, Papa broke his leg, right? I remember we had to find strong hands to help us through the winter. And when Aunt Mary wanted to leave after Uncle Ed died, we didn't let her go without a word," he added softly. "Hear me out."

A hard gaze flicked between Stephen and Grandpa. The eldest Bridge motioned him over. They spoke in hushed tones while Bree stole a peek at Noah. Or was it Luke? She hungered to speak to him.

Right as Grandpa agreed to hear Noah speak for himself, she spied Addy running down the path to the clearing. She headed straight for her sister, all the while peering at the stranger.

"Who's that?" her sister squeaked.

"He said he's Luke."

Addy made a face as if she'd caught a whiff of rotten fish. "That can't be him. Why would he say something so cruel?"

Bree shrugged.

"Why haven't they driven him away?"

Bree hesitated before she replied, "There's something familiar about him."

"He looks nothing like him. Why would an old man—"

"He isn't that old."

"But he's older than twenty. He must think we're fools to believe Luke would stumble over twenty years before—"

"Hush! He's speaking."

Noah began his tale from the very moment he woke up alone in the middle of an empty field. He described the landscape, revealing the eeriness he'd experienced running through the circle of pines and ferns where their cabin should have sat. She could feel his helplessness as he searched the forest and found no one.

Noah had wandered south, was enslaved, then freed. Eventually, he moved on and reached Boston, where he labored as a dockworker.

At that point in the story, Bree and Addy leaned against each other. Bree's bad ankle ached from standing too long, but she was enthralled, imagining the salty breeze from the Atlantic across his back as he hauled goods off massive ships. To them, his recollection felt like a moment in time, but the far-off look in his eyes revealed he'd experienced something deeper.

Noah's voice briefly brightened once he spoke of the war and his enlistment. He recounted his joy at seeing his uncles—especially Edwin—having them fight beside him, and their time in a military camp called Valley Forge. All the while, he'd wanted to tell them the truth but couldn't.

"Why didn't you say anything?" Stephen asked bitterly.

"Would you have believed me?" Noah replied.

"No." Stephen folded his arms.

"Lies are easier to believe than the truth at times. Uncle Ed almost recognized me."

Stephen's brow furrowed. "Was that a couple years ago when we were training in Amherst County?"

Noah nodded.

Stephen added, "Now that you say that, Ed did mention seeing someone who looked like Luke, but I thought he was missing home."

"Missing home isn't an excuse for seeing what isn't there," Grandpa said solemnly.

Bree took in the sky. She wasn't sure what time it was. Molly fed her baby, and the cousins arrived to stare at the stranger. Ben slept at Grandpa's feet. No one complained of missed chores or animals needing to be tended.

Noah's tale came to an end with his time in the army. The pain in his voice sliced through Bree when he spoke of Uncle Edwin's death, and how his heart broke when the Bridge men were honorably discharged.

"All that time, I wanted to come home," Noah said, his gaze sweeping over them. "And the only way to find *this* place in time was to wait until *after* I disappeared."

Grandpa's leg began to twitch, but he grasped his knee and bent his head as if in prayer. Stephen rested his hand on Grandpa's shoulder and squeezed it. Grandpa motioned for his eldest son to lean over to hear him, and the two spoke in whispers. Seconds stretched to what felt like an eternity.

Finally, Grandpa turned to them. "I cannot decide the fate of this man without praying on the matter and hearing my children's thoughts." He paused before facing Noah. "Tonight, you'll make camp next to Ivy Creek near the fallen oak. Do you know the place?"

"Yes, sir."

"We'll come for you in the morning. Will you respect our decision?"

Noah nodded again, but Aunt Em released a deep sigh with a shake of her head. The man took hold of his belongings while the Bridge folk kept quiet. Even the curious children knew better than to meddle when their fathers waited like vipers.

Before Noah left, Emily retrieved food from her apron pocket.

"I'm well, Mama. No need." He tried to refuse the nuts, but she placed them in his hand and closed his fingers. After that, Noah slipped away into the trees.

One by one, the Bridge elders rose and made their way to Grandma and Grandpa's cabin. Bree and her sister hurried after them. Poking her nose in their business was easy at first—no one had eaten a meal and she hurried to prepare supper. She kept her back to them while the Bridge men settled on one side of the room and Grandma and Grandpa rested on the other. Normally women weren't allowed to be present when there were serious matters to discuss, but no one forced her aunt to leave. Aunt Emily waited outside, hands clasped tightly as she paced the patch of dirt beyond the porch. Only Grandpa had the authority to ask Grandma to wait with the other women and children in Molly's cabin.

While Bree warmed cornbread near the stoked fire and drew up the ingredients for asparagus soup, the men began their conversation. Addy tried to help, but Grandma intervened. "Go help your cousins mind the young ones at Molly's."

Addy quickly glanced at Bree, but Bree jerked her chin to the door. Whatever she learned she'd share later—if they let her stay.

"I don't like him. He isn't my boy," John said first to Grandpa. "Something about him makes me uneasy."

"He's a fool to think we'd believe such nonsense." Stephen snuck a piece of cornbread before Bree finished warming it. Between chews, he said, "Luke used to always play tricks on us."

"But this isn't the kind of trick you play on people," Grandpa said.

Bree kept her hands steady while she cut up asparagus, onions, and parsley. Out of the corner of her eye, she spied Emily's shadow falling across the front doorway.

"He must be sick in the head. We saw many things no man should witness—death, madness, hangings," Stephen said softly. "Before we were discharged, he never acted like that."

"True. Not once did he lose his wits, but who knows what happened to him after we left the army," Grandpa said. "The men who marched to Augusta kept fighting."

"Something could've broken him," Stephen admitted. "And he probably heard us talking about Luke and thought he was the same man."

"Did he ever say anything about his family?" Grandma asked. "Where are they from?"

"He mentioned they lived near the Southwest Mountains," Stephen said. "But now that I think about it, I've never heard of a single man named Battles from around here."

"Folks come and go." Grandpa appeared thoughtful for a moment. "His family could've been from the mountains, but that's no excuse for lying or saying you're someone's missing child."

Nods floated through the room. The heat from the fireplace grew uncomfortably hot, but Bree refused to budge or remind them she was present. As much as she wanted to defend the man she knew was Luke, it wasn't her place.

Aunt Emily came through the doorway. "But what if he isn't lying? What if he's the *real* Luke?"

"Can you hear yourself, Em?" John asked. "That man is ill in the head."

"If God can make His holy son Jesus rise from the dead, why can't He send His earthly children anywhere He sees fit?" She drew closer. "You believe he's in league with the devil, but what if this is God's work? What if there was a *purpose* to his journey?"

The enticing aroma of soup filled the room. Bree stirred the pot as quietly as possible but froze after hearing her aunt's words. She had trouble believing God would be so cruel.

Emily now stood before Grandma and Grandpa. "I can prove he is Luke."

"Clinging to another woman's child won't bring yours back," Grandma said softly. "I know you wish to see him again—I do. I've lost too many babies myself, but we have women and children on this farm to protect."

"Mother Bridge . . ." Emily began.

John rubbed the back of his neck, the same way the stranger had. *Can't they see the similarities between father and son?* she thought. But then again shouldn't Luke look more like his papa?

John had a reddish tinge to his dark-brown skin and thinning hair along his temples, while the stranger had moles dotting his cheeks and soft brown skin like Emily's.

"Mama's right." Stephen approached Emily and his parents. "Papa, I know you feel the same. I say we send him on his way."

Bree's grip on the pot ladle loosened, and it fell to the floor. She scurried to pick it up. Five heads turned her way.

"Go after your sister, Bree," Grandpa said firmly.

"But the supper—" Bree said.

"I'll mind the soup." Aunt Em pried the ladle from her hand. Perhaps her aunt caught the pleading expression on her face, for Emily smiled at her. *Everything will be fine*, her aunt seemed to convey. Hadn't Emily given her the same expression every time she talked about something that troubled her?

When Bree tried to sneak around the back of the cabin, Stephen followed her. Undeterred, she took the path into the orchard, then doubled back to return from the south. Grandma would punish her for not minding, but she had to know what would become of Luke.

From behind the trees, she limped toward the house, but Stephen's presence kept her from getting any closer. He listened from right outside the door. Her stomach quaked from the mouthwatering smell of the soup. Insects fluttered around her feet, yet she refused to budge from her hiding place. Voices rose within the house, though she couldn't hear the words.

Bree didn't know how much time had passed, but she sighted the silhouette of a horned owl flapping, then landing on the cabin roof. Twilight had arrived.

Movement to her right caught her eye. Along the dark edges of the setting sun, Bree glimpsed a Negro woman, no older than herself, in a light-blue dress, standing by a line of trees.

No, not a dress—a white shirt a man would wear and a skirt; the ankle-length fabric was a vivid blue, just like a speckled robin's egg.

The woman stared at her as hard as Bree did. Bree almost looked away, but there was something peculiar about the stranger. The cut of the woman's clothing made her blink. Instead of a hem that fell to the ground, the stranger's dress reached her ankles, and her booted feet peeked out. What was she doing out here? Bree took a step forward, then the woman retreated as her mouth parted. Their gazes connected. The dying sunlight hit the stranger, revealing her shirt's lacy bodice and collar. Her gloved hand floated up to her mouth.

To Bree's right, Emily strode away from the cabin toward the orchard. Bree couldn't read her aunt's face, but she approached Emily tentatively. She glanced over her shoulder, and the strange woman was gone. As much as she wanted to ask Aunt Em about the woman, she had other pressing matters.

"What did they say?" she asked.

Emily kept moving, only pausing long enough to give Bree a few words. "My boy can stay."

Bree tried to make out the shapes within the cabin, but the fire gathered more shadows than light. She couldn't see their faces.

What had her aunt said to convince them?

CHAPTER 13

Sabrina Humbles

APRIL 1780

Six long days passed—long enough for Bree to embroider two petticoats. Instead of thinking of Luke, she concentrated on crafting even stitches to resemble tiny yet narrow leaves found on many a wildflower. After that, her hands feverishly added bluebells on a bodice. The faint tap of the needle striking the thimble on her finger filled the monotony.

During that time, no one from her household heard so much as a whimper from the man who called himself Luke Bridge. Not even Addy, who'd lost herself within the menial task of picking wool clean, visited him.

Then one morning her sister said offhandedly, "I wonder what Luke's doing today."

"Who knows. Probably working somewhere."

"Have you ever thought about him?"

"We're friends."

"I can't stop thinking about how much fun we had." Her face lit up as she went on and on about their lazy summer days when the sun had baked their backs. How they'd had nothing better to do than talk about what they wished for their lives.

The more Luke's name came up, the more Bree was certain Addy still yearned for him too.

With their pails in hand, the sisters headed to the creek, but they ended up veering toward John and Em's cabin instead. They lingered along the fence to the pasture like bees searching for early summer blossoms. Chickens clucked and pecked the ground at their feet, finding what they sought better than the sisters could. In the distance, the cabin loomed, larger than Grandma and Grandpa's, but neglect clung to this one. Weeds defiantly sprouted around the home and moss mottled the north side. A long dirty rope was nailed to the side of the house and led to an overgrown garden and outhouse.

Though John and Emily's house had seen better days, life carried on within. The wonderful smells of shepherd's pie bubbling in a covered pot reached the sisters along with the rhythm of conversation tumbling out of the open front door, giving them a taste of Luke's younger sister Fanny. At eighteen, the girl ruled the cabin the moment her parents left to work in the orchards. During the day, she took care of her younger siblings.

"If you don't fetch the wood, there won't be any supper." She had to be saying that to David.

"I don't want to," the five-year-old grumbled as he made his way to the door.

Through the front doorway, they glimpsed Fanny snatching his blouse collar and tugging back the child to swat his bottom. The boy yelped and Addy jumped.

"You better not cry," Fanny snapped. "You're not hurt. Go do as I say."

David escaped out the door and ran off to the woodshed next to the house. A tabby cat darted out after him.

Bree and Addy waited next to the fence while Fanny hurried out, then she hooked her arm around the rope since she couldn't see well. Fanny made her way to the family garden. Aunt Em's youngest, Grace, slept on Fanny's back, safe and snug within the long black cloth tied around Fanny's bosom. The two-year-old's head wobbled, but she never woke. Fanny stooped and ran her hands through the garden's oblong sage leaves and the feather-like parsley plants. The family cat rubbed against her side. With a soft smile, she scratched the top of the animal's head before she plucked what she needed and returned inside.

The sisters inched their way down the fence, ducked under the line connecting the cabin to the fencing, and walked up to the house.

When they were ten feet away, Fanny called out, "Who's there?"

"Morning, Fanny," Bree said.

"Fanny . . ." Addy murmured.

Luke's sister emerged from the house again. Her straight face turned into a wide grin. "Might as well go about your business— Luke isn't here."

"Did he leave the farm?" Addy asked before Bree could.

"No, he's here to stay—as long as he doesn't start any trouble."

"Is he really your brother?" Addy added.

"Yes, indeed. He sounds different though. Older," Fanny mused. "He was quiet for a couple days, then he mentioned things he'd missed."

A flush reddened Addy's cheeks. "Did he mention me?"

"Why would he?" Fanny often spoke before she considered the bitterness of her words.

"Fanny," Bree warned.

"From what I heard, he's been alone for a long time. During the day, he works with Papa. Then after supper, he speaks with Mama by the creek." She swayed a little, perhaps to placate Grace.

Addy approached Fanny. "Did he say anything about another woman?"

"Not yet," Fanny said, "but only the Lord knows."

Bree swallowed past a lump in her throat. He did say he'd been gone for twenty-two years. If he had a wife, wouldn't he have brought her with him?

With nothing else to talk about, the Humbles sisters left. When the time was right, they'd see Luke again.

They tried to hide their wandering, but in a small community like the farm, they couldn't keep such things to themselves. Soon enough, Grandma said to them, "Leave him be. Things are different now, but they won't always be that way. It's going to take some time to adjust."

Sunday arrived, bringing a day of rest and prayer. That morning Bree gave thanks to God for Luke's return. Wasn't it better to have him home than lost or dead? She didn't understand how he could have gone where he claimed to have been—but he was here. Even if he was meant for Addy.

The Bridge family assembled outside Grandma and Grandpa's cabin and listened to Grandpa reading from the family Bible. Luke was there too. Family members lounged next to one another while babies fussed and children squirmed, but even with the interruptions, they were all together again.

While Grandpa read from Ephesians, Bree kept her hands clenched on her lap. Her little sister leaned against her, not knowing how Bree wrestled with her feelings.

At the end of his sermon, Grandpa spoke up. "In a few days, Luke and Addison will marry. May the Lord bless them."

After the service, while the adults conversed, the children gaped at Luke. Bree's older cousins stole glances in his direction too. He used to stand with them, but now he was an elder.

Briefly, his gaze connected with Bree's and he smiled. His easy grin used to aggravate her, but this older, more refined Luke set her insides on fire. She turned away from him. He was still her friend, but in a way she hadn't expected, they were a trio again. And fate would inevitably draw them apart. It was best for her to consider Addy.

Bree faced her sister and forced herself to laugh at a joke from Fanny—even though she wasn't listening. She just wanted Addy to be happy again. Addy never asked for much, and she did her chores without complaints. She would become a great mother and wife. *Even if she took her time to finish the chores,* Bree thought with a smile.

The Sunday service ended, and as hard as she tried to forget about Luke, he plagued her thoughts. Seeing him alive and well, like a cape with different stitches and fabric, should've helped Bree cast her feelings aside, but an itch to talk to him still crept up her spine. Eventually, they'd speak to each other. And when the time came, would she be able to say her true thoughts without changing everything?

———

Over the next couple of days, excitement flittered through the farm, as weddings were a special time. The family would eat apple fritters, and a pig would be butchered for the feast. There'd be plenty of jovial conversation, and weddings promised the possibility of new children.

Bree should've been happy for her sister, but the thought

of Luke and Addy having a child together tightened her stomach into a coil and never let go. To ease her errant thoughts, she fetched water in the mornings without her sister. Addy never hurried while Bree struggled uphill with her weakened ankle, but walking alone gave Bree an opportunity to sort through her thoughts and make plans for the future.

The forest always had a way of calming Bree. When she was alone, she could hear her own breath. The sighs. The sniffs when she wanted to cry. She refused to have witnesses. She didn't mind being alone—until she met Luke by chance near the creek. It wasn't like that morning more than a week ago when she'd found him perched carefree with his legs swinging in the water, a smile on his face. Now he sat on an elevated spot at the water's edge. His face remained troubled this time, a pool of worries compared to the nearby tranquil waters.

"Morning," he said.

She gave him a nod and shuffled down the bank. Her ankle often made the path precarious. Before she could hurry through her labors, Luke stood and reached over, took the pail from her. His palm was rough, yet with a single touch he set her stomach off-kilter.

Bree swallowed and managed to say, "I can do it by myself."

"You always could do it by yourself, but I like helping you."

She waited for him to return uphill, but he sat again. Her feet remained rooted to where she stood, but she itched to walk away.

"Unless you got somewhere to be, I plan to sit here," he finally said.

"I have chores to do—"

"And you'll do them soon, but you and I need to talk."

Her mouth opened, then closed. "Yes, we need to talk."

She walked a few steps, hoping he'd follow, but he didn't. This serious Luke wouldn't make anything easy for her. With a growing frown, she found a spot to sit nearby.

"Are you still mad at me?" He laughed.

Bree tried to hold on to her stiff demeanor, but Luke's relaxed smile made her mouth stumble. "I'm not angry. You said twenty-two years have passed, but it's been only a couple days for us. Honestly, I don't understand how that's possible."

"I don't either—but what matters to me is how you feel."

Her head turned sharply in his direction. Luke had never said such things before. "I'm numb." She licked her dry lips. "And none of this makes any sense."

"No, it doesn't."

"You disappeared right in front of Addy and me, and now you show up later looking—"

"Like a filthy muskrat."

A laugh snuck out of her mouth. "What I meant to say was you appear different, but you *feel* the same."

"I'm still the same man." His face grew pensive. "But I've changed. I've been places."

"You mentioned Boston before. Where else did you go?" Anticipation of hearing more drew her closer to him. "Philadelphia?"

"Perhaps."

"You're lying."

He laughed. "I've seen many places, but Boston was the best. If I hadn't wanted to return home, I would've settled down there."

"Boston sounds like another world. Tell me more."

Luke spoke, and the city unfolded like a night-blooming flower before her eyes as he described sunrises off the bay and the bustle of the endless wharves. On any day, women and children sold baked goods or peddled flowers in the streets. They dodged horse-drawn carriages, which click-clacked as the conveyances rolled up and down narrow cobblestone roads. Bree loved every single detail.

"Why did you return?" she asked. "In a city like that, you could've made a living for yourself. Or you could've gone to England. Perhaps even farther."

He stared at her for a bit, and she couldn't discern his thoughts.

"What?" she asked.

"The thought of boarding one of those massive boats doesn't scare you?"

"Not in the least bit. If I ever had the chance—and I'm not a fool to think it's likely—I'm *certain* I'd go."

"Not me. Home is home. Have you always felt that way?"

She sighed. "This farm is my home, but I often wonder if I could find my way . . . like you did."

"Could you stay for a while? I've recently returned." He sounded wistful.

"I've wanted to leave for a long time now, but I didn't want to leave our grandparents alone. I never had the courage to talk about it. I'm thinking Richmond or Charlottesville."

He slowly nodded and scooted closer to her left side. They sat in silence again until he spoke. "Hard to believe I'm getting married soon." Regret colored his words.

"Twenty-two years is quite the engagement." Her voice was hollow, but like always, she added a smile.

"I missed everyone."

"We missed you too."

"I've waited a long time to speak with you."

Tension gathered in Bree's chest. His right hand was closer to hers than before, but she told herself that meant nothing.

"Now that I'm here, I don't want you to go." Luke paused.

"We've grown up together. Seen each other through trouble and times of good health. I don't want to lose my friend."

"We'll always be friends. Weren't you always friendly with that trader who comes by every season to barter for tools?"

"That's not the same." His relaxed expression darkened. "He's a part of the world outside this farm, and that place is far more frightening than you can imagine."

"What happened to you?"

Luke reached over and grasped her hand. She stiffened, waiting for him to release her, all the while her heartbeat quickening like a cornered winter hare.

"Plenty happened, but it doesn't matter. Why do you think I spent twenty-two years doing everything I could to get home?"

After many hitched breaths, she felt him finally let go of her hand. The skin of her palm burned for him to touch her again.

"Whatever you decide to do," he said, "I'll be there for you."

She managed a nod.

"I've been waiting many years to say what's in my heart." Luke's voice shook a little.

"And what's that?"

"That I've always wanted to be with you."

Bree's heart stumbled. Had she heard him clearly? Never in the years she'd known him had he revealed such feelings. When had he changed his mind? And why? She stared at him, wondering what he'd gain by her staying since he would marry her sister.

"You look like you want to drown me in the creek, Bree."

"How long can you hold your breath?" she asked sternly.

"I like it better when you're mad at me." Luke smiled. "You've always been the strong one. You've come a long way since I helped you and Addy twelve years ago."

She stiffened. "What did you say?"

His smile widened. "Do you remember the time before Grandpa found you? You and Addy were lost in the mountains."

She slowly nodded.

"I found you *first*."

"But I don't remember you." Her heart beat so fast, she swore she'd misheard him.

Luke told her with uncanny detail how he'd encountered the two girls, what they'd worn, and how he'd left food for them to eat.

"I tried to keep you safe," he added. "I hadn't expected to see you like this."

"Like this?"

He motioned to her left leg. "When did that happen?"

"On the way to the farm with Grandpa, a snake bit my ankle. Aunt Emily did all she could, but after the swelling went away, I couldn't walk as fast."

"How did you get the scar on your face?" he pressed.

"At twelve, I fell and scraped my face against a tree."

He stared off into the forest, past the swaying pine and birch trees, before he glanced at her leg. "I wish I'd known you'd end up hurt."

She opened and closed her mouth, not understanding. "Are you saying you don't remember?"

He shook his head. "Before I left, however that happened, your ankle and face were fine. The events over the years have changed and I don't know why."

She shuddered. How could there be another Bree? None of what he said made sense, yet he spoke of things she'd experienced and hadn't shared with him. Perhaps what he said was true.

"If I had known helping you and Addy would've hurt you, I wouldn't have changed the past. Will you do well out in the world?"

"I'm seventeen years old. I know how to care for myself, and if you can support yourself, I can do the same." She shifted away from him.

"You're the most capable person I know, but I've seen the filth out there. They prowl the streets and take advantage of the disabled. They'll see you and—"

"And what? They'll believe I can't run away? They'll think they can hurt me? I'm not scared of what *might* happen. I'm more scared of standing still, of waiting and watching the man I love marry someone else. I must find my way like you did."

Luke went rigid and stared at her. She'd never revealed how she felt before, and her admission left her breathless, yet relieved.

He opened his mouth to speak, but she forced herself to stand and take her pail. She didn't want to hear what he had to say. No matter how much she loved him, she'd never betray her sister. The more she thought about it, she wondered what had happened. Had one of his parents forced him to marry Addy? Perhaps Grandpa? There had to be a reason he had chosen Addy over her, but that didn't matter. What was done was done.

Bree marched uphill, letting the sun warm her shoulders and the song of the morning birds ease her mind. She waited for Luke to steal the bucket again, but this time, he didn't follow.

———

The days leading up to the wedding went by faster than a vengeful summer storm. The mornings were swallowed by the rush of wind, a rain's rage. In the aftermath, there was nothing left but sorrowful puddles, linens dripping on the lines, and the arrival of suffocating dampness. The morning of the wedding crept up on Bree—just like Addy, who squirmed and wiggled beside her long before the sun peeked above the horizon. Addy leaned over her and kissed her cheek.

"I'm getting married," Addy whispered.

"Yes, my dear heart." Bree faced her sister with the smile she wore every day, then she took in the bundles of flowers she'd hung from the ceiling. During the tepid summers, she loved to lie up here and get lost in counting the dried petals. Many of them were shrunken and withered, but some—the stubborn ones, like the black-eyed Susans and catmints—held firm to their shape. Time was an ever-present ally and enemy.

After stretching her arms, Bree asked, "Are you hungry?" She knew the answer. Addy never had an appetite in the mornings.

"No." Addy flashed her a smile bright enough to drive away the darkness of the days.

"You'll be hungry soon."

"Don't go." Addy reached up and took her hand. "I'm not hungry yet. Tell me the story of Mama and that little hen."

"Oh, Addy." She tried to lower her voice. "You could recite that story forwards and backwards."

"I like the way you tell it." Addy leaned her head against Bree's shoulder. "I can't remember Mother, but whenever you tell the story, I pretend she looked like you."

Before Bree could escape, Addy placed her head on Bree's lap. Warmth from her younger sister's side seeped into her, and her hands moved of their own volition to play with the thick twists of Addy's hair.

"Once upon a time, there was a red hen who followed Mama everywhere she went," she began. "The hen could fit in your palm, but she clucked the loudest and bounded this way and that, determined to follow Mama to the fields."

She covered Addy's face with her palms. "During the day, the hen hid under the tobacco leaves until the overseer released the slaves in the evening. At night, she curled up at the back of the henhouse. Alone. Cold."

Addy slowly shook her head, playing her part.

"Now, the plantation cook, a horrible woman by the name of Mala, wanted to chop up that poor chicken and serve it in a stew for the master, but Mama would have no such nonsense. She picked up the hen—"

"—and tucked the animal away in the beautiful cotton cloth she'd used to carry her children in," Addy finished softly.

"That's right." Bree trailed her fingers along the curve of Addy's round cheeks. "The hen no longer had to hide under the tobacco or sleep all alone. Mama took care of it. Nurtured it."

"She loved it," her sister added.

"Yes, but love isn't always easy. One day Mama woke up and the hen was gone. She cried and cried after searching all day. Days passed, and a week later, Mama came upon a chicken stew bubbling in the pot and the master smacking his lips from his *fine* meal. That poor woman's heart broke in two. All she had left was a tiny feather no bigger than her fingernail. She struggled to work, day in and day out, until she heard a familiar cluck from the henhouse. She crept up and peeked inside."

Addy's grin widened.

"Mama had found her precious hen, but the bird didn't need her no more. Now four tiny chicks followed the tiny hen. Her baby hadn't gone—she'd become a mama herself."

Addy's sweet smile never wavered. "That's the beautiful thing about love. It lives on."

"Forever and ever," Bree added wistfully.

They couldn't lie around and tell more stories, for on a day like this one, they had much to do. The previous evening, in preparation for the feast, Stephen had butchered a pig, and Molly had baked apple bread long into the night.

A flurry of activity carried decadent smells, sweet and savory, across the farm. Mary roasted trout over a fire, and the aroma of slow-cooked greens wafted from Emily's pots. In the middle of the pasture in front of the cabin, Grandma and Bree got Addy ready. Earlier in the day, her little sister had packed what little she owned: a shawl Bree had knitted over the past winter, a new shift, and two dresses Bree had recently mended. Bree's breath caught to see her sister donned in her wedding dress. The garment swallowed Addy's narrow waist and fell over her flat chest, but Addy glowed as if the fabric had been spun from gold.

By midday, the time had come. The regret Bree held tightly to her bosom melted away as family members slipped through the trees. Everyone gathered before the circle of stone Grandma and Bree had fashioned. The Bridges became a sea of dandelions, humming and swaying in the wind, but Bree didn't want to move with them.

This pain shall pass, she thought. *This ache you're feeling while Addy puts her hands into Luke's will eventually come to its end—just like a summer storm.*

The rise and fall of her family's voices singing a joyful noise lulled and lifted her. One moment she closed her eyes in prayer, and in the next, she opened them to see the handfasting rope wrapped around their wrists. Congratulations, whoops, and cheers filled the field, but to her, their blessings swelled as one until Bree heard nothing but the roar of her heartbeat.

It is done.

Her head swam at the thought, but a steady hand grasped her elbow. Emily pulled her away from the others as the world slammed into place. Her aunt's tiny hand offered not a celebratory grip but a consolatory one. Aunt Em threaded her fingers with Bree's and squeezed over and over again.

Bree tugged to pull them back toward the ceremony, but Luke's mother had the strength of ten men. Once the forest embraced them, Bree took in the tear streaks on her aunt's cheeks, the tremble in her hands, the empathetic line of her mouth. She held tight, feeling the familiar jagged scar on Emily's right palm.

Her aunt rarely cried. Even after a child died last year, she'd held the strength of the base of a tree trunk. Unmoving. Steadfast.

"You're going to be all right," Em murmured. "It's done now." Emily wiped her cheeks. "These are tears of joy, sweet pea."

"Tears of joy," Bree repeated back, squeezing her aunt's hands until she could clutch them no more.

Spent and relieved of her stress, Bree returned with Aunt Emily to the others. There was plenty to do and children to mind instead of seeing Addy and Luke side by side. Platters of food needed to be given to the elders. When Grace fussed in Fanny's arms, Bree swept in to sing to the sweet girl. More children gathered around her, and soon she lost the evening in laughter and games. Her ankle ached from running after them, but these children would sleep well tonight. The burdens of loss and sadness had no place in their minds.

Bree had to do the same.

Her sister was married now. Bree had done her part. Mama would've wanted her to guide Addy like that baby chick so Addy could find her own way. Luke wouldn't abandon Addy like Daddy Humbles had. That thought sprouted in her chest and blossomed there.

Long into the night, Bree's limp became more pronounced, but she danced and sang until all she could do was sit before the fire between Aunt Molly and Aunt Mary. Stephen tittered from imbibing too much cider when someone Bree didn't recognize entered the glen. Her eyes followed the boy while he skirted along the line of trees, slinking in and out of the shadows. He had to be no more than ten or twelve. With tears wetting his cheeks, the boy tentatively approached the fire, revealing his high-waisted dark-blue breeches and the ripped sleeves of his white linen shirt.

"Who's that poor child?" she caught Grandma saying.

"Must've smelled the food," Grandpa said. "Bring him here."

John rose, but Emily held him back. She motioned for Luke to join her. They approached the boy, and he rushed into Emily's arms and sobbed against her bosom. The dancing ceased as everyone stared.

"You know him?" Mary asked Molly.

"I've never seen him before." Molly shook her head and cradled her baby. "Poor child."

Emily gave the boy a once-over before she drew him off to the side, away from everyone else. Luke fetched the child some cider, and the wretched thing drank deeply. The stew they gave him vanished just as quickly. Slaves on the run posed a danger to the farm if slave catchers came searching for him and rounded them up too, but the boy's clothes, although dirty, didn't seem as worn and thin as a slave's.

"He's a quiet one," Bree remarked to Grandma.

"He might have nothing to say. Or plenty," the elderly woman replied.

"Are we going to send him away?"

"He'll sleep here tonight," Grandma said softly as the fire cast a glow on her wrinkled cheeks. She turned away from Bree. "We've celebrated a fruitful union tonight. My ancestors are restless, and I fear what he'll find out there."

CHAPTER 14

Sabrina Humbles

MAY 1780

After Bree's sister left to go live in Luke's home, the cabin took shallow breaths. The home had just as many inhabitants once the boy, whom Grandma called Olu, after her father, came to live with them, but there were too many empty spaces. The spinning wheel now sat in Addy's new home, and Olu ate from the bowl Addy had used for her meals. The quiet boy also slept beside Bree up in the loft. He struggled the most at night, sobbing until she drew him into her arms. Over and over, he cried out for his mother.

"Mama Bear, where are you?" was all he ever said.

Everyone kept asking the boy for his name, but he never gave it. He merely shook his head and cried.

Since Olu eagerly followed Grandpa and Grandma to the orchard, mornings left Bree lost in thought as she fetched the water or washed the clothes. It was better to focus on her embroidery, for there was nothing more soothing than falling into perfectly aligned stitches or watching the simplicity of a dress come to life with the promise of spring. She imagined a future Addy wearing the garment she embroidered. She'd spin in a circle, the dress mushrooming while her laughter blossomed. Her children would do the same. Bree allowed that vision of her sister's laughter and joy to trail after her while she plucked weeds from the garden behind the house and fed the chickens.

Later, a visitor appeared in the cabin doorway as she hummed the soft tune Addy often sang. Emily had sunshine in her smile. Summer planting was in full swing, and the elders rarely left the fields—Bree was surprised to see her.

"Are you well?" Bree asked.

"Yes, but . . ." Her aunt's gaze swept over the room, lingering. The cabin was tidy as always, but Emily seemed to see something she didn't. "Your cousin Fanny burned herself and my husband cut his hand. Just another day. I had to walk away before I lost what little wits I have left."

They laughed. Emily stitched up folks while Bree stitched fabric. At least the clothes didn't complain.

"Do you need anything?" she asked. "Are you hungry?"

Em took a deep breath and perched on the stool beside Bree. "We need goods for the new cabin."

By "new cabin" her aunt meant Luke and Addy's.

Emily continued. "I told John we should go to Richmond. You'll go with us, won't you?"

Bree's hands trembled after she heard the word "Richmond," but she managed to smile. "I should."

"You should? You don't sound as confident as a couple months ago."

"I still want to find an apprenticeship, but—"

"Has something changed?"

"No. All is well. Maybe I'm nervous at the thought of leaving Grandma and Grandpa alone."

"They'll be well. The boy is here now, and their children have always taken care of them." Emily scooted closer to her. "People come and go. That's the way it is."

Her aunt took a long look at her—just like Luke had.

"Yes, people come and go like Olu," Bree whispered.

Emily smiled wistfully and nodded.

"Is he faring well out in the orchard?" Bree asked, hoping to talk about anything other than herself.

"Better than I expected. The boy's tended fruit trees before, and he never makes a fuss either. Mary wishes to have him come live with her, but she'll never win a fair fight with Grandma."

"Grandpa told me Grandma was feistier than a mountain viper in her younger days."

"Has that changed?"

They laughed again, and the thought of leaving, and how she'd miss these moments, saddened her. Perhaps her smile had wilted, for Emily patted her knee and released a sigh big enough for the both of them.

"It's time for you to take flight, my sweet pea, just like Olu. I want you to be willing to work for what should be rightfully yours." Emily's voice rose in intensity. "You deserve more. And you won't find what you seek here."

Aunt Emily rocked a bit. "Did I ever tell you about how I came to live here?"

Bree swayed with her, recalling the early years after Grandpa and Grandma took her in. "If you did, I don't remember."

"I grew up not far from this place, but for the longest time, I lived near the coast north of here. The winters were difficult, but I thrived." The hint of a smile touched Emily's cheeks as if she remembered something precious.

"Why did you leave?" she asked.

Em paused. "I had to go. And one day you'll make a decision, like I did, to venture out and find your true home." Emily stopped rocking and bit her lower lip. "After wandering for only God knows how long, I encountered John and we . . . fell in love in the middle of nowhere. He kept telling me how happy he'd make me. How I wouldn't regret taking a chance on him. You can take that chance too, sweet pea."

Her aunt stood and made her way to the door. Bree wished Em hadn't used that name—there were so many memories connected to that endearment. Back then, a younger Bree had drunk up every word, every lesson. Emily's books had given her worlds Bree assumed she'd never see and experiences she'd never witness. Over the years, Emily had become not only her teacher but another mother when she wasn't brave enough to speak to Grandma. Her younger self had believed everything Emily said, but today she had doubts.

"We're leaving tomorrow at sunrise." Emily waited until their gazes connected before she added, "If you wish to come, be ready. When you're there to grasp it, the *right* opportunity often presents itself."

———

Hints of the first light drove away the milky shadows in the loft where Bree slept, but she had yet to pack a thing. Last night, she'd decided to stay. She should've slept soundly, but she twisted and turned on the straw bed. Perhaps if she waited for sleep, she'd find it.

She never did.

So Bree lay there and listened as her grandparents rose for the day. The familiar sounds of Grandpa shuffling to the outhouse tugged away any thoughts of sleeping. As if on cue, Ben barked at the chickens. *Might as well get on with living then.* She sprang to her feet to prepare breakfast. Olu woke quickly and obediently followed her.

The sky held firmly to purples and pinks as she coaxed the fireplace to life. She heated servings of the cornmeal she'd set over the dying coals last night and poured hard cider into cups. While she worked, a strong, wrinkled hand—Grandpa's—gripped her shoulder. Moments later, before Grandma accepted her bowl, her soft palm stroked the middle of Bree's back as a mother would a child.

Bree blew out a deep breath and tried to quell the tears she wanted to shed. Grandma and Grandpa never were ones to linger with goodbyes and sorrow.

"I've lost many children," Grandma had once told her. "I cannot cry anymore when I've scraped every tear out of my soul."

After Grandpa, Grandma, and Olu left for the day, she gave in and hurried to bundle what little she owned. Over the years, she'd collected swatches of cloth. Shiny buttons and discarded buckles filled the nooks and cracks in the space she used to share with Addy. The temptation to leave them behind came to mind— perhaps she'd return—but she swallowed past the urge and reached into every hiding place. She moved without thought. If she sat long enough, she'd stumble and change her mind. Soon enough, her wrapped cloth held her two shifts, her only other dress, two petticoats, and other treasures. Her sewing supplies fit deeply within her apron pockets.

Bree considered gathering the flowers she'd left hanging from the ceiling to dry, but in time she'd gather more scents, more colors for her collection. Someone else, with dreams like hers, might see the catmints and imagine the promise they'd once kept. A promise of love instead of withered dreams.

With daylight creeping toward the horizon, she had one last thing to do before she boarded the cart. Her uncles were already hitching up the mares in the clearing next to John and Emily's home. Every footstep felt like a boot was pressed against her gut. She should've eaten with the others, but a meal would've added to her discomfort. The person Bree wanted to see held Grace on her hip and watched the men. Addy waved.

"Emily said you're going to Richmond, but she wouldn't tell me when everyone's coming back," her sister said. "It'll only be a couple days, right?"

Instead of an answer, Bree pulled Addy in for a hug and savored the warmth. Grace squirmed in Addy's arms and Bree kissed the child's forehead to quiet her. She had missed holding Addy. She'd gotten used to her sibling's restless sleeping, but now Addy slept next to someone else. Her sister smelled like *him*—a blend of carpenter's resin and worn leather. A man's scent.

Bree backed away with a forced grin and grasped Addy's free left hand. "Did Emily tell you I'm looking for work?"

Addy's smile died. "No, she didn't."

"I've told you many times I've wanted to be a seamstress."

"You have." Addy's eyes narrowed. "But I'd hoped once I got married you'd do the same."

The same as in I stay here with her, she thought.

And who would Bree marry? No one had expressed interest recently.

"I probably will get married someday," Bree admitted, "but I won't learn the trade I'd like to do living here." To quiet the quiver in Addy's hand, she gave her sister a dress she'd made after the wedding. "I'd planned to give you this in the fall, but now seems a good time."

Addison held the precious dress with a clenched fist. "Leaving me like this isn't right, Bree. You're my only family."

"You know that isn't true." She lowered her voice. "And don't you dare say such a thing in front of Grandpa or Grandma. Do you understand?"

"We've never been apart before."

"If I raised you well, and I know I have since you married well, then you'll find your own way. Just like I must do the same."

A tear fell down Addy's cheek. She refused to wipe the streak away, so Bree did. "Stop crying. When I'm able, I'll come visit." The lie that Bree would return had tumbled out too easily. "This isn't goodbye, Addison."

"But it feels that way."

If Bree didn't try to go now, she never would.

"It's never goodbye for you and me." Bree slipped her hands into her sister's. "It's only a farewell until we meet again."

The journey to Richmond lasted less than a day, but the trip wasn't as pleasurable with Luke in the wagon, along with Emily, John, and Stephen. A part of Bree wanted to lose herself to the tranquil woods and the rolling hills, but they couldn't keep her from thinking about Luke.

No one spoke during the ride. Their silence was necessary for their safety. *Don't look at anyone. Don't speak to them either.* Those were the rules. They had left Albemarle County and ridden deep into Henrico. If anyone of authority stopped them, none of their freedom papers would give them permission to travel this far from home.

Buckeye, birch, and thick patches of ferns held shadows, and Bree tried not to think of how many Negroes had taken a similar journey opposite the way they had come. Stephen had talked about the many men he'd served with—how they'd escaped and fought to spite their masters. Those masters had continued to seek their property as the war waged on.

Soon enough they spied wooden homes. As the muddy road widened, Bree's spirits lifted to see more people. They drove past warehouses to the south and, even farther, the great James River. Watermen guided long flatboats and barges east and west to deliver goods. Their wagon fell in line behind a team of oxen hauling covered furniture.

The weight of Luke's stare pressed against her, but she took in the long road heading east to Williamsburg instead, noting every house and storefront. She'd never seen this many people before.

The trek east continued until they reached the far edge of town. Wooden houses, some built in haste, dotted the hills. At the end of a dirt road, they came upon a two-story home at the top of a knoll with a barn and fenced-off livestock. The home had beautiful four-pane windows. Violet and dark-yellow pansies added a touch of color to the mud-brown structure. She spied, behind the house, rows of sprouts—likely corn, based on the flat and pointed leaves. By fall, those stalks would be taller than her head.

"Where are we?" she whispered to Emily as they came to a stop next to the barn.

Her aunt didn't answer and climbed out after the men. Before Bree could do the same, Luke reached over for her hand to help her get out. She gathered her belongings and reluctantly accepted his hand.

"Where we are?" she asked him.

"Knox Farm." He reached into his haversack in the wagon and pulled out a bundle wrapped in gray cloth and placed it in her hand.

"What's this?" Before she snuck a peek at what was hidden within the folds of cloth, his mother called out her name. Emily stood in front of the house next to a Negro woman round with child. The woman, dressed in a delicate white linen dress and black head wrap, had a refined air of money. While Bree situated Luke's parcel in her apron pocket, the other woman disappeared into the house. She turned back to Luke.

"Just a gift to see you on your way," he murmured with a nod. "Farewell, Bree."

Emily called for her again, and she reluctantly left his side to join his mother.

"Leave your things," her aunt said.

"But I—"

"Later," Emily said sharply.

Bree returned her things to the wagon, dusted off her dress, and followed her aunt to the doorstep. Once there, Emily tilted up her chin and gave her a quick once-over.

"You wore your best dress. Good. Are you ready?"

"Yes, ma'am." Bree straightened her back and followed Emily through the front door. They strolled across wooden floors, gleaming and spotless, to a large room with a closed door to the right and a staircase leading to upper floors. On the other side of the room, Mrs. Knox lounged on a dark-blue settee with a rolled tobacco cigarette poised in one hand and the other with restless fingers. She picked up her cup of tea and sipped. Her dark eyes assessed Bree with a hint of suspicion.

"I didn't expect to see you until the fall, Emily," Mrs. Knox said.

"Events over the past month changed our plans." Emily's voice sounded different. There was an eloquence, a crispness Bree hadn't heard before.

Bree kept her gaze fixed on her own clasped hands, but she hungered to see their faces.

"And what events would bring you all the way here?" Mrs. Knox asked.

She couldn't resist and glanced up to watch their exchange.

"My niece is a bright girl, Bridget," Emily began, "and I believe she'd fare well with training as a seamstress. As a woman of means in Richmond, you can help her find an apprenticeship."

A smirk bloomed on Mrs. Knox's face as she caressed her swollen belly. "She might be a bright girl and all, but the town might not be the best place for her. Word has it the governor made Richmond the new capital. Competition means less income for my husband. What makes you think we can afford to feed another mouth?"

The straight line of Aunt Emily's lips formed a smile. "I wouldn't want to add a burden to your household without compensation. If you look out the window, you'll see my husband unloading kegs of hard cider. That should fetch a couple of pounds until the girl finds work."

Mrs. Knox's hand flexed over her stomach. "I shouldn't still owe you for what you did to save my husband," she whispered. "Twenty years have passed."

"A life for a life," Emily replied simply.

Mrs. Knox took a long draw from her cigarette. The smoke from her exhale slowly rose to the ceiling while she stared Emily down. The two women had a similar status, the same wrinkles gathered at the corners of their eyes, but wisdom, and a history Bree wished she knew, danced between them.

A gangly servant girl entered the house to leave a bucket of water in the kitchen, but neither woman looked away from each other. Tension gathered in Bree's shoulders. She feared Mrs. Knox might turn her away.

After what felt like hours, Mrs. Knox said curtly, "What's your name, girl?"

Bree swallowed. "Sabrina, ma'am."

"You may stay, but you will sleep with the rest of the servants," Mrs. Knox said. "You'll do as you're told until I find you employment."

She nodded. "Thank you kindly, ma'am."

The women chatted about trivial matters for a few minutes, and Bree stood there trying to contain her excitement. Emily then took her hand and led her to the door.

"Remember your place and what we've taught you." Emily gave her a wide grin and Bree knew their final goodbyes had come. "I'm proud of you. Never forget that."

"Yes, Aunt Emily."

Bree almost followed her aunt out, but the mistress of the house called her to fetch more tea. Bree's hands shook while she grabbed the kettle and poured the warm water. She'd done what needed to be done before, and she'd do it again.

"Is there anything else I can do for you, ma'am?" Bree breathed.

Mrs. Knox flicked her fingers to excuse Bree. "Gather your things and find Eliza."

With a nod, she escaped the house, expecting to see the wagon and her uncles to say goodbye, but her family had already departed. They were a speck of dust in the distance, as small as the bundle of her things left behind. Her shoulders fell, and the desire to cry snatched her breath. She could see each of their faces, but one stood out. Luke's.

Why hadn't she said goodbye to him properly? For hours they'd sat across from each other, and yet her feelings had gotten in the way. Now all they had shared were a couple of words and no more.

"Just a gift to see you on your way," he'd said.

She reached into her apron pocket and withdrew what he'd given her. Deep within the folds of the gray fabric, she found a weathered dark-blue neckerchief. Hers. The frayed edges, holes, and stains whispered of distant lands. Loneliness. Loss. Triumph. The neckerchief also held something else: three thread spools made of maple. They'd been carved and sanded with a steady hand. She ran her fingers over the notches and curves, marveling at how old her gift appeared.

He'd made these a long time ago. These three spools held love too—over twenty lost years' worth. That love was more than enough.

PART THREE

REBECCA

Cecily Bridge-Davis

JULY 1964

After piecing together Sabrina and Luke's tale, my heart ached with longing. Tucked away in my hotel room with only my scattered research papers to keep me company, I opened the cerulean tin box and took out the maple spool. While the black-and-white TV blared the evening news, I sat on the bed and weighed it in my palm, marveling at the smooth surface. Two hundred years ago, Luke had made this by hand for Bree. How could fate be so merciless? Almost five hundred and fifty miles separated Winston and me, but if I needed to see him, I could pack up my things and race home.

On the TV, CBS newscaster Walter Cronkite said, "Ladies and gentlemen, this afternoon President Lyndon B. Johnson signed the Civil Rights Act."

I glanced up from the spool. My heart raced as I shot off the bed to move closer to the television.

It was happening.

After all this time, LBJ had fulfilled his promise. Winston and I had dreamt of this day, and here I was searching for folks who'd never see it.

The camera was centered on Johnson at a desk with rows of pens and a pile of papers. After months of wishing and waiting, the moment had finally come. All that hard work of marching and boycotting had borne the sweetest of harvests: antidiscrimination was now writ into law.

I flung my hands in the air, breaking into an excited dance. Shouts rang from outside the room as word spread. Before I could escape, urgent knocks hit my door.

"We did it!" one man cried. "The bill passed!"

I grabbed my key and hurried out to join the small crowd downstairs. Folks filled the parlor and dining room, their jubilant faces worth every spiteful stare I'd encountered while marching with the Freedom Riders. My babies had a chance for a better life now.

Someone put on a record with Martha and the Vandellas' latest hit, "Heat Wave." Chairs were pushed against the wall. Claps erupted and the ladies around me sashayed to the beat.

An old Negro ambled down the stairs and threw over his shoulder a gruff "Don't know why y'all fussin' and hollerin'—nothin' gonna change," but we kept celebrating. He settled in a seat and watched us.

One of the hotel patrons, a wiry businessman from Biloxi, even brought a box of corn dogs and burgers from Pronto Pups. We danced and sang in the parlor for hours.

When morning arrived, I woke up groggy and stiff. My world had changed again overnight. And yet when I turned over to face the window, my room and its reminders remained. The morning light stretched across the census documents and biographies strewn on the table. Right before the broadcast, I'd scribbled some random thoughts about checking the records at the University of Richmond.

Twenty minutes later, after dozing off a couple of times, the fever hit to search for Sabrina again.

Maybe I'd missed something—a shipping manifest or Richmond census. I'd only find those answers if I put in the effort.

An hour later, I drove down Highway 64. Today was just as miserably hot as yesterday so I rolled down my Chevy sedan's windows while the radio blared the Ronettes' "Be My Baby." I sang along with Ronnie, Estelle, and Nedra. With each WHITES ONLY sign I passed, I daydreamed of each one of them falling to dust.

The drive was wonderful until Skeeter Davis's "The End of the World" came on. I cringed as if slapped and switched off the radio to continue my trip in silence.

Soon enough, I reached the University of Richmond campus. With my head held high in the summer heat, I made my way to the library. As to be expected, I got strange looks—even a scowl or two—from the folks I passed. The administration had only recently opened the school to Negro students.

Despite the stares, I sailed into the Boatwright Memorial Library, but accessing the restricted materials section was another matter. The frowning white woman sitting at the reception desk, a certain Annabelle McCloud, offered no welcome. I gave Miss McCloud what my aunt Hilda called a smile soaked in sunshine, even complimenting the fine blouse she wore. I then stated succinctly what I needed and how I'd overheard from other professors up in Nashville how well Miss McCloud and her staff organized their materials. For my efforts, Miss McCloud helped me sort through the documents. The problem was that few records existed of Sabrina Humbles once she reached Richmond. Correspondence between a Mrs. Bridget Knox and her cousin in Lynchburg, dated late 1780, revealed that a girl named Sabrina had designed dresses for Mrs. Knox, but other than that, I suspected I'd uncover little else. The Virginia capital went up in flames in January 1781 after Benedict Arnold, a former general, betrayed the Continental Army and joined the British.

Other than Luke's spool, I wished there was something of Sabrina for me to hold. I liked to imagine she fell in love again and remained resilient until the end of her life, passing that resilience on to future generations.

In the time it took to pore through the early Albemarle County records and investigate Sabrina, I'd lost several more weeks. Winston had become impatient, growling at the children as we spoke on the phone, and though guilt niggled at me, I couldn't—wouldn't—be slowed down. For long hours, I sat and scribbled fact after fact about Luke and his family. I wrote until my hand throbbed and I could barely clutch a pencil.

Even when I returned to Charlottesville, I couldn't stop thinking about her. There were so many unraveled threads of my ancestor's history left to catch on the wind. Sabrina was gone without a trace for Luke to find. I didn't want to believe my beloved would face the same heartache after I fell through time.

As my work on Sabrina concluded, I surmised there was nothing I could do either. Just like when the Bridges in the 1780s, and even in the 1810s, finally grasped how awful the curse could be. There was nothing any mother, wife, or father could do about something that could not be seen, tasted, or touched. For those chosen, the inevitable always came calling—like the five handwritten messages I received once I returned to the Carver Inn. The last one couldn't be ignored.

From your husband, Winston Davis:
We're on our way to Charlottesville.

CHAPTER 15

Rebecca Raley-Bridge

SEPTEMBER 1817

In the early weeks of autumn, a haze blanketed the trees, the suffocating humidity hovering close to the earth. The land grew quiet around this time. Perhaps all living things struggled in such miserable conditions.

When the heat rose to intolerable levels, all activity on Bridge land ceased from midday to late afternoon. The forty-nine souls living on this land, including Rebecca, lounged on their porches, huddled under the protection of the pippin apple trees, or slept in the cool comfort of shade. Only the foolhardy tempted fate. Two years ago, a distant cousin of Rebecca's collapsed off a ladder like wheat sliced down by a scythe. A decade before that, five boys had gone hunting for feral hogs. One of them, a Bridge boy of no more than ten years, had stood in the sun too long. Papa Raley had told her the child's skin grew so cold and clammy the boy wouldn't have known if he was in the heat or a blizzard. Two steps from his home, the child fainted and died.

"Those ignorant Bridges don't know any better, Reba," Papa had said.

He still said that after she'd married one of them.

The Raleys had come to know the Bridges after Papa took advantage of Charles Bridge's debts and bought the man's land for half its worth. Once Papa owned the property, he reached out to them and hired the younger Bridge men as laborers for his growing enterprise of ferrying goods along the James River. Papa believed that another man's folly was his opportunity, and it was up to him to use those profits wisely.

Now that Papa was dead and gone, Reba didn't have to hear his biting remarks anymore, but she remembered his sayings. *Be wary in the woods. Do not trust your eyes. Listen. Question everything.*

During this time of the year, the mugginess pricked at the skin and smeared reality. She couldn't see beyond the rolling pasture to the two cabins near her home. Murky figures came and went, but from time to time, the hairs along the nape of her neck fluttered and she turned, only to find no one there. This strange feeling would persist from late summer into fall.

The four children sitting at her feet on her porch tried to ignore the weather and focus on the arithmetic lesson she presented on a small writing slate. Half of these students were her cousin's children. Her youngest boy was inside the house. Lizzie Raley propped up her chin with her palm, her facial expression dimming. The head of her younger brother, Gerald, bobbed for the third time. At six years of age, he never wanted to listen. Reba's instruction on how to perform a carryover reached the only attentive child: her eldest son, Jimmy.

Briefly, she wished the breeze rustling the trees would cool them off instead of baking them. No matter the sweat rolling down her back, she was their teacher, and all children living on Bridge land *must* learn reading, writing, and arithmetic. Long before she'd married Herbert and borne his children, this rule had been in place, but it made little sense to her. Unless these children found employment in Richmond or Charlottesville, they'd grow up on the farm and learn a trade. For many of them, all this wasted time with letters and numbers would do them no good. How often would they need to mark their name or read what few books they had, many of them yellowed and moldy? But she did as she was told. Bridge traditions ran deep.

Not long into demonstrating how to do a borrow during subtraction, a shout rang out.

"Miss Reba, your friend Mariah's returned!" Breeches caked in dust, a boy appeared, his tawny brown cheeks puffing in and out from his labors.

Her wilted students sprang to life, but Jimmy continued to sit quietly, ever diligent. Even her eight-year-old daughter, Annie, managed to hold her tongue.

Even Reba's spirits lifted. She'd missed Mariah dearly. They were best friends, having grown up together in the same household, with Mariah working as one of the Raley family housegirls. Mariah had a laugh like morning bells and a mood never heavier than a rain cloud.

"Did she bring anything?" Gerald asked.

"I bet she got candy like last time," Lizzie said.

"Where is she?" Reba asked. For the first time today, she was feeling elated.

"She's at Grandpa Luke's place." With the news delivered, the boy hurried off, likely to repeat the gossip to everyone.

"Can we go see her?" Lizzie stood. Sweat pebbled her forehead, but her enthusiasm was infectious.

"Fine." Reba sighed. "I'm right behind you."

Lizzie and Gerald ran off as Jimmy asked, "Can I come?"

"Yes, let's go see her. Fetch your younger brother."

Jimmy stepped inside. Moments later, he emerged holding his sleepy little brother, George. At four years old, Georgie still took naps in the afternoon. Annie had discarded the garment she had been sewing to trail after him. Waking Georgie from his nap wasn't wise, but the children hadn't seen Mariah since he was born.

They left the shelter of the porch with its damp heat and marched out into the full sun. Reba winced and sucked in a deep breath. Nausea stirred in her stomach, forcing sourness to surge up the back of her throat.

"Dear child, give me peace," she murmured.

After carrying two children with ease, Georgie and this precious babe—her fourth—gave her nothing but poor health and a foul temper. At twenty-eight years old, she'd hoped her body would be used to this by now. She had a long way to go though; she wouldn't see this child until the spring lambs appeared.

Grinning, Reba took her time to follow the children and considered their good fortune. Visitors like her dear friend were a welcome distraction. Other than the two families who lived nearby, Reba and her husband rarely had any company from outside the farm.

They ventured south, sticking to the shaded areas along the well-beaten footpath connecting the pasture to the orchard. Tucked underneath the canopy of the apple tree branches, men and women rested in the shade. Flecks of light peeked around the leaves and speckled their tired faces in light and dark. Sweat permeated the air. Many of them slept, while others relaxed, their mouths agape in the relentless heat.

"Send Mariah my best," said one of Reba's Raley relatives as he wiped his glistening brow.

"Good to have her back," said another man as he fanned himself with his hat.

She gave him a weak smile. "Rest easy."

With the harvest coming in the next month, the families who worked at the orchard would be busy producing cider and preserves. She'd spend her evenings making apple butter and her mornings drying apple rings. The sweet scent of the apples' flesh would stick to her hair and the juice to her skin, and her thumb would become achy from how she held the knife when peeling away the pale green skins.

Reba and the children left the orchard and made their way to another cabin, a clapboard structure built onto another far older one. Herb had told her the first Bridge cabin had been built here, and over time the family had added rooms and such. Now Luke Bridge lived here.

Men, women, and children swarmed the house. Voices rose from the porch, and she immediately recognized Mariah's. Reba's steps quickened until she reached a few familiar faces. They included Mariah, her husband, Herbert, and the Bridge patriarch, Luke Bridge.

After Reba caught a glimpse of Mariah, they exchanged a squeal before Mariah rushed in for a hug.

"Riah!" Reba drew the younger woman close until their laughter bounced off the porch walls. "What took you so long?"

Mariah Kenner released Reba and placed her hat on Annie's head. Her best friend eased back onto her seat. Reba almost didn't recognize her in a man's shirt and trousers. As they'd grown together into womanhood, Mariah never had a woman's curves. Over the past couple of years, Mariah's thinner arms had thickened, and the gentle swell of her full cheeks had elongated. Life had etched worries into her wrinkled brow, but the woman excelled in peace of mind. According to her, troubles came and went. How you came up for air after a wave was just as important as what you did before the wave hit.

"What took me so long?" Mariah repeated with disdain. "You try walking all the way from Richmond. I ain't as fast as I used to be."

"You used to run everywhere."

"Too tired now." Mariah gave her a hard, long look. "You're shorter."

"No, I stopped growing. You *didn't*."

"It's absolutely awful in this heat." Mariah fanned herself with her hand. "It's more pleasant near the coast."

"Everything is nicer near the coast," Reba replied.

"Herb was telling me you haven't put up a fuss this whole time." Mariah smiled, revealing two dimples.

Reba glanced at her husband. He leaned against the far wall. When she strode up to him, he feigned running away. At least he wouldn't get far in this heat.

"What else have you told her about me?" she asked, her sweet voice now salty.

Her husband surrendered his stool for her. "Nothing she'd believe, wife."

She eased onto the stool and Herb came to stand next to her. Reba's youngest scrambled up to her and rested his head against her knee. Jimmy, Annie, and the Raley children played nearby, their quest for candy forgotten—for now.

"Richmond treating you well?" Reba said.

"It was until a week ago." Mariah lit a cigarette and took a deep drag. "Mr. Simmons laid off over ten seamstresses."

"Shame," murmured the oldest man on the porch. Luke had always had a quiet way about him, especially after they buried his wife in the family cemetery not far from this house, but their elder spoke fervently during conversations like these. "All of those folks have mouths to feed."

"I only need to fend for myself," Mariah said.

"Can't feed yourself with empty pockets," Herbert said.

"That's why I'm here," Mariah said. "Haven't got much to my name now."

"You'll be fine, girl," Luke chided. "Folks find a way. There'll be more droughts and bountiful harvests in the future, but if we believe in the good Lord, He'll give us what we need. Not what we deserve."

"Scraping by for a while will make you stronger," Herb added.

"Mariah doesn't care about those kinds of things anyway," Reba said softly.

Riah flicked the ash off her cigarette. "I need a home, but I don't have that anymore either."

Herb patted Mariah's shoulder. "How long you staying?"

"As long as I'm needed." Mariah's gaze flicked to Reba's. Compared to Papa, her best friend had worked for an honest wage. There was no shame in coming here.

The family chatted until Reba's hips ached from sitting for too long. She motioned for her pupils to follow her—Jimmy and his siblings trailed behind while Lizzie and Gerald took their sweet time. They reached the path to the orchard and the mischievous pair veered north to go home.

"Where do you think you're going?" Reba called out to them.

The Raley siblings went as still as deer caught grazing in the morning light.

"We're going home," Lizzie said matter-of-factly. "Mama says once our book learning is over, we should come home."

"When did we finish our lesson?" Reba asked crisply.

Lizzie stared at the ground. Her brother fidgeted.

"Can both of you complete a carryover correctly?" She hid her amused grin.

"I can." Gerald had far more enthusiasm than his sister. Lizzie's right hand clenched her dress, and a familiar grimace filled her face.

"Can't we show you tomorrow?" Lizzie begged.

As much as Reba wanted to continue the lesson, the pleas in their eyes convinced her otherwise.

"What if we stay longer tomorrow?" Lizzie added. "We'll be quiet—"

"You already don't speak much." Reba folded her arms. Perhaps she should interrupt their lessons more often.

"Sissy will listen," Gerald said. "I'll listen too."

"No sleeping?" Reba asked.

"Never," said Lizzie with a quick nod.

Now, that was a lie.

Gerald's impish grin said it all.

Reba stood there a bit, letting them believe she couldn't decide. When they squirmed, she couldn't resist laughing.

"Go on home," she said, "but I expect you to return to school tomorrow. We have much to learn before you'll be needed for the harvest."

"Yes, ma'am," they said in unison.

A scalding breeze fanned her face, bringing with it the scent of youth and sweat as the pair walked away. For a moment, the child in her womb stilled as Luke's words clung to her. Out here on the farm, many folks never got what they needed, much less what they deserved. They had no control over their circumstances so they did what they had to do. They endured. They survived. Reba spread her fingers over her belly and sighed. A peculiar unease settled into her chest. Her mother used to say it was a sign of bad omens. Reba tried to cast the thought aside, but she feared for what lingered on the horizon.

———

It was not the cool air in the morning that roused Reba but her husband. Herb slid his arms around her waist and drew her closer. Time and childbirth had stolen her slim waist and the smoothness of the skin on her thighs and stomach, but he snuggled against her, content. Heat radiated from him, but this warmth was familiar—a steadiness that forever remained and soothed her. No matter the season, they lay here together. Sometimes with a babe between them, other times with nothing but their passion and a need to stroke or kiss the other's skin.

If not for Papa Raley's work ethic, as well as his greed, Reba would've never met Herbert and found such happiness. After living for twenty years as a mulatto slave at Dunlora for Samuel Carr, Papa had saved enough money to purchase his freedom. Papa'd had a shrewd nature. And a quiet voice that penetrated the most stubborn customer. He'd lined his pocket with coins, and after he'd bought his freedom, he'd paid for Mama's too.

One morning, when Reba was no older than fourteen, Herb appeared. They'd first met when he came to her family's home during the busy fall shipping season. Papa's barges carried furniture, spices, and expensive goods to the elite whites living up-country. When she thought about it—long after marriage and children—Herb never stood out among other men. He shared the same height as the other laborers and had a calm way about him, with slumped shoulders, bowed legs, and a stoic expression.

When Papa's men arrived at dawn to pick up a shipment of

tobacco, sweat from the late summer weather already dampened their backs. Herbert ambled about while the others spoke in quiet tones.

Reba had slipped out the front door with Mama. They'd gotten up early to tend to the gardens. Pluck the weeds. Gather shocks of greens for supper. "Like yesterday, and the week before that," she complained. They had housemaids to wash their clothes and cook their meals. Downhill from their house, farmers minded the fields of corn and barley while others tended to their livestock.

"You can't tell *them* people what to do if you don't know how to do it yourself," Mama insisted. By "them people," she meant the slaves she ignored in the streets and the dark-skinned Negroes who worked in their home. "Half of them forgot what I told them twice." Mama's voice trailed off as she disappeared around the house.

Off to Reba's left, a smear of blue caught her eye. Someone had dropped a handkerchief and darted after it. Herb stooped, picked up the blue handkerchief, and drew the cloth across his brow. The wind flicked the frayed edges of the dark-blue material and the smoothness of the skin above Herb's full beard shone in the morning light. Their gazes connected, and Herbert should've looked away, but he stared. A light sparked in his eyes as if he'd seen her before. His bold glance made Reba hurry after Mama. After that moment, they didn't see each other again until Papa moved their family onto the Bridge land he'd bought.

Herbert's rough palm stroked the curve of Reba's cheek, drawing her out of the past. He reached for her, and they slept until the light from the rising sun pried them apart. They couldn't sleep with all the noise anyway. Little George carefully made his way down the ladder from the loft. The child blinked as he left the house to relieve himself.

Herb kissed Reba's nose. "Morning, wife."

"Morning, husband."

They always said that to each other—no matter the mood the night before. Disagreements came and went, but they'd always had each other. On most mornings, they settled into a routine. Reba rekindled the fire and warmed their porridge breakfast while Herbert scurried about wrangling the children to wash their faces and prepare for the day. Mariah, who ambled down the ladder next, rubbed the back of her head to wake herself. When they were younger, Mariah had never wanted to get up early.

"Is it morning already?" the young woman asked.

"According to the rest of the world it is." Herb chuckled while he tried to get a squirmy George to don a fresh shirt. The boy had soiled his last one.

Reba never asked Herbert to help her—perhaps he pitied his wife. While carrying Georgie, she crouched outside in the early mornings, her stomach lurching until it emptied itself. After Reba had fainted three times after George was born, Herb never left until everyone had eaten breakfast and the children had gotten to work on their chores.

"Harvest started?" Mariah pulled a chair up to the worn four-seater table. Little George escaped his father and scrambled into the woman's arms. "Boy, you getting too big to be running 'round."

When Mariah tickled him, George squealed and tried running away.

"Not yet," Herbert said. "You got good timing, I must say."

"I doubt it." Mariah accepted a slice of bread and bowl of porridge. "Harvesting is as hard as tailoring."

The three children finally sat on the floor with their bowls. Herb scooted George's bowl closer to him while Annie frowned and picked out the dried apple ring Reba had added on top. Annie added the piece into Georgie's bowl.

"How come you didn't return to Charleston again?" Reba asked. Before Mariah had settled down in Richmond, she'd worked in South Carolina for a few years.

"There was work for a spell, but everything dried up, so I had to start over." Mariah traced her finger along the bread's crust, her gaze briefly lost in the hearth's flames.

"I can't imagine starting from nothing," Herb said stiffly. "We spent all those years scraping every penny together to make a life for ourselves. My granddaddy was born on this land more than seventy years ago. His parents tilled the soil and planted the trees. Ain't no reason to spit in their eyes over free Negro jobs elsewhere."

"True." Mariah finished her meal and leaned back in her seat. "Land is king around here. Damn shame your daddy didn't leave you anything back in Richmond."

At the mention of Papa, Reba rose to gather the dishes. "We're better off now. That man's greed blackened his heart. You made a living for yourself back there. There's no reason why you can't do the same here."

She waited for Mariah to disagree, but her friend merely nodded. Memories of that man had a way of souring any mood. The family had another hot day coming and their chores—which they'd do on the land they'd bought back from Papa—wouldn't do themselves. Through their labors, they'd carve out a fruitful existence for the children. This was their home now and no one could take that away from them.

CHAPTER 16

Rebecca Raley-Bridge

SEPTEMBER 1817

T he next day, Reba had a full porch of students, but the six
children had the vigor of old folk. Fifteen-year-old Patience
Bridge sagged next to her younger brother, Pete, while the
oldest student, a slim boy named Nelson Bridge, stared fondly at
Patience from the edge of the porch. The boy was older than her by
a year and always followed her around. At least he got some learning out of fawning after her. Jimmy, Lizzie, and Gerald slumped
against the wall on the other side.

Today would be as productive as the last lesson.

Not long into the lesson, Patience spoke. "Is it true Miss Kenner
returned?"

"She ain't got no candy," Jimmy said dryly.

"Maybe she hasn't shown you what she got." Patience was as
nosy as her mama, but the girl spread gossip far quicker.

"Jimmy, please show everyone how you do a carryover when

adding two three-digit numbers." Reba tried not to use Jimmy to set an example, but far too often her child had to set the standard.

While Jimmy scribbled out the math on the small chalkboard, the other children feigned interest, but she could see their eyes darting beyond the porch to the dragonflies zipping about. To the lone hawk circling the pastures. To the trees rustling as their branches swayed. After Jimmy finished, the rest of the children each took the board in turn until only Patience remained.

"When we're done, can we go swimming?" Patience asked, her subdued gaze intent on the first row of digits. "The water would feel nice . . ."

Then Patience paused and blinked.

"You all right?" Reba asked.

"Just felt funny." Patience puckered her lips and squeezed her eyes open and shut.

Her brother, who glanced over her shoulder, fanned her face with his hands. "You're sweating, Pay-Pay."

When he got too close, she frowned at him. "'Cause it's hot! Get back."

"I'm helping—" Then Pete disappeared.

Patience scrambled to stand. "Where did he go?"

"I-I don't know." Reba stood with Patience. "He was right behind you."

Among the confused murmurs of her students, she wondered if they'd missed Pete running away. They waited. The only sounds around them were the cicadas' steady clicks, and midday songs of robins. She listened for the thud of footsteps, the whistle from someone passing by, or even a door slam from the nearest outhouse.

"Don't make any sense . . ." Nelson stepped off the porch. His booted feet kicked up dust from the patches of dirt. He stared past Reba's house to the nearby pasture. She couldn't see Peter hiding behind any of the trees dotting the rolling hills or escaping into the forest less than a mile away.

"You see him?" Patience asked.

Nelson shrugged, took two steps toward them, then vanished.

Patience slapped her hand over her mouth, but a tortured scream slipped between her trembling fingers. "No!"

The girl's cry pierced through Reba's stomach, leaving her mouth agape.

"What happened to him?" Jimmy whispered as his siblings emerged from the house.

Patience, Jimmy, Gerald, and Lizzie turned to Reba. Her younger children held questions in their eyes too. She tried to breathe, but she couldn't catch any air. "I don't know."

This had to be a trick. The heat must've deceived them like Papa Raley had warned.

Patience approached Reba, her eyes wide and glistening. The girl clutched Reba's skirt and spoke words Reba couldn't make out.

"Where are they?" Patience's voice had finally reached her.

"I don't know," Reba managed. "We should search for them."

They circled the house two times. Their hands wrenched open the doors to the outhouse and the barn. The root cellar proved just as empty. Not a single child hid among the neat rows of food. A breeze hit Reba's damp back and the children whimpered, not from the heat but from an awareness that something horrible had happened.

Reba felt the same.

"Did they go home?" Jimmy asked.

Patience shook her head. "Why didn't we see them leave?"

Reba's gaze swept along the shallow dips and rises of the hills leading to the closest home to the northeast. Nelson's. The maple and elm trees hid no one. Half a mile to her right, smoke rose from the cabin of Peter and Patience's family. Only the children's mother, Ruth, could be seen hanging up clothes on the clothesline in front of their summer kitchen.

Reba picked up Georgie and broke away from the children to run across the pasture to Nelson's home. The rest of the children trailed after her in tears. The wind pushed her back, but eventually she reached the fence posts protecting their gardens. A tepid breeze tugged at the stalks of corn and pulled her toward Nelson's mother, Carrie. The small-framed woman leaned over her washboard and tub. Her tiny hands moved with a familiar rhythm to scrub a shirt. Carrie's two younger children, a set of eighteen-month-old twins, played at her feet. Patience caught up and ran into Reba like the harsh peppery scent of the lye coating Carrie's hands.

Nelson's mother grinned at them. "What's wrong? Did the devil show up for schooling today?"

"Have you seen . . . your boy?" Reba struggled to ask.

Carrie scoffed. One of the toddlers at her feet reached for his mother.

On the other side of the pasture, Ruth turned around and peered at them. She had to see crying children. Gerald clung to a sobbing Lizzie. Jimmy tried to quiet a confused Annie. Ruth dropped the breeches she held and ran in their direction.

Please let him be home—please let him be safe, Reba thought.

"He should be with you for book learning." Carrie's smile withered away.

Ruth joined them and Patience rushed to her mother. "Ma, we can't find Pete," she sobbed.

"What are you crying about, Pay-Pay?" Ruth's head tilted in question.

Reba tried to explain, but every word felt like one of those fantastic tales Herb told their children during the long winter days. After she finished, she didn't believe what she had said.

Ruth and Carrie weren't convinced either. They circled Reba like mosquitos, their mouths slashes for frowns, their eyes hard and accusing.

"Children don't pass from sight!" Carrie snapped.

"They probably ran away." Ruth drew her crying daughter closer.

"But they didn't!" Jimmy stepped forward, shaking his head in disbelief. "They were there—then they weren't."

"Go get your daddy," Ruth hissed at Patience. "Something ain't right here."

"We didn't hurt them," Reba said. "The girl shouldn't go out there all alone."

"Why should she believe you?" Carrie swept in, her teeth clenched and free hand bunched into a fist. No one on the farm crossed her family—especially after her husband died two years ago. She'd birthed twins and raised three children alone since then. She fought first and settled with words afterward. "You never wanted to teach them kids. Always telling 'em to come back another day."

"Four years ago was different," Reba said. "I was feeling poorly."

"We've all been with child. You do your job for a couple months a year. It ain't hard." Ruth made an annoying clicking noise with her tongue. "Get, girl!" she yelled to her daughter.

Reba caught Patience's tear-streaked face before she ran into the woods. No one spoke. Reba searched the pasture, hoping Herb would show up too, but she stood alone with Georgie hiding his face in her skirt. Jimmy hovered nearby with a frightened Annie.

Soon enough, a brooding Joseph Bridge marched out of the woods with his daughter behind him. Joe was a man of few words. He spent most of his time felling timber for hoop poles.

After he arrived, in a clipped tone, Ruth explained to her husband what had happened. Reba waited for him to brush her off. He didn't speak for a bit, merely taking in his only daughter's despair.

"Stay here. They probably went swimming" was all he said before he strode across the field to return home. From afar, they watched him saddle up one of the geldings from the barn and ride off to the west.

After he disappeared over a hill, a nagging feeling clouded Reba's thoughts. *He won't find them.*

Reba's students weren't hiding around her house or splashing in the creek or traipsing through any part of the woods. She shivered, and suddenly George released a loud and piercing wail.

"It's all right." She kneeled and stroked the soft tawny skin of his rounded cheeks. She should've picked him up, but exhaustion left her knees weakened. "We'll go home—"

"You're not too *worried* about our children." Ruth rested her hands on her wide hips and blocked Reba's path. She threw Reba a glare hot enough to sizzle meat on a spit.

"Of course I'm worried." Reba gestured to the pasture. "But standing here won't bring them back."

"Don't you want to wait and see?" Carrie used her dress sleeve to wipe her damp brow. The boy, then the girl, mewled at her feet. "Two children are missing."

Reba eyed them up and down. Let them try to stop her.

"I'm not feeling well and my children are frightened." Reba tried to step around Ruth.

"All of us should be frightened," Ruth said. "And yet you can go home with *all* of your babies."

Before Reba could speak her mind, two breathless Raley boys came running up to them.

"Hiram's gone! Hiram's gone!" The oldest boy fought to catch his breath. "He was swimming in the creek and drowned."

"He ain't drowned," his younger brother cried. "Our mama was there and she said he's just . . . gone."

Reba's gut clenched. Hiram was a grown man at nineteen. Her husband's younger brother always had a friendly smile. Herb told her his brother loved to splash in the water from the first day his mama dipped his toes in.

And now he was gone.

Reba grabbed Jimmy's hand, feeling assured he was still here. *Good Lord in heaven.* Two boys gone. Now a third. She squeezed her eldest son's hand tight enough for him to flinch, but he didn't let go of her.

Her two neighbors fell silent. Their faces darkened as if a storm had brewed. She felt the storm too. And even her children's presence couldn't drive away the rising dread inside her.

———

After Hiram disappeared, further accusations hung unspoken, but the hard stares remained and seeped into Reba's skin. Perhaps her neighbors needed someone to blame. Word spread quickly, and when the families convened in front of Luke's cabin that evening, more glares and grimaces were thrown at her.

Reba's husband ambled up to everyone with sweat lining his brow and worry in his eyes. His calves were wet up to his knees. The water was far too low at this time of year for anyone to drown. Herbert kept asking her what had happened to Pete and Nelson, but she shook her head each time. How could she look him in the eyes and tell such a far-fetched truth? She turned to face the others instead. All the families formed a semicircle around Luke's porch. Gerald and Lizzie's parents hovered on the periphery. Questions swam in their widened eyes. Not far from them, other Bridges spoke in whispers, throwing rumors around to salt the earth at Reba's feet. Meanwhile, Ruth and Carrie scowled at her from the opposite side. Other families wandered closer with questions.

"Where have the boys gone?" one woman asked.

"Has anyone seen them in the orchard or the fields?" another said.

Ruth stepped forward when she had enough of an audience. "My son, Pete, was taken," she said with a spark in her eyes. "He was at Reba's house, supposedly learning, when the children told us he left."

A few eyes darted in Reba's direction at the mention of her name.

Ruth pressed on. "After Pete disappeared, Nelson ended up missing too. And not long after Reba showed up at my place, looking all innocent, we heard Hiram drowned."

"That ain't what happened," Herbert said firmly. "My sister said he was there, then he wasn't."

"Maybe he's downstream then," Carrie said. "Half of y'all can't see worth a damn."

"We *searched*." Herbert glared right back at her. "There's no body."

But Carrie would have none of Herbert's remarks. "Don't matter! Something ain't right here. They could be out there, half beaten, or in chains already." She spoke with bared teeth like a cornered cat. "I say we look for our children."

Murmurs of agreement rose from the crowd.

Carrie turned to Lizzie and Gerald's mother. "Your kids could be next. Who knows what's out there."

From inside the cabin, Luke emerged and shuffled to a stool. The gray-haired man eased onto the seat with a sigh.

"What if they weren't taken?" the old man asked.

When Luke tried to speak again, Carrie continued to shout pleas for help.

"He got something to say," another Bridge man called out. "Let 'em speak."

Herb left Reba's side to stand near the center of the circle. "I'll say it, Luke. This has happened before. When I was a child, I remember Pa talking about how Luke disappeared one spring day, then a few days later he returned, *twenty-two* years older."

Instead of gasps, Reba heard guffaws.

"Joseph told me that happened a long time ago," Ruth growled. "What makes you believe it's true?"

"Half of y'all have lost your common sense," Carrie said.

"It's true," Herbert said firmly.

Carrie sniffed and slowly shook her head.

"Over the years," Luke said slowly, "I've prayed this would never happen again." He gripped his knees and leaned forward. "But here we are. Three children gone, and from what I've heard, there were witnesses, yes?"

"We saw it," Reba managed.

"Did you see them disappear?" he asked.

She nodded.

His rheumy eyes stared at her as if he could see through her. "Then they're gone and there's nothing any of you can do to bring them babies back."

"W-what?" Ruth stammered. "This man ain't right in the head."

Luke added, "I went back twenty-two years—maybe they gone that far too."

Carrie slumped against Ruth. "I don't want to hear this nonsense no more. My boy was *taken*."

"My family searched for me too," Luke said, his words eaten away as protests rose. "My mother told me that everyone searched as far as Charlottesville, but they found *nothing*. I wasn't here for them to find."

Reba glanced down in shame. Herbert had told a similar story to their children about a wandering man who'd traveled for twenty years before he found his way home. Back then, she'd listened with rapt attention, but the possibility the story was true sounded deranged. They lived in the real world, God's world, and not once in the Bible had He sent one of His children into the past.

"Mama Bear, is what he's saying true?" Jimmy asked her.

"I don't know," she admitted.

"But we all saw what happened to Nelson and Pete—" Jimmy began.

"I know . . . but there has to be . . ." Reba's words trailed off. There had to be what? An explanation as to how three people were there, then they weren't? As Jimmy's mother, she'd taught him the skills necessary to survive. She'd even taught him the horrid realities of their life—how one man could own another. But time travel was make-believe and nothing else. No one could prepare for it.

"As much as we'd like to sit in this heat," Ruth said bitterly, "Carrie and I are gonna find our children. You can listen to this man and *waste* time or you can help us."

The pair strode away and many people trailed after them, offering prayers and comfort. Reba expected her husband to accompany them, but Herb watched them leave.

"Why don't you go with them?" she asked him. "What about Hiram?"

Her husband briefly exchanged a hard look with Luke.

"We need to go home." Herb clutched Jimmy's shoulder and tugged the boy to follow. "It ain't safe for us here."

CHAPTER 17

Rebecca Raley-Bridge
SEPTEMBER 1817

Early in the late-winter mornings, back when Reba was a child, she often came upon Mama Raley sitting before their hearth's dying embers.

"I can't find the splinter," Mama would mutter.

The chill added mist to their breaths, so Reba stoked the fire to warm them, then sat next to her mother. Mama always smelled as sweet as the lavender she collected in the midsummer. Reba reached for her hand, but Mama curled away, her hazel eyes flashing brighter than the fire Reba had brought back to life.

"What makes you believe you can help?" Mama grasped a needle from her sewing basket at her feet. Instead of picking away at the splinter in her index finger, she poked the pad. Blood pooled, but she never spilled a drop. She stabbed and retreated, pricked and pulled away. Then she dabbed the site with her handkerchief before dragging the needle's eye underneath her fingernail. Each

183

minuscule wound was seemingly wiped away and forgotten, but not the splinter. The stubborn shard remained elusive.

Mama's behavior confused Reba until she spoke to Papa. "Why does Mama hurt herself like that?" she asked him.

"Ignore it." His words were terse and final. "We're all scratching away at something. As long as she keeps it to herself, I don't care. You shouldn't either."

Among the Negroes in Richmond, affluent mulattos like her parents never revealed their weaknesses. They paraded around town instead, their tailored clothes heavy with perfume and their get-togethers filled with pretentious neighbors. When Mama kept wandering about the house, murmuring strange words to herself, Reba told her friends that Mama had fallen ill from charitable work. Or her mother had left for a trip to Norfolk to see kin. All these excuses formed a protective cowl over the Raley family home.

As she came to ignore her mother, she lost something precious: time. Mama Raley no longer taught her how to cross-stitch—she learned that from one of the housemaids. When her womanly time arrived, it was Mariah who gathered rags and taught her what to do.

She should've reached out during Mama's brief moments of clarity. She should've asked the things she'd always wanted to know but couldn't ask: What had it been like to grow up at Dunlora? Did Mama take after her own mother—or the white father she never spoke of? But by then, the answers were lost. Reba still had many questions and little sense of her family history because she'd remained silent.

Armed with indifference, Reba had stabbed a new sliver into her mother, a thorn of neglect.

Reba continued to remain silent on her porch as she sought her own splinter before the rooster sang his reveille. She hadn't slept well the previous night, worried over the missing children. She took a step forward. Her family hadn't woken up yet, and the shadows held firmly to their perch. This morning's cooler weather drew out wildlife they rarely glimpsed during the day. A herd of deer strode through a copse of trees nearby, while on the far side of the pasture, the bushes shifted from a fox darting into the woods. She waited for the animals to pass on their wisdom of survival, but none of them had an answer as to why this had happened to her family.

The temperature had dropped from sweltering to pleasantly warm, bringing the caress of a lukewarm wind against her face. Raindrops touched her forehead, and the deer fled under a crackle of lightning in the distance.

The empty bucket in her hand needed to be filled. She'd taken the path from her house to the well behind Carrie's home many a time, but today the splinter poked at her hand gripping the pail. She'd have to face what she feared.

No one guarded the well, but the Bridges should've started their day. Joseph and Peter usually made their way from their house to the barn about now. Pete swept their chicken coop while Joseph fed the horses. Yet Ruth's house was still.

Carrie's home groaned with the oncoming rain. A thin line of smoke rose from the chimney. Was anyone awake inside? Nelson used to tarry in the mornings, but the boy had milked Carrie's cow and fed the chickens. The place Carrie tended with love, her garden, was green and lush with crops ready to harvest, but she hadn't touched the field since her boy disappeared. Reba had the mind to send Herb over there to help, but would Carrie accept their kindness?

Reba circled around her neighbor's house along the familiar footpath. The only sounds came from their elderly collie. The animal sniffed her skirt, barked at her, then ambled back to the woodshed to resume his guard duties. She waited for sounds to emerge from the house, for the scrape and clang of pots or the thud of footsteps to reach her ears, but none came. The temptation to knock on Carrie's door and ask if her family was well tickled the back of Reba's neck. But she could still hear Carrie's spiteful words. The sear from Ruth's condemnation added an embarrassed heat to her cheeks. It was best for Reba to keep her distance and get what she came for: the water her family needed for the day.

The familiar stone structure was close. She still remembered the day Papa Raley had hired men to dig this well after he'd purchased Charles Bridge's property. Even though Papa's gesture had ensured her family no longer had to fetch water from the creek, she still felt like a prowling thief. This land belonged to Nelson now.

As Reba hurried up to the well, her stomach quivered, and nausea added a stumble to her step. Her palms grew slippery as a chill swept down her back.

Do not vomit here, she prayed. *Not where Carrie can see you.*

Five steps from the well, she closed her eyes and waited for the queasiness to pass. Murky swirls spun behind her eyelids. She was a seasick passenger on a ship that would never reach the shore. The seconds stretched out to minutes. With her last pregnancy, she'd constantly felt this way—each wave left her stuck on her pallet, dry-heaving. How easy it was to forget these miseries after she gave birth. Over and over again, she'd lain with her husband. Four times now she'd gotten with child. She often wondered what wrongs she'd committed to have to go through the weakness, the strain and burning during childbirth, and then the sleeplessness and the irritation of a screaming babe once it was born. Perhaps it was the joyous moments afterward, Annie's first words or Jimmy's arms reaching up for her, that made her bury these maladies.

Once her sickness retreated, she fetched the water. Not long after, she heard the yawn of Carrie's front door opening from around the corner. Reba added strength to her back. Any moment now, her neighbor would appear. The echo of Carrie's footsteps approaching made Reba quicken in her task. She considered what she'd say to the woman, what words of endearment she could offer, but when she turned to see her neighbor, she faltered. With only a hint of dawn, all she could see was the sternness in Carrie's features. The woman's downturned lips and hunched shoulders grew menacing with each breath Reba took. Her empty stomach threatened to rebel again.

"What do you think you're doing?" Carrie asked far too quietly as she set down one of her twins.

"I tried to be quiet." Reba adjusted her hold on the bucket, but the water sloshed over the side. "You look pale. Have you eaten?"

Carrie slowly shook her head. "You can stay away. You're not welcome."

"I know you're hurting right now—"

"No, you *don't* know," Carrie snapped. "You got a house full of children. Not a single one of them is missing."

Reba opened her mouth to speak but let the words course down her throat to her upset stomach. Her family had always used this well. They were kin, after all.

Carrie took a step toward her. "You got plenty of folks at your house—why not tell *your* boy to go to the creek?"

"That isn't neighborly, Carrie."

"Neighborly? If you were feeling neighborly, you should've been searching with Ruth and me last night." Carrie drew closer, and her other twin clung to her skirt. "A neighborly, God-fearing woman would've cried and prayed with us all night."

"I've been praying—I never stopped." She shuffled from one

foot to the other and swallowed past her dry throat. "Why don't you come by my place? Your children can eat while you sleep."

Carrie snorted. "I ain't slept since yesterday. If your Jimmy was gone, would you sleep right now?"

She shook her head.

"When the rain started, I damn near collapsed. We were soaked as dogs looking for them." Carrie turned away, giving the forest past the well her anger. "Ain't nothing out there." Even in her bitterness, Carrie trembled and wrapped her arms around herself.

"We can search again today," Reba offered.

"I'm too tired. I can't think straight." The woman released a long breath from her tiny frame. "I have too much to do."

Whatever captured Carrie's mind tugged her away. She strode back into the house. The wind picked up and bit Reba's face, harsh and wet.

———

Reba returned home to find her husband in the spot he'd occupied late into the night. Instead of searching for Nelson and Pete, Herb had guarded the house from a stool near the door. His rifle rested on his lap while he rubbed the timber surface of a relic from his childhood: a compass set in a wooden box. She'd seen him holding it before. His thumb had circled the scratched-up cover many times. But the compass was a simple thing. She eyed the gun instead, wondering how they'd reached this point. Could they kill what had taken those children? How could they fight against something they couldn't see?

Breakfast was a mostly silent affair with little chitchat. Herb kept glancing at the door. Did he expect someone to thunder through? Mariah fumbled with the firewood. The only person who didn't notice the tension in the room was precocious Georgie. The boy clapped and ran in circles around them.

"The pumpkin bug's got a pumpkin smell," he sang, "the squash bug smells the worst. But the perfume of that ole bedbug, it's enough to make you *burst*."

From her spot on the floor, Annie had finished her food, but she kept looking up at Reba, then to Jimmy. *He's gonna get in trouble, ain't he?* her frown conveyed.

Reba's eldest tried to reach for George, but the child darted away. On most days, she'd ignore Georgie or even send him outside to release the little bugs crawling under his skin, but today she preferred the *thump, thump* of his footsteps to the terrible silence in this house.

"George!" Herb threw the child a stern glare and jerked his chin to the floor. Their youngest scurried to plop down in front of Jimmy.

Herb added, "No more fussing, boy. If you're done eating, then you got chores to do. Get started on them dishes."

"Should I fetch the firewood first?" Jimmy asked.

Reba glanced at Herb and they shook their heads.

"Stay inside," she added.

Jimmy and Annie hurried to their feet. George was left behind, but he didn't sit still for long. He picked at the sole of his boot.

Herb turned to her with a sigh as the children stacked the dirty bowls and utensils. "You been to Carrie's house? Was she home?"

"Yes," she said quickly. "And she made it all too clear she doesn't want me paying any visits."

"She's probably exhausted," Herb said. "While I was out checking the house, I heard from a neighbor that she carried those twins of hers all night long."

Poor thing, Reba thought. "Why didn't she leave them with us?" she asked gently.

"After what happened to Nelson and Pete, would you have left your children with anyone?" Mariah fiddled with her empty cider cup. "She's scared like we are."

Herb and Reba glanced away—their answer was clear.

"It was late by the time the search party returned," Herb said. "We should lend a hand, if possible."

"I can milk her cow and feed the cow and calf," Mariah offered.

"Jimmy and I can do it." Herbert revealed his stoic profile to Reba as he took in the rain through their open door. His meal had long gone cold, but he hadn't asked for a warmer portion.

"Seems like everyone is spooked," he said. "Not a single soul outside."

"Maybe Hiram and the others'll come home—just like Luke." She squeezed his hand.

Herbert's jaw twitched in irritation. She withdrew her hand. One of them needed to believe their loved ones were well somewhere.

"I don't know what's going on." Her husband rubbed his chin, just like all the other times he'd worried for their children. "Luke says we need to keep on living or we won't have anything for those who remain behind."

After they'd eaten supper the previous night, Herb had left to speak to Luke again. He'd returned at nightfall and begun his guard duties. She wondered what the men had talked about, but her husband hadn't said a word. His face was stony and she assumed he'd learned nothing new. Perhaps when they had a moment alone, she'd ask.

It was still early in the morning, and even with the rain, the family had plenty to do. As to how they'd do it while keeping the children close would be another matter. The chickens and pigs had to be fed, the clothes washed, and in the garden the weeds popped up faster than Reba plucked them. Those were the daily chores.

Herb had yet to mend the fence around their garden, and the pile of wood in the shed was far too low. They needed a lot more cords for the winter months. Also the orchard harvest weighed heavy on their minds. Every hand was necessary. And yet they now sat idle and afraid.

Reba's thoughts were interrupted when her daughter touched her shoulder. "Mama Bear, can I get the eggs from the coop?"

"We'll go together with Georgie," Reba said.

"I'll take Jimmy and we'll see to Carrie's cow," her husband said.

She rose from her seat before they could leave. "Can't he stay with me?"

"He'll be fine, Reba. I promise." Herb kissed her cheek, but the warmth from his lips didn't soothe her. What if something happened to Jimmy while they were out? The very thought that her child could be stripped away cut into her deeper than any blade.

"I don't know . . ." she began to say.

"They'll need extra hands up in the orchard," Mariah said. "You two stay close to home and I can help out today."

Before Reba could grab Jimmy's hand for him to follow her out, her husband took him and left for Carrie's home. With Mariah off to the orchard, Reba had no choice but to take Annie's and George's hands to venture off to the coop. She kept glancing over her shoulder until Jimmy disappeared into Carrie's barn.

———

Reba spied her son across the pasture leaving their neighbor's barn. The boy strained to carry two buckets of milk while his father chopped firewood in front of the nearby woodshed. Why had Herb left him alone in the barn? Her husband should know better. Worry dug into her skin like sharp fingernails. That disquiet trailed after her from the coop to the lye-leaching barrel. The rain had been unreliable lately so there wouldn't be any fresh lye in the trough under the barrel any time soon.

Annie trailed after her and clutched an apron full of eggs. To her surprise, even Georgie held an egg in each hand. She didn't expect the fragile eggs to survive the trip home.

On the way back to the house, she found Jimmy hauling a bucket of cream inside.

"Your papa sent you home?" Reba kissed his forehead and wiped his brow.

"Miss Carrie had too much cream." He left the bucket in the coolest corner of the room. "He told me it'd go bad if we didn't churn it soon."

More chores at Carrie's house and now more chores at hers, but that was the way it was. The farm never stopped producing. "I can combine her cream with ours—although her butter isn't as salty as mine."

Jimmy smiled. "Your butter tastes fine, Mama Bear."

As much as his praise touched her, she knew she added too much salt.

An hour into churning the first batch of cream, a shadow crossed Reba's doorstep. Mariah had returned early from the orchard.

"Everything fine?" Reba asked.

"They said they didn't need me but wouldn't say why."

Reba knew why. Once the children disappeared from her home, evil had marked this place and everyone in it.

Jimmy finished shucking peas and got up from his spot in the corner. "Mama, you need a clean bucket for that butter?"

"Go get it for your mama." Mariah patted the top of his head as he went by. "He's gonna be tall like his daddy."

"Jimmy, stay here," Reba yelled after him. "When your papa returns, you can go get it."

Mariah's thick eyebrows rose in question. Reba recognized that look. A woman bold enough to walk alone from Richmond to here didn't hold back.

"They can't go outside?" Mariah stared at her a bit.

"Yes, they can, but I'm being careful after what happened yesterday." Her fingertips tumbled across the churn handle. "I can't stop thinking about those three babies."

"Have you heard any news this morning?" Mariah reached across the table and squeezed her hand.

"None. I wish somebody had taken them. That would be easier to explain than seeing them disappear before my very eyes."

"Folks walk away. Lord knows, they run away too, but they don't *disappear*."

"They do, Riah. I've never had any problems with my eyes, but yesterday, there had to be something wrong with them. Patience was reading and her brother was right there." She could see them clearly in her mind. It was far too vivid, far too fresh. Patience had her head down while she was doing math, her face flushed and sweaty as Pete tried to fan her. The girl's younger brother was intent on his task, his expression like Jimmy's, eager to please. Then he was gone—almost as if he hadn't been there in the first place. It had been that way with Nelson too.

"There must be some bad blood in the air," Mariah mused. "Anybody die recently?"

"Not recently."

"You never know in places like these," Mariah said. "Back in Richmond, Negroes are dying every day."

Reba didn't believe the dead lurked behind corners or tormented the damned. There had to be something else at play.

Not long after Mariah had returned from the orchard, another storm swept in from the west, darkening the skies again. If the answers were out in the forest, Reba wouldn't find them any time soon in this weather.

She opened the door to let in some cool air and found her husband had returned home too. He took up his spot again on the porch stool. She sighed. How long would they have to live like this?

Lightning briefly illuminated the pasture. The shadows across Herb's face retreated.

"How is Carrie?" she asked him.

"Not good. The babies hadn't eaten either." He shook his head. "Jimmy fed 'em, but they need better care."

She bit her lower lip. "After the storm settles down, I should take some supper over. Maybe I can bring the twins back with me. I have to do something. She's hurting."

"Then we should do right by them," Herb said gently. "Things are going to get harder."

"What are you saying?" Mariah asked.

"Luke says all this is far from over—it's only the beginning. Prepare yourself." Herbert's eyes appeared distant as he lit a cigarette, took two deep drags, then walked off into the rain, leaving only wisps of slow-rising tobacco smoke.

CHAPTER 18

Rebecca Raley-Bridge
SEPTEMBER 1817

R eba stood alone in the doorframe after Herb left. The breeze
from the rain cooled her spirits.

Prepare yourself—but how? This was no thief-in-the-night
Bible tale. She stole a glance at her babies. Did he mean they were
next? What if they lost more than one?

She peeked out the door again. Herb had slipped into the barn.
She wouldn't get any answers right now. Reba would have to wait
in this house while George stomped around the table again.

"When that bedbug comes down to my house, I wants my walking cane," her youngest sang proudly. "Go get a pot an' scald 'em hot!
Goodbye, Miss Lizzie Jane!"

That bedbug song would be the death of her. If only they could
get rid of this madness with scalding hot water. Georgie never had
a care, and she envied him.

While the rain beat against their roof, Reba considered what they could do inside. She could finish churning Carrie's cream or read the Bible to the children. She reached for the book, but Mariah drew her to sit.

"All right now, everyone." Mariah threw her a mischievous grin. "How about a game of find the thimble?"

Jimmy groaned, Annie's face brightened, and George sang even louder.

"Whoever wins five rounds gets a prize!" Mariah said.

"Whatcha got?" Annie asked.

"Anything good?" Jimmy added.

George's grand march ended.

Reba chuckled. Mariah was always hiding something good in her traveling pack's pockets.

"I'm not telling you—but I never lie when I say I got something." Mariah's feline smile deepened. "George will go first. After that, whoever finds it can go next."

Georgie bounded up to her with his tiny hand outstretched for the shiny thimble. Mariah leaned down and whispered into the boy's ear while she gave it to him.

Here we go, Reba thought. That boy would take forever to hide it.

"Let's go out to the porch so Georgie can have his turn." Jimmy and Annie rushed after Mariah.

Reba flinched, but Mariah peeked around the corner and said, "They're right here."

She nodded while her youngest proudly held the thimble for a while. He seemed to forget the game until Mariah asked, "What did we talk about, Georgie?"

The little boy giggled, a sweet and pure sound that resonated better than any church bell. Reba wondered if he planned to pocket the thimble and abandon the game.

George glanced over his shoulder to see her staring at him. He threw a pout.

"Don't worry. I won't peek." Reba grinned and partially closed her eyes, knowing very well Georgie stomped wherever he went. From the time he woke until he fell asleep, he walked like he had God's might in his soles.

The boy hurried to where they kept the tinderbox and stowed away the thimble behind the small metal box. With an upward tilt of his chin, the boisterous child scampered to the door. "I hid it! Come find it!"

"I hope *someone* finds it." Mariah ushered the others inside.

Annie rushed to the fireplace first, but Jimmy caught her arm. "There's no way he'd hide it there." He winked at her.

"But why not?" Annie's whole face scrunched up. "We heard—"

Jimmy drew her toward the loft ladder. "I heard him go up here. I'm certain of it."

When Annie always wanted to spoil the fun, Jimmy saved his brother each time. Little spunky Annie preferred to brave deeper water and explore. She was the one who came home with poison oak first—and nobody scraped their knees as often as she did. All the times she darted outside into the pitch-black darkness brought a smile to her mother's face. Not that Jimmy was afraid, only that the girl ran toward the unknown, while her older brother was far more tentative. Reba saw so much of her own father in her child— the girl had the same honey-like hue to her skin, the reddish tinge to her wiry curls forming a halo around her head. But she wasn't completely like her granddaddy—at times she had her father's quiet intelligence and kindness.

The children rummaging through the loft for the thimble filtered down to the women. Mariah leaned against the doorframe with her arms crossed. "You didn't put the thimble in your pocket, did you?" she asked Georgie.

The boy shook his head. His wide grin revealed his straight baby teeth. A baby rattler's teeth, if you asked her.

Eventually, his siblings came down the ladder and continued their search. Annie took her time and *stumbled* upon the thimble behind the tinderbox.

"Your turn, Annie girl," Mariah said.

The game began again, but this time, her daughter carefully hid the thimble among the other sewing supplies in the far corner. Annie never wanted to make things easy for anyone.

The morning carried on like that for a while. Once her children got to playing, they enjoyed themselves until they had to do chores. In the end, Annie won a piece of rock candy—which she refused to share with a crying Georgie. After an audible crunch, she swallowed the treat in a single bite.

"She's the winner, Georgie," Mariah said firmly. "You're not always going to win."

The boy still sobbed and kicked at the wall in the corner. When he flew into a rage, reprimands and spankings never reached him, and all Reba could do was make sure he didn't hurt himself. Her vengeful child tried to bite her and kick her stomach.

Mariah rose from where she sat with the children to intervene, but Reba shook her head.

"Ignore him," she said firmly. "When he's ready to behave, we'll see him again."

While the others opened an imaginary store, Reba churned the cream from Carrie's house. The steady motion quieted her fast-beating heart. She couldn't go too fast or the cream would stick to the churn's walls and not form butter. If she went too slow, she'd be turning this damn thing all day. So she rotated the handle with a focused rhythm. Steady rhythm, steady heart. But no matter how she worked at calming herself, frustration marched up her back. Dark thoughts flitted through her mind and she didn't like any of them. Why had she been given such a difficult child? Why couldn't she feel grateful for what she had, a gift many women wanted but some couldn't have? She didn't dare admit she prayed God would grant this next baby a more congenial soul.

Reba stewed and turned the handle while Mariah played the role of a shrewd shop owner. With the razor-sharp cunning of her grandpa, Annie bartered for socks and mittens with rocks as coins. She kept urging her little brother to join them, but Georgie defiantly shook his head.

"Mama Bear, make him play with us," Annie said.

"Leave him be." Reba drew in a deep breath and kept turning the handle but felt no relief. Shouldn't the third child be easier than the first? She wasn't lacking experience this time around.

The day stretched out. Reba finished churning and cut the butter into portions for both families. Her little demon child sipped a cup of buttermilk, his feet swinging with delight. A pot of stew bubbled on the hearth and everything was seemingly right with her home.

And yet it wasn't. With sweat coating their backs, everyone gathered at the kitchen table. Prayers were said, but Reba wasn't sure if God heard. Hiram, Nelson, and Pete had yet to reappear. And they might never return, no matter how much the family prayed.

After their dinner, Herb read from Psalms. He spoke of gratefulness, of the blessings they'd received, but she didn't feel gratitude—only resentment.

The evening crept toward the night. No one wanted to sleep. Restlessness hopped from one set of shoulders in the house to another, leaving them roaming like untethered spirits. Jimmy haunted the hearth. His younger sister stared blankly at her parents while her fingers formed small bunches of parsley and thyme. Reba should've finished hanging the sage to dry, but she twisted and twirled the twine. Mariah read a book until her head bobbed with exhaustion. Even Georgie didn't feel like singing.

Reba took in their forlorn faces and an idea came to mind: maybe all this was a dream and they'd wake up soon.

I doubt it, she thought.

"It's time for bed," Herb finally said. "We can't stay up all night."

"I want a story!" Georgie said.

"We've heard all of your stories, Papa," Jimmy mumbled.

"Then I should tell you about the one time I was lost in the woods," their father said.

Annie sat up straighter and Jimmy tilted his head with interest. Georgie wiggled his way into Mariah's lap.

Reba smiled. She hadn't heard this story before.

"Back when I was as old as Jimmy here," Herb began, "I was out foraging for oyster mushrooms. That particular winter had been merciless, so merciless that the ground had remained frozen long into the springtime. I'd tried to set up snares, but my traps hadn't caught a single cottontail. At the time, your uncle was too young to come out with me, so off I went east toward the mountains. Grandpa Stephen told me, 'There's always food, if you're hungry enough.' We didn't have much left. And we were all hungry." Herb paused long enough to draw a sip of cider. "A drought over the summer had killed most of our crops. That meant less feed for the animals. We didn't fare well either, so after our root cellars emptied, I wandered up and down the mountains." He sighed, but now he had their attention.

He pressed on. "When I'd left the house, the early morning fog hadn't fallen yet, but as I hunted, the clouds slipped downhill.

Deeper and deeper until I couldn't see my hand if I reached out like this." He presented his palm. "Up in them mountains, predators are looking for food too. A man who can't find his way home could find himself in a bear's belly.

"I used to always follow a footpath southward from Boone's Peak down to Wolfpit, but I couldn't find it."

"Did you starve out there?" Annie asked.

Jimmy rolled his eyes. "How could he starve if he's right here?"

"I was half starved, Annie angel," her daddy said. "It was bitterly cold there, and I walked in circles until a man appeared. He was a strange fellow. He wore a short dark-blue wool coat with shiny brass buttons. His trousers were light blue, and he carried a rifle over his shoulder like this." Herb demonstrated. "Over the years, I've wondered what he was doing up there in the mountains."

"What did he say?" Annie asked. "Did he try to shoot you with his gun?"

Herbert chuckled. "He didn't scare me. He looked as frightened as I did—but he knew something I didn't and that was the way home. The man reached into his bag and pulled out this." Her husband presented the brass compass enclosed in its wooden box. He placed it gently on the table. "After the man had helped me return to the farm, I expected him to stay, but he told me he couldn't. Now that I think about it, he was downright strange. He should've stayed and eaten. He'd even given me one of the rabbits he'd caught that morning, told me to feed my family."

"Did you ever learn his name?" Mariah asked him.

Herb thought for a moment, then shook his head. "He told me once, but I forgot . . . I was so happy to return home. Guess it never mattered."

"What an amazing story," Mariah marveled. "It's not real, is it?"

"The story is as real as this compass," Herb said softly.

Reba stared at her spouse and considered his tale. He'd never revealed how he'd gotten the old compass. She'd seen him occasionally flipping the thing or stroking it until he'd worn down the wood's finish on one of the sides. Though she wondered if he'd told a story meant to entertain his children, the pensive look in his eyes made her think otherwise.

———

The next morning, before a haze settled on the dew-drenched grass, Reba hurried out of the house. Her children, like two obedient ducklings and one stubborn chick, followed.

With the sun peeking above the horizon, the relentless heat had yet to bake the farm. The well-beaten footpath connecting the pasture to the orchard loomed ahead. This early in the day, she expected to see men and women stacking boxes and baskets around the trees for the harvest, yet there was no one around. Only the familiar chirps of warblers bounced off the trees.

On the footpath, Reba paused briefly to gesture toward a small patch of blackberry bushes. A few had been picked clean, but one had a couple berries left.

"Jimmy, take a couple of blackberries for Luke," she instructed.

From the orchard, their trek led them up to their destination. The cabin doorway was cracked open, and Reba heard shuffling footsteps. Thank goodness the family elder was home. A small dog's head poked around the door. Clover ambled up to them with his tail wagging.

"Morning." Jimmy grinned and scratched Clover's favorite spot—right behind his left ear.

Georgie ran ahead of them and bounded inside. Annie followed shortly after.

"What do we have here?" Luke called out.

"Morning, Grandpa Luke," Annie sing-songed. "Mama Bear wanted to come visiting."

"Did she now?" Luke said with a chuckle.

When Reba slipped into the house, the small smile on Luke's face faded.

"I'd hoped to see you sooner," Luke said.

Her mouth twisted into impossible knots. How did one begin such a conversation? She had far too many questions. And what if he refused to answer? She trembled at the thought. To steady herself, she took in the cabin. The nearby pile of kindling had grown far too low. Crusty bowls had been left on the kitchen table and—based on the fetid odor—Clover had relieved himself in a corner instead of outside. Luke's meager belongings, a chest, a bed, and a table, spoke of many years of use through the scuffs, nicks, and weathered wood. She struggled to imagine another Luke, a far younger one as tall as Herb who'd lived in this house with his wife, Addy, and their children. They'd had four strong boys and two pretty girls. That other family had gone about their lives, not knowing another trag-edy would befall the Bridges.

"Have you eaten?" she asked.

"Ain't hungry in the mornings," he mumbled from his usual resting spot—a rickety chair next to the table. He tried to straighten his wrinkled shirt and breeches as if she were esteemed company.

"True." She took the blackberries Jimmy had gathered and placed them in Luke's wrinkled, soft hands.

"Thanks, child."

Decades of work had eroded Luke's joints, leaving him tethered to his bed or the stools on the porch. Usually, his grandchildren came by every couple of days to bring him food or attend to the chores around the house, but the disappearances must've spooked them.

Reba gathered the bowls without a word. Annie didn't hesitate to sweep the porch and Jimmy hauled in firewood. Georgie remained rooted to the floor, drawing swirls in the dust peppering the floor. His head swayed as he sang a nursery rhyme to himself.

Reba drew in a cleansing breath before she asked in an offhand manner, "How have you managed lately?"

"Each day is like the one before," Luke replied. "Well, until . . ."

She nodded, knowing what he meant as Georgie got up and tried to rifle through Luke's chest by the bed. "George, stay out of there." She shifted to intervene, but Luke shook his head, his hand rising.

"Leave the boy be. Ain't nothing there he can hurt himself with."

She edged closer to Georgie. The boy searched for trouble like chipmunks foraging before winter. With a mischievous laugh, he plunged into the depths of the chest and retrieved women's garments. She gasped to see Addy's dresses and stockings strewn over the floor. Jimmy scurried to fetch them.

"Little fella, why don't you take a gander at this." Luke ignored the clothes and tugged at a length of leather strung around his neck. Reba couldn't make out what he held until her son spoke.

"What's that?" Georgie asked.

"That's a spool. You wrap spun wool from one end to another," Luke explained with a twirl of his finger. "Come see."

The boy's tiny hands slid down the spool. It was no longer than the length of his index finger. "It's so smooth," he marveled. "Why do you wear it?"

Luke grinned, revealing a missing front tooth. Briefly, youth shined in his eyes and smoothed the wrinkles lining his cheekbones. "We all wear things important to us. Don't you have a spool too?"

Georgie's shoulders rose and fell.

"Your mama needs to get you one—or maybe someday you can make one too." The old man gave him a slow nod. "All you need is love, patience, and a good whittling knife."

The boy's eyes brightened. "Mama Bear, can I have a whittling knife?"

"Ask your daddy." The response always worked in her favor. Herb never agreed to such requests.

Didn't matter though. Luke settled her four-year-old on the floor and taught him how to find the best wood for carving. Jimmy paused here and there while he shook out the old man's bedding. Annie took her time. The same spot on the porch had to be clean by now.

Somehow little Georgie drifted off and his head rested against Luke's knee. Perhaps it was the lilt of Luke's voice. Soon only the whistle of the wind floated through the cabin and tugged at the threadbare curtains.

The quiet pricked at her. She never liked the silence. Too many bad things happened when she least expected it. She had to introduce another sound in the room. One that cleared the fog and allowed the sun to part the clouds.

"I need answers," Reba finally breathed. "I want the truth."

"The truth changes over time." Luke's head lowered until his chin met his chest. "I'd wanted to forget about what happened, but God won't let me forget."

"Then what is the truth?" She'd considered both sides over the past couple of days—from Luke's stories to Ruth's and Carrie's rants. How could she protect her babies without knowing what she faced?

"It's all in God's hands. That's the truth. And *all* this madness is bigger than you and me," Luke said. "Right after I arrived home, my family tried to shun me, but my mama spoke." His voice hovered above a whisper.

She leaned toward him. The *swish-swish* of Annie sweeping made it difficult to hear him.

"I never knew what she said to them," he added, "until she came to me the next morning. She told me I could stay, but I couldn't forget my place in time, my role I had to play. You see, she'd traveled through time too."

"So it's generational?" Fear coursed down her spine and her unborn child stirred. "Who else knows about your mother?"

"No one—who'd believe me?"

She wanted to believe him. "Did she tell you how to stop it?"

"There ain't no stopping it. Like I said, it's in God's hands. We can only prepare."

Any Bridge could be taken. Her husband. Her children.

"Prepare how?"

He pointed to a shelf on the other side of the room. "Bring me that."

She strode up to it and plucked a foul-smelling box bound in oilcloth. "What's this?"

With the utmost care, Luke unraveled the leather ties around the box to reveal an old Bible. "Mama told me we must never forget the stories. Folks won't believe us, but we must never forget those who fell from time *and* those left behind to remember. She also said the Bridges will come to learn one child in *each family* will be lost if they are born from a Bridge man. After the child falls, their brothers and sisters'll be safe."

Each family? Her knees faltered at the thought. What did that mean for her children? Or even her husband if his brother had succumbed to the curse?

Luke placed the family Bible in her hands. "Every Bridge since

1760 is in here. This book is fragile, but a woman with schooling like you could create a new family record."

The book weighed heavily in her hands before she gently opened the butterfly-thin cover. On the first page, she discovered rows of names and dates. Many of them faded. "I don't know . . ." she whispered.

"You will know. Not today or tomorrow, but someday." He gave her a wistful smile. "I used to always want to stand still—but time doesn't stop. We're all forced to accept the tide or flow with it. You'll see."

CHAPTER 19

Rebecca Raley-Bridge
SEPTEMBER 1817

Two long days, with muted sunsets and sunrises, passed. Reba held Luke's words close to her heart, but they brought no relief. If one of her babies was going to disappear like the others, she didn't want to chronicle family births or even the disappearances. It was best for her to hide away the Bible, so she tucked the wrapped book among the precious heirlooms in her chest.

The family heard no good or bad news. The lack of any word from anyone pained them just as much. During that time, the storms retreated, but thick, dark clouds hovered like expectant mothers. Soon they'd give birth to thunder and lightning. New fallen branches would replace the debris they'd cleared away yesterday.

Reba used the dreary day to deliver bread and cheese to Carrie's doorstep. Jimmy accompanied her, sullen and silent.

"I could've done this by myself, Mama Bear," he grumbled.

She shook her head, having hidden long enough. Hadn't Carrie chastised her for not doing her part? At her neighbor's doorstep, they tucked the wrapped food behind a porch post. The fresh bread had left her hands warm. Beyond the closed door, she heard the soft *pit-pat* of the children's footsteps. She reached for the doorknob.

"Don't do it," Jimmy whispered. "Last time I was here, she didn't want me around either."

"Did she hurt you?"

"No, Mama Bear."

"If she ever says or tries anything, you come running home." Reba had said those words firmly.

They made a trip to the woodshed and retrieved wood to pile next to the door too. With all the noise they made, she expected Carrie's door to swing open and for the woman's thanks to be nothing more than a grateful *Get the hell off my property*. But the door remained shut, and in a way, that was just as harsh. A couple of days ago, they would've politely nodded or talked about all the work they'd have to do after the harvest. Once in a while, and it was too rare now that Reba thought about it, she'd find George playing with the twins.

She drew her arm around Jimmy's shoulders. "Let's go home."

"Should we leave them some water?" he asked. "I can run and bring some back."

"Good idea." Her boy's kindness was a reminder she needed to do better too.

Jimmy fetched the empty bucket stowed away in Carrie's woodshed, and they made their way to the well behind the house. Her boy walked faster as she hurried to keep up. He came to such a sudden stop that she almost ran into him. Then she spied what had slowed him down. A flat gray stone, about four feet wide, capped the well.

"Why is it covered?" Jimmy asked. "Did she do it because of the storm?"

"No." The well had never been covered.

"Did Carrie do that?"

"I doubt it."

Carrie was too tiny of a thing to haul a stone that heavy. The woman would break in two trying to lift it. Someone else had placed it there to keep her family out.

"C'mon." Reba motioned to Jimmy.

"Shouldn't we get the water, Mama Bear?"

Jimmy only knew they lived in a place where people helped one another no matter what, and she didn't want to be the one to break it to him.

"Don't bother," she told her son. "We're not wanted here."

"Why?"

"Because."

Jimmy didn't prod further. He'd heard her many a time using that reply. He knew not to press her.

They returned home, their walk far slower and silent. Their arms brushed against each other, and she was grateful he didn't add distance between them.

"Want me to go to the creek for water?" Jimmy finally asked.

"We'll go together."

Her son opened his mouth, then shut it again. He had to know why his parents didn't trust him alone, but for now he held his tongue. After he grabbed a pail, they trudged around the barn—only to see two figures circle the outhouse.

"What's Patience and her mama doing?" he asked.

"Quiet." She pulled Jimmy back behind the corner.

Ruth held a rifle while Patience searched. The girl darted ahead of her mother, opened the door to the outhouse, scoured the interior, then they turned toward the barn.

Reba tugged Jimmy back harder.

"What's wrong?" he whispered.

She pressed her fingertip to her lips.

She'd never been close to Ruth—she'd been to Carrie's house far more often—but she could read a person's eyes. Intent shined in Ruth's. The woman marched with determination—like she intended to search every corner of Reba's property, whether she was welcome or not.

"We're going home now." Reba grabbed the back of Jimmy's shirt and ran around the barn to the house. Herb had already left for the day, so it was Mariah who stood in a rush.

"Is there a bear out there?" She still held her needlepoint.

"You could say that." Reba glanced behind her, then strode across the room to pluck Herb's rifle from where he kept it on the wall. Annie headed to the door, but Reba stood in the way. "Stay inside. Don't go out, you hear?"

"What in the heavens?" Mariah turned to Jimmy.

"We saw Patience's mother out behind the house—" he said.

"And she's armed," Reba finished. "Keep them inside."

"Mama . . ." Georgie whispered, his face wrinkling.

Mariah reached for Georgie. "It's all right."

Reba shut the door behind her. She didn't want to hear the rest.

Her unborn child fluttered in her belly, perhaps feeling the nerves shooting through her. The rifle was as familiar in her hands as any tool in the kitchen, but her sweaty palms made the weapon slippery, her grip uncertain. She sat on the porch stool and waited. Soon enough, Ruth and Patience arrived. She held still with the rifle in her lap as they slowly circled the front of the house. Step by step, eyes searching. Ruth paused, and Reba held her breath. Would her neighbor dare to cross her doorstep? Would the woman demand to search the house?

Reba clutched the rifle hard enough for her hands to go numb, knowing without a doubt she'd do the same if one of her children had disappeared, but this was *her* home. The place where she kept her children safe, and she'd be damned if she'd let a woman holding a gun go traipsing through. Even if she let Ruth search, what would her neighbor demand next? For all she knew, Ruth and Joseph had put that rock in place at Carrie's behest. All that work to punish Reba's family.

At a time like this, Mama Raley would say to be careful around women like Ruth, for they had splinters aplenty. "After you've lived as a slave, you're never the same."

Growing up with Mama and Papa, Reba had seen what she meant. How Mama often ignored or separated herself from *them*— the slaves who worked in Richmond. They had to be constant reminders of her past life. How Papa demanded that Reba speak eloquently. All those lessons had been shaped to divide Reba from the enslaved. Hypocrisy had saturated their childhood home.

Reba watched Ruth and Patience slowly march around her house with the same stare she'd used for Mama. This was how it was. She couldn't forget that—she defended what her family had because she knew how treasured it was. And for that same reason, she hunkered down on that stool with that rifle until the two intruders departed.

————

Ruth was eighteen years older and far more aloof, but Caroline and Reba should've been the best of friends. Long before Charles had passed away two years ago, they'd gotten to know each other as two young Bridge wives. Through conversations at the well behind Carrie's house, they'd learned that they'd been born less than two weeks apart. They were practically spring-born sparrows with the same memories of childhood droughts and harvests.

Over the summers to come, Reba had spent the hottest time of the day in Carrie's home. Little Nelson was no older than four around that time, and Reba perched eight-month-old Jimmy on her hip. On a cooler day in early August, Carrie had flitted from her kitchen table to the pots where she boiled chitlins for supper. Hints of copper and the earthy reek of animal entrails lingered underneath the aromatic scents of onions and celery. She'd spent the morning butchering one of their fall sows, and after Reba's arrival, she'd gone out into the heat again to salt pork portions for winter meals. She hummed a sweet melody while her bare feet whispered on the wood floors. No matter how much Nelson shouted or ran about, she embodied a strange sense of calm in the center of a storm. She tended to rise to anger with ease, yet she quieted just as quickly.

"Did you try the biscuit recipe?" Reba asked.

Carrie grinned, the tiny moles dotting her dark-brown cheekbones gathering together. "Mmm-hmm. I ain't never seen Charlie empty his plate that fast—the man eats like a bird."

That past spring, Carrie and Reba had exchanged family recipes. "Herb loves it too. I can't ever make enough."

Suddenly, Carrie's face scrunched up. She reached down and grasped her stomach. "This heat got me feeling something awful. The devil's cookin' the countryside."

"Are you sick?" Reba stroked Jimmy's back in small circles as he nursed.

"When am I not sick? I never ate well as a child. Tomatoes made me deathly ill—and I never could touch peppers or eggplants."

"I haven't seen you eat those lately. Are you with child?" she asked.

"No, I'm in no hurry to have more," Carrie said dryly.

Reba chuckled. "Last I heard, God's will keeps showing up year after year around here."

The right corner of Carrie's mouth tilted upward. She reached up to where she kept her dried herbs. Carefully, she ran her fingertips along the bunches until she discovered what she wanted.

"Open your hand," she commanded. Carrie never suggested; she instructed.

Reba presented her palm and Carrie sprinkled tiny seeds into the middle.

"Why did you give me Queen Anne's lace?" she whispered.

Carrie separated out at least five seeds into a smaller pile. "Crush these and drink them with water after you lay with your husband."

"Do these really—"

Carrie motioned to pocket the seeds, so Reba accepted them. "Grammie told me it don't always work. Her daughters, namely my ma, didn't listen well. Ma had two sets of twins."

"Two sets of twins," Reba breathed. She couldn't imagine birthing two babies at once.

"Her mama told her it's about knowing your body." Carrie stirred the chitlins. "The best time to lay with your husband is right after your womanly time is over."

Reba brushed her fingertips over the bristly seeds. How could such tiny things hold the power to keep her from having another child? It felt like witchcraft—these seeds added an unnatural weight to her palm. And yet a question came to mind she hadn't thought before: Were these why Carrie had gone five years without another child?

She took in the depths of Carrie's rich brown eyes down to her knowing smile. A smile laden with secrets. Reba slipped the seeds into her pocket.

"Charlie goes down to Monticello to work every fall, and when he comes back . . ." Carrie smacked her lips with disapproval. "I ain't some hen waiting to lay eggs. Look at this house."

She tilted her chin to the single-room cabin with its rotted roof and furniture in need of repair. "Can you imagine ten children up in here? Charlie has even less money than his daddy, Dabney."

"We do what we must," Reba said softly, and she meant it. "Even if that means accepting the Lord's gifts."

Carrie gave her a sharp glance. "Not all His *gifts* are blessings." She sipped the bubbling broth, made a face, then sprinkled some salt across the top.

"You don't mean that."

"Oh, I do. Most women these days don't get blessings. Old Fanny Bridge kept birthin' babies until she was split in two. I heard she couldn't stop pissing everywhere. Until Ruth had Peter, she struggled for years to have another child, bless her soul. My twin sister died during childbirth from bleeding too much. If you want to determine when you'll receive that *blessing*, you should see to your own well-being."

After Charlie, Reba didn't visit as often. The two women didn't share recipes anymore, only shared messages about the children. Georgie asked every now and again about seeing the twins, but Reba declined—which she now knew had been a mistake. She shouldn't have hidden away from Carrie's grief. Like Mama Raley, her friend deserved better. A listening ear. A caring hand. The more she believed she'd learned better, the more she realized she hadn't.

———

A couple of hours after Ruth and Patience left, the family was trapped inside the house again with three children who wanted to play. Reba let them run through the front yard for a while, but the rain returned and forced everyone indoors. From then, the fighting began between Annie and Georgie after the boy took her doll and hit her when she tried to take it back.

"Georgie, my goodness!" Mariah separated them and swatted his bottom. "You know better." She harrumphed. "Is he hard of hearing?"

"He can hear just fine," Reba said. "He's stubborn and spiteful like my papa."

Mariah chuffed. "That man follows us from the grave, I tell you. I still wonder what my life would've been like if he hadn't owned my mama."

Years ago, they'd spoken at length on how Papa Raley had bought Mariah's mother's freedom—only to enslave her again. Now Papa's past dealings were a dirty secret, like soiled clothes rarely left out in the open.

"My mother went from one hell to another," Mariah whispered.

Reba sighed. "Hell is everywhere, and it isn't hot like Virginia. It's a cold place where people willingly hurt others. I never wanted my children to feel that way."

"They won't," Mariah said. "Herb's a fine man."

"He's perfect—bowed legs and all."

Mariah chuckled. "Thank the good Lord none of your children got his crooked smile."

"I rather like his smile. After living in a house where folks didn't smile much, a smile is like the sweetest berry off the bush. You only get to sample it once in a while, but you can savor it, remember it."

Her husband and children gave her everything she needed. It had taken five years for them to save up the money to buy back the land Charles Bridge had sold away to Papa. Now that Raley land belonged to the Bridges again, they wanted to build a vineyard. All the families would benefit from a profitable business. Maybe someday they could build a schoolhouse for the children. That would be a beautiful day in the far-off future.

If George behaved long enough to see the future, she thought.

The sky darkened as the day came to an end and Ruth had yet to return. But unease continued to circle Reba's home and dripped off the roof like the remains of the storm.

Reba kept glancing outside, expecting to see someone other than Herb. After being stuck in the house for so long, the children often stared out the door too. Even after Herb returned, he did the same. Perhaps they had apprehension curling in their stomachs like she did. She waited for someone to appear with news. Not long into their supper, a heavy knock shook their door.

Everyone stared at the door until another thud startled Jimmy. The boy stole a glance at his mother before he shifted to answer it. Reba grabbed his shoulder. Mariah reached for Herb's rifle.

"Who's there?" Herb yelled.

"It's Ludie!" A man's strained voice bled through the door. "Another Bridge child has gone missing. David's granddaughter."

Herbert got up. Jimmy's lower lip trembled as her husband opened the door and a breeze swept through the room. "What's that mean? Mama?"

"I don't know," she admitted.

Ludwell Bridge, her husband's second cousin, stood in the doorway with rain dripping off his hat. Shadows partially hid his face, but fear glinted in his eyes. A fourth child, gone.

Georgie scurried from his spot on the floor to scramble into Reba's lap. She kissed the top of his warm head. The cooler air was a welcome reprieve to the heat, if not for the news that the wind carried.

"A bunch of us are meeting up at Uncle Luke's place," Ludwell said softly. "We'll need every able-bodied man."

Herb blew out a deep breath. "I'll go."

Reba would have none of that. She strode across the room, trying to convey with her eyes that she didn't want him to go. If they stayed together, maybe their children would be spared. She clutched his sleeve.

"Are you sure you have to go?" she begged.

Her husband avoided her eyes. "Someone has to." He stroked her cheek.

"But what if . . . whatever this is comes looking for our children?" Reba kept her voice low so as not to frighten anyone, but even she caught the subtle whine in her plea. "Maybe the minute you walk out the door again, they'll face the same fate as the others."

"We can't hide forever," he said fiercely. "Don't matter where we go, where we stand, where we sit. We need to come to terms with that fact."

She clutched his shirt tighter, refusing to let go. "I'm not ready yet."

He gave her a soft smile. A whimper snuck out, and she swallowed it by covering her mouth. Her family had to be careful, but that didn't matter when she had no idea what they faced or even if she had a chance to fight against it.

With his hat on, Herb hurried out the door. Reba kept watch until the shadows engulfed him. Before she slipped back into the house, she glimpsed someone else standing on the other side of the pasture in front of Carrie's house. Lightning flashed, revealing a woman standing in the rain, the door to her home wide open behind her. Carrie wavered with the trees fighting against the wind. At her feet, one of her toddlers reached up, but the woman paid no mind. Reba could hear the child's cries and it broke her heart in two.

Jimmy and Annie grabbed Reba's hands. Georgie reached up for her too, but she pulled him close to her stomach—close to her other vulnerable child. She willed her feet to move. She willed herself to act, but she couldn't take a single step to separate herself from her children. Mariah joined her and squinted into the darkness.

"Is that Carrie over there?" her friend breathed.

"I think it is."

"Heaven above . . . that poor baby." Mariah stepped around her and pushed her aside with the urgency Reba wished she felt.

"Reba!" Mariah yelled. "Come help me!"

Any decent Christian woman would've run after them. A woman who cared for another would've gathered blankets, food, and anything else Mariah would've needed to march across that pasture and see to their neighbor. From afar, with shame raining down from the sky to drench her, Reba watched Mariah help them into their house.

CHAPTER 20

Rebecca Raley-Bridge

SEPTEMBER 1817

Herbert still wasn't home. Jimmy tried to keep George entertained with another game of hide the thimble, but all that came to an end when the door opened. Reba rose, expecting to see Herbert shaking off the rain, but Mariah came back instead.

"Is everything well?" Reba asked. Guilt still pressed on her shoulders. "There's hot water for sassafras tea."

She offered her friend a fold of cloth and searched her face for an answer as to Carrie's condition. Mariah's face appeared strained as she unraveled her damp headscarf and rested the fabric on her lap. Without it, she had a childlike quality.

"Tea sounds perfect." After Mariah sat, her face fell further. "I've never seen such a sight."

"How is Carrie?" Reba asked as she fetched the sassafras bark.

"She's lost up in here." Mariah pointed to her head. "One of the neighbors told me she'd always been outspoken, but she's withdrawn now." She shuddered. ""Those babies need better care. Both of their diapers were full, and there was filth everywhere. It's as if she's given up."

All of this sounded familiar. After Charles had died, Carrie fell deep into a sadness only time and her son Nelson's prodding could pull her from.

"She's in a bad place and all," Nelson had said, "but she'll be fine. We'll be fine. Ain't nothing going to keep us from moving on."

But Nelson was gone now. And as Carrie's neighbor, it was Reba's responsibility to help—even if she had to drag her children across the pasture. "From now on, one of us should look after them, rain or shine. We should also reach out to the other Bridges."

Summer's end was upon them; the farm families had a couple of months to fill their root cellars and prepare for the winter months. Such precious time would vanish far too fast.

Reba added the bark to the kettle and shivered, thinking of how quiet the winters felt. How the snow packed against the outside walls and amplified sounds in the house. The wintertime had a cruel way of reminding them how alone they were on the farm.

"I'll talk to Ruth tomorrow. We can take certain days," Mariah said.

No matter how much those two women despised her, everyone had to come together to help those in need—even if that meant she had to face Carrie again.

After Reba drank tea with Mariah for a spell, she waited four hours for her husband. Eventually Georgie fell asleep against Annie and it was time to send the children off to bed. She curled up next to them in the loft. Jimmy grumbled about sleeping close to her and added space between them.

"Yes, you're older, but right now is different." She pulled him back and kissed his forehead. "Go to sleep."

An ache spread across her chest. Here she was, lying in this stuffy loft while her husband was out there searching.

Reba tried to remind herself he'd come home safe, and that they'd be happy again someday. That the joy she'd felt when she married him would be enough to help weather this storm.

Soon enough, Georgie fell back asleep, his head cradled against her bosom. Annie's forehead touched her shoulder, while on the other side, Jimmy presented his back to her, but at least he was close. His presence lessened the fear pooling inside her. Reba's fourth child fluttered in her belly, a reminder that everyone was present. But for how long?

The rain pitter-pattered against the roof, the only sound besides the children's breathing. The night crept on, and soon the house went quiet. Georgie twisted and turned, crawling his way out of her embrace. Soon enough, the boy hung his leg over her waist and his mouth rested against her arm, his skin sweaty and hot. She should've reached out to make sure he wasn't too warm, or even wipe his forehead, but she didn't. Jimmy now slept on his back. An arm's length separated them. She moved closer. Breathed in time with him. A sheen of sweat coated his cheek, and she ran her fingers along the cheekbone that was no longer smooth, the curves representing his childhood shifting to adulthood. He'd become a man soon. A good man who'd care for her in the years to come. She didn't have to close her eyes to see his bright smile or hear him ask her if she was well. Again and again, he'd been the only one to bring her water when she wavered in the heat or rush to get her a stool if she needed to sit. Annie sometimes followed his lead, but dreamy Annie often preferred the company of the clouds.

Dear God, don't take my children away, she prayed. *I'll be a better mother if Jimmy is spared. I'll make sure George minds his manners and grows up well. Annie will become a proper lady like my mother.*

Reba waited for Herb, but sleep kept nipping at her. No matter how hard she tried to stay up to hold on to her children, a current of fatigue kept pulling her under.

The next morning, she was startled awake. Painful cramps snaked over her stomach, but the discomfort receded as quickly as it came. The pain was all too familiar. First was the stretching and pulling, then as the babe grew, the child nestled under her ribs began to kick and headbutt. Reba's limbs were heavy, her mouth sawdust dry. She reached out for her babies. Jimmy was there with a faint smile on his sleeping face, his chest rising and falling. On her other side was Annie. The girl's head wrap had fallen off, and her hair had unraveled from the plaits Mariah had braided. One child had crawled away from Reba. Little George lay on the far side of the loft on the floor.

Get him. The thought came to mind but then vanished like Nelson and Pete. Reba should've scrambled to grab him, but she clutched Annie and Jimmy instead. Georgie was safe. He was even stronger than Annie. Even fast sleep, George's bottom lip defiantly curled. He slept with his arms and legs stretched out as if he needed to be tethered to no one. Not even his mother.

———

Thankfully, the rain ended in the night—the late summer harvest waited for no one. While Mariah crossed the pasture to check on Carrie's cow and calf, Reba fetched the rifle and took the children out to the garden. All this rain brought field mold to the corn, potentially leaving their harvest to the birds.

Annie and Georgie fussed a bit, but Jimmy didn't complain. He'd seen many a harvest and knew what had to be done. Without instruction, he took up the scythe and whetstone. Reba and the other children trailed after him into the corn patch. Last summer, it had been Herb who'd swung the scythe, and she'd followed him, bundling the sheaves. He'd twisted at the waist, his back muscles flexing with each movement. Now her boy worked his father's field, briefly pausing to draw the whetstone against the dulled blade.

The sun beat down on their backs and a cooler breeze whistled through the birch trees—if she hadn't thought about it, today could've been like any other summer day.

As the day progressed, the heat rose and the haze returned, blurring the stalks they had yet to cut. A shadow rustled the yellowed crops. She squinted, waiting to see if someone had followed them, and yet the form moved away. Briefly, the blur cleared, revealing the top of a worn hat—one she'd never seen before. The dark-brown, weathered fabric was made of a dull material, while a narrow brim surrounded a rounded crown. Just as soon as she saw the strange sight, it disappeared. Papa Raley's warnings came to mind: *Do not trust your eyes. Listen. Question everything.*

She listened for the sound of retreating footsteps but heard none.

"You see someone coming, Mama?" Annie asked.

She shook her head. "It's nothing."

After they'd bundled the cornstalks, Reba and her children drank water and rested for a spell, but not for long. The overgrown garden waited. First, she got to weeding. Jimmy stooped close to her and tucked fully grown sage into his sack. Annie gathered green beans, her brow wrinkled in concentration. Two steps away, after Reba finished weeding, she kneeled before a row of lettuce and kale. Her hands worked of their own volition to pinch off the vibrant leaves around the outer edges, while her eyes followed the children.

Annie had finished fetching beans and moved on to the squash. She twisted the shiny plants off the vine with a quick flick of her wrists. Inch by inch, she wandered away—only to jump to the next row, where Reba couldn't reach her.

"Don't you go too far away, Annie!" Reba said, sharper than she'd meant to.

Not far from them, Georgie meandered up and down the rows with his basket. Eventually, he came upon the ripe tomatoes and shoved tiny red ones into his mouth. Even the sour green ones disappeared.

"Mama, why are tomatoes red?" Georgie asked.

"I don't know," she admitted. "Maybe the tomatoes get a sunburn."

"A sunburn? Then how come the corn doesn't turn red too?"

Annie laughed. "Corn and tomatoes are two different vegetables."

Georgie shrugged and kept picking. Once he'd eaten his fill, he picked a couple and offered them to Annie.

His sister opened wide and Georgie pushed the vegetable into her mouth. "Tastes good. You want one, Mama Bear?"

"I'm not hungry," Reba replied. "We still need to keep working, girl."

Now that George had fed his sister, he abandoned his work to slap the watermelons. The fruits' field spots had yet to go from white to buttery, and he tapped them as if they were a baby's bottom.

"You're a bad boy!" Georgie said. "You're gonna get a spanking!"

"What're you doing?" Jimmy snapped. "Get back here and stay close to Mama."

While Reba watched her eldest stomp over to his brother to grasp the boy by the wrist, she exhaled. Not one but two exasperated breaths.

Reba was tired of feeling ashamed. Just like she was tired of feeling nauseated and pulled in every direction except the one she wanted to go in. She edged Jimmy out of the way.

"Stay close to me, Georgie," she said softly.

"Why, Mama?" he asked between chews. His breath smelled of mint, sour green tomatoes, and innocence.

"Because" was all she said.

———

Reba and her children spent hours in the gardens and fields. Her lower back and hips ached, but the time eased her mind until she'd forgotten about Ruth's visit, the cover over the well behind Carrie's house, and disappearances no man or woman could explain.

All that ended when they returned home. Reality swept in as she prepared supper—along with a dull cramp that kept streaking across her abdomen. She stroked her belly as if such a movement would soothe it. This child wouldn't whisper into this world but come shouting and screaming.

Swaying and begging for peace didn't help, so Reba slipped out the door. With each step, pressure built in her lower stomach, a sign she needed to relieve herself.

"I did too much today, didn't I, little one?" she breathed.

Puddles from yesterday's showers still filled the pasture. Reba half expected to see Nelson and Peter waiting outside, but no one was there. She hurried to the outhouse, not bothering to sidestep the puddles. The warm water seeping into her boots was a reminder she was alive and well.

When Reba slid her hand through the knotted rope tied to the outhouse door, a new dampness slid between her thighs. She hiked up her dress, noticing the dots of crimson speckling her petticoats. *Please, no.*

She reached down, knowing what she'd find. Her fingertips brushed against her inner thigh and her trembling hand revealed the truth. Clot-filled blood ran between the cracks and crevices of her hand to darken the puddles at her feet.

Dear God in heaven, that's my baby. She stumbled up the single step. Waited for the pain to come, for the agony she'd seen other women experience, but the feeling never arrived. All that hung in the air—while she sat in that filthy place—was a hollowness as empty as her womb would become. And in that emptiness, a new feeling sprouted: relief. Absolute relief.

What had Luke said? *The Bridges will come to learn one child in each family will be lost.*

"Thank you, God," Reba whispered. "For sparing my other children."

CHAPTER 21

Rebecca Raley-Bridge
SEPTEMBER 1817

Herb returned after everyone settled in for the night. Her husband's news broke her heart even further: The girl was never found. It took far too long for Reba to put what happened into words.

"I think I might lose the baby," she whispered.

Herb drew Reba close until they faced each other.

"I'm praying for a better outcome but . . ." She shifted until her nose and lips rested against his collarbone. Over the years, whether it was hot or cold, Herb's clammy skin offered a familiar comfort. She squeezed her eyes shut. A single inhale came out as a whimper.

"We've been blessed for many years, wife." With his index finger, he gently drew circles on her back. "We'll be blessed again."

"I know." Her breath quickened. Before she cried again, she tried to match Herb's steadiness.

Scratches and tiny thuds stirred outside the house next to the barrel where they kept food scraps. Herb stilled. Alert. Both their heads turned toward the sound. Probably the fat-bellied coon Herb had failed to catch. The sounds receded and Herb relaxed again.

"Do you remember when you fell last year?" he asked offhandedly. "It was springtime."

"A little."

"You were holding Georgie and you tripped over Jimmy's toy."

"That boat . . ." Briefly, she couldn't resist smiling.

"I was sitting on that porch cleaning my tools. You were crossing the pasture from Carrie's place when it happened. Thought you'd fallen into a hole." He went quiet for a spell before he continued. "Seemed like the tall grass swallowed you up. I never ran so fast. When I got to you, Georgie was crying, and you were lying there bleeding from a cut on your forehead. Took you a long time to wake up too."

"I don't remember any of it."

"You don't, but I do. It's trapped in my head," he said. "I was uneasy for the longest of time until I had a dream 'round Christmastime."

"What dream?"

"It was years into the future. You and I were sitting next to the creek with the other Bridges. A couple of Raleys. We were watching the children swim. Annie was older, as tall as you are now. Our boys—all four of them—were playing in the water. Barely recognized 'em."

"Four boys?"

"Yes indeed. You and me and our blessings."

Reba was tempted to ask if her husband had seen the other missing children in his dream, but she didn't have the heart to ask. There'd been enough loss around here to last twenty lifetimes.

The next day the overcast sky refused to weep with Reba. She stared outside and waited for raindrops to pepper the porch, for dew to dampen the fields, but the rain that refused to leave a couple of days ago wouldn't return.

So she sat. The hush in the house trickled into her, ever the reminder of what had happened, of the rags placed between her legs to catch the blood. Sorrow had sliced through her like a deep and unyielding serrated blade. Even if Herb had dreamt of other children, she still had thought of what she would name the babe, considered the clothes she needed to mend, and the simplest things. Like would the child's nose be small like hers, or its cheeks high like Herb's? Would the baby have birthmarks?

Mariah served the children porridge and warm bread. "Mama's tired," she told them.

Exhaustion wrapped itself around Reba and she closed her eyes, cradling the feeling close until a shadow passed in front of the door. She squinted to see Mariah stride across the porch. Then her friend spoke in hushed tones with Ruth of all people.

"I heard Reba lost the baby," Reba caught her neighbor saying. "I came to see if she needed anything."

Ruth turned away from Mariah to approach the door, her face ashen with the sadness Reba should've carried. But in the same instant, Reba wanted to cry with *joy*, to shout a prayer of thanks to God for sparing Jimmy, Annie, and Georgie. The shame rolled over her and squeezed more tears from her eyes.

Dear God, forgive me, she thought.

"I heard what happened from Herb," Ruth said. "How is she doing truly? I'd hoped she wouldn't lose one like Joseph and me."

"I don't know," Mariah admitted, taking a step back. "It happened last night and we're still trying to come to terms with it."

"She was four months along, wasn't she?"

Reflexively, Reba stroked the gentle curve; her child was still there, unmoving, yet soon it wouldn't be. Her hands trembled and she clenched them into fists. The women spoke of her as if she didn't sit right in front of them. But hadn't she done the same since the last time Ruth had lost her baby? Last spring when the sheep were heavy with lambs, Reba had ventured across the pasture with food in hand and prayers in the same manner. She'd sincerely meant her words of condolence, even if she hadn't completely understood the depth of the loss.

"Joseph and I send our best," Ruth said. "If there is anything we can do—"

"We can pray for the other families. I hope no one else is taken," Mariah said firmly. "I tell you, this land is cursed. No matter what Herb says or that crazed man. Something ain't right here. I don't know if God took that baby or if it was taken like those other children, but none of this is natural."

After offering more words of comfort, Ruth left, only to return an hour later with Carrie and her children.

Reba slowly tried to rise. Carrie said softly, "Don't get up. Rest easy."

Her neighbor floated into the room, her eyes distant and clothes disheveled. Carrie eased into the seat next to Reba. Without glancing at Reba, she patted her hand with sympathy. The woman's daughter climbed into her lap while her son leaned against her legs with his thumb in his mouth. Ruth settled on the opposite seat, remorse evident in her drawn-up shoulders and eyes trained on the nicks in the table. Mariah's gaze flicked between the two, ready to act if one of them misbehaved.

"I never thought, whatever this thing is, that it would take the unborn," Ruth began.

"It's the devil's work," Carrie murmured. "Don't matter how

old those children were. Hiram was a grown man. And now this one . . ." Her voice trailed off as her gaze darted across the table.

Reba opened her mouth to speak but couldn't form words through the sawdust caught in her throat. Mariah passed her a cup of water. The tepid fluid quenched her thirst. "So what happens now?" she whispered.

"I don't know." Carrie wrung her hands. "I still don't know what to do."

"Ain't nowhere left to search, so here we stay," Ruth managed, wiping away a single tear.

Reba wanted to take in their faces, but if she did, she knew she'd be swept away and left breathless with grief. So the women stewed in silence. They allowed the wind to rattle the front door. The buzzing from the cicadas filtered inside.

"I asked Joseph about leaving," Ruth said quietly.

"It's only been a couple of days. He might come back," Carrie said. "And where you gonna go? Up north, they don't want colored folks anyway. Last I heard, Negroes couldn't go to Ohio."

"This place don't feel right anymore," Ruth whispered. "I turn every corner expecting to see Pete, but he's never there. Everything feels dirty in here." She brushed her hand against her chest. "And I can't scrub it clean."

"Some stains can't be cleaned," Carrie said.

And some splinters can't be removed, Reba thought.

"We haven't made a decision yet . . . and winter's coming in a few months," Ruth said. "Maybe by spring things will be different."

"How long does it take?" Reba managed to ask. "For things to feel different?"

A hint of a sad smile touched Ruth's lips. "A mother's pain is forever. But the sharpness retreats. Sometimes gradually. Sometimes bit by bit. Having Joseph with me helps—even if he's not the talking type."

"You should talk to Herb," Carrie said to Reba wistfully. "You have a good man. He takes care of you."

"I think he helps you around the house too much," Ruth said.

Reba paused to clench her skirt. "Herb takes good care of me, as he should."

"True, but that ain't right." Ruth leaned forward as Mariah rolled her eyes. "Women should stay in the house and men should be working. You see, they're on the outside and we're on the inside," she said with an air of authority. "That's how it should be."

"Should be?" Carrie grunted. "I know plenty of men who don't do half the work I do at my house. I don't need them."

"Do you want another man?" Reba couldn't help but ask.

Carrie pursed her lips, then smacked them. "They're only useful when I need my bed warmed. That's when I don't mind them being *inside*." A smile brightened her pretty face. "And afterward, the man can head on *outside*."

Reba laughed. Ruth tried not to. Mariah guffawed and covered her mouth. Soon enough they were all laughing. Why did it take all this madness for them to sit and comfort one another?

The tightness in Reba's chest eased. She was ready to speak her truth. "I should've been more serious, more insistent," she managed.

Carrie's head rose. "What are you talking about?"

"I'm talking about our children. When I taught them, I could've done things differently." She tried to swallow past the cotton in her throat. "Carrying a child is a part of life. We all must do what we can for the betterment of others."

"Indeed," Ruth murmured.

Reba attempted to gather scattered thoughts. "Come this spring, we should work with the Raleys to build a proper schoolhouse. We shouldn't wait."

Ruth slowly nodded. "Joseph can build desks for them."

"A proper place for the children sounds wonderful," Carrie added.

"In time," she said, "they'll have arithmetic books and chalkboards."

Each woman sounded off, one after another, with the supplies their children would need. The vineyard could be built in the years to come. They had all the time in the world, didn't they?

A quiver circled Reba's stomach. She trembled as she pulled herself away from a melancholic train of thought. Had her baby moved? No, it was the porridge surging up her throat. She rushed out the door and emptied her stomach onto the grass.

A warm hand pressed against her lower back and stroked. Carrie's tiny, splayed hand had the span of a hummingbird's wings, but her palm was comforting.

When she was ready to return to the house, Carrie helped her back inside. It was Carrie who sat with her while Georgie played with the twins. Reba wasn't sure how the day passed as people went in and out. Now and then, she rose to attend to the chores, but a hand was there to force her to sit again. By the end of the day, the bleeding had ended, and her baby still hadn't moved.

"A mother's pain is forever. But the sharpness retreats. Sometimes gradually. Sometimes bit by bit," Ruth had said.

Reba carried those words into the next day. Then the next. Gradually, she got up from her spot before the hearth to pace the house. She swept the floor. Hung the bundles of herbs up to dry. All with the purpose Luke had shared: Didn't the living need to move on?

A week later, Mariah said to her, "I caught a pheasant. Want to help me cook it?"

"You might not want that," Reba admitted. "Herb learned how to roast a chicken from his mother, and she taught me how to *not* burn it."

Mariah laughed. "Then I'll cook it."

She assessed the hearth. If they wanted a fine meal tonight, they'd need more wood.

"Can I help, Mama?" Georgie asked, abandoning his sister, who played by herself and sang off-key.

"Go tell Jimmy to bring me some firewood," Reba said.

With a squeal, Georgie bounded out of the house and tore out into the yard. He returned with his brother not far behind him.

"You needed me?" There were beads of sweat on Jimmy's forehead and dirt caked under his fingernails. He'd spent the morning cutting firewood for their winter supply.

She smiled. "Georgie was supposed to tell you to bring me some wood."

"He didn't. I'll go get you some, Mama Bear!"

Reba looked him up and down, noticing his torn trousers and filthy shirt. "When's the last time you changed your clothes?"

"It's been a while," he murmured.

"The hole in your breeches has gotten bigger," she said. "Your clothes will grow legs and throw themselves into the fire."

With a groan, Jimmy hurried up the ladder. Moments later, he returned in a fresh linen shirt and a pair of dark-blue breeches. As he made his way out the door, she leaned over to kiss him. But before her lips even reached him, her precious son vanished before her eyes.

Annie was still softly singing her song, but once Reba screamed, her voice fell silent. Reba searched the kitchen, but her son was gone. Just like Nelson. Just like Peter. Just like Hiram.

Georgie began to cry, and Annie whimpered before she wailed. Reba couldn't hear them over her own screams.

———

No funerals were held for the missing children. There were no bodies to bury. During that time, Herbert and Reba numbly went through the motions of living. Her beloved husband refused to speak to anyone for two days. After losing his brother and now two children, he had nothing left to say.

Reba distracted herself by harvesting Carrie's corn with the scythe. The jerk and twist of her arms was like rocking her babies while she separated the stalks from the earth.

The Bridge family Bible remained in her chest. The very thought of drawing it out to mark her boy's name inside struck her very soul. Perhaps with time she might find the strength to consider Luke's request.

Buckets of apples piled up in the barn. Little Georgie stuffed his cheeks and gorged himself while Mariah and Reba did what had to be done to preserve the harvest.

Not once did her friend mention what had happened. Mariah let her tears fall, and the woman stopped soothing her when she couldn't stop crying out for Jimmy.

God has punished you, and rightfully so.

If she hadn't prayed for his safety, this wouldn't have happened.

Punishments or not, Georgie still wanted his mother. That afternoon, he drew Reba away from her errant thoughts as he parted her stilled hands to try to climb into her lap.

"Leave Mama be." Mariah reached over to pick up the boy.

George squirmed out of her arms, ran up to his mother, and leaned against Reba to kiss her belly.

Horrified, Mariah snapped, "You're being a pest, Georgie!"

"I'm kissing the baby," the boy said proudly.

Reba's blood ran cold—she hadn't told him yet that his sibling had gone to God. But right then, she felt a stirring in her lower belly. No, it wasn't her stomach but movement in her womb. The child flexed again, its life assured and strong.

She released a long breath and motioned for Georgie to sit in her lap. "Yes, come kiss your mother like you did the baby."

Georgie rained kisses on her cheeks. They were blessings for the baby and her too. She closed her eyes and said a new prayer. A request for forgiveness. Then a prayer for Jimmy—for if Luke's words were *true*, Jimmy had landed somewhere out there. He was still home. That was her only solace. Her boy lived on *somewhere*.

And she hoped someone had opened their arms to welcome him.

PART FOUR

CECILY

Cecily Bridge-Davis

DECEMBER 1924

While conversing with Amelia—no, I was certain she was *the* Emily Bridge—I knew I had to tell her my tale. She had to understand how I came to sit before her in her aunt's parlor and why she had to make the brave, though difficult, choice to alter the timeline to help women like Rebecca, like me, and herself too. Rebecca's meticulous notes had started my journey. Without her entries in the family Bible, I couldn't have retraced my family's steps. I was thirty-nine now—an unimaginable age after living thirteen years in the past. My wrists were arthritic from years of writing, and a few strands of gray wove into the hair at my temples. My journey to reach this seat had been long. I could've despaired over what I'd lost, but the twenty-one-year-old woman peering at me had an opportunity no other Bridge who fell through time would ever receive. She had a chance to live a normal life.

Amelia crossed her legs and the fabric of her navy-blue dress rustled. "You still haven't told me why I should violate the most important Bridge family rule and interfere with the past."

"Yes, it's the reason I'm here." My tea had long lost its heat, but I sipped the drink. "I can't prevent the family curse, but I can change *your* role in it."

My stomach twisted, as it always did when I recalled the revelation I had discovered during that early summer of '64. "Every profound event in world history has a tipping point. A series of decisions can send thousands of soldiers to their deaths. An infection in a small town might bring the world to its knees. Little things can become significant. I've always sought the tipping point for the Bridge family. And at that place of convergence, I discovered my fate and my purpose. It was to find you."

CHAPTER 22

Cecily Bridge-Davis

MAY 1964

For the past month, the letter with Aunt Hilda's last will and testament had added an unbearable weight to Ceci's purse. The handbag glared at her from her desk drawer at work. The weathered envelope's three pages—which she'd committed to memory—poked at her when she ate lunch in the quad between the buildings. On her drive home, after her students' final exams, the bag practically mocked her from its spot on the front seat of her Chevy. To her family, it was a boon, but to her, it symbolized closing a door on kin she'd never known.

The twenty-six-year-old professor knocked her bag off the seat to the floor. After the Chevy's engine roared, she turned on the radio.

There. Much better.

She bobbed her head to the beat of Sam Cooke's latest R&B hit, "Another Saturday Night." The singer always reminded her of her husband, Winston—though her husband couldn't sing worth a damn.

Before she left town for Charlottesville, she had groceries to buy, and her husband had forgotten, yet again, to pay the electric bill. She couldn't resist laughing as she pulled out of the staff parking lot.

"I got it," Winston always said.

For years, her husband had taught electrical engineering at nearby Fisk University. He could recall some obscure, albeit boring, formula at will. Due dates, not so much.

The radio belted out more butter-smooth R&B hits, propelling her from one errand to another. Little Anthony serenaded her through a quick stop at Piggly Wiggly for groceries while Ike and Tina Turner ushered her home up Torbett Street. Her family's quiet street in northwest Nashville was just over a mile from her work at Tennessee State University and the first major purchase she'd ever made with her husband.

Black children darted back and forth between the long bungalows. All summer long, they'd play kickball and baseball, just like Winston used to do in Charlottesville. Back in late '54, he'd been the new kid in town. He was the tall, broad-shouldered boy who graced Burley High School's halls with his slow smile and quiet intelligence. Ceci and Winston had crossed paths at a fall carnival, and they'd been together ever since. Attending college in another state should've separated them, but she never thought they'd come to Fisk together, let alone end up as parents. Didn't life always work that way? Unexpected moments peppered between the menial ones?

She pulled into the driveway and her boys, Jason and Lloyd, slipped out of the house, the screen door banging behind them. Not long after her giggling six- and four-year-old children escaped, Mama Davis appeared, holding her housecoat closed over her thick body.

"I told y'all about slamming that door," she snapped.

The boys paid her no mind. Jason shouted, "C'mon, Barney! Yabba dabba doo!"

"I don't wanna be Barney this time!" Lloyd moaned. "I'm Fred."

As Ceci shut off the engine, she called out the rolled-down window, "Get these groceries now." Their prehistoric play would have to wait a few more minutes.

A chorus of Yes-ma'ams followed her as she grabbed her brief-case and entered the house.

The mouthwatering aroma of a slow-cooked pot roast seeped out of the kitchen right off the living room. Her mother-in-law's favorite soap opera, *As the World Turns*, blared from the television, but Ceci ignored it to trudge over to the desk next to the door. She caught Mama Davis's quick footsteps approaching. It never took long for her small but stout mother-in-law to fuss over her. "Why you got all that food? We'll be fine." She sternly looked Ceci up and down from the opening connecting the rooms.

"Winston and the boys will be all right, but you shouldn't be carrying heavy things." Ceci surrendered her high heels and rubbed the back of her neck. Another day done.

Her mother-in-law gave her a glassy stare. "When you gonna start packing? You about to grow roots at this rate."

"I know," Ceci whispered.

The screen door swung open as her mother-in-law was about to speak again. Winston had a way of arriving at the perfect moment. He strode into the room, his pressed dark-brown suit *still* wrinkled, and glanced at his mama. "What did I miss?"

"Your wife ain't packed a thing." Mama Davis grinned. Mother and son exchanged a knowing expression and Ceci frowned.

Guess her husband's timing wasn't *that* good.

"You've had that letter for weeks now," Winston said. "Did you give your exams to the department head like you said you would? I thought you planned to leave right after class." His bushy eyebrows rose in amusement. Even after a long day teaching, he could lighten a mood with that mischievous twinkle in his eyes. "You could be halfway to Knoxville by now."

"Oh, hush! My department head has the exams, and that land ain't going *nowhere*." Ceci eased onto the family sofa across from Mama Davis's mustard-and-orange floral-print chair while the boys put away the groceries.

"You should go so you can see what's out there. Maybe it'll even be something that can help us." Her mother-in-law gave her a reassuring smile. "That land is your boys' legacy now."

"I'm going, I'm going." All these years, she'd assumed her father's family had left nothing behind. After Ceci graduated high school, her aunt had sold the Ross farm and hauled their belongings over to Nashville. Apparently, Aunt Hilda hadn't sold everything. "I just won't be there for long. I go in, put up a FOR SALE sign, then I come home."

Mama Davis chuffed. "Life don't work that way. Especially with kin you ain't seen for the longest time. How come you ain't seen anyone with they hand out?"

"Good question." Ceci folded her arms and rested her head against the sofa's cushion. She'd shared many things with her mother-in-law, but the moment she'd escaped Virginia to go to college, she'd left the Bridges where they belonged—buried with their secrets.

———

After packing four pairs of pants, five summer dresses, four blouses, and one Green Book, Ceci wasn't finished. She had yet to put together a bag of her toiletries and the two wigs she preferred to wear when her hair wouldn't behave. With care, she added some old family photos, in case she ran into any relatives, as well as her aunt's pearl earrings. Might as well have Aunt Hilda come with her in spirit.

A silhouette crossed the open doorway to her bedroom.

"No, you don't have to come with me." She crammed another lightweight pair of slacks into the bag as her husband's arms slipped around her waist. His lips brushed against the sensitive spot at the crook of her neck. She tried to hide her smile. "I don't have time for that either."

"So you're saying"—he kissed her shoulder—"that I'd keep you up all night long?" His warm exhale set her at ease.

She abandoned her packing and twisted into his embrace. She wished she could bottle this moment—the pleasant tingle of the stubble on his cheek when she rested her face against his, the splay of his fingers spread across the small of her back. She'd remembered these tiny things over the years. She wouldn't take her marriage for granted like her colleagues. They gossiped in the faculty lounge, fawned over the newest hires from the East Coast. She didn't have time for foolishness.

Ceci had a good man at home.

"We could make a weekend of it," he suggested. "Eat lunch at The Midway. Maybe walk down Main Street and see if the Ivory family still owns that bakery with those cakes you like."

To quiet him, she tilted her head up, and their lips met. They were right next to the bed, but she didn't like the way long good-byes trailed after her. It was much easier to live in the moment. Each cry and each laugh over the years could whisk her away into the past, just like H. G. Wells's *The Time Machine*. She had thousands of bottles and she couldn't wait to grow old with Winston to fill many more. She kissed his nose. Breathed in his Old Spice aftershave. He perched on the edge of the bed and settled her on his lap.

After spending many a season rocking toddlers on her hip and chasing after rambunctious boys, a break would be welcome. In a couple of weeks, she'd return to spend a summer of early mornings at the local Negro pool, library visits, and endless episodes of *The Flintstones*.

She had all the time in the world.

CHAPTER 23

Cecily Bridge-Davis

MAY 1964

Traveling alone always had a way of dredging up the past. Especially in the middle of the night. The mind drifted, constantly seeking an anchor to pass the time and poke holes in the monotony.

Ceci trained her gaze on the endless stretch of Highway 40, her fingers flexing on the steering wheel. Stretching her neck repeatedly didn't keep her thoughts from wandering. For the first two hours she sang—whether she liked the song or not. She counted advertisement signs. When the radio stations disappeared up in the Appalachian Mountains, she recited funny lines from last week's *The Ed Sullivan Show*.

This wasn't the first time Ceci had talked to herself, growing up an only child in her uncle and aunt's home. She had a full tank of gas, some spare gas in a canister, and for her safety, she wouldn't stop until she reached Charlottesville in the morning. One of her co-workers had made this trip last summer and warned her to be wary of sundown towns marking the path there.

"There's not a single Black soul for miles in Cookeville," her colleague had said of the small Tennessee town. "Keep your head down and don't stop unless you have to. Those eight hours will be over in no time."

The rain began in the third hour. Ceci had eaten one of the meatloaf sandwiches Mama Davis had packed for her and downed a bottle of lukewarm lemonade. With her stomach full, she only had the shadows cast across the highway from her headlights to keep her company. With the pitter-patter of water hitting the roof and the soft sounds of the Ronettes flowing out of the radio, the Chevy worked its way up and down the narrow mountain passes. The tall pines extended their arms toward the road, their branched fingers seemingly reaching for her.

The forest was a special place—Ceci had fond memories of exploring it with her best friend Winnie as an adolescent. But the part near Bridge land had always been off-limits. Folks gossiped about it from one corner of Charlottesville to another. They whispered over afternoon sweet tea about hauntings and mysterious figures in tattered clothing that would slip out of sight on heavy fog days. Granddaddy Ross, Ceci's maternal grandfather, said they were the souls of Bridges seeking solace from generations of torment. Her mother's sister, Aunt Hilda, was decidedly less empathetic, telling Ceci they were mournful creatures.

When Ceci was fifteen, she overheard from her nosy tenth grade teacher that the widower at the local Negro grocery had married a Bridge, but he never visited his wife's grave nor spoke of her.

Ceci didn't know what to believe, only that she wondered what lay beyond the hidden path her family passed on the way to church in town. Week after week, Granddaddy's rusty Ford sedan tumbled down the road, and she could swear he always slowed at that spot.

Aunt Hilda kept her eyes fixed on the road ahead, but Ceci always had to look. She had to see if she could glimpse one of those ghosts her friends mentioned. Maybe they would appear half alive, half dead, just like the creatures in the fantasy tales she read in those *Amazing Stories* magazines. The very thought brought a shiver of anticipation down her back. Yet to her disappointment, every trip from their farmhouse off State Highway 29 to their Baptist church was as boring as any other Sunday. They left the farmhouse as a family twice per week. Ceci loved to escape the countryside for the neat rows of brick buildings downtown. The movie theater, the ice cream parlor—that's where all the fun stuff was. At least attending church meant she could sit next to Winifred, just like she did in class.

When the Ross family arrived at church, Granddaddy would amble in first, followed by her aunt. Many were eager to greet her grandfather. As a veteran from the First World War, the old man didn't say much, but folks listened when Samuel Ross spoke.

At one Sunday service in particular, sweat beaded parishioners' necks, and ladies fanned themselves to drive away the late-summer heat. The choir's pianist, an older blind woman, caressed the keys to the opening notes of "He Is King of Kings." The melody floated sweetly up to the rafters as parishioners found their seats.

At the far back, a set of pews usually sat empty. Winifred had told her the Bridges used to sit there. Now only unfamiliar faces eased in and out of them.

Questions weighed heavy in her chest, but she never spoke the words out loud anymore.

"Aunt Hilda, what happened to Mama and Daddy?" Ceci had asked the previous year.

That question got her the *look*. Whenever she annoyed her aunt, the woman blew out a long breath and her brow furrowed, the wrinkles creasing tighter until the only thing that remained in the room was the unspoken truth. Her schoolteacher had admitted her mama died during childbirth, but her daddy was another matter. No one ever mentioned her parents in passing. No one shared memories of better times or reminded her to pay her respects at the local Negro cemetery. It was as if they had never existed in the first place. She was a Ross now and that was that.

Ceci and Winnie sat in their usual spot in front of the empty Bridge family pew. Granddaddy Ross worshiped near the front. Three rows ahead of the girls, Aunt Hilda gossiped while the reverend and his deacons conversed at the pulpit. Sometimes they had Sunday school, but since their teacher'd had her baby boy recently, the children fidgeted and squirmed beside their mothers and their siblings. One toddler even made a break for it down the main aisle before his big brother shooed him back with a light swat on his bottom.

Her friend leaned over to whisper in Ceci's ear. "Wanna sneak out again today?"

"Can't." Ceci fanned herself, anxious to escape the heat but locked under her aunt's keen eye. Any moment now, Reverend Williams's wispy voice would replace the piano. The man could never hold her attention. "My aunt said I'd taste that switch if I was out playing in the dirt. Said a young lady shouldn't be getting dirty."

Winnie shrugged, her wide eyes blinking behind her thick eyeglasses. Both wore their Sunday best, and Aunt Hilda would have her hands on her hips and a growing frown the moment Ceci returned with dirty shoes, a wrinkled pleated skirt, or dark smudges on her face. No matter how hard the girls tried to avoid the puddles or mud, the outside stuck to them like those prickly burdocks.

The reverend and his army of deacons stood. The piano's pleasant music ended and, along with it, any hope of escaping the sweltering heat. To Ceci's left, Winnie clicked her tongue in displeasure. At the far end of their pew, Mr. Pruitt's slippery gaze swept up her bare legs.

"Nasty old man." Winnie slowly shook her head.

There were other Mr. Pruitts in the room, many of them smiling and shaking the girls' hands for too long—just like the reverend.

Before Reverend Williams had married his current wife, he was another Mr. Pruitt. The single women filled the seats to listen to his honeyed words, but the church leader preferred to compliment the younger sheep in his flock. As the reverend made his way to the pulpit that day, Mr. Pruitt grinned. Winnie tugged down her plaid pencil skirt and crossed her legs at the ankle.

That didn't stop that filthy, filthy man from leering.

Ceci leaned forward and scowled at him. That man was as old as her granddaddy, yet he had the nerve to wink at her.

Reverend Williams stretched out his greeting, and instead of letting the choir sing, he braced against the pulpit to capture their attention. "The Negroes down in Richmond should've kept Edwin Randolph on their city council, the only Black man who spoke up for us. Over ten years have passed since he warned us. He told us marches and mobilization are the only way to bring about change. Not locally but as a nation."

A chorus of amens echoed throughout the pews. Fans shook with renewed vigor. Winnie scooted toward the end of the pew, a smirk dancing on her face.

Meanwhile, the reverend's voice rose to capture the congregation's rage. Up in the front, Aunt Hilda's hand shot up in agreement.

Granddaddy gave an approving nod, while Winnie edged toward freedom. She had a clear path to the other end—until her mama glanced over her shoulder. Winnie froze.

Caught like a raccoon at dawn, Ceci thought with a grin.

"We need to act," Reverend Williams shouted. "Our children should be in those white schools. The Supreme Court already held their vote. It's unconstitutional for the children to walk past Lane Elementary over to Jefferson."

Claps erupted.

"It's unconstitutional for the children to walk past Lane High School over to Burley."

The fervor rose, and stomps shook the floor.

He paused a moment to make his point. "Inaction is not an option. If not in Richmond," the reverend said, "then in Birmingham, where they shot that boy. If not in Chicago, then in Atlanta, where those innocent girls were violated. Five of our brothers are heading down to Richmond to have their voices heard." He beckoned folks forward with a sweep of his hands, and five men shot to their feet. The Rosses had never protested Jim Crow laws, and yet to her surprise Granddaddy Ross followed four spry-looking middle-aged men to the front.

Winnie was on the move again. She tugged on Ceci's wrist to join her, but Ceci didn't budge, her eyes locked on her grandfather's thin figure among his younger peers. A sliver of fear pulsed through her.

"I am a man," her granddaddy had once said. "I expect a man's dignity. Wasn't that what this country was founded on? Equal rights for *all* men? I gave my body and soul over in Europe, but over here, I ain't no better than a dog." His wisdom always came from his rocking chair or by the light of their lamps. Never had Ceci seen his private convictions manifested in public. "I ain't gonna wait forever to live as a human being. They need to watch out—'cause someday I'm gonna *take* what I deserve."

Once the volunteers assembled, the deacons circled the men to cover them in prayer. Another tug at Ceci's wrist interrupted her thoughts, and she freed herself. There'd be no mischief this morning.

"Why aren't there more men up there?" a nearby woman asked another. "Sam's getting up there in years. Ain't he got a bad leg from the war?"

The sermon, the singing, and the praise kept Ceci rooted to her perch. She didn't feel like singing or clapping. Half of her was trapped in this world; the other half took flight in imagination. Would her granddaddy stand his ground if fights broke out? And if he did, would he live to tell about it?

After church ended, the congregation seeped out into the cooler air, but Ceci didn't welcome the breeze against her face. She hurried over to Granddaddy Ross and took his hand. His skin was dry, yet the grip was firm.

"You listen good today?" he asked, his expression assured.

"Yes, sir."

The Ross family trudged back to the Ford, albeit with stops for prayers for Brother Ross, "to see him on his way to God's work." As they made their journey back toward home, her grandfather pulled off to the side of the road—right at the scarcely marked access to Bridge land. He sometimes stopped at this spot each Sunday. The old man ambled out, leaning hard on his good leg.

"What's he doing?" Ceci whispered to her aunt.

Out here in the woods, only the songs from robins accompanied her grandfather's soft footfalls. He strode out of the sun and up to the birch trees. Did he need to relieve himself? But he avoided the shelter of a nearby bush and marched up the middle of the overgrown path. Gnat swarms and thickets partially hid what lay beyond. He stared down the road for the longest time.

Ceci held her breath, her gaze sweeping from one end of the road to the other. Would a ghost appear in the corner of her eye? Just when she thought he'd stood there for too long, Granddaddy marched with purpose to the trees lining the narrow road, then he yanked away the vines.

"Should I go help him?" Ceci asked. Maybe she'd see something. Her aunt shook her head.

The elderly man revealed what could've been a wooden mailbox. Ceci squinted. Dark-green vines were curled around the rotted post and box. Perhaps they clung to the only evidence the Bridges had lived here. Granddaddy reached into his pocket and took out something shiny. Light briefly glinted off the surface before the object disappeared into the mailbox. He returned to the car, and they headed home.

———

Ceci never returned to see what her granddaddy left behind that day. Nor did she ever get to ask him why he did it. Samuel Ross got in a car with other volunteers to Richmond and didn't come back. Her aunt never told her what happened—Ceci had to overhear the news from her bed when Reverend Williams came by the house two days later.

The reverend's nasal voice bled through the walls. "Our brothers bravely protested at a segregated train station. Brother Ross stepped in to protect the younger folks, but we lost him in the shuffle."

"How do you lose someone?" Her aunt's voice rose with pained furor. "God took my husband in '49 and now my daddy's gone. What do *you* think happened to him?"

"I suspect he was killed," the reverend said. "And we'll never find him."

To escape her aunt's loud sobs, Ceci turned onto her side and faced the wallpapered wall. She counted each nick and notch between the red posies dotting the surface. A single tear slipped down her cheek. Even now, she could still remember every flaw on that wall.

As she drove to Charlottesville, her anguish still trailed after her. The feeling was as real and as vivid as the wall in her mind. Granddaddy Ross wasn't coming home. His fate would remain a mystery.

CHAPTER 24

Cecily Bridge-Davis
JUNE 1964

O n a crisp Monday morning, Ceci trudged over to McIntire Library. Since arriving in Charlottesville, she'd passed the white-columned brick building every day on the way to the county office, but she'd yet to go inside. Maybe she feared what she'd find. It wasn't as if she hadn't buried herself in the research trenches before. She briefly smiled as she climbed the steps, strolling between large clay pots filled with bright flowers. As she entered through the double glass doors, the cool air hit her face and the welcoming scent of weathered pages brought her home.

No matter the location, she'd always loved libraries and what they represented: a galaxy of worlds hidden between the covers. Those worlds had no boundaries, and heroes faced adversity only to persevere in the end.

Ceci weaved her way around the card catalog cabinets. Much had changed. The shelves used to be oak, not these industrial metal ones. The frail wooden chairs were gone. Now comfortable chairs swathed in orange upholstery beckoned the patrons to curl up with an adventure or two. The chairs reminded Ceci of how she'd loved lounging around with the latest science fiction title while Winnie drew in a worn notebook.

Ceci found the crescent-shaped circulation desk at the back of the main hall. A woman manned the special collections counter. The woman glanced up when she approached.

"May I help you?" the woman asked with a thick Spanish accent. The pin on her chest read MABEL.

"I'd like to examine issues of *The Daily Progress* for the years 1938 and 1939. Do you have those?"

The woman's thin lips quirked. "Indeed we do. And back then, the paper released each issue once per month, so your search shouldn't take long. Let me get your machine set up."

Ten minutes later, Ceci sat in front of a microfiche reader. She spotted what she was looking for in the February issue of 1938.

12 SLAIN AT LOCAL FARM, CHILD KIDNAPPED
By Reed Carlson

CHARLOTTESVILLE, V.A., February 26th — Tragedy struck a farm north of Charlottesville. Twelve Negroes, both men and women, were found dead in their homes. There are no suspects. According to the fourteen survivors, a single man's rampage swept across the five homes on the farm as he set fire to the structures, then the assailant kidnapped a child by the name of Owen Bridge, 5. The man fled south and took the child with him. The victims include: Ralph Bridge, 28, Douglas Raley, 57, Dennis Bridge, 56, Ernest Bridge, 45, Ernest Bridge Jr., 19, Alexander Bridge, 26, Audrey Freeman, 23, Ursula Bridge, 65 . . .

A man had murdered her daddy, Alexander Bridge. Ceci brushed her fingers across the name.

She reread the final paragraph not once but three times. A man had murdered not only her daddy, but her uncle, her cousins, her grandfather. She sucked in a razor-sharp breath. Ceci imagined a far grander man than two simple words in an article with an attention-grabbing headline, without photos, and with few details.

Her neck cracked as she twisted in the seat away from the machine. From the other side of the room, Mabel took a step toward her. Ceci's hand rose. She'd be fine, and now she knew how the Bridges had died.

For the next hour, she scoured *The Daily Progress* into 1939 for more details, but nothing popped up. The lack of news left a bitter taste in her mouth. The man who'd murdered twelve innocent souls had vanished. She read the names again. Other than her father, one of the other names stood out. She'd seen it on one of the pieces of paper she'd retrieved from the Bridge family Bible. The 1955 receipt was for the purchase of a suit by a man named Owen Bridge.

———

The yellowed piece of paper had never stood out among the Bridge memorabilia Cecily had collected. For all she knew, it could've been used as a bookmark. The receipt was four by six inches in size. The gothic black-and-white print framing the text in the middle drew her eye, reminding her of advertisements from the late 1800s. Someone had penned in cursive the company's name, Stallworth's, and the establishment's founding date at the top. The upper-right corner was frayed, as if someone had folded it back and forth many times—perhaps to hide the bloody fingerprint underneath.

Back in May, she'd glanced at it a couple of times, then shoved the document aside to browse far more intriguing research materials. But now she flipped the receipt over to read the handwritten text she hadn't scrutinized before: "Found where Owen was taken in Ralph's house in '38. A man left this."

So the kidnapper had left evidence behind. The word "this" had three sharp strokes underneath. There was something familiar about the swoop of the cursive *O* and the precision to the *F*. She'd glanced over her granddaddy's shoulder as he'd written notes as a gardener for one of the professors at the university.

The article didn't mention the Stallworth's receipt. No surprise there. Back in those days, Black folks had to handle things on their own. Not only that, a ludicrous name and date at the bottom of the receipt listed the customer as Owen Bridge, an address in Charlottesville that hadn't existed yet, and a purchase date of October 1955. That would've gotten a laugh back in '38.

It made Ceci laugh too. First, that ancient mailman's tote, found with survival tools in it, which would be a clear help to any traveler coming across it, in any era. Then there were those peculiar family rules on a paper found inside the bag, including "Never interfere with past events." Plus the far-fetched family legends from her childhood, like the mysterious figures in tattered clothes who would slip in and out of sight in heavy fog. Now she dealt with a paradox so stale it could've inspired an episode of *Captain Video and His Video Rangers*. She didn't believe those time-travel TV shows either.

Madness. All of it.

She had other things to do. Spending the day tracing every line and curve on a scrap of paper wasn't a good use of her time when the farm still needed to be put up for sale. If she kept dragging out returning home, she'd have to deal with Winston showing up and hauling her away himself.

The next morning, Ceci headed over to *The Daily Progress* off Main Street to put in an ad for the property. She tried to keep her eyes on the road, but she couldn't resist peeking at the Stallworth's storefront.

I'm not going to stop in there today, she thought. She wasn't about to stir up a hornet's nest over what was likely a mistake. One of the Bridges might have left the receipt in the Bible by accident. She was better off doing what she needed to do. Order the newspaper ad, get the land sold, and get the hell out of here.

Ceci managed to get the ad into next week's paper. She added a skip to her step, pleased she could check off a task from her endless list. But Stallworth's waited down the street. The glass door even swung open, and two customers departed, chatting among themselves. All she had to do was go in there, present the receipt, then have a good laugh when she learned the Bridges were nothing more than pranksters.

She drew closer and peered inside. Every surface in the store had seen better days. The chipped paint on the window distorted the advertising for a flannel suit. Cigarette burns marred the doorframe. And no one had swept the space under the awning in a long time. Ceci hesitated twice, but the unanswered questions pushed her through the door. She'd never have another opportunity like this one. Might as well figure out what it all meant.

Once inside, she approached a man who looked no older than herself. He appeared to fumble through sets of small drawers against the far wall.

"Will be just a moment, ma'am," the man said. "I can't seem to find those fabric shears. Mrs. Booth won't be none too pleased if she shows up for her husband's slacks and they ain't ready."

"I had a quick question, but if you're busy I can come back another time." By "another time," Ceci meant not at all.

"Not a problem." He turned to face her. "I'll find it and get the slacks done just fine. A customer is a customer."

Ceci fished the receipt out of her purse and presented it.

"Well, look at this." He examined the proof of purchase, even turning it around to the other side with her grandfather's note. "Where did you get this?"

"I inherited my daddy's land. While I was looking around, I found this receipt." She feigned a grin, trying to play it cool. "Do your receipts go back that far?"

"Definitely not. How is it so old? And it's got Stallworth's name on it too. Are you sure this was found in 1938?"

"Not really. My granddaddy wrote that note. He died in '53."

"Strange." He scratched the scruff on his cheek. "Did it take a ride in a time machine? Maybe visit them creepy blue people like in that movie from a couple years ago?"

"Sounds about right." She snorted—she'd fallen in love with Rod Taylor after seeing *The Time Machine*. "Your store didn't open until 1951, right?"

"Yeah, my uncle opened the place over ten years ago. The date on the receipt is right, but there's no way this could've been found back in '38. Someone's playing quite the prank on you."

Finally some semblance of the truth. "Yeah, it's probably a prank." She slipped the receipt back in her purse. Time to leave before she embarrassed herself further. "I will take my leave so you may finish those slacks."

They said their goodbyes and she managed a hasty escape.

On the way back to the motel, she couldn't stop thinking about the receipt. Once she returned to the room, she opened the family Bible. Instead of tucking the receipt inside, she examined the roster of her ancestors' births and deaths. Some people, in particular a James Bridge, had a birth date and no death recorded. Instead, the word "gone" was used and repeated elsewhere. At first, she'd thought they died or perhaps moved away, but after talking to the clerk, an ominous idea came to mind. Something horrific had happened to the Bridges, and it bordered on fiction instead of science.

CHAPTER 25

Cecily Bridge-Davis
JUNE 1964

Ceci was drowning in revelations. The slain Bridges, the mysterious receipt, and now her cousin might've time traveled. The errant thoughts left her lightheaded and curled up on the hotel bed's orange-and-brown blankets. A noisy fan tucked in the window opening blew the tepid afternoon breeze across the room and ruffled the papers on the table she was using as her desk. Sounds of Preston Avenue, and the memories they triggered, filtered through. Two blocks down, over on the Fourth Street corner, she'd held Winston's hand for the first time. A week before that, they'd crossed paths at Trinity Episcopal Church's annual street carnival. Ceci had glimpsed him from behind—his wide shoulders and the profile of his turned head as he walked with his friends. The Ferris wheel's flashing lights and the twirling merry-go-round nearly concealed him, but she'd stared, enamored.

Winston always had bragged to others that he'd seen her first from afar. He'd fallen in love before they spoke. But no, she'd strolled around the ride in his direction, telling herself he wouldn't be as handsome from the front. They'd come face-to-face and he'd be like any other boy in town. Her anticipation rose with each footstep. *Can't look too eager*, she thought. But her smile quickly surfaced when his smooth voice bled through the brassy merry-go-round music.

"The Dodgers need to move Jackie back to left field," he'd said to one of the three boys. "He's wasted at third base—"

The other boys from her high school kept walking, but the new boy had spotted her. Unsure what to say, she blurted, "That man is good enough to play *any* position."

Instead of passing her by, Winston darted into her path.

"Is that so?" he said. "What makes a pretty girl like you believe that?"

Ceci stepped around him without a word. His friends stood slack-jawed as Winston trailed after her and they disappeared into the crowd. Over seven days, the two high schoolers exchanged secrets and promises. Winston revealed he wanted to be a professional baseball player so he could take care of his mama. Cecily spoke of her dream to attend college and not end up as some housewife having babies.

"You do things your own way, Ceci," he said. "Don't see any reason why you should change."

Those endearments carried them to a dim corner, away from the glare of the nearby Paramount movie theater, where Winston Davis brushed his tentative lips against hers.

What she wouldn't give to return to that corner. Instead, here she was, lying with doom at her doorstep, cornered by questions.

Ceci forced herself to get off the bed. She paced from the table covered in her papers to the far wall. Three steps there, three steps back. When she returned to the table, her gaze swept over the facts she'd accumulated. The family Bible was opened to the first page and propped up against a stack of books. Beside it, she'd left the family tree she'd drawn the other night. She stared at it, past the arrows from names to notes, past the smudges from where she'd erased mistakes. Each name with the word "gone" flicked at her.

There was a pattern here. Only one child from each family unit disappeared in a generation. And the time travelers were only born of Bridge men and not Bridge women.

Daddy had been born from another Bridge, but he hadn't fallen. His sister Teresa was the one to go--just like his uncle Jonah. According to the "gone" data, each Bridge fell before that age. Did that mean Cecily faced the same fate since she was twenty-six? She slowly shook her head at such an absurd thought, but she couldn't drive it away. The faces of Winston, her boys, Mama Davis, her many friends, flashed before her eyes—what if she lost all of them? But she fought to hold on to logic. In the real world, the technology to support time travel didn't exist. Yet.

To anchor herself in the present, she touched the receipt she'd left on top of the family Bible. The facts stacked up one by one. If her granddaddy's note was *real*, then the receipt was found in 1938 at her uncle Ralph's house—which meant her uncle's home, or part of it, had survived the fires. Only Owen, if he had traveled in time from 1955 to 1938, would've been able to leave the receipt behind. So why did he kill those innocent people, his own family?

And if he took *himself*—how could such a thing be possible?

She shook her head in horror. Logical reasons swam to the surface. That man could've been anyone. A liar. A con man. Maybe one of the Bridges had crossed the wrong person. Back in the day, some folks settled problems with vengeance instead of words. Hadn't Granddaddy Ross gotten into a fight every now and then?

Only a horrible human being would do such a thing. Something terrible must've happened, and this man, this imposter, had exacted his revenge.

———

All folktales had a beginning. Ceci had to find the eager storytellers, the older folks willing to share the oral histories. With ease this time, Ceci returned to the rutted dirt road and approached the half-rotted bungalow. The midday's clear skies revealed a structure surrounded by trees and bits of rusted metal from bicycles hidden among the overgrown shrubbery.

The elderly woman she'd met on her way to the Bridge family land was sitting in the same rocking chair. As she got closer, Mrs. Gladys Hale's hand rose in greeting.

"What you still doing in town?" Instead of the harsh welcome from last time, Mrs. Hale's voice revealed a hint of amusement.

Ceci took another rocking chair facing the front door. The seat groaned but held her weight. Faint gospel music could be heard through the screen door into the house. Since it was late in the afternoon, Mrs. Hale's grandson Lee Lee, who appeared to be no older than twenty, prepared his grandma's supper.

"Catching up on things," Ceci replied. "How are you today?"

Mrs. Hale cast a side-eye in her direction. "You here for supper? Lee Lee caught some catfish and he's making soup."

"No, ma'am. I know this was a long time ago, but do you remember the boy who was taken? The Owen Bridge boy?"

She squinted briefly and batted away a fly. "Course I do. I prayed for God to cover that child in the blood of Jesus."

From within the house, Lee Lee lit a Camel. He shuffled back and forth in the tiny summer kitchen as he minded the meal. The cigarette smoke wafted outside, and Ceci's fingers flexed. She'd quit after she got pregnant with Jason, but every now and then, when her life hit the side of a speeding train, she'd give anything for the bitter taste and relief from a deep drag.

Cecily turned again to Mrs. Hale. "Did anyone ever search for him?"

"Course we did. The ones who'd survived went up and down them woods. They still had blood on they clothes. And they eyes . . . ain't never seen anything like it."

Lee Lee's slow crawl in the kitchen picked up as he ladled soup into a bowl. He emerged from the house and gave his grandma her portion. "Want some?" he asked Ceci.

She shook her head. She hadn't eaten since breakfast, but she wasn't hungry.

Mrs. Hale chewed slowly, working through the soft catfish bites. Between chews, she spoke quietly. "Them Bridges been through so much. Oh, child . . . They were a strange bunch." She slurped her soup. "My brother worked with your uncle up at the university. He said those Bridges were like roses, but like the wild kind."

"What did he mean by that?" Ceci said, rocking back in her chair.

"He said wild roses grow without being cultivated," Mrs. Hale said. "They can sprout up almost anywhere. And if they can grow, they'll survive. Most of them Bridges stayed put and survived just fine, while other families 'round here died off."

"I see."

"When I was a young girl, Sam Ross, your granddaddy, was always roaming up and down these hills. He was a good-looking fella, but he only had eyes for one of them Bridges." She smirked, flashing a row of gums. "A man like him wanted them tiny gals, not a tall girl like me. He was always looking for his little flower, his sweet little Amelia. Said he'd strike gold up in the mountains someday and he'd build a place for them, but that never happened."

She paused to slurp. "You see, some Bridges disappear. And I ain't talking about moving up north. Sam told me he'd heard about the stories from his friend Isaiah. Now that I think about it—that poor man disappeared too. I thought they was tales to frighten us children. I shouldn't have believed him, but who wouldn't want the attention of a good man?"

Ceci nodded, knowing all too well how the teller of a tale was just as important as the tale itself. Shadows crossed the woods in the distance, but she couldn't make out the forms.

"Did you see them up at the farm?" Mrs. Hale paused in the middle of her meal, drawing Ceci away from the past.

"See who?"

The old woman's thin lips formed a small smile. "One of them Bridges. Some of them come back, and I don't mean for a visit."

Ceci stared at Mrs. Hale to see if she was trying to trick her. She had to be. "Come back?"

"That's what Sam told me."

"And Owen . . ." Cecily almost swallowed the words.

"Oh, he came back too, but not like the other ones."

Ceci planted her feet and eased forward in her seat. If the receipt was legitimate, then Owen could've been living in town while she'd grown up. He must've kept to himself. She'd never heard of him before. "Why did he come back?"

"Guess he's drawn to this place." Her patchy white eyebrows rose. "Just like the rest of us. I heard his mama's cousin back in Richmond took him in, but . . ." She smacked her lips. "The devil can jump from living under one house to another. That lady got a bunch of money from whoever left Owen on her doorstep. One would think she'd see to that child, but their dogs ate better. He grew up poor as they come and showed up in town looking like a bum. When was that, Lee Lee?"

"Ten years ago," Lee Lee called out from inside the house. It seemed he'd been listening the entire time. "That was back in '53. I remember 'cause that's when the textile factory had that big accident."

She nodded. "Owen kept saying he needed to be close to his daddy's land."

"Why?" Ceci left her chair and planted herself at the woman's feet. She'd told herself to keep her distance—Mrs. Hale was a stranger. But she had to know why a certain chill had settled in the middle of her back.

"Don't know," Mrs. Hale said, "but I say he knew he was born here, and he had to wipe away the stain. Can't hang new clothes on the line if your house ain't in order."

"Did you hear anything else about him over the years?"

Her face wrinkled. "Not really. He was a quiet boy, and I bet he wanted to buy back his daddy's land. I heard Sam somehow got everything after Dennis Bridge died. Then after your granddaddy was killed, it went to your aunt since she looked after you too."

Ceci returned to the rocking chair, feeling her stomach clench

271

tight enough to snatch her breath. Mrs. Hale had Aunt Hilda's blunt tongue. She could've stretched the truth, but Ceci sensed the hidden threads unraveling from the fabric of the Bridge family's story. If "Never interfere with past events" was indeed a rule of time travel, then her cousin had violated it.

CHAPTER 26

Cecily Bridge-Davis

JUNE 1964

The next day, the world had moved on outside her door, but Ceci still couldn't face it. Once she'd learned the truth about her family's time-traveling curse, Ceci wept until her cheeks were hot and raw, then sank into a numbness and slept. That very morning a woman and her husband, their footfalls light and their voices tinkling like chimes, had lingered in front of her door. They'd gushed about extending their honeymoon another week. How they couldn't stand the idea of being apart once they returned to Biloxi. "Let's go here," the man had said. "Let's see this or that." The promise of a happily-ever-after had floated down the hall and disappeared.

Time sloughed off after that. Each agonizing second fell away, losing relevance and meaning. It was only hunger and the need to relieve herself that finally drove her out of bed, then out of her room. She ambled down the stairs, passing the Carver Inn's receptionist.

"Ain't seen you in a while," the woman said brightly. "You hungry?"

Ceci ignored her and wandered down Preston Avenue. The afternoon heat hit her hard once she left the shelter of the trees. Block after block blurred together with at first residential homes, then businesses. Two Black women leaning against a yellow VW Bug waved her way, but Ceci kept going. Past the busy parking lot outside the Safeway grocery store. Down the gentle sloping hill into downtown. She bought some cigarettes from a vending machine outside of Gleason's Bakery off First Street before she briefly glanced into the window. Laughter and conversation from a Negro man and three children spilled out. If she closed her eyes, she could imagine somewhere in Nashville her husband and children probably spending the day at the pool. Winston would be sitting there reading some technical book while the boys swam. After wrangling the kids at the pool, he often took them to the ice cream shop for a treat.

Just like this family.

A woman carrying her dry cleaning plowed into Ceci. The woman's pillbox hat fell off and rolled until it hit a nearby sedan.

"Hey!" The stranger's face twisted into a snarl. "You shouldn't loiter in front of businesses."

"Pardon me." Ceci's body moved to pick up the hat. After a slew of apologies, her feet carried her a block north up First Street until she finally reached Lee Park. She'd spent over a month here, yet she'd never taken the time to cross the park from one corner to another. Instead of walking through, she briefly soaked in the cool air under the maple trees. *Keep moving*, she reminded herself. She strolled down the wide walkway leading up to Robert E. Lee's monument and considered a path down the steps to the street again, but she plopped down on a bench instead.

The world continued to spin as she lit a Camel and sucked in a deep drag. The smoke was rough on the back of her throat, but a heady feeling circled her chest and her discomfort eased. Nothing like a good cig to take her mind elsewhere. The day thinned like wisps of smoke until she'd emptied half the pack.

Shame she'd started such an expensive habit again. She glanced at the pack in her hand. Might as well toss the thirty-five cents in her pocket into the nearest bin.

"Mrs. Davis, is that you?" an older man's voice asked from behind her.

Cecily turned to see the inn's white elderly porter shuffling in her direction. The man wore the same shirt and slacks every day, but he strode down the corridors of rooms with purpose, almost as if he never forgot his marching orders from the Second World War.

"You got a phone call earlier," he said with a hint of concern. "You're usually up at Hank's eating around this time. What're you doing sitting here all by your lonesome?"

What was she doing? She took in the nearby statue: Robert E. Lee perched on top of his horse Traveller. Two young men from UVA were stationed in front of it, handing out GO WITH GOLDWATER AND MILLER IN '64! presidential campaign pins.

"Enjoying the view?" she managed to answer, however unconvincingly.

"Didn't you grow up here?" He laughed. "Ain't much to see."

There was plenty to see. If she closed her eyes, she could recite the location of every bench and shady spot. She could imagine the cars buzzing past the library on Second Street. All these distractions kept her from picking up a phone to call Winston. She had to say something—and not sound like she'd lost every lick of common sense. Ceci needed *time* to form a plan, and time was the *one* damn thing she didn't have much of anymore.

"Someone called for me?" Might as well get past the pleasantries. She got up and motioned for the porter to join her.

"A gentleman was asking about the Bridge farm. Said he was a serious buyer. Good news, yes?"

So someone wanted the land. That was quick, but then again, Charlottesville had grown since she'd lived here. Who wouldn't want over sixty-five acres for a farm or commercial use? A brief feeling of elation swept over her—didn't a potential buyer mean she could return home and forget about the Bridges? Before the sun set, she could toss her notes into the trash, pack her bags, and jump on the road. That sounded nice. Simple. She didn't have to be present to complete the sale.

And yet somehow she had a feeling she wouldn't see Tennessee any time soon.

———

A winery had made a high four-figure offer on the farm. Ceci couldn't help but imagine the down payment for a newer house back home. Maybe they could set money aside for Jason's and Lloyd's college education too.

All she had to do was sign the purchase agreement, and yet she hesitated up at the courthouse, her hand hovering over the signature line. If she sold the property, there'd be consequences—not just for her but also for other Bridges arriving from the future.

Are those folks out there? she thought. *You're assuming time travel is real.*

Even if a single time traveler didn't show up on the property, the evidence remained. The survival packs were likely still out there, given the many X's on that map. Owen had left a 1950s receipt in the 1930s. She couldn't stop the curse. If she fell through time, she'd end up in an unfamiliar place without the safeguards on the property.

She put down the pen.

"Plans have changed," she said to the buyer's agent. "I'd like a new deal for twenty acres on the northern edge of the property instead of the original sixty-five."

———

A week later, mid-June had swept in as Ceci's Chevy pulled up to the Bridge farm's entrance. The early morning heat coated the countryside with a suffocating humidity, but she had work to do. Thanks to her negotiations, the cabins and apple orchard remained in Bridge hands.

Instead of letting her bones petrify in that lonely hotel room, she settled on clearing the winding path from the main road to the one cabin she'd already visited. First, she attacked the overgrowth around the mailbox. Over a decade of twisted vines and stubborn bushes had enveloped the spot where her granddaddy had stood all those years ago. While she toiled, she listened for the supposed ghosts her aunt Hilda had warned her about. None of the specters ever lent a hand. Didn't matter though. Ceci had hauled manure from their barn to Aunt Hilda's gardens, scraped burned crud from pans, and gutted catfish for suppers. All that dirt under her fingernails meant she'd put in an honest day's labor, and it showed. The patch of land fought back, but soon enough, she glimpsed what she'd been looking for: the remnants of a rusted metal mailbox. Both sides of the box were dented inward as if time and the weather had attempted to expose the secrets inside. However, the flap was shut, protecting the contents through the years.

Carefully, she drew the lid downward. The single screw holding the mailbox door in place gave way and disappeared into the ankle-high grass. She held the door to her chest and peered into the mailbox's depths. A couple of abandoned spiderwebs guarded the prize, but she plucked her find with a joyous squeal. At last! She had it. Once Ceci touched the smooth surface of a rock—yes, a rock—her laughter turned to cackles. She'd done all that work for a cruddy piece of goethite small enough to fit in the middle of her palm. The speckled crystal had a tarnished pistachio-green tinge with flecks of glossy minerals interspersed with rough edges. Granddaddy Ross used to spend hours in his chair on the porch, his wrinkled hands busy polishing his finds with only sandpaper and a melancholic hum from between his lips.

"God created this rock," he'd once said, "but He also granted me the breath and will to change His creation. This circle begins and ends with change."

A fine goethite like this one wouldn't have an emerald's value, but its shine could rival any fine jewels.

She searched the mailbox for a note or any extra clues as to why he had left the rock in the mailbox, but there was nothing. Did Grandpa leave this for someone?

Mrs. Hale's words echoed through her head. "Some of them come back, and I don't mean for a visit."

Ceci slipped the rock into her pocket. Maybe someday she'd learn why Grandpa had left it there.

After far too many hours, she had cleared a path to the house. The next day, a caravan of trucks and cars stumbled up the road, many of them local Black business owners. Carpenters got to work replacing the rotted flooring on the porch. Then Lee Lee's brother showed up. He owned a hauling company. Four of his men got rid of the broken or rotted furniture. Ceci could finally air out the house, but the place wasn't empty for long. Mrs. Hale's niece had passed away recently, and the Hale family needed to sell the poor woman's furniture to pay for the funeral. The table and chairs from the Hales needed minor repairs, but everything else, like the beds, end tables, and dressers, would help make the home cozy again.

Not long after the hauling company had gotten to work inside, a group of high school boys began clearing the overgrowth around the nearby barn, outhouse, and chicken coops. To her delight, she unearthed an herb garden behind the house and a well underneath a stone cover.

"There's still water in there," one of the high schoolers declared proudly. "I can clean it up for more money."

Ceci hid her smile and bartered with the boy until they agreed on a fee. The local boys had found plenty of work on the property and she didn't blame their entrepreneurial spirit. While it would take some time yet for the modern niceties such as electricity and water service, things were off to a good start.

At night, she slept at the Carver Inn, and when she got hungry, she could stroll down the street to eat, but spending the day on her paternal grandfather's land gave her peace. 'Cause thinking led to tears. Sooner or later, she'd have to call Winston and tell him everything, but only after she had enough evidence—which meant more research. And the Bridges still had stories to tell.

Days passed and July snuck up on Cecily. She continued her research until that fateful day when the Civil Rights Act was signed on July 2. After dancing and celebrating long into the night with the guests at the Carver Inn, she slept and woke up with a renewed vigor. She just had to know if she'd find more records about Sabrina in Richmond.

After weeks of research where she'd found little evidence on Sabrina Humbles's whereabouts and work to clean up the Bridge farm, Ceci returned to the Carver Inn. The receptionist stopped her near the doorway.

"You need to reach out to your husband. He says you haven't called him back." The short and portly woman stood no higher than Ceci's shoulders, but the spark in her reprimand tugged her down a peg or two. "Thank goodness he hasn't been calling all over town for you."

"Thank you." Ceci accepted the receptionist's five pieces of paper and escaped to her room. She knew what the notes said. The cutting remarks on them were likely sharp enough to slice her fingers.

Once in the cool darkness of her room, she peeked at them, knowing the reunion with Winston would happen but dreading what needed to be said. She'd learned all she could from Amelia, Sabrina, and Rebecca. Now it was time for the Davis family to learn her fate too.

CHAPTER 27

Cecily Bridge-Davis
JULY 1964

Wow, this place is better than camp!" Jason yelled. Lloyd's laughs followed not long after.

"I wanna see the apples," Cecily's youngest added. "Can we eat 'em?"

"There'll be plenty of time." Winston hauled two bags out of Mama Davis's beat-up Chrysler automobile. The car's rusty muffler had announced their midmorning arrival. "Get on up there to see your mama."

Cecily grinned from a well-shaded rocking chair on the porch, *A Wrinkle in Time* in hand. The Davis boys always made an entrance.

They darted from the car and barreled through the front yard. Jason ran up to her first. She extended her arms and laughed at the sight of Lloyd trying to keep up with his older brother's stride.

"Mom!" Jason called out. "Mom! Mom! Mom!"

She laughed when they nearly knocked her over. Their giggles sprinkled her with profound pain.

"Did you behave for your daddy?" Her cracked voice betrayed her feelings. She forced a smile.

"Yes," Jason replied.

Lloyd gave his usual nod. He kept glancing at the house, probably curious to see what trouble he'd find.

"You okay, Mama?" Jason asked.

"I'm fine. Just happy to see my boys," she murmured. She squeezed them again as her youngest squirmed to free himself. "Why not sit for a bit? Did you wash your face and hands this morning?"

The boy shook his head.

"Mama, can I go look inside?" Jason asked softly.

She peeked at his hands too. Not much she could do. "Go on now."

Today Ceci would let them make mud pies. She'd let them run through the house from one corner to the other, banging pans. After all, they were her boys. She hurried inside after them.

And of course it was Jason who discovered the toys on the kitchen table.

He examined the baseball glove and ball. "Are these ours?"

His little brother didn't bother to ask for permission and scooped up a wooden cash register set. After last Christmas, her youngest always made them stop at the Fisher-Price display. Thanks to a heavy dose of mom guilt, today was his lucky day.

"Go ahead." She turned to Jason as Winston came in. "Surprised you didn't jump through the wall to get to those."

Her husband left the bags near the doorway and strode up to her. He slipped his arms around her, and she pinched her lips together. *Not yet. Not yet.* She couldn't cry yet. Her heart squeezed as she pressed her cheek against his.

Why can't time stop for just a little while? she thought.

To quiet her nerves, Ceci backed away with a short smile. "How was the drive?"

"I haven't been up this way in a long time, and much hasn't changed." Winston's features brightened.

Yes, the world would change, and she wouldn't be here to witness it. To push the errant thought away, she turned from her husband and picked up the bags.

"Mama, can I play outside?" Jason asked.

"I wanna go too," Lloyd added.

"Go on." She turned to Winston. "Are you hungry?" she threw over her shoulder.

"We stopped overnight at Ronald's place and his wife fed the boys breakfast before we rode up here." Winston was staring at her hard. His eyes had formed slits as he leaned against the kitchen table chair. She'd seen that face before when he stooped over his papers at his desk. He was calculating.

"I should still get something started," she said. "Who knows when they'll be hungry."

Ceci's body moved of its own volition, and she gathered the ingredients for a vegetable soup. The work kept her shaking hands busy until Winston ended the silence.

"When did you start smoking again?" he asked. He eyed the ashes in the ashtray next to her notes on the table.

"Not that long. It's been stressful out here and old habits die hard." She shrugged and tried to add levity to her voice. "I'll quit once we're on the . . ." She fished her mind for the next set of words, and they refused to rise to the surface.

Winston pulled out the chair, the sound of the wood dragging against the floor drowning out her inconsistent chops. Even these damn carrots didn't want to make things easier on her. She waited for him to speak—to finish her sentences like he used to do—but he said nothing.

"Did you know that Pronto Pups is still open?" She poured water into the pot and scooped up the vegetables. "And the place where we went on our first date up on Fourth Street and Main? It's still there."

She headed to the cupboard to fetch a stirring spoon, when arms slipped around her waist from behind. The caged panic in her chest escaped its bonds and reared its sharp teeth. Her mouth dried and her eyes blinked as the wall she'd built to protect herself crumbled and fell to her feet. A sob escaped her mouth.

"Whatever it is, I need to hear it, sugar," Winston said.

"I found my daddy. He was murdered."

He twisted her around to face him, but she couldn't look him in the eyes. From where she stood, she'd rather look through the window at her boys playing.

"I'm so sorry, baby," he murmured.

"I'd like to say that's it, but the Bridges . . ." She broke away from his arms and strode over to the portable Coleman stove and turned down the gas. "There's more."

She pointed to a thick manila folder on the table.

"What's this?" He opened the folder and retrieved the first page.

"It's my assertion, and the evidence to support it."

He scanned the page twice, his straight lips slowly opening in disbelief. "W-what is this—"

"Before you ask, just read it. From beginning to end."

Winston Davis didn't move. He stared at her, his eyes poking holes in her demeanor.

"Say something," she bit out.

He looked away briefly. "Anything I'd say wouldn't sound good."

"Try me."

He slowly shook his head, then blew out a long breath. "Do you think I'm a fool? You've been gone all this time, and you show me this *bullshit*?"

The pages in the file folder of "bullshit" fluttered as Ceci's husband thrust it in her direction.

"You've been gone over a month," he said. "Fewer and fewer phone calls. And now you want me to read some report?"

"There's too much to explain, but all—" The tightening in her stomach grew painful and she flinched.

"Page one has a family tree." Winston riffled through the folder and opened it in the middle. "'The accounts of a Rebecca Bridge, which include birth dates and disappearances, corroborate with local census and newspaper articles. A historical record of "Free Negroes and Mulattos" in 1833 shows . . .' Why should I read this madness dressed in sanity's clothes?"

There. That was the question he should've asked. "Because you love me and the unbelievable requires a leap of faith."

Wrinkles flexed on his forehead and his jaw jutted back and forth.

"Do you still trust me?" she whispered.

The weight of that word "trust" circled the room. All Ceci could do was wait.

After a resigned sigh, her husband returned to his chair, and flipped from the first page to the second.

While the soup bubbled in the pot, the stack of read pages grew, but the focused expression on Winston's face never wavered. He went through the papers as if he had to grade them before Monday.

Ceci abandoned the summer kitchen. Unpacking her family's bags seemed best. The sound of pages flipping floated from the kitchen while she tucked away the boys' things in the second bed-room. She avoided looking at Winston's back when she left his bag in her bedroom. Instead of returning to the parlor, she got on the bed and curled into a ball.

Hours later, with the sunlight outside dimming to a honeyed yellow, she woke with Lloyd beside her. She pressed her face against the stubble on the back of his head, just like when he was an infant. Back then, the curls had been softer and tickled her nose.

Tears blurred her eyes. She sniffed and stiffened, refusing to go there, refusing to think about what would be.

A warm hand softly shook her shoulder, drawing her away from the moment.

"What time is it?" she murmured.

Her husband stood beside the bed and glanced at his wristwatch. "Three thirty."

"And Jason?" She sat up, careful not to disturb Lloyd.

"Jason's out in the orchard." He picked up their youngest. "I'll be back."

Winston disappeared around the corner to take Lloyd to the other bedroom before joining her on the bed. It felt strange since he was on the wrong side—he always slept on the right.

"The verdict?" she whispered.

"Now, if I say you're of sound mind—and right now I'm not so sure—you have compelling evidence to support your family's time-travel phenomenon. But for every argument, I can think of an explanation."

Ceci was ready for this part.

"What if the Bible's 'gone' references were fabricated?" he asked. "Your whole argument has no merit without them."

"Some of them could've been fabricated, but why would any-one concoct a scheme at this grand of a scale?"

"Mass hysteria?" His eyebrows rose.

"There's over a century of records," she added, "including newspaper articles from Richmond to DC corroborating the disappearances noted in the Bible."

"'Gone' can mean anything. People *leave*. Folks find jobs or their family dies, and they relocate."

"Yes, people leave, but not at this scale. And all these disappearances are connected to one family line. Isn't that suspicious?"

Winston threw question after question her way, never stumbling in thought, and her brain whirled from the sheer weight of the information she had accumulated. She'd followed the Bridges' lives since they'd bought the land. She knew them. Felt them.

Winston didn't.

"None of this is *real*, sugar." He threaded their hands together, and she bit her lip to keep herself from recoiling. "It can't be."

"But it is." She let go of his hand to touch the freedom papers she kept in her pocket. They were just as real as anything else.

"If time travel *is* real," she whispered, "and we ignore what I showed you, what will happen if it's true?"

He rubbed the back of his head and drew out a long exhale.

"If it's true, then I *gotta* prepare. Just like my ancestors." She leaned toward him to rest her head against his shoulder but then she pulled back.

Her husband slowly shook his head again. "Do you understand how all this sounds from my perspective?"

"Unfathomable . . . I thought the same thing."

"I find it hard to believe you have less than a hundred sixty days until some curse kicks in."

Her birthday on January 5 held new meaning now. "Probably less than that."

He gave an unsteady laugh. "You need to stop doing all this.

You're probably scaring yourself for nothing. We got plenty of money from selling the land. I say we hang out, have a nice extended sabbatical as a little family vacation, and by New Year's, we go home."

So he'd met her in the middle. Now that she thought about it, after reading so many science fiction and fantasy stories, she would've been far less kind had she been in his shoes.

"What about your job?" Her voice trembled.

"I'll handle it. I ain't had much time off since grad school, anyway."

The sounds of the screen door banging bounced into the bedroom. Jason was back. Her husband leaned toward her. The soft kiss to her forehead had to be a peace offering, a promise that everything would be all right.

CHAPTER 28

Cecily Bridge-Davis
JULY 1964

N o more working," Winston said firmly as he took Ceci's pencil.

Her husband folded his arms and blocked the midmorning light shining through the parlor window. Shadows darkened the worktable and hid the scribbled facts and figures.

It wasn't as if she'd returned to her research after he and the boys arrived last week. Every single evening, she clung to her babies tighter than the stubborn ivy crawling up the side of the house. Jason snuggled up to her, while Lloyd would have none of her fussing. Not one iota. She would try to pick up the child and sing *The Flintstones* theme song, but he would escape to go play.

"Don't make that face, sugar." Winston smiled and returned her pencil. "Before you call Hitchcock and plot my murder, we're gonna do something as a family. While you sat petrified in that chair, I went out and grabbed some lunch."

So that was what she smelled. She hadn't eaten yet, only prepared her usual lavender tea for breakfast.

"Why can't we eat inside?" she asked. "I still need to figure out if Emily and Amelia Bridge are the same person."

"Does that matter right now?"

He had a point there. She glanced out the window to see her boys milling about in the front yard. How long had they waited for her? She rose from her seat.

"Let's go." She took her husband's hand, and after Winston retrieved the bag of sandwiches and a picnic blanket, they left the house.

The sky remained murky in spots, but the shade offered shelter from the damp heat. Even with the warm weather, the walk was pleasant. Back when she'd toiled to clear paths, the shrill call from the common redpolls kept her company. Hearing her children's shouts and laughter sounded better than anything.

She used to always hold hands with her husband like this, just like the last time they'd headed up to Michigan on vacation. They'd left the boys with Mama Davis and traded the Nashville humidity for cooler temperatures. One of her friends from the Nashville group of the National Council of Negro Women had spoken highly of Idlewild. How Black folks could swim and lounge with comfort off the lakes or catch a first-class show at the Paradise Club. After they'd arrived, they'd spent the whole time exploring the town from one end to the other. The sanctuary from oppression had left them at ease—enough for Winston's professional demeanor to falter.

Ceci's grip on her husband's hand tightened as she realized how little they'd spent time alone after their academic studies had ended. Once the boys were old enough, the Davises had traveled as a family unit. From the get-go, Ceci and Winston had agreed to give their children the world they'd been denied.

They ventured north now, sticking to the shaded areas along the footpath connecting the glen to the orchard. Jason darted ahead.

"The ground is on fire!" He ran faster and his little brother squealed to hurry after him.

"Fire, huh?" Ceci said with a smile. "And I bet you're safe *under* the trees?"

"Of course. Didn't you play that game?" Winston winked at her.

"We knew better. We stayed in the shade and played in the trees."

Soon enough, the orchard appeared. Many of the trees' branches didn't bear fruit. There were far too many limbs.

"Miss Cecily," Lee Lee had said, "someone needs to come down here and prune them trees. Need to open it up to light and let all that heat out."

At the time, she'd shrugged off his concern. Yet today, as they weaved around the first row, she wished she could've seen her family orchard in its heyday. Back then, the trees would've been shorter, and one wouldn't have blended into the next.

The family discovered an opening to a field on the other side. The stilted breeze tugged at the tall grass and wildflowers. Not far from them, a husk of a home remained partially hidden through thickets and trees reclaiming the land. She hadn't ventured here before, merely sticking to the main cabin.

"Where you wanna eat, Jay?" Winston asked.

"Right here." Jason gave the spot a quick jump.

"Nice and shaded. Good job." Her husband spread out the blanket. "Now, before we eat, I say you gotta pay the Tickle Monster."

Jason broke into a wide grin and backed up. "Oh no."

Lloyd knew the game and bolted. The boys squealed as Ceci and Winston raced after them.

"You're fast, but you're not fast enough," Ceci called out, briefly catching Jason to tickle his back. They ran in circles around the field, in and out of the woods, and finally they circled the old cabin before collapsing on top of the blanket.

Ceci wrapped her arms around Jason. Her firstborn rested his head against her chest and murmured, "Love you, Mama."

"I love you too."

From the other side of the blanket, Winston grinned at them and handed out lunch. "You wanna eat, you need to sit up." He gave the boys a stern glance.

"Can we play some more?" Lloyd asked. The boy had a history— even under Mama Davis's watch—of grand escapes from the dinner table. No more than five bites into his hot turkey sandwich, Lloyd had wrapped up his meal.

"Can I go play?" He even wiped his hands on his pants and sat at the edge of the blanket.

"Don't you wanna sit here with your mama?" Winston asked the boy.

Ceci reached for him, but he scampered off the blanket until the sunshine enveloped him.

Her eldest son inhaled a couple more bites of his sandwich and followed after him.

"You too?" Winston chuffed and stretched out his legs to rest his head on her lap.

"Are you comfortable yet?" She still held her food over his head.

"I will be as soon as you stop waving that thing all over the place." He leaned up and snagged a dangling tomato slice.

She ate her sandwich with one hand and splayed the other across his cheek. Winston reached up with his free hand to run his fingers down her neck. He followed a trail of sweat across her clavicle down to the V between her breasts. His hand came to a stop when he bumped against the pouch she'd wrapped around her torso and hidden under her shirt.

The boys' voices retreated as they slipped through the trees on the other side of the field.

Ceci stared after them, watching the children dart back and forth through the brush. A hush settled over the meadow, and a support beam in the cabin's carcass collapsed with a thud. She couldn't deny the chill down her spine.

"Who do you think lived there back in 1938?" he asked, pulling her out of the moment.

"Not sure. My grandpa Dennis owned all of it then, but he didn't leave—" She swallowed the final word as a vision of Owen storming through the houses came to mind. She glanced away from the structure, but she couldn't help but imagine her cousin pounding on the door. And when no one answered, Owen stormed inside with a gun in hand. Gunfire lit up the house's interior as screams were cut short.

"You good, Ceci?" Winston tapped the hand she had rested against his cheek, then intertwined their hands again.

"Not really." She swallowed against a dry throat. "This place was a haven for the Bridge family, but a lot of horrible things happened too."

"Damn shame."

"It is a shame. Their tragedy was wrapped up in overgrown trees and trapped behind cracked windows."

"But you found it."

"Yes, I did, but if I go, it'll be lost again." Her husband stiffened against her lap, but she kept talking. "I want you to continue my work on the Bridges. I mean it, Winston." She chewed on her upper lip. "When the time comes, I need you to mark my name in the Bible."

"You know how I feel about this."

"I'm serious."

"Can you hear yourself right now?"

She snorted. Reason had trailed after her, mocking every far-fetched theory until only the spectacular remained. "At this point, I want the unbelievable to happen so I can stop doubting myself. I've sat in that house asking myself if time travel could be possible within the bounds of what we understand."

Ceci rambled on while Winston stayed silent.

"I don't know," he finally said.

Neither did she.

"All I do know is anything as big as this needs an observer," she said. "One of my ancestors took on this task, and you're the only person I trust to do the same for me."

Her husband jerked his head in what she hoped was a nod. "I'll think about it."

An hour later, they packed up the blanket, the mood heavier and thick. The remains of the old dwelling loomed next to them, its shadow covering them as they departed.

This time Ceci and Winston returned to the cabin with a gap between them. Their boys walked ahead of them. She promised herself she'd spend the rest of the summer with her children. She promised herself she'd never mention the Bridges or time travel again. As she briefly turned back to the orchard, she promised herself she'd never regret her decision.

CHAPTER 29

Cecily Bridge-Davis
1911

S uddenly, night became day.

Tucked away in the quiet of her bedroom, Cecily fell from midair to the cabin floor. Her head hit first with a thud, followed by her back. Pain snaked down her spine as she squinted at the early morning light breaking between the cracks of unfamiliar curtains. Instead of yellow ones with daisies, the fabric was faded white. All four corners of the room remained the same, and yet one of the room's occupants had defied the laws of science.

It's happened.

Her mind screamed those words on repeat. She was one of them now, the fallen, those who'd time traveled. *Gone.*

Bile surged up into her throat, and she crumpled onto her side to purge her stomach. The bed she'd shared with her husband was now gone, replaced by a brass bed on the opposite side of the bedroom, with the doorway out to her left and the window to her right. The small form of the bed's occupant snored, their head covered beneath a faded blue-and-brown quilt.

Ceci mewled and crawled toward the brass bed, her knees bearing the brunt of the wood floor's knots. The air in the room was far too cold, and she felt naked and exposed in her nightgown. On her way to the door, she crept past a dresser that hadn't been there before. The bed's occupant—a woman, Ceci supposed by the chemises and housedresses strewn on the floor—coughed. Ceci's nose rankled against the foul odors soiling the nearest dress that she picked up, which was a lot more than her half-dressed behind wore. She sniffed. The sour, sweaty aroma would've knocked out a grown man.

Wake up, Cecily. Get to the damn door.

She scrambled around crushed cigarette butts and an empty wine bottle to find her only way out. Dull footsteps approached the door. She stood, her heart racing. The steps halted outside.

The woman under the stained quilt coughed loud enough to shake the bed. Ceci stiffened. Where the hell would she go?

The woman on the bed cried out. Ceci waited for the stranger to rise, but she only sniffled.

"Oh, Lord," she moaned, coughs shaking the bed again. "Please take me home."

The sounds from the kitchen grew louder as someone shifted pots and pans.

"Bertie, come find me," the woman begged.

The clinks and clangs diminished. The footsteps approached the door again, then a soft knock shook the white-painted wood.

"Ma, you hungry?" a girlish voice asked from the other side.

The woman whispered incoherently in response.

"Isaiah is making hotcakes, your favorite," the girl added. "Want to come see?"

Isaiah?

The girl's mother rolled across the bed to the edge. Ceci tensed, watching the woman's shoulders for movement.

Instead of spotting Cecily and throwing curses her way, the woman faced the window.

It was time to get out of here. Now.

Whoever had knocked on the door had retreated, and soon enough, the voices of two people, a boy and a girl, withered away after the cabin's front door swung open and shut. Ever so slowly, Cecily turned the brass doorknob. The tarnished metal squeaked, but the door opened without rousing the bedridden woman. Ceci slipped into the hallway before hurrying through the parlor. All the furniture in the rooms, from the parlor to the summer kitchen, had played a game of square dance. The built-in shelves weren't yet built. Two armchairs now sat opposite the front door. They appeared utilitarian. The kitchen and the parlor's end table held no clues. No notebooks, no newspapers, nor any hints as to the date. Simply a kerosene lamp here and there. From underneath the end table, she snagged a red, threadbare hardback. A quick peek at the copyright page for *Eisner's Ecology* revealed a date of 1895. Based on the binding and faded text on the pages, the book could've been ten years old or more.

Damn it all to hell, she could be sixty years into the past.

She left the book on an armchair and opened the front door. A frigid breeze cut to the marrow of her bone. "Fuck."

Winter had seized the pasture beyond the door, covering the nearby barn and chicken coop in bright yet sparkling snow half a foot deep. Footprints from Isaiah and his sister led northward toward the orchard. She needed to find a survival pack—but how? She needed better clothes.

Ceci glanced at the dress she still had in her hand. The thin fabric was useless. She dropped the dress and scrambled to find clothes. In the bedroom next to the room she had escaped, she put on a man's shirt and trousers. Her fingers trembled as she buttoned up the shirt halfway. *Keep moving*, she kept reminding herself. A set of work boots next to the bed would have to do. They were oversized, but she didn't bother to tie the laces. The Bridge siblings could return at any time.

She couldn't find another coat in the room, so she settled for the quilt over one of the beds. Briefly, she considered leaving something of value for her thievery. She twisted her wedding ring on her finger, but now wasn't the time.

Survival first. Restitution later.

With the quilt draped over her shoulders, Ceci hurried out of the house and followed the footprints leading to the orchard.

The map she had discovered, with its X's for the locations of survival packs, came to mind with vivid clarity. She had to find one of the packs.

Breathless, Ceci shuffled through the snow, searching around the fourth tree in the second row. Nothing. She checked the third row. Nothing. Panic began to suffocate her senses. She darted to the fifth row, where she crossed paths with a lone woman, dressed in a long dark-brown coat and knitted cap at the far end.

Though excuses percolated inside her, Ceci could only emit a squeak. She retreated until her shoulder brushed against a low-growing branch. She twisted to cry out, but found no one there.

"It's all right," the woman said, extending a mitten-covered hand.

Cecily continued her backward march, clutching the quilt tight enough for her fists to go numb.

"If you just got here, you shouldn't be outside. It's too cold." The middle-aged woman didn't question her state. "I'm Ursula. You don't have to speak, honey. I can take you to a safe place."

This woman knew—she was a Bridge. Ceci had scribbled her

name down before in her many notebooks. But this delicate woman, with her thin frame and large eyes, couldn't be real. She would die in 1938, right along with her daddy. Ursula lumbered up to her as Ceci retreated.

"It's all right." The woman edged closer. "You don't want to freeze to death, do you? I live nearby."

Ursula carefully touched her cheek. Ceci shuddered. She had wondered what might happen if they touched—if Ursula's hand could wrestle her awake from this nightmare.

"It's all right," Ursula murmured. "Come with me." She took Ceci's hand and guided her to the other side of the orchard. No more than twenty-four hours ago, Cecily had chased her children here, next to a dead house. More tears fell as she climbed up the fresh set of muddy wooden steps, numbly entered through a door painted in soft red. Cecily felt herself melting, falling away into disbelief. She'd imagined she would be strong. Every time, she'd played out a scenario where she marched to a pack and ran off. She'd never thought it might play out differently.

The inside of the house had a single door to a bedroom, along with a summer kitchen and parlor with chairs and a kitchen table. The home was a bit untidy, except for the messy kitchen. The clutter in the cooking area threatened to spill into the parlor. Smudges from soot and ash darkened the linoleum floor around the cast-iron Acme stove in the kitchen and the odor of rancid grease carried throughout the house. Faded copies of *McCall's* magazine littered the plaid cushioned sofa and chair in the parlor.

Ursula tugged for her to follow. "Come sit."

Her gentle hands drew Ceci to one of the chairs at the cluttered kitchen table. "You can warm up for now." She smiled again, revealing a chipped incisor. "Don't you worry none 'bout saying anything. I can get you fed with clothes and such."

Ceci's blurred gaze followed Ursula as the woman hurried to add a kettle of water to the stove.

She waited for relief. Yes, she'd wake up soon. Any minute now her body would lose all feeling and this reality would float away. The woman disappeared into the bedroom, leaving her to sag into the wooden chair. A bump on the seat poked her thigh—an all too real feeling, along with the faint scent of cinnamon from nearby. The kettle whistled sharply.

Ursula returned to set it aside. Then with soft eyes, she placed a pretty sweater and skirt in Ceci's hands. "This belonged to my sister, Jane, but you look about the same size as she was. Stay right here."

Jane Bridge. Born 1882. The facts came too quickly. She'd spent more time researching instead of with her own family.

"Don't you worry. You can stay here as long as you need to." Ursula wiped at her damp cheeks. "It's okay to cry. God hears your pain."

No one heard her pain. No one could make this better.

For the longest time, she cried at the table. A clock on the other end of the room struck nine. Then ten. She kept stealing glances at a newspaper on the other side of the table.

If she snatched it, she'd know the truth.

If she ignored it, perhaps she'd wake up.

After a deep breath, she reached across the doily-draped table and slid more *McCall's* magazines to the side. From the bottom of the pile, she withdrew *The Daily Progress* she'd seen. One of the January 19 headlines read, "A New Novel by Miss Ellen Glasgow." She blinked as she recalled watching the 1942 movie made from Glasglow's award-winning book *In This Our Life*. Through her tears, the stencil blurred again and those four numbers, 1911, remained in the aftermath. Winston wouldn't be born for another *twenty-eight years*. And if, *if,* she ever held her precious boys again, she'd have to wait nearly fifty years.

Fifty damn years.

The seconds, the hours, then the decades ahead punched the middle of her chest. She tried to inhale and stuttered.

So much lost.

Her right to vote, gone. And the Civil Rights Act that Lyndon B. Johnson would sign was also over fifty years away.

"Breathe, honey, breathe." Ursula's words bled through her din. "The good Lord saw fit to give you breath. Use it."

What good would your breath do if you'd left your heart fifty years in the future?

CHAPTER 30

Cecily Bridge-Davis

FEBRUARY 1911

Ceci didn't know how long she stared out the parlor window. She'd slept on the armchair with her neck bent in surrender, her eyes dried empty, and her soul scraped raw. Thankfully, Ursula passed through the rooms like a ghost. During their meals at the tiny table, the woman chatted about her day, but she never pushed Ceci to speak. Nor did she quiet Ceci when she cried again.

Meanwhile, the outside changed. The sun rose and set. The snow gave way to spring rains, then a summer heat wave. She would've welcomed rain rather than sunshine, but the swimming pool weather persisted, perhaps mocking her pain.

None of this could be real. The green-and-gold rug Ursula traipsed across every morning didn't resemble the antique one from her aunt's home. The two children who crossed the glen in front of the house weren't Amelia and Isaiah Bridge. Those names were faded ink on a piece of yellowed paper. They were ghosts.

And yet here she remained as Ursula roused her from the seat. "Got to work for your breakfast this morning, Miss Meg."

Ceci slowly shifted in the chair after hearing the name she'd supplied to Ursula not long after she'd arrived. Choosing the moniker from the heroine of *A Wrinkle in Time* seemed apt. She shifted again, her limbs creaking from the lack of movement. She ran her hands over her hair, finding the coarse curls matted and parched. Her host zipped from one side of the house to the other, opening the curtains in the summer kitchen.

"C'mon now." Ursula poked her shoulder. The woman's quick steps meant business. "You fending for yourself today."

"Yes, ma'am." Ceci's words held no weight. The sorrow sticking to her bones tugged at her to stay in her chair, but somehow she rose.

Step by step. Slow breath in, slow breath out. That was how she washed her face. Slipped another woman's leather boots—those had belonged to Jane too—onto her feet. Ursula waited by the door, her stern gaze never wavering.

"We're gonna scoop the molasses out of your slow-cooked porridge this morning." The woman giggled with a hint of a smile.

Fully dressed, she followed Ursula out the door into the high humidity. The Bridge farm always had a tranquil underpinning. Beneath the rolling hills and flecks of trees hid the unseen threat of time.

Ursula stormed through the darkness, a sweet hum from between her lips as they trudged around the house. Two structures, an outhouse and a chicken coop, had replaced the empty field she'd walked across with her family. Chickens milled about the A-frame coop, squawking and skirting away at Ursula's arrival.

In the future, a young Ceci would trail after her grandpa Ross to another coop to gather eggs. He'd towered above her, and his tin bucket of feed had swung with each step. His birds, which had the strangest names of Chicken Pot Pie and Chicken-'n'-Gravy, had harassed Ceci at every opportunity. The most evil rooster of them all, who lived well into old age, had been aptly named That Bastard Bird.

Ceci held the warm eggs and smirked at the thought of that damn bird, hounding her as if she dared approach the coop. Those were the good old days.

"Looks like you got one." Ursula grinned. "Time to cook these." She gently tapped under Ceci's chin, then gestured to her own small basket.

The minute the pair returned to the house, Ceci's steps slowed again. The chair beckoned her like a throne in need of a ruler, but Ursula pressed her tiny palm against Ceci's back.

"Can't wait to fry these up," she chirped. "Oh, the smell gets me every time."

Ceci managed a nod.

"How do you eat yours . . . where you're from?" The woman pushed a bit harder to quicken Ceci's arctic shuffle. "You seem like a fried-eggs-and-ham kind of lady. My grandmama loved some buttered ones."

Ursula left her standing in a corner of the kitchen while she fussed over her Acme cooker. She opened the stove's feed door and added bits of wood. Over the past couple of months, Ceci had watched the woman ignore the grime and old grease caked on the stove.

"Can't stand filth," Aunt Hilda always used to say. "Might as well set the table on a filthy floor."

Speaking of floors, on the way inside, Ursula had tracked her muddy footprints all over the checkerboard linoleum.

"Can you believe my grandmama added scoop after scoop of butter and sweet cream? Then that woman put all that on *top* of some bread." Ursula sucked air between her teeth as the butter sizzled in the cast-iron pan. "Granny should've ate a bowl of cream and been done with it."

She turned around to reach for the eggs Ceci held. "Do you like cream?"

"Yes, ma'am."

"Good, 'cause I love it." Ursula freed the eggs with a practiced *thwack* and sprinkled salt and pepper on top. The abandoned shells left a gooey pile on the counter. Ursula ignored it and began to sing.

"Put your arms around me, honey," she crooned. *"Hold me tight. Huddle up and cuddle up with all your might."*

Ceci glanced from the mess on the counter to the woman. Finally, she crossed the kitchen in two strides and gathered the refuse. A buoyancy in her gait she'd missed added strength to her steps as she tossed the shells into the compost bucket behind the house. Then she picked up the broom from the kitchen corner.

Ursula swayed to a beat only she heard, singing in a pitch higher than Little Anthony could ever achieve. *"Oh! Oh! Won't you roll those eyes? Eyes that I just idolize."*

"What are you singing?" Cecily swept up the crumbs hiding along the floor next to the counter.

"It's called 'Put Your Arms Around Me Honey.' Isn't it great?"

"Sounds wonderful." She wished she meant it.

"Music and the good Lord above make me happy."

Music used to make her happy too. She'd never hear the Ronettes again, never dance to Ike and Tina Turner's music either.

"Where did you go?" Ursula touched her shoulder. "I was getting to the good part."

Somehow Ceci had returned to the seat in front of the window. "I got tired," she admitted. "Do you need anything?"

"Why, Miss Meg, I had you up a moment ago. Would you like to sing with me? We can pick a different song."

"Not right now."

"Fine then, but you're gonna need to rest up if you wanna get out of here," she said softly. "A cousin of mine is heading into town at summer's end, and I know Dennis wouldn't mind if you came along. Want to get out for a spell?"

At the mention of her grandfather's name, Ceci's heartbeat sped up. She had yet to see him or her daddy. Why hadn't anyone crossed Ursula's doorstep since she'd shown up? After Ceci had arrived, the clothes and quilt she'd stolen had disappeared—most likely returned to their owners.

"Do you want to go or not?" The way the woman tilted her head, Ceci would've thought she was one of those parakeets.

"I'm from the future . . . Would that be wise?"

"You'll always be from the future, honey," Ursula said. "Are you gonna run into yourself?"

"No, ma'am. I likely never will."

Her nostrils flared from a delicate sniff. "Then it don't matter. You got living to do."

CHAPTER 31

Cecily Bridge-Davis
AUGUST 1911

The morning brought apprehension and an endless curtain of rain. Thick clouds outside the parlor window promised Ceci's trip wouldn't happen any time soon. She folded up the blankets from her pallet near the stove and prepared a pot of hot water, all for her grandfather's arrival. She imagined him striding through the rain up to the door, his hat dampened from the storm and his face covered in a sparse beard.

"How long you been awake?" a voice asked.

Ceci turned to see Ursula in a white nightgown with a shawl around her shoulders. This early in the morning, strands of her white and black hair had escaped the three braids she'd tied the night before.

"Not long," she lied. "The storm woke me up."

"You usually sleep in." Ursula turned around to plod over to the kitchen. "Not much of a storm, if you ask me."

"No, it isn't. I've seen horrible snowstorms in these parts."

"Indeed." Ursula paused to give her a once-over. "Are you sure you want to wear those clothes into town? That old thing?"

Not long after adding a bit of kindling to the stove, Ceci had washed up and put on one of the housedresses the woman had given her. The back hem had frayed and the flowers on the bodice had faded, but the clothes fit right.

"It's clean," Ceci replied. "I can buy something new once I sell a few things."

"You could buy something when we're in town, but when Bridges go to the Lord's house, or elsewhere, we look our best."

She'd been wearing two of Jane's housedresses while washing her underwear daily. When she added what Ursula had called "that strange contraption on your chest" to the wash, she considered burning it, but she couldn't part with it. The woman had yet to offer her anything else to wear, and it was time for her to get her own things. Especially since her host was far too short and Ceci couldn't fit into any of her hosiery.

Cecily rose from her seat. "If there's a Negro business that buys goods, I have some pearl earrings to sell."

Ursula looked horrified. "Now, why would you need to sell your valuables?"

"I need the means to take care of myself . . ." Ceci trailed off.

"Hmph." Ursula flicked her fingers to motion for Ceci to follow her into the dimly lit bedroom.

She plodded after the woman. A single kerosene lamp illuminated one of the corners. Like the rest of the house, the room was untidy, with clothes scattered across the floor and knitting materials strewn over one side of the double bed.

The first time Cecily had come in here, she wondered what kind of life Ursula Bridge had led before Owen killed her at the age of sixty-five. Had the woman slept next to a husband on this bed?

Had she comforted her grandchildren on long afternoons in the kitchen? Ceci had discovered no evidence of a man, nor any children's clothing, only the remnants of Ursula's sister, Jane, stowed away in a cedar chest.

"My sister left everything behind," Ursula murmured. "Brushes. Jewelry. Her clothes are old but well made." The woman strode through the room, checking the drawers in a bureau, then she shifted her attention to the cedar chest under the only window. "I'll never forget the day after she left. Daddy kept crying while Mama kept cleaning. Nobody wanted to collect Janie's things." Her voice receded to a whisper. "Nobody wanted to remember how much they missed her or how they were hurting."

"Are you sure you want to give this to me?" Cecily asked.

"I thought it would be easy to take out a couple of things, you know, a dress or two, but I don't have the heart to do more myself, to be honest. Lord knows I tried."

From the depths of the chest, Ursula retrieved thin outer garments and what appeared to be a corset, the color of an old pearl. "All this belonged to my sweet Janie," she explained.

Ceci stared at the clothes, recognizing the shirtwaist top and ankle-length skirt from older black-and-white photos, but she'd never studied what the women back then had worn underneath. She'd never considered how they put them on or how they kept them clean.

"How do I . . ." she began to say before Ursula fussed at her to take her housedress off. It didn't take long for Ceci to abandon her bra for the corset and a chemise made from stiff cotton and linen. Jane had had a wider waist but narrower hips. With effort, Ursula adjusted the straps until Ceci had an ideal fit.

"Look at you." The woman backed away to admire her work. "Now let's get you into this blouse and skirt."

By the time Ceci was fully dressed in a shirtwaist and navy skirt, her heartbeat quickened at the thought of finding a mirror to see what she looked like.

She touched the lacy bodice and thought, *This is my life now. These are the clothes I must wear.*

Ursula sniffed in her direction. "Smells a bit musty, but it should be fine." She blinked and turned away.

As Ceci waited, she wondered what her boys were up to. If they were searching for her, hoping for her return.

She forced herself to speak. "I really appreciate the clothes."

"They're already here. Why waste them?"

"But they remind you of her. I can tell."

"People come and go, Miss Meg. They're born. They die. We can't change that."

No, Cecily couldn't change that. Not far from where Ceci and her family ate their lunch, Ursula's house remained, but the woman had been long gone. Briefly, Ceci considered telling her what would happen twenty-seven years from now. The Bridge family rule to never interfere kept her mouth shut.

"No matter what, I need to repay you for everything you've done for me," Ceci said.

"Repay me for what? For taking care of *my* family? That's what Bridges do."

Cecily's gaze hit the window and the rain beyond. The corset pushed her back to straighten. "I feel so damn empty. I'm getting nothing done, and I don't know how you've put up with me."

"I ain't put up with anything." Ursula surprised Ceci by drawing her arms around her. She had to stoop to accept them. "After my sister left, I prayed and prayed for her to be comforted by a woman like my aunt Leah."

Ursula rocked a bit and Ceci swayed with her.

The woman murmured, "Back in those days, my daddy's sister was the strong one. Little did I know, when I thought my auntie was ignoring how hungry we were, she was hiding and giving *her* food to one of the fallen. And once they were ready, they moved on."

"Did you ever find out who it was?"

"Never did. Aunt Leah believed, like I do, that the Bridges have an obligation to shoulder the burden you're experiencing right now. I can't lessen your pain, and you're gonna carry those wounds until you return to the Heavenly Father." Ursula stroked her back like a mother would a child. "But I can get you out of that chair. Do your hair. Feed you a hot meal. Janie would want me to do that."

Ursula smoothed back Ceci's Afro and chuckled. "This head needs some help, child."

An hour later, the woman finished straightening Cecily's hair with a hot-pressing comb in the summer kitchen. It had been over ten years since she'd sat in Aunt Hilda's parlor for a similar treatment. The burned-hair smell and head twisting transcended time. Ceci ran her fingers through her shoulder-length curls and let out a long breath. There'd be no more wigs for a while. Not the kid she'd recognize.

"Now you look like you have purpose," Ursula remarked.

"What do you mean?"

Ursula cupped her cheek. "Your purpose now isn't to take Jane's place but to move on from it."

———

Ceci saw puddles had formed in the patches between the tall grass as she opened the front door to glance outside. One thing she knew for certain was that wagons these days didn't do as well stuck in the mud. All she could do now was wait.

By the time the skies had cleared, she resigned herself to taking off her nicer clothes and returning to scrubbing the laundry, but Ursula peeked outside and declared, "Time to go. He should be waiting for us by now."

Ceci must've frozen in place, for Ursula added her hands to her narrow hips. "We can't get out of this house unless you start moving them legs. C'mon now, Miss Meg."

All she needed was one "C'mon now," and the skin on her cheeks cracked from a wide grin. Ceci picked up a velvet clutch purse and reached inside for something—she had to remind herself car keys wouldn't matter for another forty years.

The two ladies had to make their way along the footpath from Ursula's cottage through the orchard. From there, the path wove through a glen to the house she'd arrived from. A copse of trees hid a cabin and a delivery wagon in the front, but bits of color from the home's red shutters bled through the birch trees.

The pitter-patter of raindrops falling from the canopy of birch and elm trees accompanied them and quieted Ceci's fast-beating heart. She stared through the trees, attempting to pierce through them to spot the house and its occupants on the other side. The person she truly wanted to see perched on the edge of the delivery wagon's driver's seat. A sign attached to the side was painted with the words BRIDGE MASONRY.

Was that *him*? She considered asking Ursula but held tight to patience. A couple more minutes wouldn't matter. She slowed down to stand in the woman's shadow. As she drew closer, the man's features came into view. She had his high forehead and full cheeks.

Right around this time Dennis would be about thirty years old—he was practically her age, a grown man with a wife, two young children, and a newborn.

She stared at him until she seared his likeness into her memory.

As her boots sank into the wet earth, Ceci thought about how every single atom in her body had traversed not millions of miles but a couple hundred yards to reach this point. Everyone else traveled from one place to another while trapped within the boundaries of time. She'd escaped the temporal dimension to witness this moment.

When the man spotted the woman in front of her, he tilted his head her way. "Mornin', Miss Ursula. I thought I'd have to send Isaiah over to fetch you."

"Not necessary," she replied crisply. "I knew you had business in town. Whether it's snowing or raining, Dennis Bridge finishes what he starts."

Cecily stood off to the side, her gaze resting on the rutted mud from the wheel tracks. She nervously touched her upswept hair and smoothed down her skirt.

"Dennis, this is my friend Miss Meg. She came this way from down in Nashville."

"Miss Meg." He jerked his chin in greeting, then extended his hand to help her into the wagon. The bed had a row of seats on one end and bags of supplies on the other. Dennis had a strong grip and guided her up the side step.

"How are you this afternoon?" Cecily managed to say.

"A bit tired," Dennis admitted, "but I got a new baby at home."

The year was right: 1911. Her father had been born that spring.

Once Ceci and Ursula were seated, Dennis set off for the main road. The wagon jostled and slipped over the uneven road, but the two Bridges chatted about the rainy weather while Ceci kept stealing glances at her granddaddy's back. She wanted to ask where he lived on the property, what his wife and children were like.

Ceci shifted her focus to her new home. The narrow path leading from the Bridge land opened onto a mud-slicked road. A single mailbox, this one dark green with chipped paint, marked the spot she'd visited before.

Seeing the unpaved road felt surreal, as if someone had smeared the present into the past. They rode for a while before a bungalow appeared along the road. That place would be long gone in 1964. More country farms appeared and vanished. Roads weaved slightly left or right compared to the last time she'd driven her Chevy up and down these hills.

Once they made it downtown, she understood—yet couldn't fathom with her own eyes—how much had changed. Jefferson Elementary still stood on the same spot on West Main Street, while the Paramount and Pronto Pups weren't there, of course. A part of her expected to see all the modern vehicles—the Chryslers, Chevys, and Fords—but they had been replaced by chugging, noisy Model Ts. It was as if she'd stepped onto a movie set.

As they drew closer to what should've been the city park, she counted each cross street, waiting and hoping for the open field and Robert E. Lee's statue.

But it was all gone.

"While Dennis handles his affairs," Ursula said softly, clutching Ceci's hand, "I want to treat you to lunch."

"I'd like that."

Ceci's granddaddy dropped them off in front of Smiley's Eatery off Preston Avenue. As he helped her off the wagon, he said, "The folks here make the best meatloaf, but their biscuits ain't too good."

She thanked him, wishing she could say more before he drove away. She hurried down the damp pavement after Ursula into the restaurant. Black diners, eating their afternoon supper, nearly filled the six tables. Ursula didn't wait to be seated and headed to the back. Instead of picking an empty table, she took a seat across from a well-dressed gentleman in a striped, dark-brown sack suit and black Homburg hat. Ceci sat in the free chair to Ursula's left.

"I've been waiting for four hours," the man said stiffly.

Ursula dabbed away the sweat on her cheeks with a handkerchief. "And you would've waited even longer with all this rain, Ozzie."

The man shifted toward Cecily, but Ursula interrupted him with a shout to the waiter. "Two afternoon specials, please."

"Sis, I need to catch the evening train," the man added.

"And you'll catch it. Miss Meg hasn't eaten out since her arrival."

The man frowned and inclined his head in her direction. He appeared to be in his mid-thirties and had a refined edge to his words. "Forgive my sister. I'm Oswald Bridge."

"Margaret," Ceci said, slightly distracted by the goings-on in the eatery. "I'm Margaret Murry."

"Well, Miss Murry, I wish I could say welcome, but I suspect you'd rather be elsewhere."

"That's an understatement."

Ursula reached under the table and gripped Ceci's knee. "She's here and she'll be fine. What can your friends do for her?"

"Not much, but I'm working with other Bridges who have means. They've formed a collective of sorts to secure funding to help the fallen and those left behind."

Now the conversation had her attention. A waiter arrived with glasses of water. A hush fell over them until the man left.

"So far, we've helped five gentlemen resettle in DC, where I'm living now as a physician," Ozzie explained. "Others have found jobs in town, or we've paid for their transportation elsewhere."

Ceci took a slow sip of her warm water. During the long hours that she'd stared out the window at Ursula's house, she'd often thought of what she'd do next, but none of her plans was concrete. She wasn't supposed to exist yet. She was no one.

"Whatever you'd like to do, it's important for you to not reveal your true identity or anything of the future," Oswald said. "We will help you find a new name and secure the necessary government registration."

Ceci's and Ursula's food arrived. The waiter placed a steaming platter with meatloaf, country-style potatoes, and french peas on Cecily's place mat. The sad biscuit on top of the peas had charred edges. Even gravy couldn't fix a stony biscuit. Ursula got to work sampling the food while Ceci turned to Ozzie.

"You were saying?"

"In order to adapt," he began, "you'll need a trade."

"Before I . . . came here, I taught history at a university."

Oswald's face sagged. "You were a professor?"

Tennessee State hadn't been founded yet, and the likelihood of someone hiring her at another university was low.

"I can speak with my associates to see if anything is available nearby," he said, "but you may have to start out as a schoolteacher."

"I need to work." Ceci had to force herself to pick up her fork and knife. She stirred the peas around before she took a bite of meatloaf. It wasn't too shabby. A bit salty, like Mama Davis's food, but the very act of eating food in a restaurant gave her a moment of clarity. She had twenty-seven years to come up with a way to change events just enough so Owen doesn't end up murdering her family. But before she could do that, like Ursula had said, she had living to do.

Oswald spoke to his sister. "Do I need to say it?"

"Say what?" Ursula didn't glance up.

He reached into his suit pocket and fished out a couple of bills. He slid them across the table. "Get Miss Meg some new clothes. She can't be wearing Jane's."

His sister stopped mid-chew. The look she gave him was laden with daggers, and after swallowing, she said, "You been swimming too long with the rich fish up in DC."

"Here we go."

"Jane's clothes are old, but they look perfectly fine."

"You know that's not what I'm saying, sis."

"She needs to *save* money right now."

"Miss Meg can still do that, but I'm talking about *you*."

"I swear, Ozzie."

"It's been almost ten years. Give those clothes to charity—"

"It's that easy, huh? Just toss 'em out with the trash, and maybe I should move up north too? Is that how I'll *forget* her?"

Oswald's impassive face briefly revealed his frustration. "You always know where to cut deep, don't you Ursula Renee?"

She didn't reply and stabbed the meatloaf. The metal fork hit the plate with a loud clang.

He added, "Putting me in my place won't bring Jane back."

"Nope," she said with her mouth full. "All you had to do was come down here and help. I know what I need to do."

The siblings continued their conversation in hushed voices. Ceci put down her utensils and placed her hands in her lap. The cottony material of the skirt—Jane's skirt—was smooth to the touch. Such a simple thing roused festering wounds. Those two sounded as if they could go back and forth all day, but Ceci didn't have to listen. Somebody had to move on. Might as well be her.

"If you'll pardon me," she said softly, "I need some fresh air. I'll be right back."

Ursula nodded as Ceci grabbed her clutch and left.

Once outside, she stared down Preston Avenue. Past two little Negro girls playing jacks in front of a house-painting business that would be a Safeway grocery. Past the Wood Carriage Company and the King Florist Shop. These storefronts were before her time, her previous time. They held no memories and meant nothing to her.

An older man driving a cart full of flowers pulled up next to the florist. Two women spilled out of the shop, a shower of Italian preceding them. They greeted the gentleman before he got down to unload the goods. As he worked, the scents of chrysanthemums and roses floated down the road. Aunt Hilda had loved late-blooming flowers.

"Ceci, there's nothing better than mums," her aunt used to say. "No matter the weather, those pretty little ladies keep their secrets all summer only to share them come fall."

A wooden box stuffed with yellow chrysanthemums tumbled from the back of the cart. Petals sprinkled across the road. The driver picked up the parcel, but a bunch of flowers wrapped with twine remained in the red clay dirt. Half in, half out. Abandoned and forgotten.

Ceci took a step forward—only to turn back to the restaurant's window to see her wide-eyed reflection staring back at her. She could go anywhere, but without thinking, she set off south down Preston until she reached her first four-way intersection. With no street signs to guide her, she let her memories from '64 tug her down what had to be Main Street. From there, her pace and spirits picked up. She counted the blocks. One. Two. Three. At the fourth intersection, she looked around, her soul as invigorated as her body. White children played tag in front of an Italian grocer while across the street a couple left a bakery. Not a single detail reminded her of her time, and yet she could feel Winston approaching from Fifth Street. He'd have his hands stuffed in his jeans pockets and a wry smile on his youthful face.

Her glove-covered hand brushed against her lips. She swore she'd never sit and wait. Somehow, someway, she'd see Winston again.

CHAPTER 32

Cecily Bridge-Davis

DECEMBER 1924

Around this time of the year, when the snow fell and families adorned their mantels with holiday trinkets, Ceci always told her students to reflect on the past for the sake of the future. None of them knew how deeply she did the same.

Within the quiet of her private room at a boardinghouse not far from Howard University, she packed her trunks to the crackle of the fire in her fireplace.

She used to hang up three socks in the hope Santa Claus would return her family to her, but lately she'd hung up something else on the wall next to the fireplace: her plans for Amelia Bridge. Ever since she'd identified the young woman, Cecily had covered a large swath of wall with her past research. Most of her notes and records from 1964 were still there. Over the years, time had both muddied and clarified the waters of memory. But as Ursula had predicted, she'd learned to move on. Her journeys had taken her to Chicago,

New York, and then finally Atlanta. From there, she'd heard of an opportunity to teach classical history at Howard University.

Right next to her chemises, she added her suffrage sashes. She didn't need them anymore, but the marches, along with the times she'd listened to great orators like Marcus Garvey and Ida B. Wells, were one of the things she cherished.

Her attempts to change the past, not so much. In 1917, she'd sent a sum of money to Owen's parents to improve their situation, but nothing came of that. Last year, she'd even written a letter to Ursula, explaining what would happen in 1938. The letter had been returned to her unopened. Either the murders couldn't be prevented or she had to take drastic measures in the next fourteen years.

And then she met Amelia Bridge a couple years ago. Once she'd confirmed her suspicions about her former student, she'd spent many long nights planning a new timeline. This change had to be *big*. Bigger than a letter or a grandiose confrontation.

Based on the data she had gathered, the curse had always been with the Bridge family like some peculiar mutant gene, from Zachariah all the way down to his descendants. It simply had manifested itself in 1817 with Nelson, Hiram, and the others.

But Luke was different for some reason.

As to why his fall had happened forty years before the others, Ceci didn't know.

What she did know—based on Luke Bridge's attempt to alter the timeline—was one change had the potential to make an impact in the future. Amelia would always have to go back in time since she was her own descendant, but if a small change were made far enough back, every event afterward could be slightly different.

For example, Emily could avoid having Luke. She could live a fruitful life, and her descendants, including a future Amelia, would time travel to a different sort of life. The family would adapt like before, but the legends of Luke and Emily would be replaced by something else.

The first step would be convincing Amelia to go back in time somewhere other than the Bridge farm in Charlottesville. Pretty soon, Amelia would turn twenty-two. All Bridges fell before twenty-seven. The girl might have a couple more years left in the 1920s, but Ceci believed Amelia's fall could happen any time now. Her student could go all the way to Maryland or Massachusetts, but she might not make it. The woman's best bet was Pocahontas Island, an early Negro settlement south of Richmond. If the woman agreed to help her, they could be in Petersburg by this evening. Ceci had far too much to do. A headache threatened to form whenever she thought about changing the family's long history in Virginia. An altered timeline meant innocent lives could be wiped away. Emily's descendants might never exist as they do now.

Ceci grabbed her satchel and shut the trunks. It was time for her to call the boardinghouse porter to fetch her things. She had to catch Amelia before the young woman took the midday train to Charlottesville.

The trip to Amelia's didn't take long. Soon enough, a brisk wind nipped at Ceci's face as her cab deposited her and her trunks outside the Bridge household. Cecily closed her eyes until the pain had backed off. Then she straightened her back and knocked on the door.

PART FIVE
EMILY

CHAPTER 33

Amelia Bridge
DECEMBER 1924

After Professor Mayberry revealed her true identity and her plan, Amelia scooted off her seat and stood by the fireplace. Her former teacher had to have lost all common sense. She glanced down the hallway to the kitchen. If the professor gave her any trouble, she'd call for Clara or Mr. Parks. Millie's guest had yet to shift from her spot on the divan.

"We shouldn't tamper with time," Millie said firmly. "Can you imagine how much could go wrong?"

Mrs. Mayberry had that knowing smile, a veneer she often had shown during her lectures. The side of her mouth tilted up and her cheek twitched with amusement. "Dear girl, I've lived in the early twentieth century for over ten years now. That's a long time to do *a lot* of damage."

"Have you altered the past yet?"

"By being here, I've already changed things." Mrs. Mayberry

shrugged. "As for my life in 1964, I'll never know. Might be for the best."

She added, "What I do know is the actions I've taken since 1911 haven't affected me until this point. It's almost as if I've *always* existed here."

Millie crossed the room to stand behind the armchair. She gripped the top to steady herself. All this was too much.

Professor Mayberry continued. "What I'm trying to say is, I lived my life as I saw fit. You can do the same. Case in point, what will you do when you return to Charlottesville?"

"I'll wait it out on the farm."

"Then what?" The woman's eyebrows rose. "You'll time travel and just *see* what happens?"

"I have no choice. I'll find my way . . . wherever I end up."

"You will end up in 1758." Professor Mayberry had said those words with authority.

"So you say," Millie replied. "But you could've concocted all of this out of thin air."

Mrs. Mayberry opened her satchel and retrieved a large envelope. She opened it and placed a photo on the table. "I thought my explanation would've been enough to convince you, but you're a woman of reason." Professor Mayberry waited for Millie to take it before she added, "I rather like that about you."

Millie carefully examined the photo of what had to be an old document. The photographer had gotten as close as possible, revealing every detail. It took a moment for her to understand the elusive cursive, but there it was: a 1771 Albemarle County freedom paper registration for Emily Bridge. In the notice, a thirty-five-year-old Emily had stated she'd been born free and moved to Virginia from New York in 1758. Not only did the scars match up but the ages too. If Amelia fell through time to 1758, she'd be twenty-two then. Thirteen years later, she'd be thirty-five in 1771.

A hollow spot formed in Millie's chest and spread until her breath caught. She sagged into the seat. Her grip on the photo briefly tightened before she remembered what she held. "How did you get this?"

Her teacher poured more tea into her cup. She added two sugar cubes and a spoonful of cream. "Would you believe me if I said I knew where to find it? It was with a bunch of county records in Charlottesville."

Millie thought for a bit before she spoke. "Say that I am Emily Bridge, and I could do what I wanted. What if I go back to this Pocahontas Island and I end up killed?"

"You're stuck in a time loop, my dear," Mayberry said. "You do have some freedoms, but there are constraints too. You must give birth to your ancestor David, Luke's younger brother, but I'm proposing one change that *might* benefit you and the other Bridges. What if you didn't immediately meet John, and therefore not have Luke?"

"That's a big change."

"Yes, it is. But think about it. Say you do go home to Charlottesville right now. You will sit at the farm and wait to fall. Once you're back in 1758, you will marry a man and bear his children over twenty years. You will never finish your medical training. You will live your life knowing every major event, including when you will die. Is that the life your brother would've wanted for you?"

Millie stiffened. "It's what God intended. And anyway, there's no institution that would accept me in 1758."

"Not an institution, but what if you made a life for yourself before you returned to the farm? You're a bright woman. What if you used 1758 to 1761 for yourself?"

Millie's bunched shoulders relaxed.

Professor Mayberry continued. "Up to this point, you have

written your story. You left the farm after your brother fell. You earned a degree in biology—something most Negroes in this time period will never have. You could've been a doctor like your uncle too. If you follow my directions, you can continue to do as you please. Then when the time is right, you can return to the farm, and history may continue as intended—after you've made one change."

"One change." Amelia turned away from the woman to face the window. She had much to think about and not much time to do it. She glanced at the photo, imagining what Emily's life had been like back then. Millie couldn't help but see her own face as Emily stood before the county clerk.

A frightful swallow tickled the back of her throat. *Will I remember this day—this very parlor—in 1771 when I register myself?* she thought.

"There is one more thing I must tell you before you decide," Professor Mayberry added with a small smile. "There are mysteries in our family's history that even I haven't solved. In particular, the curse's origin. I believe the Bridge family has always had it and the phenomenon simply manifested in 1817 with Nelson, Hiram, and the others. Now, when it comes to Luke, that's when things get interesting. I don't know why he fell forty years before the others. He's an anomaly and we may never understand. Or perhaps it's for you to find out. Something unexpected will happen, and you may learn how everything connects together."

Millie turned away from her teacher and focused on the decision to be made. She could wait on the farm—just like she did when she and Isaiah waited to fall—or she could continue to forge her own path.

Millie had never faced such a difficult decision before, so she sat quietly and weighed her options.

When Clara arrived with a fresh tea service, Millie finally rose from her chair. "Professor Mayberry, it's time for us to catch that train to Petersburg."

CHAPTER 34

Emily Bridge
MARCH 1758

During the days of preparation with Professor Mayberry, Amelia's teacher had never told her about the silence. The quiet left Amelia, now Emily, uneasy. After she fell through time, it was the stillness that welcomed her. The clanks and thuds of heavy machinery and the steam train's urgent whistle calling to board were gone. There was only a profound quiet encompassing all, even the spaces between the cattails and the dribble of early spring flaking away above the current of Swift Creek. Thick evergreens and oak trees filled the land as far as she could see.

None of the tales passed down from her family spoke of the moment *right* after. That free-fall feeling when one missed a step off a street curb. Her aunt Ursula had once told her of a woman who'd crossed her doorstep thirteen years ago. The woman had "arrived," as Auntie had called it, in barely a stitch of clothing with wild eyes and lips stretched thin in grief.

"No other Bridge has fallen this far back," Professor Mayberry had said. "You represent a new start. The opening to the old Emily's tale is no more—you rewrite history now."

If she were lucky, she'd have a happy ending.

Emily stooped to one knee to retrieve a compass and a change of clothes from her pack. The wool coat, white blouse, and skirt she wore would draw unwanted attention. In time, she'd repurpose them. As she changed clothes into a simple cotton dress and petticoat, all the while shivering and shaken, she kept alert. She wouldn't have to deal with wild animals during the daylight hours, but the night would bring other dangers.

Tonight there might be nowhere to go. No haven from the overcast sky or the bite from the evening's draft. She returned to the creek to fill her jug. With a couple of cattails for dinner in hand, she used her compass to walk westward. Swift Creek fed into the Appomattox River to the west, but she wouldn't find the Pocahontas Island peninsula with its namesake settlement in that direction—so she ventured southwest.

There was nothing to see but untouched land. Signs of spring life popped up in the rabbits emerging from their winter dens and the fragile buds peeking from the trees' branches. Perhaps she'd arrived in late February or early March. A lone eagle's nest reigned over the barren woods from high up in some elm trees. The bird peered at her, its eyes following her trek through the naked branches. While she walked, she plucked the leaves from winter-hardy, edible plants. The tension in her shoulders eased when she came across stinging nettle and field chickweed. Each leaf meant she'd survive another day.

But less than a half hour into walking, she couldn't help but glance at her watch. She laughed—did she really think it'd be that easy to figure out the time and date? Perhaps she'd pass a paperboy with today's news too.

By the time she spied trails of chimney smoke in the distance, Emily's legs ached. All those years of taking public transportation in the city had left her soft.

The flat land left little mystery to the location of Pocahontas Island. Six to ten dwellings were scattered along the northern part of the riverbank, a smattering of homes compared to the budding township of Petersburg across a bridge to the south. To the west, she spied the lower end of a small, forest-covered atoll called Flea Island.

Emily stuck to the outer confines of the Pocahontas Island houses, many of them homes with straw roofs and buildings for pigs and sheep. The smell of roasted meat wafted from a house to the north.

She shivered against the wind hitting her back and made her way around a house with dust for a yard and thin chickens underfoot.

Professor Mayberry hadn't said much about how to find shelter in Pocahontas.

An older Negro man appeared at the door with a sullen expression and little pity in his eyes. She wouldn't find a warm welcome here. The two small houses farthest to the north, with trees hugging the back, drew her eyes.

As she considered where to head next, she saw a light-skinned middle-aged Negro woman shuffling to a well. The woman huffed and puffed as she carried her pail. Em quickened her steps to the same destination. The woman paused, eyeing Emily with suspicion, until Emily gave the woman a short smile.

"Good day to you," Emily said, her feet moving almost to a run. Hopefully Professor Mayberry was right about how folks greeted one another in these times.

Emily reached the well and tried to keep her breath even.

The lady struggled to pull the rope to draw up the bucket.

"Do you need help?" Em asked.

She'd ignored the fourth rule—don't speak to strangers unless absolutely necessary—and yet she couldn't stand there like a fool.

The woman disregarded Emily and kept her gaze fixed on each tug and pull. Her light-brown skin blanched as she struggled to get the bucket to the top. She stood half a foot taller than Emily with a dark-blue dress and pale white neckerchief. Tufts of curly white and black hair peeked out from under the scarf on her head. The woman's hand shook as she grabbed the bucket handle. Emily edged closer—something was wrong, but then again in these days who *didn't* have something wrong with them? She'd seen such labored breathing from her brother and the patients at her uncle's practice. Perhaps the woman had a heart issue—not that the woman would let Emily examine her.

"Phoebe, what are you doing?" a woman called.

Emily turned to see another woman standing in the doorway of a nearby house. Her eyebrows were drawn to dark slants against her forehead and the skin of her dark-brown cheeks was cast in shadow.

"Oh, Tabitha, could you stop griping for one day?" Phoebe lugged the bucket back toward the house. Water sloshed over the sides, leaving tiny pools in the dirt. Emily stayed at the well, wishing she could follow.

Em escaped into the trees to the north, passing a second home, a sod house. She peeked through the trees to check Phoebe's progress.

That poor thing needed a doctor.

Phoebe finally disappeared into the house, and Emily resigned herself to focus on minding her own affairs. She decided to gather kindling for a fire—once night came, she wouldn't have daylight's protection.

Soon enough, she had a fire going and her tiny cooking pot bubbled with roots she'd foraged. Right now, she was warm enough, but anyone could be a threat. She considered spending the night in the woods. And then perhaps in the morning she could find work on the Petersburg docks. She'd spied folks hauling goods off boats, unable to discern the enslaved from free men.

Emily took a deep breath to steady herself. For now, she had to listen, observe, and learn.

And get herself a pistol somehow.

She guffawed at the thought of trying to load a weapon with lead shots and gunpowder. She'd likely fumble the damn thing and end up shooting herself instead. Her hunting knife would have to do for now.

Isaiah, did you end up in a place like this one? she thought. Over the years, she'd dreamt of him landing in the 1800s. He'd disappear into the Canadian wilderness, or perhaps head out to the Pacific Northwest—somewhere safe from slavery.

And yet amid her dreams were nightmares: he ended up on a tobacco plantation back in 1792, or he landed in Richmond in the stockyards of 1817. No matter how free he was in his mind, many of the white men he'd encounter would see him as an inferior being, without intellect and unworthy of freedom.

The trees' protection didn't keep the wind from nipping at the flames of her kindling. She wished she had a brighter light so she could read before she slept—*if* she managed to sleep. Emily reached into her pack.

"I don't think it's wise to bring modern reading materials from the future," Professor Mayberry had told her. The woman hadn't faced Emily at the time, but Em had caught the it-won't-go-as-you-expect tone.

"Why not?" Emily had replied.

"We're trying to change the Bridge family's future. Dumping definitive evidence of time travel isn't wise."

"I can remove the copyright page and choose a book that was already in existence."

In the end, Professor Mayberry agreed to a newly printed copy of Dante Alighieri's *The Divine Comedy*. The irony of choosing a book about a person's descent into hell had made Emily laugh. But it would be a welcome distraction.

The corner of the book's cover brushed against her fingers while she rifled through the pack. She'd never carried this much before. Even when she'd had a pack as a kid.

Gone were the days of bright red wool polo coats and expensive cloth-top boots. Strapped to her belt was a field ax. It was small yet handy for chopping wood or cutting meat. She also had flint and steel for fire starting, a whetstone knife sharpener, needles, thread, petticoats, scarves, and cloth for her monthly time. She'd left so much behind, like her mama's pearl hair comb. Professor Mayberry had promised to return it to her mother.

The sky deepened from a murky gray to sullen purple, and the first signs of a late sleet wet Emily's cheeks. A calico cat with prominent whiskers approached her, but thought better of it and scampered into the safety of a nearby barn. Indeed, the colonial age had rolled out a warm welcome far better than any postwar parade.

She rolled up and stowed away everything. Her makeshift tent wouldn't keep out the rain, but at least she'd be spared most of the chill.

As the sun retreated below the horizon, she tucked herself under the tent and took in the two houses across the small field.

The sod house seemingly disappeared in the darkness while the larger stone-end home had lights bleeding through cracks in the door. Was everyone safe inside, eating a warm meal? That larger home had one shutter-covered window. The howling wind muffled the conversation within, but Emily imagined the inhabitants were comfortable enough yet cognizant of the dangers outside their door.

Emily drew her ax to her chest and decided to do the same.

CHAPTER 35

Emily Bridge

MARCH 1758

When Emily woke up to a horse's shrill whinny the next morning, the muscles in her back and legs ached. She fought to open her eyes. When she finally pried them open, she saw a middle-aged woman on the other side of the small field. Tabitha, as Phoebe had called her, wore a black cape and unassuming dark-blue dress.

Armed with a stony expression and a scar across her upper cheek, Tabitha moved with deft experience as she saddled the mare.

Emily grimaced. Her stiff fingers shook as she tossed kindling onto her nearly dead fire. She crept out of the tent, only for Tabitha to pause and look her up and down with a scowl. The woman had good eyesight.

Em jerked a nod in Tabitha's direction. At least the woman's glare hadn't killed Emily in her sleep. Tabitha filled the saddlebags, mounted the horse, and rode south across the bridge into Petersburg.

Emily stared after her, wondering what this woman did for a

living. She shuddered to imagine how many people must've walked by while she'd slept.

Before she ate her breakfast, she rubbed heat into her palms. Living outside would take some getting used to. The pleasant smell of burning wood and the heat fanning her face fed energy into her limbs. This was her new life now.

Emily began her day. She sipped water from her waterskin and balked at the sticky film in her mouth. Though Colgate's toothpaste left a peculiar taste in her mouth, she would've much preferred that over gargling and spitting water. For breakfast, she ate some dried duck and wrapped up her precious reserves in her neckerchief.

It took her far longer than usual to get moving—just like old times back on the farm. What she wouldn't give to smell fresh bread. Or hear the scrape of the spatula against the pan when her brother flipped over the hotcakes. Even a lukewarm boiled egg would taste better than gnawing on leathery meat.

She gathered up her supplies so she could set out for the forest to the north. The weather hadn't warmed, but the clouds from yesterday had blown west, leaving skies bathed in blue with faint white smears. A breeze off the Appomattox River nipped at her skirts and spread a chill through her cotton stockings.

After marching north for some time while collecting dry branches, Emily turned around and realized the Pocahontas Island township had vanished far behind her. Briefly, she let a tempting and terrifying thought germinate in her mind. With free will in her pocket, she could go anywhere. She could see new places before she had to meet John and give birth to David.

She could keep walking north until she reached the northern colonies. But after that, then what? She had a couple of years, then she had to return to the farm. A decision had to be made, so she made one.

Returning south, she spotted Pocahontas again. It was time to find work. The many plantations along the river employed free Negroes and whites, but which places would offer a friendly face versus those that posed danger? She had no idea how to know.

Emily emerged from the forest, once more near Tabitha and Phoebe's home. A herd of sheep had migrated from the house directly to the west and veered around the well, where now a lone Negro man drew water. Two women worked the herd while another man stoked the fire for a blacksmith's home. While she had been gone this morning, Pocahontas had come to life.

Back on the Bridge farm, someone would've called out to her in greeting. But at the thought of calling attention to herself, the word "Mornin'" died in her mouth.

The spot where she'd camped the night before welcomed her back instead. The very thought of having the whole day to herself, with no obligations, made her laugh.

Maybe I could keep walking until I find the South Pole, she thought. *Professor Mayberry would be proud.*

Emily stopped laughing when she glanced to her right and noticed someone lying near the house's wood lean-to. The calico cat she'd spied yesterday sat near Phoebe's head. Em glanced toward the open doorway. Was someone else home?

"C'mon," she breathed. Had anyone else seen Phoebe fall? No one shifted around the other houses in the glen. Only the sheep and chickens had been witnesses.

Emily picked up her skirt to keep her dress from catching on her feet and ran to the woman. No more than a couple feet away, she noticed Phoebe was still breathing.

Thank God, she thought as she leaned over to listen.

"Hello?" She pressed her ear to Phoebe's chest and waited for a steady rhythm. The pulse echoed a rabbit's frantic beat. Next, she examined Phoebe for any injuries.

The woman's lips parted with a whimper before her eyes opened to slits.

"You fell." Emily pressed her warm palm against the woman's cheek.

Phoebe tried to rise, and Emily pressed her hands against her shoulders. "Don't get up yet. When was the last time you ate?"

"Don't hurt m-me." The familiar lilt of home echoed in Phoebe's words, but Emily caught a twinge of an English accent.

"I'd never," Em said softly. "I was over there when you fell."

Phoebe tried to get up again. This wouldn't be the first time Emily had a reluctant patient.

"This has happened before. I'll be fine," Phoebe said.

"You *will* be fine lying here until your symptoms improve." Emily wiped the woman's clammy brow. "Did you break your fast this morning?"

Phoebe pursed her thin lips. "I had no water for cooking, so I fetched some."

"But you didn't eat." Emily got up. "Don't move until I return."

Em backed away at first, expecting the woman to try to escape, but Phoebe stayed put as Emily ran to fetch her pack. From inside, she retrieved a few pieces of dried apple. Professor Mayberry had shared taffy with her during their train ride down to Petersburg, which she'd pocketed without eating, but a produce seller with dried fruit at the train station had caught her interest. She palmed three generous pieces and went back to Phoebe.

"Here, eat this," Em said firmly.

Phoebe eyed the food with suspicion. "What's that?"

Just like when Em had to take care of her mama during her spells, Emily brought the food to Phoebe's mouth. After a hesitation, she accepted the first slice.

"I ate a bit of venison, but—" the woman began.

"But you're still tired," Emily finished. "Some folks need porridge, fruits, and such in the morning or they'll fall ill."

"You sound like Tabitha," Phoebe grumbled.

"Your friend knows what she's talking about." Emily grasped the woman's wrist and found her pulse steadier this time. "Let's get you into the house. You should be right as rain very soon. I'm Emily Freeman. What's your name?"

"Phoebe . . . Phoebe McDonald."

Emily draped the woman's arm over her shoulder and helped her to her feet. "There we go. Don't go too fast," she instructed.

The woman finally smiled, revealing a mouth full of small teeth and generous gums. "Not that I'd ever run anywhere feeling like this."

They were halfway to the house when Phoebe spoke again. "The last time this happened, Tabby told me I'd be face down in the dirt, but I wasn't."

"Tabitha has sound advice," Emily replied. "You should mind your health, or you'll spend an afternoon in the cold."

"She complains too much, I say. 'Phoebe, keep standing like that and your legs will swell again.' 'Phoebe, you don't eat enough.' On and on and on."

Em hid a smile. Folks in 1758 were just as ornery as those in 1924.

The door to the house was open, so she helped Phoebe inside and guided her to a bed to the right. The calico cat plodded in after them. While Phoebe eased onto her side, facing the wall, Emily's gaze swept over the home. The kindling pile was too low. No one had emptied the chamber pot nor swept the floor nor beat out the dust from the bed's blankets. A familiar foul odor, one of neglect she'd remembered from Grandpa Elijah's home, came to mind. As his arthritis worsened in his knuckles, the man couldn't lift his spoon to his mouth most days.

After crossing the stone-end home from one end to the other, Emily stood in the middle. If she spread her arms out, this single room spanned three times her outstretched arms. Phoebe and Tabitha lived in a house no bigger than her parlor back home.

A cough from Phoebe pushed Emily into action. She took a cup from one of the many shelves against the wall and scooped out water from the bucket.

The woman gulped down the drink. "I was so thirsty."

"Yes, that can happen after a diabetic episode."

"Diabetic? What's that?"

"When we eat, we're given strength from food. Some of us can't digest food properly, and during certain times of the day we need to eat more or less food."

"That makes sense. Are you a midwife like Tabitha?"

Emily hesitated before she spoke. "No, I'm not."

Phoebe's gaze followed Emily as she sat on a chair before the fire. She leaned back against the chair and let the fire's crackle lull her into a moment of rest. Refreshed from the heat seeping deep into her bones, she eventually sucked in a breath and stood.

"Now that you're feeling better," Emily began to say with a bit of an English accent like Phoebe's, "I should leave you to rest. I need to get my belongings."

"I'm too awake to sleep, to be honest." Phoebe scratched her forehead under her head wrap, revealing long corkscrew curls. "Say, where are you from? You sound like you're not from around here."

"I'm not."

"You look like one of the slaves I used to know from back in Maryland. Have you ever been there before?" Phoebe squinted at her as if she'd scrutinized every pimple on Em's forehead. "That woman fussed at everyone, but nothing she said made sense."

"Sounds like my aunts back home." Emily edged toward the door.

"You like onion pie?" Phoebe asked.

"I've never had the pleasure."

"I came across a fine onion the other day." Phoebe got up far too quickly, wobbling a bit, but her face lit up as she strode over to Emily to grasp her wrist. Phoebe tugged Emily over to a basket and fumbled through the goods inside.

Emily accepted the onion with a chuckle. "It's rather early in the season for onions to get this big. Did this come from south of here?"

"I believe so."

The scaly leaves on the onion's outside crackled as Em examined it. "Someone spent too much time guarding this fella from pests."

"They probably sang to it," Phoebe said with a grin.

"Or sat on it like a hen."

They cackled while Phoebe filled her weathered hands with tiny potatoes and apples. Emily waited with that massive onion in one hand. Phoebe added a paring knife to the other.

"Are you going to cut it?" Phoebe said to Emily as she lugged an oven kettle by the handle and settled it on a nest of bright coals. "Should be warm soon."

"Are you well enough to cook?" Em asked.

"I'm much better." Phoebe removed the lid and left it off to the side. "I'll sleep well tonight with a belly full of pie."

"That's a good idea. Will the lady who left earlier return soon? What was her name again?"

"That's Mrs. Tabitha Oyo. She's off to Mrs. Mackenzie's lying-in. Who knows when the baby will come." Her eyebrows shot toward her scalp. "The last babe almost killed the poor thing."

"Seems like Mrs. Oyo won't have it easy."

"She'll be fine. She's one of the best." Phoebe glowed with pride.

After fetching her pack, Emily spent the morning into the afternoon helping Phoebe. They fashioned the barley dough for the pie and prepared the spices and filling. Once Emily rested the lid on top of the pot, she waited for Phoebe to shove her out the door, but the woman kept yammering on until the skies darkened.

Emily's subtle hints about needing to leave missed their mark until she caught Phoebe nodding off. "I should head off and let you rest."

"Nonsense!" Phoebe snapped. "A godly woman like yourself shouldn't be out there with the devil's ilk. Every month ships from England bring more convicts to town."

Phoebe even slid into another topic: the nosy church matrons in the parish. "Those bothersome biddies up at the Blanchard Church say we should be rid of the prostitutes, but I believe every woman deserves a livelihood." She blew out a disgusted exhale. "Those self-righteous women have never spent the night with rocks in their stomachs. Let them live one week without, and I guarantee they'd be willing to, as they say, 'soil' their righteous bodies to eat. Don't you agree?"

"Yes." Short answers had saved Em from lengthy debates all day.

"No one can understand poverty unless they've had nothing. Not even their freedom."

By the time Emily formed a pallet of blankets before the fire, Phoebe was too tired to gossip any further. The woman shuffled over to the double bed and slept. Emily could've read, but she had trouble keeping her own eyes open, so she gave up and did the same.

Yet hours later, when the morning should've tugged Emily from slumber, it was Phoebe's choking gasps in her sleep that kept her up all night. One moment, the woman's snores bounced off the dried mud walls, and in the next, Phoebe fell as silent as a corpse until her body shuddered with its next breath.

Emily's restless vigil lasted until the rising sun shone through the cracks around the cedar door. She tried to close her eyes and bury herself beneath her blankets, but a frantic knock on the door forced her to her feet.

"Who goes there?" Phoebe asked, her voice thick with sleep.

"It's Matthew Abramson," a man said sharply. The visitor spoke with a thick accent Emily couldn't place. He wasn't an Englishman.

Emily scrambled off her pallet and hurried over to the door. Behind it, she found a Negro man. A tall one at that. The top of her head met him square in the chest. As hard as she tried not to stare at his handsome face, she gaped at him.

The man cracked a smile. "May I come in before I bleed to death?" He gestured at a bloody apron he held against his forearm. Bloodstains darkened a jagged rip down the sleeve of his brown waistcoat.

"Of course, of course." Em's stomach formed knots as she got out of the way, taking in his wide shoulders and narrow waist.

"Is Mrs. Oyo out?" the man asked.

Phoebe rose with a grimace. "She left yesterday."

"Then I'll find Dr. Hobbs." He turned to leave, but Emily reached out to grab his good arm.

"Don't go," Em said. "I can help."

Phoebe joined them. "Yes, this is Miss Freeman. She helped me yesterday."

"Fine then." Matthew returned to stand before Emily.

With trembling hands, Emily placed her hand over his, grasping the cloth he held against the wound. She pulled the cloth back until the five-inch laceration down the middle of his forearm peeked back at her.

"What happened?" she asked him. "That had to hurt."

"A broken beaver trap got me good." His breath fanned her face and brought the strong scent of coffee.

Em breathed it in—only to turn her head away at the thought of her own breath.

Lord help her. She'd eaten all those onions. Bite after bite.

"You should be more careful," Emily added to push herself back to task. Any time she imagined Uncle Ozzie standing behind her at his clinic, her recall improved. "How much does it hurt when I press the other side?"

"A lot," he admitted with a wry face.

Rather refreshing to have a patient tell the truth.

After washing her hands, Emily flushed the wound clean with water from the bucket, then she set about finding medical supplies. "Apply pressure again. I won't be long."

Mr. Abramson would have to wait longer than a little while. Emily glanced over the shelves and the scattered supplies of jars and tiny wooden boxes. It was like walking into another woman's kitchen to search for a fork.

Thankfully, Phoebe asked, "What do you need?"

"A thread and needle for stitches and boiled cloth for the dressing."

"She keeps them here." Phoebe unrolled a linen cloth from one of the shelves to reveal the supplies Emily needed.

"Wonderful." Emily searched over the dried herb stalks hanging from the hooks under the shelves. She found the woundwort first, and with a quick sniff, she confirmed her find through its astringent smell. *Perfect.* Emily rolled and kneaded the plant between her fingers until she had enough small pieces. Satisfied, she added them into the midwife's stone mortar with a bit of water to form a paste. Yes, she could do this. The nervousness in her stomach quieted a little. During her second year at the clinic, her uncle had drilled suturing skills into her head. And after handling patients from a couple of nightclub brawls on U Street, she'd gained confidence.

"Take a deep breath," Emily told him. "I'll go as fast as I can." She focused on the wound and her hands moved with a practiced precision to apply a buried suture.

"My sister Penny told me Mrs. Oyo was looking for an apprentice," he said. "Are you her latest one?"

Em paused, then forced herself to continue. "Oh no. Miss McDonald was kind enough to let me stay here last night. I'm leaving today."

Emily caught Phoebe's stiffened shoulders from the other side of the room.

"What will you do after you leave?" Matthew hissed as the needle dug into his flesh.

"I don't know," Em admitted, "but I will be well."

"You should work at the apothecary in Petersburg," he suggested. "Mr. Graves is getting old and could use help."

"Thank you. I'll go there when I'm able." Now that Emily stood so close to him, she found it hard not to glance at his face. His nose was perfectly straight, while his cheeks were long yet curved enough to make him appear youthful. Was he around her age? Briefly, his full lips formed a slight smile. She glanced up again after her final stitch to see amusement shining in his eyes.

"Why don't you ever appreciate keen-looking boys?" her cousin Henrietta used to say back at Howard. "You're smart and likable. Why don't you speak up?"

Though she'd admired plenty of handsome, smooth-talking fellows in DC, none of them could've donned this man's frayed waistcoat and worn it like a king.

"It will hurt for a couple days," Emily instructed. "Keep your arm dry, and if you're able, change the dressing every day with clean fabric."

He nodded as Emily let go of him. Perhaps she could indeed live off her skills in this place.

To her left, the door opened with a hard *thwack*. Tabitha Oyo stormed inside with her black cape wrapped tightly around her. She took one look at Emily and her eyes narrowed. "What are you doing in my home?"

CHAPTER 36

Emily Bridge
MARCH 1758

Tabitha strode into the house and hung her cape on a hook near the door. "I won't repeat myself. What business do you have here?"

"Tabby, that's the girl we saw two days ago," Phoebe said.

"I'm well aware of that," Tabitha replied, gentler this time.

"Morning, Mrs. Oyo—" the man beside Emily said.

"Mr. Abramson," Tabitha said curtly.

Matthew and Tabitha spoke with a similar accent. Emily wondered if they came from the same place.

Tabitha marched across the room in three strides and snatched his arm from Emily's grip. Using her wide hips, she bumped Em out of the way while she examined the fabric. "What did you do to him?"

Emily backed up. "He cut himself on a trap. I cleaned the wound and applied stitches."

Tabitha carefully removed the wrap and squinted at Em's work. "What did you put on this?" She rubbed her fingers against the swollen, reddened skin around the abrasion, wiping away the tiny green woundwort buds.

Emily stared at the dirt floor, suddenly back in Uncle Ozzie's clinic. "Warm water, a bit of mint to reduce infection, and woundwort to promote healing."

Tabitha gave Emily a dark look and presented his arm. "Who do you think you are? Barging into my home, without my permission—"

"If you'd stop complaining," Phoebe snapped, "I can explain."

Tabitha's hand shot up. "You and I will speak in private later." The woman spat venom at Emily while she flushed out Matthew's wound. "Mr. Abramson is *allergic* to woundwort."

Emily's mouth dropped open. Oh God, she could've unwittingly killed him. All the usual steps, taking a patient's history and performing an examination, had fallen aside as she scrambled to stop the bleeding. She should've known better and asked questions as she worked.

"It only itches a little, Mrs. Oyo," Mr. Abramson said, flashing Emily a straight face. "There's no harm done."

"Healers are not to harm their patients," Tabitha said to Emily. "I don't know where you came from, but you have no business meddling in the healing arts."

Phoebe scooted off the bed. "I fainted outside, which I'm embarrassed to admit, but Miss Freeman helped me."

Tabitha's features briefly softened. "I told you—"

"And I didn't listen, as usual," Phoebe said quietly. "I'm fine. The girl complained enough for both of you."

Emily kept stealing a glance at Matthew, who edged toward the door with Tabitha still holding on to him. His face hinted at amusement. Perhaps he didn't hate her—for now. He hadn't keeled over yet, but even she spotted the fingernail-size welts forming on his forearm.

Emily retreated until her backside hit the far wall. While Tabitha rewrapped the man's arm, Em burned with shame.

"I'll take my leave." Emily gave a curt nod to Phoebe.

"Wait a moment, Miss Freeman," Phoebe said. "Tabitha might be a burly bear, but she isn't that bad."

"I'm much worse," Tabitha interjected.

"You barely got out of bed yesterday morning, Tab," Phoebe said. "I couldn't help but think over the past day how Miss Freeman would make a fine apprentice to learn your trade and take over as midwife."

Tabitha gave a full-bellied laugh in response. "You've known this stranger for how long?"

"She's been here since you left to take care of the Mackenzies."

"And that doesn't mean she has the knowledge, Phoeb," Tabitha replied. "The last girl—"

"She was lazy, yes. And the girl before that couldn't remember anything, but you told me you wanted a woman with skills as a healer."

Tabitha's head slowly turned to Emily. "Didn't you say you were leaving?"

Emily quickly folded up her pallet and picked up her pack. She hurried outside. The cold air bit the back of her dry throat. *Well, that didn't go well*, she thought.

She searched around the house to see where Matthew had gone, but he'd disappeared. She strode over to the place where she'd slept two nights ago. Sleeping on the ground in the house had proved far better, but then again, she couldn't expect such an easy arrangement. Then she recalled what Matthew had said about the Petersburg apothecary.

Maybe her time in Pocahontas had come to an end. And if she never had to see Tabitha Oyo's face, that might be a good thing.

Emily set off south down a path for Petersburg, which lay on the other side of the Appomattox River. A breeze ruffled the muddy waters, bringing the foul odors of dead fish and damp vegetation. She crossed the bridge and passed the busy port, taking in the crowded waters with ferries, flatboats, and coasters. A single schooner took up most of the space at the pier, and workers hauled crates off the ship. Foremen barked out orders as passengers disembarked first, then slaves in chains. The men and women wore filthy, threadbare clothes. Two women shivered and huddled close to each other. Emily tried to glance away but couldn't.

She'd only seen old photographs of slaves. But these people were real with flesh and sweat.

Professor Mayberry had lectured her on how to interact with her enslaved brothers and sisters, but how did one truly prepare for such a sight? How could you witness someone's subjugation without feeling disgust roll through your stomach, without vitriol pumping through your veins?

"Walk away," her professor had said. "Keep your head down, Miss Bridge, but *never* forget what you witnessed."

Emily avoided the shipyards, walking between the empty tobacco barns. By late summer, they'd be full of cut stalks drying in the sun. She recalled seeing a plantation back home near Charlottesville, but not many folks cared about the history associated with them—only the possibility of finding work.

On this side of the river, Petersburg thrummed with life. At least a hundred people lived here, compared to the smattering of wood homes in Pocahontas. Sturdy stone-end homes, both dated and recent builds, were scattered along the riverside. Between them, chickens and sheep wandered. The town also had a church, and not far from that, a gallows and pillory. She peered at the weathered wooden post, wondering when it'd last been used.

The market house off the river had a meager crowd of five people. Many of the stalls were empty. Most of the vendors ignored Emily to sell their parcels and baskets of butter, eggs, and such. The colder weather didn't keep folks indoors. Early spring sheep needed to be sheared and gardens turned over for planting.

A fishmonger stood before his barrels of fish. When their gazes connected, he shouted, "Fresh trout and eel!"

She shook her head and quickened her steps. Deeper into town, she passed two white ladies gossiping while out on a stroll. Emily shuffled to follow them, but not too closely. She had no idea where she was going. Even back home she wouldn't have asked them for directions. There were no street signs here or advertisements. She'd have to wander for a while until she came to the right place.

Twenty minutes of wandering later, she came upon what had to be the apothecary Matthew had mentioned.

Through the cracked-open door, she glimpsed racks and clay pots with herbs. She opened the door and peered inside, finding little light except for the glow from the hearth on the other side of the room.

"Hello?" she called out.

An older white gentleman rose from a seat near the hearth. "Does Mr. Bolling need another tincture?" he asked, his voice choppy from his missing teeth.

"Pardon?"

The man squinted. "You're not Patsy."

"No, sir. I've come to inquire about work." Emily's voice

squeaked a bit. Her confidence had up and flown away. "I was told you may be looking for help."

"You sound like a fine young lady, but I do not need help." The man returned to his seat, his frown saying much more than a curt "Good day."

"Good day to you, sir." She left yet another house to head back into the cold, only to run right into Matthew.

"There you are!" he said, revealing a grin that set her heart aflutter. "Miss McDonald was looking for you and I told her where I'd sent you."

"Why? Has something happened to her?" She glanced at his hand and arm to see if he had any swelling.

"She's fine." He shifted to block the wind. "At least I sent you somewhere I could find you. According to Miss McDonald, I made a mistake sending you to Mr. Graves."

Emily laughed. "I don't know what Miss McDonald is going on about—I got quite the warm welcome from him."

They strolled northward down the dirt road away from Blanchard Church, then back toward the Petersburg bridge. She had nowhere to go. Might as well start walking somewhere.

"From the way you talk, it sounds like English is your mother tongue," he remarked, "yet you sound . . ."

"Different? Peculiar?" she finished for him.

"I wouldn't say that." His eyebrows rose. "I find it pleasant."

"I don't like how high-pitched my voice sounds sometimes."

"I beg to differ."

Was he flirting with her? "How about the way you sound?" Emily asked. "English isn't your first language."

"My sister and I come from Africa. Are you from there too?"

"No, I was born here. I can't imagine traveling that far."

"It's not as far as you'd think. There are greater distances to travel."

Emily stole a peek at his profile, wondering where in Africa he came from. Maybe he was from Liberia, or another place in West Africa.

As they passed porters carrying furniture onto a ship, a thought came to mind, and she had no idea how to broach the subject: Was Matthew a slave? She wasn't sure how she might ask such a question.

"Miss McDonald told me you should return to her house," Matthew said. "Do you want to go?"

"Mrs. Oyo doesn't want me there. Why should I?"

"Mrs. Oyo can be *too* direct, but when Miss McDonald spoke to me, she said she believes you have a chance to learn from Mrs. Oyo. I believe you do too."

Emily hid a smile. "I don't know."

"Think about it on the way," he suggested. "I won't be far away in case you need help again."

"Where do you live?"

"I'm in the house next to Mrs. Oyo's."

So he lived in the nearby sod house.

As they approached Phoebe and Tabitha's home, she asked, "Will you get in trouble with your employer for helping me?"

"It's not a problem. During the day, I work for the Millwell family and they owe many favors to Mrs. Oyo." He stopped near the property edge. "Go in before Miss McDonald scolds me for not finding you."

"Thanks again, Mr. Abramson." A feeling Emily hadn't experienced for years took hold: relief and warmth. If Phoebe could help her find work, or even a place to stay, Emily would be grateful. She'd considered the docks or checking the plantations, but Em didn't want to venture to the farms just yet.

Emily knocked on the door. She caught a soft-spoken "Come

in" and walked inside. It wasn't Phoebe waiting near the hearth but a glowering Tabitha. The look on her face suggested she had every intention of sending Emily back the way she had come.

———

None of Emily's professors had stared her down like the midwife of Pocahontas Island. The woman said nothing after Em entered the home, merely continued her task of preparing a meal. It was as if this stranger knew every mistake she'd made in medical school. Emily had met physicians and nurses like Tabitha before. They didn't second-guess their decisions as often as she did.

"Miss McDonald sent for me," Emily began to say. "Is she well?"

That got a snort from Tabitha. "She's well. You, however, are another matter."

Emily glanced at the midwife's hands, for they were as small as hers, yet the corded muscles on Tabitha's forearms flexed with strength as she removed the plucked chicken's skin.

"Phoebe told me I've gotten bitter in my later years," Tabitha said. "That I'm still carrying what happened to us back in Annapolis."

Emily wondered what she meant, but she knew when to keep her mouth shut.

"One of the things I learned as a slave was to never trust anyone. The only thing you can trust is for people to show you their true nature. I've pondered on yours." Tabitha sprinkled dried rosemary and thyme on her table, then rolled the chicken through the herbs.

Once she was done seasoning her food, Tabitha grimaced as she leaned over to add dough to the bottom of the baking pot. Emily had seen that pained expression before, but as to what ailment Tabitha had, the woman hadn't given many clues.

"How old are you, girl?" the woman asked crisply.

"Twenty-two, ma'am." Emily's birthday had passed, as usual, without any sort of celebration, back in January.

"You should know better." Exasperated, she tapped her chest. "I've had fifty-two years to make mistakes and learn from them. You have a lot to learn."

Tabitha kept working. "Tell me everything you did earlier today, then tell me what you did *wrong*."

Emily stood straighter. With ease, she recounted every detail. Through a fast-drying throat, she finished with "I should've asked him questions while I stopped the bleeding."

Once the midwife added her chicken to the cooking pot, she motioned for Emily to follow. "Outside. Now."

Em's insides quaked. Perhaps the woman meant to toss her out after a real beating.

She followed Tabitha to the wood lean-to, where the midwife took a pail from a hook attached to the wall. "Grab the extra bucket."

Emily did as she was instructed, while the chilling wind drew tears from her eyes.

"I can tell you learned from an English physician like I did," Tabitha said matter-of-factly. "But book learning and a litany of Latin words doesn't teach us common sense." While the midwife drew water from the well, Emily stood there, bucket in hand, with her gaze set on a small patch of green on the ground. The midwife gave every grisly detail as to what she'd done wrong—how the stitches were crooked and the twine she'd used for the sutures wouldn't hold well in Mr. Abramson's line of work as a trapper and field hand.

Once the woman filled her bucket, Emily hurried forward with the next one. Tabitha added water up to the brim and then left both pails beside the well. She marched right back to the house.

Emily glanced at the buckets, then back to the midwife.

Move it, Millie, she could hear Isaiah say.

Em grabbed the handles and followed Tabitha. For the rest of the afternoon, she boiled linens, hung fresh early spring herbs upside down to dry, and replaced the soiled hay in the mare's stall in the nearby barn. By the time Phoebe returned shortly before dusk, Emily knew where most things were stored.

"Where have you been?" Emily asked her. "I was worried."

"I'm a washing lady over at the Bolling farm. I would've been home sooner, but Tabby told me to stay away while she 'chatted' with you."

More like tormenting, Emily thought.

"Can you stay?" Phoebe whispered to her.

"Don't know."

"Tab's a slow-to-warm kettle." The woman touched her shoulder in sympathy. "Don't worry."

Emily left the cabin to fetch more wood. At dusk, Pocahontas Island grew still. No lights flickered through dim windows. The village slept. Tabitha could work Em's hands raw from sunup to sundown, but the unknowns outside the house frightened Emily more.

CHAPTER 37

Emily Bridge

APRIL 1758

A morose March came and went, but the biting rain and murky clouds remained, leaving the countryside crestfallen.

Six months ago, Emily had left Miner Hall every morning to hurry across campus to her Embryology and Physiology lectures. Now she rose from a pallet on the dirt floor in front of a fireplace, her back stiff from sleeping on the unforgiving surface. The soot from dying fires caked her blankets, but she preferred the draft through the cracks in the cabin walls to her tent.

Getting up early was just another day for a farm girl. Before Tabitha or Phoebe woke up, Emily brought the fire back to life, emptied the chamber pots, and served a meal of oats she'd left in a pot to cook overnight. Phoebe always looked forward to eating Em's meals, but not Tabitha, who always said she cooked better.

The midwife hadn't been called yet this month to bring another baby into the world. Like yesterday, the midwife slept in and ate after Phoebe fussed and poked at her.

Emily had begun to leave a portion by the fire to keep it warm for her host.

"Anticipate and mitigate any problems" was one of the earliest lessons her medical school professors had taught her.

Tabitha's face scrunched up as she rolled off the far side of her straw-mattress bed. Each day, Emily had seen her clutching her right side. The woman never let Phoebe or Emily brush against it. Emily stared Tabitha down while her fingers tackled menial work. This time she helped Phoebe boil linens for the Bolling household. The site, right under where her rib cage should end, appeared too high for appendicitis or a liver infection. Perhaps she'd fallen and hadn't recovered.

Tabitha's slow march took her over to the chamber pot, where she turned away to release her morning water. Once the woman was done, Emily scurried over to grab the pot and empty it outside. A quick glance inside the pot revealed no blood or dark urine. When she returned, the midwife slipped a pouch of pain-relief herbs into a teacup. The woman took a seat at the table, her eyes focused on the steam rising from the cup, when a knock shook the door.

Before Emily could answer, the midwife belted out, "Who's there?"

The door opened and a middle-aged Negro man in a stained black waistcoat said, "You're needed at the Bolling farm. My daughter-in-law's throws have come."

"The last I saw Penny, she looked about ready. I'll be there soon," Tabitha said.

Penny was Matthew's sister. Emily tried not to turn around to show interest.

"Thank you, ma'am." The man departed after delivering the message, leaving a hush within the cabin until Tabitha spoke.

"Fetch my apron," the midwife said.

Emily snapped up from her spot in the corner opposite the bed. The fatigue in the midwife's movements vanished as if the woman had swept them out the door. Tabitha stood with an audible groan, then hurried to dress.

Don't expect to go, Emily reminded herself. She wanted to head out and see the neighbors. Over the last couple of weeks, she'd thought of Matthew. While she fetched wood or water, she'd expected to see his face from afar. While she foraged for herbs, she'd hoped to cross paths to chat. So far, luck had not been in her favor.

This morning wouldn't be any different. Emily kept glancing at the midwife while she wrapped scissors, linen scraps, and other tools into a leather pouch for Tabitha's apron pocket.

Once the midwife slipped on her boots, her stern gaze finally focused on Emily. "Don't dawdle, girl. Let's go."

Em bit her lower lip to keep from smiling. The time had come. She draped a heavy shawl over her shoulders and scurried out the door. No one had to tell her twice.

The pair strode north, away from Pocahontas. The quiet forest swallowed them. The only evidence of their travels was their footprints through the damp grass.

"Where are we going?" Emily whispered.

"North," Tabitha said. She wouldn't say anything more than that.

After they climbed to the top of a steep hill near the river, an open field revealed their destination. On the other side of the incline, they came upon cleared land with wooden and limestone buildings off the Appomattox. It was the Bolling farm. Four single-story stone-end homes huddled at a distance away from an imposing two-story farmhouse on the other end of the glen. Patchy footpaths in the grass separated the barren, tilled soil from the evergreens. This late in the morning, laborers should've tended to the tobacco seedbeds, but only a lone man, his limbs long yet skeletal, stood in the middle of one of them. Em couldn't look away, almost holding her breath for the moment he'd bolt from his prison. But the man never did. As they approached the homes, Em tried to curb the anticipation in her stomach. If Penny was about to give birth, Matthew wouldn't be around. Even back on the Bridge farm, men kept away. And yet she couldn't resist steeling herself when they turned the corner around the first house.

Matthew wasn't the first man she'd taken a liking to. During her junior year at Howard, she'd often daydreamed of a fellow who sat in the back of her advanced biology courses. He didn't say much and wore decade-old suits. But when his deep voice filled the room—she just loved the sound of it—he added humor and insight to the boring lectures.

Ever the dutiful spy for Aunt Alma, her cousin Rosie had told Emily, "Mother would never approve."

Now that Emily thought about it, a man's clothes didn't matter. It was how he carried himself—whether he greeted everyone like family or laughed without a care. After speaking to Rosie, she'd let her classmate slip away. The moment the man accepted his diploma, he'd returned to New York City, taking any chances she had to act on her feelings.

When they reached Penny's home, a hive of activity was buzzing around it. Three children no older than five tried to peek through the open entryway. A middle-aged Negro woman left the house and shooed them away. A flood of conversation—including complaints from a younger woman—spilled out.

"Something isn't right," a woman moaned. "My back hurts."

"That baby wants to come out," an older woman replied. "Keep walking, child. You'll see the babe soon."

Without knocking, Tabitha walked in. Emily followed.

The four women in the house didn't greet the midwife. One

lady in the corner continued to work at spinning wool, while another cleaned a pile of corded wool. A stocky woman fussed over a pot at the hearth; the heavy scent of her meaty soup wafted through the home.

The expectant mother, dressed in a cotton nightgown with a brown shawl around her shoulders, paced across the wood floors between the bed and hearth. Penny Green's hair was braided and free from the gray caps all the other women wore.

The matron who'd left earlier returned with a bucket of water. "Good day, Mrs. Oyo," the woman murmured.

"How long since her throws started, Mrs. Green?" Tabitha asked.

"Since last night." Mrs. Green left the bucket next to the bed. "This is her first, so I had my husband fetch you this morning."

Penny swayed as her face contorted through a contraction. "Can't we wait, Mrs. Oyo? Mrs. Hunter's baby died last month."

"Everything'll be fine." Tabitha cupped the woman's cheek with tenderness. "I've birthed children during full moons, after milk spoiled. No matter the sign, the Lord's will shall be done whether we give in to superstition or not."

The midwife set her rolled-up apron on the only table in the room, then she unfurled it. Closing her eyes as if in prayer, she then ran her fingers across her tools. "Today is a good day for a birth," she whispered.

Penny approached Tabitha from behind. "*Iya-iya mi* told Mama to drink chamomile to stop her labors. It didn't work for me."

Everyone in the room chuckled—except for Emily. She was puzzled why no one had told Penny chamomile would have the opposite effect.

"You can wait all you like," Tabitha said with a knowing smile. "That child will jump into your arms whether you like it or not."

Emily stood near the door, out of the way. She glanced at Tabitha for the first order, but none came. Back at her uncle's clinic, she'd learned to read his movements. How to clean and prep the beds for examinations. Pregnant women had visited the clinic, but none of them had given birth there. Hours of memorization from textbooks hadn't taught her a thing about the realities of childbirth.

Penny's mother-in-law picked up a smaller pail and bumped into Emily, forcing her to scurry out the door.

"Sorry, ma'am," Emily said.

"I've never met you before," Mrs. Green muttered before she dumped the dirty water in the grass.

Em returned inside to find Tabitha next to Penny on the bed. The midwife had completed a quick exam to determine the baby's position. Emily wished she could've seen what Tabitha had done.

"Rest for now," the midwife said. "The baby should be here by the morning."

Mrs. Green pointed at Em. "Who's that?"

"My new helper." Not once did Tabitha glance at her. For now, Emily was nameless, a "helper" meant to stay out of the way until needed.

Penny mewled, her face contorting as another contraction hit. There'd be no anesthesia here—nor the earlier forms of pain relief, such as chloroform or ether. In Uncle Ozzie's clinic, she'd treated grown men writhing in pain. Those men got pain relief, yet Penny would get nothing but soothing words and reassuring touches.

After that, hours passed as they waited for Penny's baby. Emily was cast adrift to sail where needed. She moved when called upon and hovered near the door when others attended to Penny.

Plenty of folks passed Em on the way in and out. The door swung, from two girls bringing them a late lunch of warm mince pie to a Green relative letting Mrs. Green sleep for a spell.

Those with true intentions, compared to the nosy folks peering inside, tended to Penny's chores. No one asked for permission. All women worked during the travail. Emily watched another Negro woman, at least ten years older than herself, tackle the cleaning, all the while minding her toddler clinging to her bright red petticoat.

When Emily left the cabin to fetch water, the sun edged toward the horizon. Her gaze swept over the farm for Matthew. He had yet to check on his sister.

"What are you doing?" Tabitha snapped from the doorway.

Emily had lost time daydreaming on her way back. "I have the water."

"From where? The well back home?"

"Of course not."

Em returned to find Penny squatting on the birthing stool with the other women surrounding her. A frowning Tabitha stooped down in front of Penny to catch the child. Two other women, including Penny's mother-in-law, braced her shoulders and arms.

Good God, she'd almost missed the birth.

Emily tripped over a notch on the floor but managed to stay upright to leave the bucket by the hearth. Eyes wide, she rushed to wash her hands in the chilled water. There'd be no time for soap, for the midwife barked out orders.

"Push," Tabitha said, then softer, "That's it. The head is crowning."

Emily stood to Tabitha's left, ready to act.

"It hurts so much. Take it out," Penny pleaded.

"I know," the midwife said. "You're almost there."

"I can't. Can't." The woman panted, then screeched in pain.

After a couple more pushes, Tabitha's head twisted in Emily's direction. "Tools. Now."

"Which one?" Emily fetched the apron.

When the midwife snatched the knife, Emily steeled herself.

"Hold her tight." With practiced precision, Tabitha applied a cut to widen the birth canal.

Penny hissed as her babe's head slid out.

"Bear down again," Tabitha instructed.

All around the room, encouragement rang out, along with cries of joy from Mrs. Green. Meanwhile, Tabitha grabbed a scrap of linen at her feet to wipe away Penny's excrement.

"You're doing well." Tabitha secured the emerging baby with one hand and handed off the soiled cloth with the other.

Emily tossed it into a pile of dirty linens as the baby slid out, face down. The midwife guided the child out with one hand under the baby's head while the other supported the baby's backside. The precious baby girl gurgled, then screamed in the midwife's arms.

"Well done." After cutting the cord, Tabitha turned to Emily. "Take the child."

"Praise the Lord!" Mrs. Green called out.

Emily grabbed a blanket and took the child.

"Hello, little one." Warmth surged through Emily's limbs, and she couldn't resist grinning. She'd done it. She'd witnessed her first birth.

While Tabitha massaged Penny's stomach to expel the afterbirth, Emily rested the baby on the table for a brief exam. A quick swipe to remove debris from the baby's mouth and nostrils revealed the child had quite a healthy cry. Em marveled at the child's tiny ten toes and thick head of hair. The sweet girl wasn't pale, and she didn't have blue fingertips. No struggling for breath either. She was perfect.

By the time Emily finished swaddling the babe, the matrons had put Penny to bed. A crowd had gathered outside the door.

"Bring the baby to suckle." Tabitha rested in one of the chairs now. She hid a grimace and leaned to her right. Had she pushed herself too far?

Em crossed the room to lay the child in her mother's arms.

"Do you have a name for her?" Emily asked Penny.

"Not yet." Penny gave a weary grin. "My husband wanted a boy named after his daddy, but he'll have to wait for the next one."

"Didn't you tell me your mama had all girls after your brother was born?" Mrs. Green leaned over Penny to help her breastfeed.

"Six girls after Matthew," Penny murmured. "I should name her Ibilola, after my *iya-iya*. She was the first daughter, like my child."

"*Iya-iya*?" Emily spoke slowly to pronounce it correctly.

"That's what she calls her grandmother," Mrs. Green explained.

"It's one of the tongues from our homeland." Tabitha had closed her eyes, and her chin rested against her chest. "Year after year, I hear it less."

"The name is nice." Mrs. Green reached over to stroke the baby's forehead.

"My beautiful Lola." Penny nuzzled the top of the girl's head.

While the women spoke, Tabitha beckoned for Emily to come to her. "Help clean up, then eat."

"Do you want to eat now?" Emily asked. "You look exhausted."

The midwife flicked her fingers to shoo Em away.

With plenty to do, Emily gathered Tabitha's tools. She'd sanitize them properly back at the house. For now, she assisted others in cleaning up. No one spoke to her, even as a familiar face entered the house and took off his tricorn hat. It was Matthew.

"Have you sent word to my husband?" Penny asked him as she shielded her chest from his view.

"Not yet. He's due to return tomorrow." Seeing Matthew melt before his niece added a grin to Emily's face.

"Come meet Ibilola." Penny glowed through her fatigue. "Little Lola."

Emily couldn't resist joining them. "Your sister's baby is beautiful," she remarked.

Penny chuckled. "She has her daddy's nose, but that's about it. Lola is an Oyo girl through and through."

"Oyo?" Em asked. "Are you all related to Mrs. Oyo?"

"No, it's where we're from," Matthew explained. "Mrs. Oyo took on our homeland as her last name."

The siblings stared at each other until Penny turned away with a pained expression.

"You'll be fine." Matthew touched the top of Lola's head. "I'll be fine."

"Does that matter? Has it ever?" Penny asked.

"Is something wrong—" Emily began to say.

"No, everything is well." Matthew retreated slightly. "I came to see the child, and now I must return to work."

"What about leaving for good?" Penny's voice grew quiet. "Are you still going to go?"

"You know I have to." He said his farewells to his sister, then departed. Emily left behind him.

"Are you heading back to the Millwell place?" Emily asked once they were outside the house.

"I am."

"And what about after that? Penny said you're leaving."

"Not yet. It will take a while, but I'll go when I have enough money." He turned to the forest past the fields. "Now that Penny had her baby, I can leave Virginia."

Emily nodded, although her heart sank knowing he'd leave someday. Eventually, she'd have to go too, but a part of her would've liked to have gotten to know him better.

CHAPTER 38

Emily Bridge
JUNE 1758

Long before the sun rose, Emily and the midwife stood shivering before eight departed souls lying under coarse gray blankets. A great fire had risen like a wraith in the night and consumed a house in Petersburg. A wagoner's widow and her precious children had perished.

"We must prepare them for burial," the midwife said quietly. "Their family is upriver. They'll come for them in the morning."

"Tell me what I need to do." Emily had repeated that phrase many times, and like the other days, her heart hurt whenever a child died.

Pain or not, this was her new life now under the midwife's tutelage.

The starless night passed with Phoebe keeping torches lit while Tabitha and Emily stooped down before each blanket and blessed the body with care. Before each patient, the midwife murmured words Emily couldn't understand. A prayer perhaps. After a while,

Em spoke those words too. Emily liked to imagine the midwife asked for God's favor as she gently wiped the grime off the toddler's cheeks or replaced the eldest girl's charred dress with another.

In the morning, a cart arrived with sullen white men. They thanked the midwife with two coins and hoisted their loved ones into the wagon. Before they could take the smallest child at the end, Tabitha picked up the babe, cradled the child against her chest, and arranged him with care next to his mother.

Emily didn't have an ounce of strength left, but she stood beside the midwife until the cart disappeared over the bridge into town. Smoke still darkened the skies to the southeast.

This place had given her far too many firsts. Birth and death walked hand in hand.

Less than a week later, Emily escaped the house to forage and clear her head. There was plenty to do. This morning, she couldn't find precious wild rose petals. A month earlier, she'd spied the elusive dark-pink plant hiding among the river-edge thickets, like the naughty flash of one's shift underwear.

It was on days like this that she wished she could steal the petals from a neighbor's garden back in 1924. So many of the well-to-do folks in the U Street neighborhood grew them to impress the other families. A fistful of those plants would've lasted her an entire season.

After Emily found the critical herbs on her list, she still needed at least two bunches of valerian. The umbrella-like flower had calming properties she could tap into. Foraging always had a soothing, valerian-like effect on her senses. She could pretend she was back in 1924. When she could hear nothing but the whip-poor-will's familiar call from the treetops, Em imagined the Bridge farm was just past the birch trees on the way to Petersburg.

A whistle from behind her made her glance over her shoulder. Matthew, this time with deep-brown skin and a wide grin, waved in her direction with his right hand. In the other, he held the reins to a mare hauling pelts and small parcels.

"How have you been, Miss Freeman?" he asked.

"I've been good, Mr. Abramson." She slowed her pace, unable to resist returning his smile.

"Busy morning?" he asked.

"Just searching for plants, but I can see you've been busy too." She glanced at the pelt pile, recognizing the familiar rings from coons and the thick beaver coats.

"Mr. Millwell sent me all the way to Cobbs to get these. Can we trade? Your load looks much lighter."

"No thanks." She stuffed her hands into her apron pocket, suddenly conscious of the dirt under her fingernails and the mud smearing her sleeves. Had their time apart not helped? He'd disarmed her with ease. Of course they walked past some marshmallow plants, and she needed those. A part of her hoped he'd wait, and he did. Even the horse grazed on nearby grass. The stubborn flower had deep roots in the thick soil, forcing her to chip away at the earth. An easy silence settled between them, so she kept working until she freed the white-petaled flower.

"About time. Stubborn beggar." She got to walking again, and Matthew strode up beside her.

"Not for someone like you."

"I've never met an herb I couldn't dig up," Emily said. "With time, of course."

They walked a bit more. When her side brushed against his, she added space between them. Again and again, they drifted back and forth until they found a sweet spot. All she had to do was turn her head to see him.

"May I ask you a question?"

"Yes."

"Back in Oyo, what did you do?" she asked.

When Matthew didn't immediately answer, she added, "You don't have to tell me."

"My family fled our village after a rival chief took over," he said slowly. "He planned to kill my uncle along with his relatives. Most of us stayed over there, but a few, like my sisters and myself, became apprentices."

"How did you find that kind of work without speaking English?"

"My eldest sister knew their tongue. She made the arrangements for us to work five years for passage. I thought she was coming to America with us, but she was sent to England."

"Are you done working off your debt?"

"I finished two years ago, when I turned thirty. Felt like much longer."

So many questions came to mind. She wanted to know everything about him. Was his sister coming here someday? Had she written any letters? Matthew sounded like he still missed his homeland. She'd give anything to know if Isaiah thrived in his new home.

"You're free now to do as you please," she said. "There's something wonderful about knowing you can go anywhere, see anything."

He adjusted the load from his backpack. "There's much to learn out there. Much to experience if you're willing to see the world. My family rarely left our village, but we had all sorts of stories and lessons about our ancestors. Those tales taught me not to fear the unknown but to embrace it and find my way."

"I'd like to hear a couple sometime."

"It will be nice to tell them," Matthew said, flashing that easy smile of his. "Now that I'm so far away, I'll never hear them from my aunts again."

Emily nodded, thinking of the Bridges and how Professor Mayberry considered the family Bible more precious than anything. But those records went back only so far—the Bridges' story began long before Zachariah and Gertrude set foot in the colonies.

"I don't know my family's history before we came here either, but we all can take root anywhere and find our purpose." She fell silent for a moment, feeling the weight of her journey. She'd never had a chance to grow roots and settle down, but she'd thrived, accomplished things.

Matthew smiled at her with his eyes, and she couldn't resist saying, "Why do you look at me like that?"

Oh God, can I rip my mouth off? Emily scurried to walk faster.

She could feel his eyes on her back. There was no way he was frowning this time.

"On the way to Cobbs, it rained the whole time," he said quietly. "After a while, I was miserable and cold, but I couldn't stop thinking about this lady I met. She makes me laugh, and she smells like the bitter plants she picks."

Did he just say she smelled like weeds?

"When you stitched up my arm," he added, "you had this scent I couldn't place, but I liked how it wasn't subtle or soft like a flower."

"That was mint." At least he hadn't mentioned the onions.

Something inside her bloomed like the white rose petals in her apron, a warmth rivaling the June heat caressing her cheeks. Matthew had thought of her.

"Are you leaving again soon?" she asked before a more intrusive question came to mind.

"Not any time soon."

She glanced in his direction and found him content.

They walked for a spell until the familiar fields of tobacco and flax appeared. She expected him to veer off with the horse toward the Millwell place east of Petersburg, but he followed her right up to the midwife's house. At the doorway, he hoisted his pack off his back using his right arm instead of both.

"Why aren't you using your left arm too?" she asked. "Something wrong?"

"Still hurts, but it's my fault."

She pursed her lips. That man probably would've left the rags on his arm until the fabric jumped up and danced a jig.

"Let me see it," she said firmly.

"Not today. I have to deliver these."

"You have enough time to walk with me, but you don't have enough for me to see your wound." She folded her arms.

"I'd never do that to a friend."

Did he think he could fool her?

"I'll let you see it tomorrow," he finally said.

"Fine." Emily marched to the front door. "You'll either show up or you won't, but if we're friends, it's better to admit you're not fully healed."

Matthew bid her goodbye with an amused glint in his eyes. "I'll see you at first light then, Miss Freeman."

CHAPTER 39

Emily Bridge
JUNE 1758

Emily found Matthew waiting outside her door at sunrise. The mid-June heat had kicked in, bringing enough waves of humidity to dampen anyone's spirits, yet he bathed half in shadow, half in the sun next to an evergreen near the house. Clouds of gnats were the only creatures bold enough to dance in the light around him.

He greeted her with a nod and trailed after her to the well.

Having his eyes on her backside unnerved Emily at first, but he followed her diligently, and helped carry the bucket back to the house.

Only moist air circulated through the house, so she took care of his wound right out front. While she unraveled the cloth around his arm, she fixed her gaze on the middle of his chest. Any higher might've betrayed the thoughts caressing her mind. Was the curve of his cheek as smooth as it appeared? What would happen if she cupped it to run her thumb against the smooth stubble?

She peered at the cut, finding less angry-looking welts than before. She ran her fingers over his forearm to search for inflammation and he quivered. The movement had been subtle. A brief flash. But she'd caught it and stilled.

"Is something wrong?" Matthew asked.

"Everything looks good."

Just like you, she couldn't help but think as she wrapped fresh cloth around his arm.

"Thank you, Miss Freeman."

Day after day, for the next two weeks, as the heat rose to intolerable levels, he waited next to that evergreen. On her way out of the house one morning, Emily caught Tabitha saying, "What's that man doing?"

"You know very well what he's doing," Phoebe said, a mischievous gleam to her hazel eyes. "He's come calling on Emily."

"He needs to do better," Tabitha said dryly. "It's about time for him to take her out into the woods and stop dawdling."

Emily escaped the house to Phoebe's laughter. She couldn't tell them such talk wasn't proper. They simply didn't care. Later that night, Tabitha even added, "You know where babies come from, don't you, girl? Women need affection sometimes. Why should we ignore our needs?"

The midwife had a point. Em had come to learn that plenty of women eligible for marriage got pregnant *before* their nuptials. All the lessons she'd learned about chaste colonial families had said little about real relationships between lovers.

A couple of days later, Emily woke up with a question poking her like a stone left in her boot. What was she doing with Matthew?

And if she did give in to how she felt, what would happen next? The man planned to leave town for good someday. She had to leave for Charlottesville in a few years too. While growing up on the farm, she'd imagined she'd marry a man she loved. They'd have children and make a life for themselves. She couldn't hold this feeling close and let it grow into something not meant to be.

She'd never marry Matthew.

The very thought made her linger at the front door. She was supposed to run an errand for the midwife, but Em didn't want to see his face, knowing they could never be more than friends.

When Emily finally headed outside, she noticed Matthew snoozing with his backside to the tree. She considered sneaking past, but she couldn't resist leaning down in front of him. It was nice watching his relaxed expression, the slow rise and fall of his chest. She wondered what he dreamt about.

She waited a bit before tapping his boot. "I considered letting you sleep, but the mosquitos have had breakfast, lunch, and dinner on your arms."

He took a deep breath and stretched his arms wide. She wanted to fall into them. "I don't mind."

"Mrs. Oyo is sending me to the shipyards on an errand. Want to come with me before you go to work?"

He got up and the sunrise's glow touched the top of his head, burning his tight curls with a reddish tinge. Emily turned away to face the forest. Matthew Abramson was far too handsome.

"Of course," he said. "Let's go."

He joined her march toward town.

A gap separated them, yet with only a slight tilt of her arm, his hand could brush against hers. As they followed the path toward the shipyards, she tried to think of an offhand topic. How the harvest wouldn't be as good this year due to the rising temperatures. Or perhaps she should bring up how cholera had become a problem in town.

Boring. Everything she thought of was boring. Her cousin Rosie had always thought of something witty.

"Have you ever worked on a plantation before?" he asked.

"Never. You?"

"I think I've done everything. Corn. Barley. Before I learned the trapping trade, I was a farmer."

"What haven't you done?"

"Not everything, apparently." He inched closer until her shoulder brushed against his side. "Does Mrs. Oyo need another apprentice?"

"Goodness no." The very thought of waking up next to Matthew on the dirt floor brought heat to her cheeks.

He laughed, and she couldn't resist joining in. Matthew made any conversation easy. She didn't have to fawn over him like her cousin Etta would do or brag about her uncle's wealth like Rosie. They could just be. That had to be enough for now.

The pair made their way down to the shipyard, where Emily fetched the parcel the midwife had been waiting for.

She expected him to drift away—maybe even come up with an excuse to go about his business—but he waited next to her.

"I'm returning home," she finally said. "Will I see you again tomorrow morning?"

"Why do you ask? Are you tired of me yet?"

The question took her aback. All these weeks he'd never asked.

"No, I'm not," she admitted. Saying those words out loud felt good.

"Then you'll see me again, Miss Freeman."

Instead of turning around to depart, he backed away, and their gazes tangled. The warmth in her chest spread until she reached Pocahontas Island and heard the blacksmith call out in greeting to an approaching man.

"Mr. Bridge!" the blacksmith said. "Never thought you'd arrive before the summer ended."

Her joyous smile died. Anyone could have that last name, but she hadn't met a single Bridge since her arrival. She twisted around the corner to watch a Negro gentleman wearing a weathered green waistcoat and brown breeches shake hands with the blacksmith.

"How was your journey?" the blacksmith asked.

"Long, as to be expected," the man replied, "but I was grateful you were willing to let me work for what I need."

"My father always trusted you. Said I'd never find a man as hardworking as Zachariah Bridge."

"Can you say that to my wife? Gertie says I never do enough."

The world wavered and dimmed at the sound of her distant ancestors' names. Why was her future father-in-law here of all places? She collapsed against the cabin's wall. Nearly one hundred miles separated her from the Bridges. She'd meet them soon enough—but right now, just for a little while, she'd wanted to taste freedom before she bent to fate's will.

She stumbled until she ran back to the house, checking behind every corner for someone else. With her luck, maybe John was in town too. Now that she knew what Zachariah looked like, John might have similar features. According to family legends, Emily met John Bridge around Charlottesville and settled down on the farm before Luke was born in 1761.

She'd be forced to choose, and in the end, she had to marry John.

By the time she reached the midwife's home, she couldn't shake the fear of uncertainty. No one could drive her away from Matthew. Not fate or twisted up timelines. And yet when she closed the door and rested her head against it, she couldn't help but picture the Bridge family orchard, a vivid and breathtakingly beautiful sight.

CHAPTER 40

Emily Bridge
JULY 1758

One late-summer morning, Emily left the house to darkened skies. She had much on her mind—especially after seeing Zachariah Bridge arrive in town. Those thoughts vanished as the screaming wind snatched at her skirts, forcing her to scurry to the wood lean-to. With her arms full, her gaze swept over the countryside. The squalls picked up and dragged branches over the hills. In their garden, the crops withering under the excessive heat were carried away.

A storm was coming—a big one. She felt it in her bones.

Not far from the midwife's house, Matthew's sod house stood like an unwavering stone, but she'd seen photos in the newspapers with leveled homes and cars hurled about.

A light flickered through the cracks in the door. Thank goodness, he was home. A good storm would fill that house to the brim. The rising panic in Em pushed her. She dumped the wood and sprinted over to his house. Emily tried to enter, but he'd barricaded himself inside.

"Matthew!" The wind swallowed her screams. She hit the door with her fists.

Moments later, she caught him stirring and the door wrenched open. He pulled her in.

From the outside, Matthew's home had few amenities like a rain barrel and woodpile. On the inside he had only a pallet and a stone pit for a fire.

"What are you doing? It's not safe out there." He was shirtless, with his breeches unbuttoned to below his belly button.

She stared a bit before she caught herself and turned her head away. "You can't stay here. It's not safe."

"I'll be fine." He fastened his breeches.

"No, you won't." Emily searched the dirt floor and found a linen shirt. "Put this on—oh no, use this one. You're coming with me."

He donned the shirt and boots as she escaped the house to a downpour. In seconds, the hard rain pelted her face, soaking through her cotton cap. Matthew enveloped her in his arms, resting his forehead against the crown of hers. She clung to him until they were safe in the midwife's house.

Phoebe was at the window, peering outside. "How bad is it out there?" she asked.

"It's not good." Emily reluctantly let go of Matthew.

"What's going on?" Tabitha murmured from the bed.

"There's a bad storm brewing," he said. "Let me secure the house."

While he shut the shutters and brought in the wood Emily had abandoned, she got the inside of the house ready. They had plenty of food from late-spring crops and the means for light.

When Matthew returned, wet and shivering, Emily handed him a blanket.

"Thanks," he murmured.

"How is it out there?" She almost reached up to wipe his face.

"If the storm doesn't pass soon, the river might flood."

"We've seen rain like this before, Mr. Abramson," the midwife said calmly. "It will pass soon and we'll be well by the morn."

As the outside world rattled the single window in the house and howled through the cracks in the walls, Matthew sat on a chair before the fire. Emily took the opposite seat and settled in for a long day. Tabitha rested in the bed while Phoebe kept trying to look outside. The midwife frowned at the behavior but kept quiet for now.

Em's sigh filled the house. She glanced at Matthew, only to see him staring at the fire. She considered reading and grabbed her book. It was at times like these, when Emily remembered all the niceties of the modern age, that she longed for the dim light from a kerosene lamp to read. God knew she'd race down to Petersburg, storm and all, to fetch some Kotex pads from the pharmacy compared to the filthy rags she had to use.

She drew closer to the fire and squinted at the worn pages of her book. At least she'd managed to buy another one from a peddler in Pocahontas. It wasn't much better than *The Divine Comedy*. Professor Mayberry was probably laughing at her right now.

"What are you smiling about?" Matthew asked.

Emily burned to speak the truth. "I'm thinking about people back home. The ones I'll never see again."

The midwife ambled across the room, appearing wistful as the storm battered the roof. "Everything's always better back home. But, then again, even if home doesn't have good memories, it's the first place you thought you were safe."

"Where did you learn the healing arts?" Emily asked, looking to fill the time.

"My master was a physician educated in England. The warts on his backside had more value than him. He saw me as nothing more than a fetch mule, a bed warmer when his wife couldn't tolerate his grumbling. That man had no intention of teaching me anything other than the difference between a forceps and tweezers." She reached down to motion for the cat to come to her. The calico obliged her for a good scratch.

She stroked under the animal's chin in lazy circles and continued. "In Annapolis, we had fewer doctors trained in England back then so well-to-do men learned under him. Their ears and eyes were open—just like mine." She snorted. "None of them had an ounce of sense. He once had an apprentice who repeated everything he said. That fellow couldn't tell one end of a patient's arse from another."

"Fools, all of them," Phoebe agreed.

"Did you live in the same house?" Emily asked Phoebe.

"At first, we did," Phoebe replied. "We were bought around the same time, Tab and me. That was such a long time ago, but she even remembers what my Nanticoke mother looked like. Sadly, I don't." Phoebe's voice briefly trailed off, but then it returned, louder. "Once our master fell on hard times, he sold me to another household."

"Damn bastard." Tabitha spat on the floor, then cursed in her mother tongue.

Matthew chuckled. Em would have to ask him later what she'd said.

"Your master or the new man who bought her?" Emily asked.

"Both," the midwife said firmly. "Other than Phoebe, only the master's wife treated me with decency. That poor woman died in childbirth not long after I gave birth to a stillborn."

They sat like that in the dark while the storm rampaged outside. Bits of the roof surrendered until the rain seeped through. Puddles formed on the dirt floor, on the tables, all over the herbs hanging from the storage shelf above the bed.

Emily and Matthew gathered some pots to catch the dripping water. The quiet left her uneasy. "How long were you a slave?" she asked the midwife.

The question made Tabitha pause, the scar on her upper cheek flexing. Even Phoebe turned to her friend. Matthew's face grew pensive.

"I was born one," Tabitha replied, "and if Master'd had his way, I would've died in bondage."

And yet she was here, and not in Annapolis. Emily wondered if Tabitha had won her freedom or escaped.

Before Em could open her mouth to speak, a foot-long section of the roof came crashing down onto the bed. Everyone scrambled, with Tabitha cursing and Phoebe squealing. They grabbed any boxes or blankets, getting further soaked in the process. It would be a long night until the storm passed.

By the next day, the storm had escaped to the east, leaving the countryside drenched and forlorn.

Emily woke up, her back groaning from her sleeping upright on the chair, but she wasn't alone. Matthew sat on the chair right next to her, and her head rested on his shoulder. Someone had covered them with a blanket. She shifted to get up, but didn't want to. Matthew was there, his body warm and firm against her cheek. She turned to his face. He was close enough for her to count the two moles along his collarbone. With a smile, she imagined tracing her fingers from one spot to the next. Would he like it if she touched him there?

"You're awake," he mumbled with his eyes closed.

She got up before he could see her embarrassment. "Yeah, we should get up. Looks like there's work to do."

Light shined through a hole in the ceiling and revealed the muddy ruins within the house.

"That's not good," Emily said.

"No, it isn't," Tabitha said. The midwife and Phoebe huddled together on top of the chest in the corner.

"I should go take a look outside," Matthew suggested.

Minutes later, everyone left the house into the damp heat. The sight stole Em's breath away. The Appomattox had spilled over and raked the countryside, leaving a wet mess of despair and dripping clotheslines of torn garments. The blacksmith's and the stone mason's homes had collapsed nearby.

She hoped the elder Bridge had survived the storm unscathed.

Even worse, poor Matthew's house resembled a wet mound of mud and debris. Her heart sank at the sight. He had nothing left but his life. Thank God he hadn't stayed there.

Emily had seen winter storms bury half of Charlottesville in snowdrifts. Her uncle Bertie had even mentioned that once the flooded Rivanna River had turned the town into a swamp, but she'd never seen or imagined anything like this.

"This is . . . devastating," Tabitha whispered.

"I've only seen tornadoes do this," Phoebe said.

"Maybe that's what it was," Tabitha replied.

As Emily took in the destruction, she recalled the photos and gossip after a great storm struck the Gulf of Mexico in 1919. She supposed a tornado or hurricane-force winds would've done such damage.

Matthew returned. His expression was somber. "I found Lucy wandering outside," he said to Tabitha. "She's a bit skittish, but I tied her up to the post in front of what's left of the smithy."

Soon enough, Emily would see for herself if Zachariah had

fared well. If God were merciful, the man had returned home to his family.

"Thank you, Mr. Abramson," the midwife said. "Have you heard anything from the constable? Does anyone need my help?"

"I don't know yet," he admitted, but the weary look on his face said much.

"We have work to do, Emily," the midwife announced.

Emily thought she'd have to remain at the house to clean up with Phoebe, but the midwife gave orders as she stuffed what little dry cloth and tools they had into an apron.

"I'll go across the bridge into town," she said, her voice weaker than usual. Her breath appeared too shallow. "You must visit *each* house on this side of the river. Help the injured."

"Yes, ma'am."

Tabitha motioned toward a chest in the room. "There're old shirts in there. Use those for bindings and wound care." She walked to the doorway and rested against the frame.

In the middle of ripping up one of the garments, Emily peered harder at the woman. Something was wrong. "Are you sure I shouldn't go with you?"

"No." The woman disappeared out the door.

The midwife wouldn't slip past her that easily. After dealing with her mama's antics growing up, Emily wouldn't let Tabitha just ignore her. Emily hurried out the door to find Matthew hauling debris into a pile. Tabitha strode up to him, murmured words Emily couldn't hear, then she left.

"Are you going to let her leave like that?" Emily asked him. "She looks tired."

"Do you think anyone tells Mrs. Oyo what to do?" The fatigue in his eyes faded for a moment. She wished she could comfort him.

"Not really."

"Where are you heading?"

"Might as well check the closest houses first," she said.

"You'll need help to get inside George Mills's house." He tossed a branch into the pile, then wiped his hands off on his breeches. "Give me a moment."

Not long after, their slow-going trek across Pocahontas began. As far as Emily could see, families, many of them bleary-eyed and weary, stood outside or did what they could to unearth their homes.

"It will be a long day," she breathed. A warm hand wrapped around hers. Matthew squeezed gently. She returned the gesture, grateful to have him by her side.

CHAPTER 41

Emily Bridge

AUGUST 1758

It took weeks for the parishes along the river to recover. For the Appomattox to recall the overflowing banks inward. For drowned fields to dry out. Great trash piles dotted the country-side, with ever-present reminders of the neighbors Emily had met: the broken wheel to the Ironside family's wagon, filthy shirts with the inescapable blacksmith marks, and a tiny cotton-filled doll wearing a muted gray dress. So many things had been lost. But none more valuable than the lives the storm had ended.

Emily surveyed the land outside the midwife's home—a bit rough around the edges due to the chipped stone walls and the hole in the roof. The midwife's new "roof window" left a lot to be desired. Her home's newest occupant, namely Matthew, had volunteered to fix it.

If he hadn't been here, she would've hauled herself up there, skirts and all.

She couldn't resist smiling, remembering this morning, when he turned around in the corner to change from his linen shirt to a work tunic. Having him nearby had been nice. There were too many opportunities for his hand to brush against hers. For her eyes to open in the morning to see him staring at her from his sleeping spot near the hearth.

You will be leaving Pocahontas someday, she reminded herself.

She'd learned not long ago that Zachariah had left town before the storm. A blessing and a reminder of her inescapable future.

Emily cast aside her dreary thoughts to focus on fixing what was left of their garden. The root vegetables had survived, but many of the other plants had been ripped out of the ground. With another mouth to feed in the house, she had to get things back in order. On the way to the garden, she passed Matthew. He stared at the roof as if he was having second thoughts.

"Are you sure you want to help?" She shuddered at the thought of anyone going up to such a precarious place. "I can tell Mrs. Oyo you don't want to do it."

"Too late." He turned toward the front door where the midwife stood with a smug grin and a bowl of breakfast oats in hand.

"What's all the chattering?" Phoebe peeked around the other, shorter woman and immediately grinned. "What are you two talking about," she asked him, "so close together?"

"Nothing much." He took a respectful step back from Emily.

"Of course," Tabitha chimed in.

Em swallowed past her embarrassment and hurried off to the garden. Her aunts back home didn't hold back from teasing her either.

From the morning into the afternoon, Matthew patched up the roof and fixed the broken firewood lean-to while Emily prepared a pot of hash. She even scraped up the ingredients for some maple nutmeg cookies—one of her brother's favorite treats. Over those hours, she never spoke to him, yet having him nearby, knowing he'd eat the food she prepared, gave her a thrill. A little dread too. He hadn't eaten her food before.

Once the meal was done, the four of them broke bread at the table. Emily had arranged each place setting and lined up the bowls and spoons, all of them misshapen and scratched, with the kind of care Aunt Alma would've fussed over.

Tabitha's right eyebrow rose as Phoebe sat.

"Are we having a proper lady's meal?" Tabitha used her hand to wipe off imaginary dust from the table.

"No, just dinner," Em said, ladling generous portions into the bowls.

"We're proper English ladies now, Tab." Phoebe picked up her spoon, blew the steam off the hash, and took a delicate bite.

"All we need are napkins," the midwife said.

"Delicate lace ones," Phoebe added. "And we deserve a roast too."

"Any will do."

"Oh no, no. I demand the finest pork. An animal to rival the meals those biddies in the church always say they're eating."

"You mean the ones who scoff and spit at the so-called lesser folk? The pigs deserve better."

The two women laughed while Matthew glanced at her from across the table, his eyebrows raised and a slight tilt to his lips. Did he find them as funny as she did? He used his spoon to bury the burned parts on the top, then he took a hearty bite.

She took a bite too and grimaced at the mushy, overcooked potatoes. At least she hadn't burned the cookies.

The two women chatted about the town's business, specifically the parish's most outlandish rumors. Emily imagined another world, where after a day of hard work, only she and Matthew returned to this table for a meal.

This perfect world didn't have flooded homes with bewildered parents crying over their dead children, or the screams of a horse that had to be put down, or the anguish from a boy who couldn't find his grandfather.

Em glanced up from her flooded thoughts to see Matthew had emptied his bowl. He leaned back with folded arms, his shoulders relaxed. His smile easy.

It was moments like this one that always shined light on the darkest ones.

————

By the end of the month, much of the debris had been cleared, along with the heavy stench from the fires burning the moldy tobacco and barley. Life had to go on—births, deaths, and folks had to work or they wouldn't eat.

Emily spent her days replenishing the midwife's herbs while the midwife attended to the sick and Phoebe worked at the Bolling home. It was all a spoiled mess. Two precious pouches of toothache plant and anise hyssop had flown off, likely through the hole in the roof, along with pain-relieving black crowberry and wild yam.

At least she could forage for the plants. She checked a small box where the midwife kept the mullein buds and found it empty. Just like so many other containers. Much would need to be replenished before winter. Em couldn't imagine all the ailments to come, nor the fact she couldn't waltz on down to the local pharmacy for aspirin.

"You frown a lot," a voice said from outside, jolting her from reverie.

She glanced up to see Matthew approaching the house.

"I frown because something is always amiss." She'd taken to using "amiss" more often since she'd heard one of the ladies in town say it. "How has your day been?" she asked him.

"Thanks to your hospitality, I'll be well rested for the season."

Her hands slowed from plucking the leaves into a pile. "The trapping season? Isn't it too early for that?"

"Oh no," he said. "In the early fall, we hunt for ducks. After that, the deer. By the time winter comes, we'll start trapping then."

Emily's heart sank, but she kept her hands moving. "Will you miss having a roof over your head?"

"That and more." When Matthew spoke, his gaze unnerved her until she looked away.

"I wish you luck," she managed to say.

"That's it?" He took a step closer.

What more could she say? Folks were a revolving door in her life. Either disappearing into the past or moving on to better circumstances.

"Don't sleep next to bears?" she whispered.

He stood there playing with a dandelion between his fingers. Finally, he asked, "Will you be here when I return?"

The question made her pause. "This is my home now."

"Do you promise?"

Her smile faltered. "I believe nothing is guaranteed."

"No, it isn't." He was closer now. "But if I'm lucky, will you still be here in the spring?"

"Like our friendship," she said softly, "I think I can guarantee that."

"Are we friends?" he asked.

He lingered and she fought to swallow. Slowly, he leaned down until all she could see was him. All she could feel was his rough breath against her lips. He was so close to her mouth. A sharp inhale away. Then his lips captured hers. The kiss wasn't tentative but possessive as his arms circled her upper back to draw her close to him.

She fell into Matthew, and her first kiss was everything she'd hoped it would be.

By the time they parted, his heated gaze left Emily breathless and yearning to kiss him again. He waited a bit before he backed away. When he turned around to leave the house, she seared his kiss into her memory to savor over the long winter.

CHAPTER 42

Emily Bridge

FEBRUARY 1759

Almost a full year had passed since Emily had fallen. All around her, the evergreen forest tried to crawl out of winter's icy maw, but even with the bitter cold, her foraging habits remained. On this particular morning, she ventured northward from Pocahontas to hunt for medicinal herbs. After a half hour of walking, she reached Swift Creek and an abandoned sod house with stone markers behind it. The tiny mounds rose like torn knuckles above the dead grass.

The home immediately reminded her of Matthew's. She wondered if he planned to build a new one after he returned.

She circled the dwelling twice for nettles but found none among the sunken mud walls and kicked-in doorway. Em's gaze swept over the nearby riverbank. Better to search there for food, but she considered what hid behind the door. Before she changed her mind, she darted inside. With little light from the overcast sky, she couldn't see much. Defiant weeds and mushrooms battled for space on the dirt floor. She took two steps deeper inside. The home still held warmth but little else. At the other end of the house, a wind gust tugged at a lone spiderweb attached to a broken wagon wheel's spokes. All life had abandoned this place.

What kind of family had lived here? Had they huddled close to the hearth during the winter, telling tales? The sweet yet subtle scent of a fresh birch log tossed on the fire crossed her thoughts. At another fireplace back in 1915, she'd listened to tales from her best friend, her big brother. She used to think there was nothing better in the world than the first taste of freedom after a long winter. Not that they didn't have fun back then. Isaiah loved to leave rocks in her boots or dead beetles under her blankets. She got him back by sewing the armholes shut in one of his shirts.

Emily sighed as her gaze swept the soddy. Her first winter living with the midwife had passed the same. Quiet. Reflective. Without the sounds of family or close friends, she had nothing but her thoughts—and her failures—to ruminate on. She'd recalled the times when, on the way to church on Sundays, she'd passed the Bridge cemetery. The Bridges never slowed down to pay respects to the dead, but at least one of her uncles had tried to prune back the vegetation. The forest always pushed back. She'd walked past two gravestones. Isaiah never had paused either, but the sight of those mounds had dug under her skin and never escaped.

Real people are buried there, she'd once thought. They'd worked from one day to the next, mourning their loved ones, until someone else had buried them too.

Emily would've never thought that each time she walked to the orchard, she'd passed the other Emily's grave. *Her own grave.* That the remnants of her mortal body, minus her soul, rested under her feet.

How was that possible?

Emily left the sod house and circled to the back. She approached a single stone and plucked away the surrounding grass. With her coat sleeve, she added a smoothness to the dimpled gray rock. *There.* The rock stood out now. If someone else passed, they'd see this grave among the others, and maybe they'd remember the nameless soul resting here.

February became March, and after the snow disappeared, Emily often sat before the fire knitting wool stockings with Phoebe. Far too frequently her mind drifted to Matthew and their kiss. Each time she spied a lone figure walking through town or when someone knocked on the door, a sliver of hope danced down her spine. That hope fought with fate.

By mid-April Emily finally crossed paths with Matthew next to the Pocahontas smithy. After spending the afternoon tending to a family stricken with scarlet fever, she'd looked forward to propping her feet up. She peered at him in his tricorn hat, patchy beard, and new dark-blue waistcoat, and her heartbeat quickened. If he would've shown up this morning, he would've found her in better spirits—and not dressed in a soiled cape with a ripped hem. She tried to wipe away the smudges on her face.

The Negro blacksmith and his son glanced up from their farrier work on two mares, but they resumed their work when Emily and Matthew veered away from their smoky brick hearth.

"Good day to you, Miss Oyo." He squinted from the bright sunlight and waited.

"Nice beard, Mr. Abramson." She still hadn't gotten used to the last name the locals used for her.

She itched to wrap her arms around him, but they were out in the open. There were far too many prying eyes.

"How long have you been back?" she asked. *And why haven't you been by to see me?*

"Not long." He scratched the back of his neck. "Now that the trapping season is over, I'm working at the Bollings'. It's tobacco planting time."

She snorted. So he'd probably seen her from afar while she was worried he was out there struggling. Had he not *once* thought about seeing her?

"You're not as happy to see me as I am you," he said.

"You look well. I'm pleased."

"Your face doesn't say that."

"Should I be more pleased? I remember *someone* asked me if I'd be here when he returned. Here I am, and you couldn't even say hello? Good day?" She tried to sound serious. "I'm bumbling around like Charlie Chaplin, tripping over my feet."

His grin spread wider. "Who's Charlie Chaplin?"

"It doesn't matter."

"I think it does."

She bit her lower lip to keep from sighing. "I was worried about you, and I would've appreciated a visit." Hell, a quick knock or a wave from afar would've worked.

Matthew took off his hat. "You're right. I shouldn't have waited, but I needed a bath. I bought a fine coat too."

He continued. "My father told me a man should be at his best when he gives a lady a gift for the first time." He reached into his pocket, then presented his palm. In the center of his calloused hand lay a bracelet strung with tiny turquoise stones.

The ice on her tongue melted to warm her cheeks. She closed the gap between them. "Where did you find turquoise?"

"Why am I not surprised you know what it is?" The stones clinked together as he rolled his hand back and forth. "While outside Wilmington, an Iroquois man had many things to barter from the south. This was one of them.

"You're smiling now," he said. "Good. You like it?"

He untied the strings and motioned to wrap them around her wrist.

She extended her arm. "It's breathtaking. Why did you buy this? You should be saving up to leave Virginia."

Matthew leaned toward her, bringing the fresh scent of sunshine baked into linen. He slowly tied the strings and his fingertips brushed against her wrist. Once he was done, she took a step back, but he held on. She glanced up from the bracelet to see heat in Matthew's eyes. The same heat from when they'd kissed.

"I didn't expect you to bring me anything," she managed.

"Then I should do it more often. I like it when you're happy."

His words stole her breath.

"I made good money this winter," he said. "After another year, I should be ready to leave Virginia. What do you think?" he asked carefully.

"That's wonderful."

He seemed to muse over her reply before he said, "Would you ever think of coming with me?"

Matthew's question stabbed her gut with a hot blade.

"I can't," she said, stumbling over her words. "Things have changed over the winter. I have to return home someday. No matter what."

He nodded and turned away. "I'd hoped you'd come with me."

"I'm sorry."

"No need to be. My aunt told me I must always be ready for change. No matter the outcome." He put on his hat and bid her good day.

This time when he walked away, she didn't watch him go. She didn't want him to turn around and see her in tears.

CHAPTER 43

Emily Bridge
MAY 1759

Matthew had made great progress on his sod house. Through the house's dirty window, she watched him haul sod from a nearby field. Stack after stack grew. When night fell, he left to sleep at the smithy.

Not once did he cross the midwife's doorstep again.

Phoebe didn't say a word. Even the outspoken midwife clammed up on the subject. For that, Emily was grateful.

She thought about taking off the bracelet, but every time she reached for the ties, she almost cried. A month ago, things were different. She didn't want to think about the *after* without Matthew.

During her meals with Phoebe and Tabitha, she often thought of bringing him a hot bowl of food, maybe a few words of encouragement, but her head—the far more steadfast part of her—kept her from marching across the glen to speak to him.

To keep her hands busy, she prepared a hope chest. In two years, she'd fill it with knitted blankets, cooking utensils, various trinkets she'd earned through bartering, clothes for her future children, and books. She loved a good book and she had plenty of time to gather these things before she had to go, and the midwife of Pocahontas Island still had much to teach her.

AUGUST 1760

Over a year later, while protected under the shade of an evergreen, Emily perched on a stool before five baskets of peaches. She chewed her lower lip. Nothing tasted sweeter than canned peaches from the grocery store, unless you had more than you could use.

The Talbert family, who'd welcomed twins last week, had paid the midwife and her apprentice with food instead of coin. At first, Emily couldn't wait to bake tarts and sweeten their stews with the ripest fruit. But—and there was always a but—she had *no* idea how to preserve food without glass jars. For the last two years, Em had only helped salt the pork or harvest the food from the garden.

The midwife had handled everything else until this year.

Right before Phoebe had left for work, Em had asked her for instructions.

"Tabby always did what needed to be done," the woman had said. "She ordered. I followed."

"So what did she do with the fruits and vegetables?"

Phoebe's face scrunched together. "Hmm, well two years ago she buried the eggs for the winter. Then she salted the pork and eggs the year after that . . ."

With no recourse, Emily was left to sit in the heat and consider her options. None of them included bothering the midwife. Maybe she could ask a neighbor instead. Through the house's open door, she barely heard the woman's breaths. The midwife didn't rise by midmorning anymore, nor did she wander about in the night due to insomnia.

She moved only when someone needed a healer.

Emily rose from the stool and wandered over to the doorway to peek inside. Within the dark confines of the house, no one stirred on the bed. Tabitha rarely shifted from her spot facing the wall.

"Are you hungry, Mrs. Oyo?" Emily called out softly. "You didn't break your fast." She'd almost said "hotcakes." If only she was back home. Before her ma's delirium worsened, the sweet, yeasty smell of bubbling dough used to convince Ma to walk among the living.

"Not hungry" was all the midwife said.

Emily took a step into the house but stopped as she remembered the last time she'd tried to examine Tabitha. The woman had scowled at the sight of Em's outstretched hand, her gaze as dangerous as a cornered cottonmouth.

"Don't you *ever* touch me," she'd warned in a tone she'd never used before. It was direct. Final. "Before I set Phoebe free and ran away with her, I cut my old master real *good* for trying to touch me again. Try it and see what happens."

"But you're sick," Emily had said, her voice rising. "I need to see what's wrong before you get worse—"

"I been past 'worse' a long time ago. Leave me be."

Em's desire to uncover the truth pushed her to the bed. Perhaps she'd find the midwife asleep. She took her time, her footsteps tentative and soft. By the time she reached the midwife's bedside, sweat beaded on her upper lip and dampened the middle of her back.

Tabitha's inert form was pressed against the wall, leaving a single space where Phoebe would usually lie. Emily had seen this sight many times before through a cracked open door into Ma's room.

She leaned forward. Carefully. Slowly. With the tips of her fingers, she gripped the gray wool blanket's edge and pulled back to expose the woman underneath. Tabitha's wiry hair was unbound and clipped short. Her back was bowed, and her shoulder bones poked through the yellowed cotton shift. A mixture of body odors mingled with the scent of the fresh straw they'd replaced a month ago. Emily placed her hand on the midwife's right side, finding the woman's rib cage in that area swollen and deformed. Before she could pry further, the midwife's head jerked toward her.

"What did I tell you—" she breathed.

"I need help with the peaches," Em said.

"Liar."

"Mrs. Oyo!" a voice called out.

Emily started and turned to see a teenaged Negro boy gasping for breath right outside the door.

"Yes?" she said.

"Momma's baby . . ." he began to say as his shoulders sagged. His gaze flicked to what was left of breakfast's oat bread on the table.

"Have her throws started? Where're you from, boy?" The midwife sprang to life and inched over the bed to push Emily away.

Another opportunity missed. Em fetched the boy some water and bread.

"Downriver off Wintycock Creek." He guzzled down the water and inhaled the offering.

"I know the place." Tabitha scowled from pain as she swung her feet over the side of the bed, but Emily moved faster.

"I can find it." She pressed down on the woman's shoulder to keep her from rising from the bed. "Anything I need to know?"

"It's her sixth," Tabitha said stiffly. "Last two babies were stubborn and breech, but this one might arrive before you set foot in that house."

Emily grabbed what she needed. Before she left, she glanced over her shoulder to check on Tabitha. The midwife no longer faced the wall and the sour expression she threw at Emily pushed her out the door.

Less than an hour later, Emily stood at the Petersburg port. The boy had remained behind to rest overnight. Without the young man, she needed someone to ferry her upriver. There were plenty of men, many of them eager to line their pockets with coin before the winter arrived. She had resigned herself to employing one of them when Ian Green, Penny's husband, stepped forward.

"Are you searching for someone?" he asked.

She explained the situation.

"Let me find Matthew—he can help you."

"No need." She'd been busy all summer after an outbreak of cholera swept through town. Every now and then she'd glimpsed him from afar, but they hadn't spoken to each other since she'd rejected him. As much as she wanted to see him again, it was best for her to focus on her midwife training. Her skills would benefit the Bridges in the years to come.

"We got a shipment bound for a township off Wintipomack Creek," he explained. "If you can wait until we finish loading the boat, Matthew can take you up there. After he's dropped off the goods, he can bring you back."

"Thank you, but I don't want him to go out of his way."

"Bah!" Ian's wide chest shook as he chuckled. "My Penny would have me sleeping outside if I let you pay for passage. It's nothing."

She opened her mouth to protest, but he'd already left her side.

With the plans made, Emily waited for the flatboat to be filled with small-animal pelts. Apprehension filled her senses at the idea of seeing Matthew again, let alone traveling with him.

But soon enough, Matthew appeared. He strode over, wearing

nothing more than a linen work shirt and breeches. Sweat damp-ened his brow, but he smiled at his brother-in-law. Had she in-terrupted his work? The two men spoke quietly and she steeled herself, expecting him to decline or even walk away, but he gave a short nod and got to work. Before the sun hit the top of the tallest evergreens, the flatboat was filled, and Emily joined Matthew on the vessel. He kept things cordial when he took her hand to help her on board.

"Have you ever been downriver this far before?" he asked.

"Can't say I have. I feel like I've been everywhere else at this point."

He almost smiled. "You're well-known now. When people say Oyo, I know they're referring to you."

She stared at everything other than him. A lone herder coaxed his goats to the riverbanks. She took in the old man, from his labored gait to his weathered features. She tried to do anything but look at the man beside her.

"I wouldn't say I know as much as Mrs. Oyo at this point, but I'm learning. Many people have been sick lately."

"A lot has happened around here," he agreed.

They were quiet for some time. She took the moment to think about her prep for the birth instead of what would happen when they had to camp for the night. Maybe they'd always be this awk-ward together. Or maybe, someday, they could be friends again.

The sun had long set by the time Matthew decided to make camp. Emily disembarked and shifted to place rocks for their firepit while Matthew secured the boat. By the time she got the fire going and had set a pot of beans to warm up, a stillness accompanied the crickets and night owls. Matthew sat on one side of the fire while she took a spot on the other.

A few feet felt like a thousand miles.

Someone had to speak. "Are there any tribes nearby?" Emily asked.

"I heard the Arrohattoc used to hunt here a long time ago, but once the English came, they disappeared. Most days, I see the Monacans and Powhatans. They're good folk when you respect their land." He caught her concerned expression and added, "We should be fine, but I plan to stay up late and keep an eye out."

Matthew filled his bowl and ate. Mosquitos buzzed around their heads, and the crackle of the fire refused to penetrate the silence.

"Terribly hot these days," he mused. "I'll take a blizzard over the heat."

"I don't like either. Give me the spring or fall and I'm a happy woman."

"You sound like Penny. She never liked the snow. Said it was strange."

"Why did she say that?"

"It doesn't snow in my homeland." His expression grew wistful as he tossed more sticks on the fire. "As a child, I remember rain. Every spring the rivers flooded, but we ate well."

Matthew stared at the fire while Emily tried to fix her eyes elsewhere. Both of their bowls were empty, but her feelings—which she'd thought she'd buried—filled their campsite. Time stretched out as the birch in the fire broke down into glowing pieces.

"Are we going to do this all night?" he asked with a short laugh.

"Do what?" she replied.

"We used to talk to each other easily. At least I thought so. Will we always be this way?"

"Nothing's wrong." She swallowed past a long exhale.

His eyebrows rose and he tilted his head in question.

Emily bounced back and forth from what she wanted to say versus what she should say. Before she could respond, Matthew said, "Can I ask you something?"

His face was earnest. She couldn't look away.

She nodded as he rose from his side of the fire and sat next to her. The urge to bolt for another perch hit, but she refused to move.

"Why did you move over here?" she asked.

He chuckled a bit, and her nervousness eased a little. "I have something to say, and I don't want *that*"—he motioned to the fire—"to be between us. I want to see your face."

"Go ahead." She wasn't ready, but she had to hear him out.

"A year ago, you told me you're returning home, wherever that is, and I'm assuming you're not coming back. What I want to know is, did you really want to go there, or did you want to stay with me?"

Emily tucked her trembling hands into her apron pocket. "I've always *had* to return home, but . . . I met you, then I fell in love." The words were there. She just had to say them. "I wanted to say yes to you that day. I would've followed you forever, Matthew."

Matthew's hand rose to cup her cheek. His thumb traced a path across her lips, and she almost floated away.

"You love me?" His voice was lower, deep enough to slide down her back and rest at the base of her spine. "I asked you to go with me because I love you too."

"How many times do I have to say it?"

"Maybe after you say it enough times, you'll believe it and come with me to New York in the spring."

Her heart sped up. Would she be willing to leave Tabitha and Phoebe behind if the opportunity came? Another bigger question remained: What would happen if she chose him over Amelia's future?

She freed her hands from her apron and glanced at them. They were once Amelia's. But when Matthew slipped his hands into hers, she knew the answer. Matthew Abramson was worth any what-ifs she'd come across.

Millie loved him.

"I believe it," she whispered. Her drift in his direction was subtle, a shifting of shoulders, a turn of her cheek toward his. When she brushed against the stubble on his chin, sparks danced across her skin. Their lips were mere inches apart. With her head tilted toward his, their bodies were too close to prevent the inevitable from happening. He captured her lips, and any reservations she had disappeared.

Tentatively, she wrapped her arms around his neck, unsure what to do, but knowing nothing else felt right.

If the sun hadn't risen, and the promise of a late summer storm hadn't sprinkled across their bare arms and legs, Emily would've lain naked in Matthew's arms forever. She nestled against him, her lips resting against his bare chest in an eternal kiss. His heartbeat thrummed against the tip of her nose. This was everything. Bliss. Serenity.

The warm drops pattered the leaves over her head before they slipped off to dampen her arms. Matthew ran his hands up her back before his left hand drifted over to shield her face from the rain.

"We should get up," he murmured.

"We should," she agreed as she snuggled closer, enjoying his warm skin against hers.

"Still tired?"

"I'm wide awake. Just want to savor this before I return to the real world."

He got up. "Aren't we already there?"

She admired the corded muscles in his buttocks and back as he put on his breeches. "Now we are," she said with a mock frown.

A couple of minutes later, Matthew had the fire going again while

Em washed up at the river and got dressed. This early in the morning, dragonflies darted at the river's edge, their tiny forms swaying on cattail tips. She'd give anything to spend the day with Matthew. They'd fashion simple fishing poles like the older fishermen off the Appomattox and watch the river, or life in general, go by.

With a sigh, Em abandoned her daydreaming. She had a mother in labor not far from here. There'd be plenty of summers, swimming holes, and quiet picnics in the future.

With Matthew. She'd think about the Bridges another time.

Emily glanced over her shoulder to see him folding up their blankets.

As she made her way over, his gaze caught hers. His eyes formed slits as he took her in—swallowing her whole. That was the same heated expression he'd worn right when he'd touched her intimately . . . She was gonna have a problem if he kept looking at her like that.

"Are you ready to go, wife?" he asked softly.

"Wife?"

"Should I say 'friend'? I like 'wife.' Maybe you'd prefer it if I said *iyawo* instead."

"But we're not—"

"Do we have to be married in the English church for me to call you that yet?"

Yet. The word held promise, which she'd never thought she'd experience. She finished packing her bag, recalling how her cousin Henrietta had had an engagement party and announcements in all the Negro papers in DC. All that fanfare had preceded a wedding in one of the most expensive halls on U Street.

None of those things had mattered to her then. Only that word from Matthew. That beautiful word "wife" sounded sweeter than any engagement ring, parties, or impending nuptials.

"If you and I are husband and wife . . . what does that mean after we get back?" Emily asked, unable to face him.

Matthew thought for a bit before he answered. "As much as I'd like for you to stay with me in the sod house, it's too small."

"Do you want me to ask Mrs. Oyo and Miss McDonald if you can stay with us again?"

"No, no. We should go to New York as soon as possible. From there we can begin a life together the right way."

She couldn't smother the laugh that snuck up next.

"Why are you laughing?" he asked. "Are you happy? Do you like my plan?"

"Yes." There was much to think about. Tabitha, Phoebe, and the faces of everyone she'd come to know came to mind, but no one could take this wonderfully giddy feeling away.

"Good. If I have to work again, we can't leave until spring comes, but we *will* go. You and me."

"You and me," she repeated.

The journey upriver didn't take long, and before midday they'd reached Goodes Bridge and a set of homes sprinkled right off the river.

After he dropped her off, she expected him to pull away, but he waited. His easy grin and hope carried her up the hill to the houses.

SEPTEMBER 1760

After the tobacco harvest was completed for the season and Matthew left to go trapping, Tabitha just lay in her bed and never smiled again.

Every now and then she moved, turning over to bathe in the sunlight through the open window. But she simply stared outside. Her eyes were empty and her skin ashen as flies marched across her forehead.

"Isn't it lovely outside?" Emily hurried over to swat the bugs away. On the hotter days, she read from one of her books, fanning the midwife to keep her cool.

Tabitha didn't answer, even when the shadows shifted and the sunlight shone directly on her face. To protect the midwife's eyes, Emily closed the shutters. What was she supposed to do when Matthew returned and Tabitha was still bedridden?

A month later, her guilt grew heavier. Emily discovered the midwife had soiled herself. After that, the woman couldn't move to use the chamber pot. No book from Emily's expensive university education had taught medical students how to deal with the end. Not death itself but the days, the hours, and the minutes leading up to the last breath. How do you comfort them? Prepare them for the end? With no one to speak to about her fears, Emily had no choice but to learn as she went along.

Especially the day she realized her monthly hadn't arrived. The previous month, she'd boiled the rags and left them wrapped in her pack, but October swept in and she hadn't used them yet.

As winter's chill returned and deepened, more symptoms snuck in, confirming her suspicions. She couldn't stand the smell of lye, nor the foul odors from the outhouse. Phoebe had failed to notice, but one morning the midwife's empty gaze sharpened to clarity. While Emily replaced Tabitha's soiled linens on the bed, the woman opened her mouth to let her thoughts be known.

"You're with child." She'd spoken in a whisper with the weight of twenty stones.

As much as Em wanted to deny it or give another excuse, what would it matter? Most women around here got pregnant before marriage. The pious chastised others from their church pews while their daughters met their beaus in the woods.

Emily touched her flat stomach. For now, only the women in the house knew, but after December the village would know. She didn't fear her condition though. She feared her fate. Professor Mayberry's plan to change history had happened, but she would've never approved of this.

Emily's baby would be due in the spring of 1761—the date Luke's birth was marked in the family Bible. But this baby wasn't John's. It was Matthew's and she had yet to meet her fated husband.

Em closed her eyes and made her child a promise. Once Matthew returned in the spring, she'd be ready to leave Virginia, never to return again. Somehow she'd figure things out. Even if that meant destroying what was meant to be. She just needed more time. The very thought made her laugh. Wasn't time the source of all these problems?

CHAPTER 44

Emily Bridge

MARCH 1761

Warmth should've returned to the countryside, but winter storms persisted, and ice blanketed the water around the river's low-lying islets. The clouds blocked off the sun as Emily's dread deepened. That familiar strain from that-which-cannot-be-prevented settled in the middle of her chest and grew along with her unborn child.

A longer winter meant Matthew might delay his return. A part of her, the hopeful sliver pining for greenery and sunshine, dreamt of him huddling underneath his fur blankets with an easy smile. His companions would have buoyed moods from a plentiful trapping season.

"Are we going home soon?" he would ask the others.

In yesterday's dream, he showed up, eyes wide at seeing her belly, widened hips, and rounded face. This time he hadn't bathed in the river or dusted off his newer clothes. He came to her as he'd left her.

Instead of a knock on the door interrupting her, she lost her concentration in the middle of reading *Robinson Crusoe* to Tabitha. Hours of work had gone into the barter for the popular book.

"Sorry about that." Em scanned the page to find where she'd left off. "'I learned to look more upon the bright side of my condition, and less upon the dark side, and to consider what I enjoyed rather than what I wanted,'" she read, "'and this gave me sometimes such secret comforts, that I cannot express them—'"

From the bed, Tabitha's face contorted as she coughed. The woman squeezed shut her eyes and tried to hold still but failed.

Em stiffened, often wanting to offer comfort, but she remembered the midwife's warning. There'd be no examinations—which meant no treatment. Since her patient refused her care, she settled for what could be done. Emily scooted off the seat and rose to make pain-relief tea. She added a kettle of water to the fire and fetched the tiny wooden box where Tabitha kept her pain-relief supplies. Em opened the box and nearly cried. Not a single scrap was left. She'd let her fears distract her. She'd gone to town yesterday, and the day before that. She could've fetched more. For all she knew, Matthew was probably roaming the woods.

God knew she had more important things to worry about.

Emily draped her cape over her shoulders. "I'll return soon. There's something I need to attend to in Petersburg."

Around this time of the year, the world outside the door should've woken up from winter's slumber, but instead, Emily had to contend with slick, muddy paths and a nippy wind biting her cheeks. She pulled the cape's hood over her head and walked faster.

At the apothecary—which had a new owner now that Mr. Graves had passed away last year—Emily purchased the needed herbs, along with valerian. For the past three months, she'd sprinkled a low dosage into the tea to ease the midwife into a heavy sleep.

On her way out, she saw a familiar face on the other side of the field. It was Penny.

Matthew's sister carried a covered basket while her toddler was strapped to her back with a bright red cloth. When the young mother caught sight of Emily, her expression shifted from detached to stricken.

"Mrs. Green!" Em hadn't seen her since last year when the family had moved upriver, away from the Bolling place.

"Miss Oyo . . ."

Emily rubbed the child's back as the little girl played with her fingers. "It's wonderful to see you and Lola. What are you doing here?" she asked.

Penny stole a glance at the swell of Emily's stomach before she glanced away. The woman stood there without speaking for far too long.

"I must apologize for not sending word," Penny finally said, her voice breaking. "Especially since you're with child. There's something I must tell you."

When she saw the sadness in Penny's eyes, Emily asked, "Tell me what?" Fear had crept into her voice.

"It's about Matthew. He's missing."

"What do you mean missing? How long have you known?"

"It's been a month." Penny sobbed now and Lola mewled upon hearing her distraught mother. "They were deep into the western territory, much farther than they'd ever been. Ian said they were in good spirits. They'd caught more beaver than last year."

Em faced the river, unable to look at Penny any longer. There was a man on the opposite side of the river fishing. His dark-blue waistcoat was worn, and his eyes defeated.

Penny continued. "Ian said while they were checking coon

traps my brother just vanished. One moment he was there, then he wasn't."

The river in the distance blurred as Emily's fingertips went numb. The man standing on the bank on the other side blended into the icy water.

"It doesn't make any sense," Penny murmured. "The men searched for him, but they found nothing."

Penny's voice faded away as Emily retreated. If she stood there another second, she'd sink into the ground. She'd disappear like Matthew. Like Isaiah.

"Miss Oyo, where are you going?" Penny called out.

Emily pressed her hands against her belly and kept walking until she arrived back at the house. Phoebe had returned from her workday and tended to the spinning wheel. She didn't even glance up at Em's arrival, her ghostly hands repeating motions her muscles had memorized over the years. The whole house was drowning, and no one wanted to come up for air.

Somehow Em ambled over to one of the chairs. She waited for tears to come, for her anguish to burst forth like Penny's, but she simply sat there while the revelation sunk its teeth into her: Matthew was *gone*.

Her love hadn't disappeared down the river or slipped into a crevasse. His fate seemed too familiar—could he have disappeared through time too?

She intertwined her trembling fingers as she sagged against the seat. There had to be another explanation. Maybe Matthew had run away north. Maybe he was in danger, and escaped into the wilderness. He couldn't be a time traveler like the Bridges. Her baby wouldn't share the Bridges' fate.

Even as her grip tightened, Emily couldn't stop shaking.

It's not true. It's not true.

But the words held no weight in her heart: What if this child was a boy? What if he was Luke? Not John's Luke but the child John would raise as his own.

She could hear Professor Mayberry's passionate speech, the words crashing through her.

"There are mysteries in our family's history," the professor had said. "In particular, the curse's origin. I believe the Bridge family has always had it and the phenomenon simply manifested in 1817 with Nelson, Hiram, and the others. Now, when it comes to Luke, that's when things get interesting. I don't know why he fell forty years before the others. He's an anomaly and we may never understand. Or perhaps it's for you to find out. Something unexpected will happen, and you may learn how everything connects together."

God help her, it all made sense. As a Bridge woman, her children shouldn't fall, and yet if Matthew was the father and a time traveler, her baby might have the curse too.

Her hands gave way, and she bent over, feeling faint. While she sucked in deep breaths, she could see her future with Matthew, the one Professor Mayberry hadn't intended, and she groaned in profound pain. She thought of her baby, who'd be born soon. The child might disappear like Isaiah, like all the other Bridges. Everything *almost* fit—except she wasn't at the farm with John.

"Emily, are you all right?" Phoebe rose from the wheel.

Emily didn't answer. She shuddered until her whole body shook.

———

The next morning, Emily woke up to Phoebe screaming, cursing, then begging.

Tabitha had died.

Emily was curled up on her side on the far end of the bed. She

stared off to the other end of the cabin, from the door the midwife had always waltzed through to the shelves where her mentor's
reproachful lessons had penetrated even Emily's distracted days.
Even though Tabitha Oyo had returned to her ancestors, bits of her
remained, and those traces dug a hot iron into Em's heart.

"Are you paying attention, girl?" Tabitha had snapped a year
ago. "You always have this faraway look like half of you is here
while the other half is up in the clouds."

The midwife was right back then and even now. A part of her
would always cling to 1924 and the loved ones she'd left behind.

Someone had to get up. Phoebe needed to eat, or she'd have
another diabetic episode like yesterday.

Emily cried instead.

Over the next couple of days, Em and Phoebe became phan-
toms, restless in their wanderings from outside to inside. As much
as she wanted to sit in the midwife's chair and fade away, her obligations forced her to move, forced her to wash Tabitha's body
and say her ancestors' prayers for a safe journey back home. Em
registered her death and arranged for burial. All the while, Phoebe
refused to get up.

Time passed. Swimming in loss had a way of blurring clarity,
but when there was a knock on the door, Emily answered it. Babies
continued to be born. The townspeople needed medical care.

But a decision had to be made. Each day, her stretch marks
lengthened, and her wrists swelled as her body prepared for birth.
She couldn't ignore the inevitable. Even back in 1921, during one of
Professor Mayberry's classroom discussions, she'd received a warning.
One of her classmates—she couldn't recall his name—spoke up and
seared the words into her head.

"Man is inherently flawed," he'd said. "We make the same decisions we believe will benefit humankind, but these decisions only benefit ourselves."

Yes, she was flawed.

Yes, she could never forget the pain of losing her brother. Yes, she was scared of returning to the farm to face John. She was pregnant and ready to give birth, but she had to go back.

The day after Tabitha was buried, Emily returned to the house. Her pack was waiting in the corner. She'd diligently arranged everything right after Matthew had left. Now the pack served as a reminder of what she'd lost.

As to how she'd broach the subject with Phoebe, she didn't know.

"Phoebe, it's time."

"What do you mean?"

"It's time for me . . ." She struggled to add life to what had to be said. "It's time for me to go home."

"I thought you might say that." Her face drooped as if she'd aged twenty years. Every bite she'd consumed for the last couple of days had been from Em's spoon to her mouth. "When Mr. Abramson kept coming around, Tabitha said you'd get married. Settle down somewhere else." Her voice thickened. "She told me not to get attached. You didn't have to hide like a hunted animal like we did."

Emily wrapped her arms around her. Luke squirmed in her belly and Phoebe sighed.

"Maybe you should wait until the baby's born," Phoebe said softly.

"No, it's time." Emily let Phoebe go. "I should go home before my throws begin."

"Home?"

Emily realized she'd never named where she'd come from. The women had never pried.

"Northwest of here. I was born on a farm near the Southwest Mountains."

"How will you get there?"

"The only way possible. With one foot in front of the other until I reach my destination. And you're coming with me." She'd decided that not long after Tabitha had passed.

"No, I'm not." The look Phoebe gave her had the same finality as the midwife's declarations. "I can never leave this place. Up there, I'm Loretta Hastings. Down here, Tabby made a safe place for Phoebe McDonald, so here I stay."

Emily squeezed her hand, but Phoebe didn't answer in kind. "I'm leaving in the morning. Think about it, will you?"

The woman turned away from her as she said, "There's nothing to think about, but I will."

Over the quiet day, Emily busied herself with packing and tidying. Phoebe baked loaves of oat bread and tucked the wrapped portions into Emily's belongings. Em hoped by sunset Phoebe would gather her own things, but she never did.

Night came and Phoebe and Emily went to bed. Just like the night before, no one took up Tabitha's space next to the wall.

When Emily rose the next morning, ready to leave for Richmond, only the calico cat remained on the bed. The spot where Phoebe had lain on the edge was empty.

CHAPTER 45

Emily Bridge
APRIL 1761

A long time ago, before liquor had poisoned Alfred Bridge's mind, he'd told his daughter that the city of Richmond was full of hidden Negro graves and tormented souls. As a ten-year-old, Pa had ridden into town with Granddaddy Elijah and witnessed what he'd called *that* place. Folks spoke of kin who'd lost family members to the auction block at Shockoe Bottom, Richmond's eight blocks of slave markets. Back in 1882, Pa had witnessed the remnants, while now Emily took in a fog-shrouded warehouse that would continue to stain the neighborhood for decades until the slaves were set free.

"Every single Clark, including my mama, came through that place," Granddaddy Elijah had told him.

Emily stole another glance at the two-story barn—a tentative one, as if the building's doors would open like a teeth-filled maw and gulp her down in one bite. She forced her swollen ankles to keep going. She'd traveled far over the last two days, and her hips were stiff from traveling by boat up the James River from the Appomattox.

This early in the planting season, the port swelled with flatboats and lighters unloading cargo, but the fog swallowed everything past two hundred feet.

Her stomach rumbled from hunger. Time to eat again. She rifled through her bag, counting three tiny food parcels.

Lord knows I could empty every food stall on this street, and nothing would sate this child, she thought.

Briefly, she closed her eyes to find the quiet she'd enjoyed back in Pocahontas. The same river-fish stench curdled her stomach, but there were fewer wooden homes. Fewer signs of the civilization she'd left behind in 1924.

A lump formed in the back of her throat and grew each time she tried to shake a familiar feeling she'd had three years ago. She had no place to go for the night. No warm bed or meals waiting in the parlor with the tinny sounds of the radio playing in the background. Just the shouts of porters in English, French, Spanish, and other tongues she couldn't place.

She considered her options instead of pivoting on her heel and begging for passage back to Pocahontas.

Emily walked faster, even when her babe pressed against her bladder. The incessant *tap-tap* would have her running for the woods soon. She wrapped her clasped hands under her belly to ease her torment.

There. Much better.

By the time she reached a T intersection, she hoped to find the path leading to Charlottesville. Three Notch'd Road, Grandpa Elijah had called it.

"You can go all the way from Richmond up to the Shenandoah Valley," he'd said. "There's nothing but God's country out there."

The urge to sit grew stronger. Now wasn't the time. With the thick fog, she had to trust other means to find her way home. She retrieved her compass to determine the way west. If she waddled her wide behind another mile or two, she could shelter for the night under tree cover.

Once she found her bearings, Em finally found the well-beaten road she'd sought. As she walked, she stooped to forage by habit. At first, she leaned down to grasp stalks of stinging nettle. On the way up, she wheezed to stand as Luke pressed against her diaphragm. By the second plant, she gave up with a hearty laugh. It would've been far easier to have her boy in her arms than to carry him around like this. Her laughter carried her onward until the lighter feeling in her chest was replaced by an awareness she had to be alert. She paused each time she heard the rickety sound of an approaching wagon's wheels, or the hard thuds from a horse with a rider. Those sounds guided her to safety until she caught a frantic conversation up the road. Emily approached an opening in the forest and peeked through the thick birch trees.

"How do you expect me to get us home?" a woman's voice snapped.

Weakened grunts came in reply.

"Stop it, Victor. You're in no condition to fight me."

Em took a step closer. Off to the side of the road, a wagon with boxes covered in blankets had crashed into a tree. The horses jerked and neighed against the stuck load, but the wagon didn't budge. A Negro couple sat in front. The woman wearing a white head wrap cradled the head of a man twice her size in her arms. At the sight of Emily, she wiped away a tear on his chin. The lightness at the corners of the woman's eyes deepened until her frown added a clear message: stay away.

Perhaps they were transporting goods for their master, or in a rare circumstance, they were free Negroes traveling elsewhere.

Emily remained on the opposite side of the road, her gaze set on the incline coming up. Step by step, she drew closer.

She wouldn't speak to them. She'd mind her own business too.

Even Luke squirmed to stretch his feet against her ribs.

See, she thought, *even your unborn child knows better.*

By the time she'd passed them, her breath had quickened from marching uphill. It was the incoherent groans—a rattling cough— from the man that tugged, then yanked at her skirts to slow down. She knew that chorus all too well.

What are you doing, girl? She could imagine the midwife's stony glare. *Use your book learning and decide. Do not dawdle.* Tabitha Oyo would've blocked her path until she burned from shame instead of fear.

Em had yet to take one look at him, but she'd seen others like him dying in their beds. Those with dysentery passed away in a pool of their feces. Others with measles or smallpox sweated through their blankets as horrific pustules erupted all over their bodies.

Most of them died and spread their contagion to their caregivers.

She couldn't help but think of Luke. His face, or the one she hoped he'd look like, namely Matthew's, came to mind. She splayed her hand over the spot. Retreated a step, then another.

Em faced the stranger as she drew her neckerchief over her nose.

And that woman looked ready to strike her dead. Her head twisted, revealing a scowling yet dignified profile.

"Go away!" Her shout carried up and over the hill.

The closer Em got to them, the venom in the woman's gaze deepened, until Emily stood before them.

"Do you want to die?" the woman barked.

The tip of the blade she held in her right hand peeked out from behind the man's barrel chest.

"He's ill." Emily kept her voice calm, although a quiver snuck in at the end. "I'm a healer and mean you no harm."

"What can you do?" The stranger scoffed, glancing at her belly. "You'll need a doctor before he does."

Em rolled her eyes and edged closer. "Then I'll keep you company. You can keep doing whatever it is you're doing, and I'll give birth."

"Bridget . . ." The man's rapid blinks coincided with the sharp breaths he fought to take.

"He's feverish and weak," Emily bit out. "How long has he been sick?"

"When our men loaded up the wagon, he was sweaty and tired, but he's always been that way." Bridget's brow furrowed. "For the last couple of days, he has complained of aches and his eyes looked peculiar."

"Peculiar as in a yellowish tinge?"

"Yes . . ." The word stretched out in exasperation.

Emily didn't need to hear much else. "He might have yellow fever. Has anyone else in your household gotten sick?"

Bridget stared up the hill again and her jaw worked as if she chewed on her thoughts. "The men who were supposed to take these boxes up to Shadwell didn't report for work this morning."

Carefully, Emily heaved herself up the side of the wagon and pulled her neckerchief from her mouth.

"What are you doing?" Bridget leaned away.

"Helping you. He's not contagious. The mosquitos around here are the problem." Emily examined Victor to confirm he had jaundice. She added, "Why did you let him leave home if he was sick?"

"I did no such thing. My husband is a fool like all Knox men. No one showed up to take care of the shipment, so he decided to go by himself. He didn't look well, so I came with him."

Now that Em sat next to Victor with Bridget on the other side, she noticed the woman didn't hold on to her husband. Victor had collapsed to the side, against Bridget, and the woman couldn't get him off without pushing him over the other side. At least that hadn't happened. Yet.

"He needs bed rest. Do you live close?" Before Bridget could answer, Emily began to climb down again.

"Is there nothing you can give him right now?" Bridget asked.

"No, he needs rest." Emily strode around the horses and wagon. From far away, it had appeared as if the wagon had crashed into the trees, but a wheel stuck in the mud had stranded them. "Do you have any planks in the back?"

"I don't know."

"Any blankets for Mr. Knox?"

The woman shook her head.

That didn't surprise Em either. While the couple sat, the fog retreated as she searched for the means to free the wheel. A quick check under the blankets over the boxes revealed a single filthy board and tools tucked away against the side. Thank goodness she wouldn't have to dig the wheel out.

Bridget remained silent, not so much as twitching as Emily worked the board underneath the stuck wheel. Em guided the animals back and forth until the wagon was freed.

Bridget grabbed the reins and squealed with joy the moment the wagon was turned around and back on the road. "Well done!"

"That was the easy part," Emily said. "Take him home and send him off to bed. No more work. Give him soup—"

Her face fell. "You're not coming with us?"

"I was on my way home." She even waved, but that didn't stop Bridget from speaking.

"In a couple hours, it will be dark. You should stay with us until morning."

Emily paused. The fog-free road up ahead waited, but Victor Knox hadn't endured the worst of his illness yet. That much she knew.

She must've hesitated too long, for Bridget added, "Please come with us."

Another day wouldn't matter. A warm meal would give her strength for the miles she had left to walk. Emily climbed onto the back of the wagon. The hill vanished again as she returned with the couple back to town.

CHAPTER 46

Emily Bridge

MAY 1761

Three days in Richmond became three weeks.

Long before sunlight pierced through the narrow window in the stuffy servants' quarters, Emily crept out of the room. She knew every loose board on the wooden floors, and her footfalls remained silent. She couldn't afford to be discovered and deterred from leaving. She'd taken this path many times past the Knox couple's closed bedroom door. Day in and day out, she'd nursed him back to health.

Someone shifted within the Knoxes' chamber, and she paused, alert and fearful. Two weeks ago, she'd caught Bridget staring at her stomach. After that, the woman kept yammering on about getting this or that for the baby. How the child would be raised with care within the Knox household, and Bridget would sacrifice her precious time to care for the babe so Emily could continue to nurse her husband back to health. The final nail in the coffin came yesterday afternoon, when Victor had gotten up to see to his business affairs in town. Emily decided it was time for her to do the same.

Soon enough, Emily reached the front door. Even the family's maid hadn't yet risen to tend to the kitchen, and Em plodded through a dim room.

Right outside the door, the tension circling her stomach eased. She'd made it. Each step away from the two-story house at the top of a knoll propelled her to go faster.

She didn't look back at the tranquil barn or the construction on the new chicken coop. The Knox family's growing wealth in the shipping business would've made this home an ideal place for her child—if she would've been given a choice.

Free will was such a beautiful gift.

Emily didn't know how far she'd walked out of Richmond, for the sky opened to rain. Without an umbrella, the rain soaked through her clothes, but she kept moving and rubbed the fabric stretched over her extended belly. Her boy had yet to drop—for which she was grateful—but such a long trip would push her body closer to her child's birth.

Two Negro families traveling to Shadwell to work as carpenters on the plantation invited her to ride along. She joined the others in the back.

"You've done well, my sweet boy," she whispered as the wagon rocked her. Each mile the cart traversed drew her closer to home.

Many hours later, in the middle of a humid night, a gentle shake to her shoulder roused Emily from sound sleep.

"I did not want to wake you," an older man said in rough pidgin English. "Go now. Bad men follow."

Em didn't need to be told twice. Whether Negroes were born free or held freedom papers, ill-intentioned folk stalked the well-trafficked roads.

"Thank you," she whispered.

The old man bid her goodbye with a short nod and a hopeful, toothless grin. "Careful."

Em waddled off the road into the safety of the woods. With little light except the faint glow from a cloud-covered moon, she had no choice but to veer west for an hour before heading northwest again. The temptation to set up camp gnawed at her, for a brisk wind and ominous clouds warned of more rain, but she was close.

So very close. Less than a couple more miles, in fact.

Anticipation made her giddy, and her belly responded in kind with a sharp contraction. The squeezing pain in her abdomen sucked the air from her lungs and her knees buckled.

"God, no." She staggered to the nearest tree and leaned against the birch tree stump. Time passed, an ever-present companion, as she sat there. What else could she do but wait? No one would celebrate her arrival, and the Bridges weren't expecting her either.

All she could do was rest against the wet earth and pray her body didn't do what she'd witnessed many other women do for the last three years: expel a child.

So Em waited. The squeezing teetered off before sneaking up on her again when she dozed off. By morning, Emily woke up and Luke was still safe and sound in her womb.

The rainfall returned, but with the familiar landscape around her, from Wolfpit Mountain to the Rivanna River, she extended one of her hands to feel the soft taps of the rain against the middle of her palm.

Aunt Ursula always said she loved the spring rains the most.

"It's like watching manna fall from heaven," she'd said. "You can't tell me you don't like opening a window, feeling that crisp, clean air against your face, and feeling at peace. It's like I'm closer to God. I'm closer to the beginning of everything."

Mud weighed down her boots, but eventually she came upon Ivy Creek. With a giddy grin, she approached the water. She'd already soaked through her shoes. Wet stockings wouldn't matter. Carefully, she crept down the bank, anchoring her feet with each step. Her precious Luke strained against her stomach again.

"Let Mama get down," she chided.

Another pain rolled across her stomach. She tensed up to breathe through it. When she opened her eyes, a muted glint shined from the middle of the creek. She waddled over, careful not to slip in the ankle-deep water. She reached in and plucked out a shiny rock—a goethite.

She burst out in a deep laugh until her side hurt. It looked just like the rocks Samuel Ross had loved to collect with her brother, but it couldn't be. But then again, hadn't fate mocked her all these years?

More than one hundred and fifty years from now, Isaiah and Sam would be exploring these lands and they'd come across rocks like these.

And Sam would think of her.

The thought left her reeling at the grand scale of time compared to her speck of a life in the middle.

As the spring rain dripped from the forest canopy overhead, she followed a single raindrop off a drooping leaf until it drenched a dry patch of earth. She imagined the life-giving fluid kissing a single oak tree seed. The tiny plant had survived falling from its mother tree where it landed in the soil. Away from the motherland, away from the shelter of branches. Over the winter, the snow seeped through the frozen earth and added tiny fractures on the seed's surface, but come spring, a miracle would happen.

A single drop of water, seemingly guided by the hand of God, fell as intended onto a square centimeter of grass—only to begin a tree's life that would stretch upward for hundreds of years. That tree would bear seeds when the time was right, and the cycle would begin again.

Emily crawled up the opposite bank. On the way up, she pressed the rock into the soft earth.

"Maybe you'll be brave enough to give it to me next time, Sam," she whispered. "You'll save on postage."

The rain showers turned into a light drizzle as she ambled westward, until she recognized the familiar rise and fall of the land close to the Bridge farm.

She'd arrived, and with it, she'd soon cross paths with John Bridge. Matthew's face came to mind, and instead of a pain-stricken longing, joy touched her heart. She would see him again. Not in this lifetime, but in over one hundred fifty years a woman named Amelia would be whisked away on a great adventure. That adventure would lead her to 1758, where she'd meet the love of her life. For that adventure to happen, Emily had to be here. At this moment, at this second in time.

She smiled, knowing Matthew wasn't dead. She truly believed it. Every now and then, wherever he'd landed, he'd think of her. Just like she thought of him.

Emily ventured deeper into Bridge territory. Soon enough, she'd see the beautiful apple trees again with their flowering plants in full bloom. Matthew would be there with her, through their son, to witness another planting, another harvest. Hope blossomed here, and she'd rather be nowhere else in the world.

AUTHOR'S NOTE

The Fallen Fruit is a work of fiction, but many of the places and events did occur as described. A few of the facts, however, have been changed to fit the narrative. Most importantly, the Bridges' property called "Free State." The idea for the Bridges' story was initially about a family of freeborn Blacks in Charlottesville, Virginia—namely mine. The time travel aspect emerged a bit later.

Back in 1779, a Black woman named Amy Bowles-Farrow had bought land from a local merchant named William Johnson. Although eighteenth-century free Black Virginians could vote and own property, once the tobacco industry (and later cotton) boomed, slavery became enshrined in American society. Plantation owners in Virginia utilized slave labor, and over time the option to buy or earn one's freedom disappeared. During this time, many communities created laws limiting Virginia's free Black population, and forced their citizens into poverty. Others were driven out of the state altogether. My sixth great-grandmother managed to carve out a life for herself and her children after completing an apprenticeship and earning her freedom. The land she bought became Free State many years later. Free State residents engaged in farming and various trades, amassed private property, and bartered with their white neighbors. Following the Civil War, their modest community grew, becoming home to the

Free State Colored School and the Central Relief Association, a local benevolent society, by the early twentieth century.

The residents of Free State were just as fascinating as Bowles-Farrow. One of her sons, Zachariah Bowles, was a soldier in the American Revolution, and his wife was Crita Hemings, a former slave and the sister of Sally Hemings from Thomas Jefferson's Monticello plantation.

With such a rich history to draw upon, I couldn't wait to see how I could bring such fascinating people into my story, in particular for Luke Bridge's time as a private during the American Revolution. I based him off Shadrack Battles, another distant relative of mine, who fought in the 10th Regiment during the American Revolutionary War. Shadrack is listed on the Valley Forge muster rolls, and he was ill, along with many of the other troops, from January to March 1778. It was quite the challenge to explore Shadrack's service, but bringing his experiences to life was an honor.

ACKNOWLEDGMENTS

The Fallen Fruit was a labor of love and I have many people to thank. First, I must thank my agent, Jim McCarthy. Jim and I have worked together for over ten years now, and his passion for his clients is undeniable. I'll always fondly remember our conversation where he told me the Bridges' story was the one I needed to tell.

Several editors have ushered this book to publication. Jennifer Baker acquired my work, and I'm grateful for her initial insight and wisdom. My current editor, Alexa Frank, along with Francesca Walker, further elevated Jennifer's vision and helped me craft the best book possible. I must also thank the outstanding team at Amistad and HarperOne/HarperCollins: Judith Curr, Tara Parsons, Abby West, Yvonne Chan, and Lisa Zuniga. Additional thanks to art director Stephen Brayda for his phenomenal work on my cover and to my copyeditor, Dianna Stirpe.

To Sarah Jude for her invaluable help over the years. You were there when my career began, and you continue to offer guidance at the important moments in my career.

To Jessica Scott for your wisdom and your encouragement. Our conversation in 2018 changed the trajectory of my career and I'm thankful to have you as a friend.

To Megan Kelly, Amanda Bonilla, Sela Carsen, Amanda Berry,

and Heather Reid for your feedback on my early drafts. You went above and beyond, Megan. Thank you so much. Additional thanks to Fola Coker for answering my Yoruba language questions.

To Stephanie Dray, Eliza Knight, Laura Kamoie, and Jeannie Lin for your wisdom and friendship as I navigate the world of historical fiction.

To my Zeta Phi Beta sisters from Spring 1996. You represent finer womanhood, and I strive to follow your example.

To the 2023 Historical Novel Society Conference "Circle of Trust" crew. Our insightful late-night conversation left me invigorated and inspired for years to come.

To my mom: thank you for the many years of encouragement and eagerness to discuss my book ideas and offer feedback.

To my husband, Segun, and our three children, Ade, Deji, and Ronke, my thanks for your patience while I lived in my office to write this book. I'm also eternally grateful to Segun for answering my endless medical questions. I'd willingly go back in time to fall in love with you again.

BOOK CLUB QUESTIONS

1. What themes or messages did you take away from the book?

2. Time travel plays a central role in *The Fallen Fruit*, causing the Bridge family to experience their lives out of chronological order. How does this unique narrative structure affect your understanding of the themes of fate and free will in the novel?

3. Luke's time travel during the American Revolution leads to moments of joy, tragedy, and confusion. How does the author use his time-traveling condition to explore the fragility of the human existence and the impact of choices on our lives?

4. The novel raises ethical questions about changing the past and influencing the future through time travel. How do Cecily, Luke, and Emily grapple with these moral dilemmas, and how did it make you reflect on the consequences of your own choices?

5. Sabrina's relationship with Luke is doomed to failure, given his fate as Addy's husband. Did you root for them anyway?

6. Cecily asks Amelia to change the timeline in the hope that Cecily might be reunited with her family. If you faced the same situation, would you alter the past to be with your loved ones?

7. When Cecily reveals the truth to her husband, Winston, he is upset and confused. What would you have done to convince him?

8. If you knew you would fall through time like the Bridges, what would you do to prepare?

EMILY'S NUTMEG MAPLE COOKIES

MAKES ABOUT A DOZEN TWO-INCH COOKIES

1 cup butter (2 sticks), at room temperature
1 cup sugar, plus some for sprinkling on top
1 egg yolk
½ cup Grade B 100 percent maple syrup
¼ teaspoon nutmeg, plus some for sprinkling on top
2½ cups flour
1 teaspoon salt

First, mix the butter and sugar in a large bowl until fully combined. Next, stir in the egg yolk and maple syrup. Mix everything together until well blended. In another bowl combine the nutmeg, flour, and salt. Add the dry mixture to the butter/sugar bowl in two batches. Next, shape the final dough mixture into a flat square and chill for two hours.

Preheat the oven to 350°F. Add more flour to a clean surface, then roll out half the dough. Cut out the shapes and place the cookies on a baking sheet. Bake for 10 to 15 minutes. The cookies are done when the edges are light brown. Sprinkle a little bit of nutmeg and sugar on top for a dash of love.